LOVE NEVER DIES

S.J. PESUT

First—I want to thank my dearest friend Karen Walker. She was always encouraging and would never allow me to say that I could not do this. Her family Betsy and Chrystel let me use their names in the book along with Karen. Walker farm was named after her.

Second—I would like to thank my brother Gary Pennington, who said that he would be glad to read the book and let me know if this was something people would want to read. Although the content is not something he would normally read, he told me that he could not put it down. He called me a "Kick Ass Author." I love him for that!

Third—I want to thank my beautiful daughter Tamara Meyer for all her support and encouragement. After she read the book, I love that she also called me a "Kick Ass Author." She stood by me through the whole process.

Fourth—I want to thank Marty, my wonderful husband of 50 years, who always encouraged me that I could write this book. He has continually supported me in everything I have done, and this is no different. I know he is proud of my accomplishments and loves me with no end. I love him with all my heart and could not have done this without his support. So, a special "thank you" to him!

Last but not least—I want to thank all my friends on the internet who have been excited about getting this story into book form. Special thank you and love to my Holland daughter Anne Te Lintelo along with Lyle, David, Mike, Steve, Rob, Luca, Vicky, and Colleen, who were always positive about my writing. Much love to my friend Dr. Anne Reddy, MD, who has become part of the family, for all her medical advice in the story.

CONTENTS

Wyoming Bound

Jamie Walker packed for the Three M Ranch in Wyoming to buy a stud for breeding. He was anxious about this one because the stud horse had just won several races and was sought after for breeding purposes. The owner of the ranch, M. Morgan, had accepted Jamie's offer of $1 million. He had not met the owner yet because their conversations had all been by email and phone calls. Jamie was looking forward to their meeting because the owner sounded quite interesting. He had a very deep, sexy voice on the phone, and Jamie thought it might be nice if this guy turned out to be gay. But, with Jamie's luck, that was probably not going to be the case. He had not had a good relationship in several years.

He finished packing and had his driver bring the limo around to the house to take him to the airport. Jamie didn't like all the things that were expected of him since he was a wealthy man, but sometimes it came in handy when he didn't want to drive himself. Besides, he didn't want to put the guy out of a job.

He arrived at the airport in Cheyenne, picked up his bag, and went outside to meet the ride that M. Morgan sent to pick him up. When he stepped outside, there was a gorgeous cowboy standing by a truck, looking as though he was waiting for someone. Jamie hoped the cowboy was waiting for him. This man was making Jamie very aware of his presence: an athletic build of 6 feet 2 inches tall; long, dark hair; and beautiful, sapphire-blue eyes. He wore tight jeans that showed a well-formed and muscular butt, a black shirt, and a black cowboy hat.

Jamie could hardly contain his thoughts: *God, this man is what every man or woman would want in their bed. He is the epitome of what a man should look like!*

"Are you Jamie Walker?" The man spoke with a sexy, deep voice.

Jamie could feel a twitch in his groin that told him this could be dangerous. "Yes. Are you my ride to the ranch? I have business with the owner."

"Hop in."

They drove in silence for about 14 miles into the country. When they arrived at the ranch, Jamie was impressed by the sight of an elegant, three-story mansion, which appeared at the end of a long driveway. This was not at all what he had expected. He assumed the place would be a typical horse ranch owned by a typical horse breeder.

Obviously, this M. Morgan is extremely successful, judging by the size of this house, Jamie thought.

The man driving spoke up, pulling Jamie out of his thoughts: "Go in and make yourself comfortable, Mr. Walker. You are expected."

Jamie went in and found himself in the largest room he had ever seen. The furniture was masculine and massive, made of richly hued rosewood, and a strong, sweet aroma wafted through the room. It was obvious that no woman lived here because there were no frilly curtains or dainty decorations. This was definitely a man's house. He wondered when he was going to meet Mr. Morgan.

Just as he was wondering this, the gorgeous man came into the room and walked up to him. "Would you like a beer?"

"Sure, but can I see your boss, Mr. Morgan? I've come a long way, and I need to talk with him to see the horse that I've bought. Is he not here?"

"Yes. He's here … I am Marc Morgan."

Jamie almost lost his voice. "*You* are M. Morgan?" He knew that he sounded ridiculous. "Why didn't you introduce yourself at the airport? Why all the mystery?"

"I'm sorry for that, but I'm not a man of many words, and I was trying to size you up a little before we talked."

Jamie had to admit that this was a great turn of events. This man was Marc Morgan, and he was gorgeous, and it appeared that there was no woman in the house. Jamie wondered if that was a good sign.

Marc called for his staff to bring them beers and sandwiches.

"Please have a seat. We can eat something, and then we can go out and see the horse you've bought."

"When I do business with someone, I like to know a little about them," Jamie said. "Do you live here alone?" Jamie knew this was an inappropriate question, but he had an urgent need to know. This man was hard to ignore.

"No. I have a full staff living here—a cook, two maids, and a manservant who also drives for me when I want him to."

Jamie noted that he did not mention a wife. This was encouraging.

"Why did you want to know this?" Marc asked.

Jamie was suddenly embarrassed. "Oh, I don't know. Just curious." He knew this was a stupid answer, and Marc noticed it also. *What is your problem? Get your act together*, Jamie thought.

Marc was now very curious about Jamie. *Is he trying to find out something else about me that he's not asking?* He was aware of how uncomfortable Jamie was becoming. Marc decided to change the subject. "Jamie, finish up your beer, and let's go out to see your horse."

They walked to the beautiful stable buildings and met the horse's groom Keith. It was Jamie's opinion that the stables were kept as clean as the house, which confirmed that Marc Morgan was indeed very successful and no doubt worth millions. Jamie appreciated this as he was very wealthy in his own right. Once again, he was brought out of his thoughts by Marc's voice.

"Keith, will you bring Shadow to the exercise ring so that Mr. Walker can see what a magnificent breed he is?"

As they were leaving the stable, Jamie tripped and fell into Marc. Marc caught him before he fell and held him in his arms.

When Jamie looked up, he met the sapphire-blue eyes, and what he thought he saw briefly was desire. Was his dream going to come true or was this just wishful thinking? Was Marc gay? He sure didn't seem eager to let Jamie go.

Jamie heard this sexy voice asking him, "Are you okay?"

He pulled away from Marc and gained his composure. "Yes. Thanks for saving me from making a fool of myself sprawled out in the dirt."

"My pleasure, I assure you," Marc said with a smile on his face.

Oh, my god! What a sight when he smiled, Jamie thought.

They were in the exercise ring, watching Shadow being led around for Jamie to see. Jamie was not paying much attention to the horse though; instead, his mind was on the way Marc smiled at him and held him that extra second. He was so deep in thought that he did not hear Marc.

"Mr. Walker ... Jamie! Are you not interested in Shadow? I can assure you that I have the appropriate certification proving his genetic quality. Have you changed your mind about buying him?"

"No. I still want him. I want you too."

"*Excuse* me? What did you say?"

Jamie was so embarrassed that he had said this out loud. "I meant that I want you to show me more about what Shadow has done in the last year. Do you have the races that he's won?"

"Yes, of course — what kind of a breeder do you think I am?" Marc asked teasingly. He knew what Jamie had said and was not going to forget about it. *He is attracted to me, which tells me he is gay and so gorgeous!*

"Oh, no ... I did not mean to imply ..." Jamie stopped talking because he knew he was not making any sense. "I'm sorry to have offended you. Please, let's close the deal and let me get on my way home. I've brought a cashier's check for the agreed-upon $1 million for the horse, so let me sign the papers and I'll get out of your hair."

"Whoa, city boy! We don't do things that fast here in Wyoming. We take our time with everything we do." Marc was playing a little with Jamie.

Jamie's first thought was, *I just bet you do — one can only hope.* Luckily, this time he did not say it out loud. "Well, how long will this deal take?"

"As long as it takes me to get you naked and all ready for me," Marc would have loved to have said. Instead, he said. "Let's go back to the house and talk some more. I like to know the people I sell my horses to."

They walked back to the house slowly, both in deep thought. Jamie wanted to get closer to Marc, and Marc wanted to get just as close to Jamie.

"What does 'Three M' stand for?" Jamie asked, just to have some conversation while walking back to the house. "I noticed your ranch is called the Three M Ranch."

"It's from my name: Marc Montgomery Morgan. Three Ms."

Stay Awhile

When they arrived at the house, Marc called for the cook to start supper for two.

"Is steak okay with you, Jamie?"

"I can't stay for dinner ... I have to get back to my farm. I have a herd of horses needing my attention and a couple of mares expecting any time. I also have a deadline for the draft of my next book, so I need to get home. Sorry! If we could complete the sale now, I can make the arrangements to ship the horse and catch the next flight home."

"Jamie, I told you that we don't do things quickly here. I like to get to know who'll be taking my horses. I told you that outside. Did you think I was kidding?"

"No. I didn't think that, but I thought you understood that we need to do this faster than what you're used to because I am on a time schedule, and I do need to get home." *I should get out of your presence soon before I make a complete fool of myself and attack you,* Jamie was thinking as he sat down to sign the papers of the sale. *God, how much more do I have to endure? He is making me into a bumbling idiot!*

"Jamie, I'm sure that you can make some calls and have someone take care of things back at your ... uh, farm, is it? I really would like you to stay. I was going to set up the guest room for a few days. I want you to get to know your horse. He's worth staying for, I assure you."

I'm sure you are, Jamie thought, and then said, "I'll see what I can do."

"Good. Steak okay?"

"Yes, that's fine."

⁓ Jamie got on the phone and called his farmhand Derek. He gave Derek the instructions and told him to call if the mares went into labor. Jamie had built himself a wonderful home on the other side of the family pond and started raising horses. His property was still part of his grandmother's farm, which she had left him upon her death. The house was being used by his farmhand because it was closer to the stables than Jamie's house.

Derek told Jamie that he would call if he needed him to come home. He was a little curious as to why Jamie felt the need to call because Jamie knew he would be handling things at home. Derek wondered what this was really about. *Oh, well, he's the boss. I'm sure he'll fill me in when he gets back.* Derek liked Jamie very much but had not opened up to him about his feelings. Jamie had always been great to him, and Derek didn't want to spoil their friendship by coming out to him.

❧ Supper went without incident, and the two men retired to the study. They discussed Shadow and what he would do for Jamie as a stud. Everyone was clamoring to buy this horse for stud service because his lineage was the "who's who" in racing circles. They also discussed how Jamie would get the horse home. The one thing they didn't discuss was the elephant in the room. Jamie was extremely nervous being around Marc, and it was putting a strain on him.

Marc walked across the room toward Jamie and stopped right in front of him. He was so close that Jamie could feel his breath on his cheek.

"Jamie, why are you so anxious to get away from me? Why do I make you so nervous?"

"I think you know the answer to that, don't you? You kept me here just to see how I would react to your being this close … right?"

Marc didn't say anything. He just moved one step closer and pulled Jamie into his arms. Before Jamie could react, Marc's lips were on his, making him respond. Jamie had never felt a kiss like this one. It shook him all the way to his toes. Marc pulled away, leaving Jamie feeling abandoned.

He looked at Jamie and told him, "I am so sorry for that! I never should have taken these liberties with you. We just met. I'll have my manservant show you to your room. We'll sign all the papers in the morning, so you can catch your flight home. Goodnight, Jamie." Marc excused himself and left the study.

Jamie stood in the same place that Marc had just kissed him. The servant came in and told Jamie to follow him. Jamie obeyed. When he got to his room, he sat on the bed and wondered what had just happened. *Why would Marc do this to me? What kind of motive would he have to treat me like this? I don't even know him!*

Jamie did not sleep very well. At one point, he thought he heard footsteps outside his bedroom door, but no one knocked or came in. Somehow, he knew it was Marc, but obviously he decided against coming near Jamie again.

 Jamie came down to breakfast and Marc was waiting for him.

"I have the papers here for us to sign, and then my driver will take you to the airport. We'll ship Shadow to you before the week's end." Marc was being very standoffish and cool. No smiles or any sign of the man who practically begged him to stay the previous night.

Jamie signed the papers and went up to get his suitcase. He did not see Marc again before he left the ranch. All the way home on the plane, Jamie was trying to figure out what had happened. *What a strange man, this Marc Morgan is. Oh, well. I'll have no reason to see him again, so get over it, Walker.*

Rejection Hurts

Jamie went directly to the pond when he got home from the airport. This was his place to think and relax. He lay in the grass, looking up at the sky, and daydreamed.

Derek came up to Jamie and said, "Hi, Jamie. What was that about when you called me from Wyoming? You knew I was taking care of things here."

"I had to make it look like I needed to be at home."

"Can I ask what was so important that you needed to lie and ended up staying another day? Did the owner of the horse have a reason to keep you there?"

"Why are you asking me so many questions about it, Derek?"

Jamie sat up and looked up at Derek. Derek was fighting an internal battle, trying not to tell him that he was jealous of this stranger that kept Jamie away from the farm. Derek looked sad and Jamie noticed it.

He stood up and faced Derek. "Tell me what's going on with you."

"I'm gay, and I'm very attracted to you, Jamie." The words poured out, like a floodgate opening, and the words would not stop coming. "I've felt like this for a long time, and I'd give anything I have if you felt just a little something for me."

Jamie looked at Derek as if he had not seen him before. Derek was an extremely attractive man with light brown hair and hazel eyes, which changed colors with whatever he wore. He was 6 feet tall and very nicely built, which probably came from all the hard work at the farm. And he was standing there, wanting Jamie, unlike the strange man named Marc, who basically gave him his walking papers.

"I can see that you're shocked," Derek said, "and, if you can, please forget what I said. I don't know why this came out. I never intended you to ever know this."

"Wait, Derek — did I say that I didn't want to hear what you had to say? I'm actually glad that you told me. What would you say if I told you that I think we should go out on a date and have dinner and some drinks? Maybe then we can see what happens."

Derek was almost speechless. "I would *love* to go out on a date with you. I don't care where we go."

"Okay! Now, go back to what you were doing, and I'm going to the stables and saddle up a horse for a ride. I need to feel the wind on my face and clear my head."

Jamie took out one of the stallions that loved to run. He was running away from feelings that he needed to get over. He also thought about Derek. Could he have a relationship with him? *I'm willing to try*, he told himself. *At least he wants me.*

᙮ Marc was having a horrible day, and he was angry with everyone. The servants took the brunt of his unhappiness.

Why am I doing this? A guy named Jamie? How can I have these feelings so quickly? Marc had never wanted anyone like he wanted this man, and it was ridiculous because they didn't even know each other. The kiss really shook him up and made him crazy. He had to send Jamie away before he made a fool of himself. It was all for the best. *I'll send the horse to him and that will be that.* He kept trying to rationalize his actions.

᙮ Jamie was getting ready for his date with Derek. They would keep it lighthearted, with no strings. They would eat and then hit some of the bars. It should be fun. *Wait*, he thought, *who am I kidding?* He knew this was unfair to Derek, but Jamie needed something to concentrate on, so he wouldn't think about Marc.

Derek came into the house. Jamie took a look at him and was taken aback. He had never noticed that Derek was a real hunk. "Whoa! You look *amazing*!"

Derek was so happy that Jamie thought he looked hot. He tried hard to look great for him. He wore a sage-green shirt and tan slacks. Jamie noticed that the shirt made his eyes a vivid green, causing him to look dangerous and sexy. Jamie kept staring at him and thought, *Wow — why have I never noticed Derek before my trip to Cheyenne? This is going to be fun. Someone who looks like Derek can definitely make me forget Mr. Marc Morgan tonight.*

Jamie put his arm around Derek and said, "Let's go paint the town!"

They went to dinner, and then hit a gay bar. Jamie asked Derek to dance, and he took him in his arms. Derek was in heaven, having Jamie holding him so closely. He could feel his body as they moved to the music. Derek had drunk a few margaritas and was feeling good. Jamie was getting turned on just moving against Derek. He wanted to do a little more than dance. Rubbing up against Derek, he could feel his cock getting hard. Jamie grabbed him by the cheeks of his butt and starting grinding into him. Derek was also getting hard and wanted to be naked with Jamie and have Jamie's gorgeous mouth on his very ready cock.

"Let's go home, Derek. I want to show you how much you have moved me tonight."

Derek reached down and grabbed Jamie's crotch. "Moved you like *this?*" He then took Jamie's hand and placed it on his own hard cock. "I am *so* ready to go back to the farm with you."

As they were driving home, Derek reached over, unzipped Jamie's pants, and pulled out Jamie's cock. It was extremely hard and thick. He bent over and took Jamie into his mouth.

Jamie almost wrecked the car with that move. "Oh, my god, Derek — what are you *doing?*"

Derek raised up and asked, "You mean you don't *know?*"

"Well, yeeeeesssssssssss!" This was all Jamie could get out.

Derek was already back to work. Jamie was moaning and having a difficult time keeping the car on the road. It didn't take too long before Derek was getting rewarded for his efforts.

"God, that felt good, Derek. I needed that so much. You have no idea."

"There's more where that came from, if you're willing."

Jamie drove the rest of the way home with as much speed as the law would allow. He decided that they should go to his house instead of his grandmother's place where Derek lived because, even though his grandmother was gone, Jamie still felt funny about having sex in her home. When they got to the house, Jamie wanted to get Derek in a more undressed state. He took Derek in his arms and started unbuttoning his shirt. He took one button at a time, stopping to kiss his lips lightly, and then started on the next button. Derek found this quite erotic. He was on fire and wanted to hurry to the next phase, but Jamie had a different plan, taking everything very slowly.

All of a sudden, Jamie realized that slowing down and taking his good ole time reminded him of a previous conversation with Marc: "We take our time with everything we do." *What are you doing, Walker? Is this really what (or whom) you want?*

~ Like an omen, the phone rang. Before Jamie could get to it, the answering machine picked it up. He heard a deep, sexy voice, which he recognized immediately.

"Mr. Walker, this is Mr. Morgan. I just wanted to let you know that I am driving Shadow to you in the next couple of days. Let me know if this is not convenient. You know the number. If I don't hear from you, I will assume that it's okay, and I'll start out. It will take me about two days. Thanks for being so patient with this transaction. I know you're anxious to get your horse."

That's not all I am anxious about, Jamie thought. He turned to Derek and said, "I'm sorry, Derek, but I can't do this."

"What? Why have you changed your mind? Did I do something wrong? I thought you wanted me as much as I wanted you. You sure acted like it in the car."

"I did — but now I just can't do it."

"Oh, I see. You get a phone call, and everything is stopped. Well, that's fine. I don't want to be with someone who doesn't want me too." Derek buttoned up his shirt and excused himself. He had wanted Jamie for such a long time, but he was not going to prostitute himself if this was not a mutual situation. He realized that the voice on the phone bothered Jamie. *So this whole thing with staying in Wyoming an extra day was about this sexy voice. At least I had a taste — literally! — of what it would have been like to be with Jamie for a short while.*

ॐ Marc hung up the phone and was disappointed that he didn't get to talk to Jamie instead of his voice on the answering machine. He had made the decision to bring Shadow to Jamie himself because he couldn't stand the thought of never seeing Jamie again. He had to see if there was a strong chemistry, like a magnet pulling them toward each other. It seemed beyond their control. *So why did you send him packing, you fool?* Marc thought. *He's what you want, and you knew it then! Why didn't you go into his room that night when you stood outside his door? You are your own worst enemy, Marc Morgan.*

ॐ Jamie tried to sleep that night, but sleep eluded him. All he could think about was that Marc would arrive in a few days. *God, Jamie! You have it bad.*

Driving to Berea

Marc decided that he should bring Keith with him to handle Shadow until Jamie got used to him and until Shadow adjusted to his new surroundings.

"Keith, I need you to go with me to Berea, Kentucky, to help with Shadow. So, if you would, get him ready to travel and pack a bag. We'll be there for about a week."

Marc paced the floor that night because he couldn't stop thinking about seeing Jamie again. He hadn't heard from Jamie, so he knew he was up for having him bring the horse. That was a good sign.

� Jamie could not get it off his mind that Marc was leaving the next day for Kentucky. He wanted to see him very much. He too was not able to sleep, but he hadn't slept much since the phone call.

ᛣ Early in the morning, Marc and Keith loaded Shadow into the horse trailer and started off for Kentucky. Marc had butterflies in his stomach, thinking about seeing the beautiful blond who had taken over his every waking thought.

"Keith, do you think that, with stops along the way, we could make it to Kentucky in one day? I used MapQuest, and it's 1,259.67 miles to Berea, so it'll take about 18 hours and 51 minutes, without stops. If we start at 4 a.m., we should be there around 11 p.m. if you include all the stops."

"What's the hurry, Marc? Shadow will need some breaks in the travel. We should stop and lead him out of the trailer and let him walk around a little. Do you have to get there sooner than what you originally said? It'd be better for the horse if we stopped overnight — but if you need to get there sooner, then I guess we could do it."

"Well, I'd just like to get there sooner. The sooner we get there, the sooner we can get back. I have a lot of work on the ranch that I can't leave unattended for too long — but then I don't have to tell you that."

"Are you sure that's the real reason for this fast track to Berea? It couldn't be about Mr. Walker, could it?" Keith had noticed the tension between them when Jamie was at the ranch. He suspected that they were dancing around each other, trying to figure out what they both were feeling. Keith was gay and saw all the signs of Marc being gay. But, until this Walker guy came, Marc had not shown any attraction toward another man.

"Excuse me! I don't think that is any of your business. You just keep your mind where it should be — with Shadow. I will take care of Mr. Walker." *Boy, that is the truth. I will take care of Mr. Walker,* Marc thought.

"Okay. I sure didn't mean any disrespect." Keith stopped talking and just watched the road.

They drove for hours, only stopping long enough for gas, bathroom breaks, and food, and to exercise Shadow. Marc was driven — like a man on a mission, Keith noticed. Marc knew he was being ridiculous about traveling like this, but he couldn't stop himself. He wanted to see Jamie.

They arrived at Berea at 11 p.m. Marc told Keith to walk the horse. He would give Jamie a call to tell him that they were there and to get directions to the farm.

Jamie answered on the first ring. *God, Walker! You are really giving it away that you're anxious to hear from Marc.* "Hello, this is the Walker homestead." Jamie spoke more calmly than he thought he would.

"Hello, Mr. Walker. This is Marc Morgan. I've arrived in Berea. I know it's late, but I want to bring the horse to your ranch tonight, so that he can move around. He's been in the trailer for most of the day. Can you give me the instructions how to get there?"

"Come down the main drag through town. When you start seeing country, turn at the first road. You can only turn one way. Come down the road until you see the first house — that's the farmhouse; the stables are in the barn right behind the house. My house is a little farther down the road. We'll be waiting at the farmhouse for you." Jamie was so nervous that he could hardly contain himself. *How will Marc act when he sees me again?*

Jamie called down to the barn and told Derek that Marc and Keith were on their way to the farm. Jamie checked in the mirror to see how he looked, and then headed over to the barn.

When Jamie walked in, Derek did a double take. Jamie was wearing a beautiful brown sweater that brought out the brown and gold flecks in his eyes and skin-tight jeans that didn't leave much to the imagination. Derek thought he looked good enough to eat. All of a sudden, he resented this Marc guy because he was going to get what he wanted and almost had. Things had been a little strained between him and Jamie, but they were working past it. He knew that Marc was what Jamie wanted — that was very obvious when he heard the deep, sexy voice on the phone.

Marc and Keith were driving up to the barn when Derek came out to help with Shadow.

Keith noticed how great Derek looked right away. "Wow! I think I'm going to enjoy this week."

Marc asked him what he had said.

Keith just looked at him and answered, "Nothing."

Marc climbed out of the truck and started helping with Shadow. When Jamie walked out of the barn, Marc almost dropped the gate to the trailer. Jamie looked so amazing that he took Marc's breath away. *How can any one man look that good and still be real?*

Jamie walked up to Marc and put out his hand. "Welcome to the Walker farm."

Marc took Jamie's hand and shook it but didn't let go. They both stood there, looking at each other.

Marc looked at Jamie's lips and thought, *I want to kiss you so much!*

Jamie could read Marc's mind and said aloud, "Me too."

Marc shook his head a little and let go of Jamie. Jamie grinned because he knew that Marc wasn't expecting that comment.

Marc turned to Keith, trying to shake off the excitement he felt with Jamie's comment, and said, "Keith — let's get Shadow unloaded."

Derek walked around to the back of the trailer to help. Jamie introduced him to Marc, and then Marc introduced Derek to Keith. They shook hands, and then went into the barn together to get Shadow settled. They put him into the stall that Jamie had made for him. Derek noticed Keith looking at him and realized by the way he was checking him out that he was gay.

This could be fun, Derek thought.

"Let's go into the house and get something to eat. Are you two hungry?" Jamie asked.

"Yeah, we could use some food — and maybe a beer, if you have one," Marc responded with more control than he thought he would have.

Jamie stuck his head back in the barn. "Derek, come in and eat with us when you get Shadow settled."

"I'll help you, Derek," Keith said a little too eagerly.

"That's okay, Keith. I can handle it."

Keith looked disappointed but decided to let it drop. The three men went into the house, and Jamie got out some sandwich stuff.

Derek finished up and came in just as they sat down to eat. He noticed that an empty seat was next to Keith. *Cool. That works for me. He is really cute — a little eager, but cute.*

Marc and Jamie were talking about the horse, the drive here, and any other small talk they could think of. Both were very antsy about being together again. Jamie could feel Marc's knee against his and noticed that he didn't try to move it. The spot felt like it was burning. Jamie wanted to touch his knee and move his hand up Marc's inner thigh.

Marc must have been reading Jamie's mind because he laid his right hand on Jamie's knee. Jamie made a small groaning sound, which encouraged Marc to go further. He moved his hand up Jamie's inner thigh, getting really close to Jamie's groin.

Jamie wondered if Marc was going to stop there. *Oh, my god! What is he trying to do to me? Can't he see that I want him and need him?*

Marc knew what he was doing to Jamie, and he felt the same. He was not going to push Jamie away from him this time. He was determined to have what he craved. He had to think of some way to get him alone.

Jamie opened the door to the notion. Trying to get his voice to stay steady, he said, "Marc, I'd like to walk you to the pond and show you how beautiful it is at this time of night. I would also like to show you where I live."

"You don't live here?"

"No. This was my grandmother's farmhouse, and I didn't want to live in it. I wanted a place of my own. Derek lives here."

Keith automatically looked up. *Oh, boy. This is really going to be fun!* Derek's and Keith's eyes met with this revelation.

"About the walk — I think Keith and I should get settled into a hotel before we do anything else." Marc said this but hoped they wouldn't have to leave.

Keith was disappointed that Marc had even suggested it. He wanted to stay at the farm and grinned when he thought of what could come up between him and Derek.

"You are not going to stay in a hotel!" Jamie said. "We have plenty of bedrooms. My grandmother's house has five bedrooms and mine has seven. I think we can put you up. Derek, why don't you take Keith upstairs and show him one of the guest rooms? Keith, you should probably stay here with Derek because you guys will be working with the horse. If you don't mind, Marc, I would like you to stay with me at the main house because we'll have to talk business regarding the horse. Are these arrangements suitable with both of you?"

"Sure, that's awfully nice of you," Marc answered. "It'll be easier to take care of business this way. Maybe by staying here, we can get things done sooner, and Keith and I can get back to Wyoming sooner." Marc knew that this was not going to happen, but it is what he wanted Jamie to think.

୬ Derek took Keith upstairs and showed him where he could stay. As they entered the room, Keith asked Derek if he was gay.

Derek looked him in the eye. "You know I am. You know I saw you checking me out, and I was not offended, so what do you want to do about this turn of events? It looks like we're going to be left on our own."

"Well, I would like to get to know you better, Derek. Maybe we can start with another beer and a little conversation."

"That works for me. Let's go back down to the kitchen. We'll talk and get more comfortable with each other."

Derek was getting a new chance. He knew Jamie was into Marc — the tension was so thick that you could cut it with a knife. So why shouldn't he see what might develop with Keith? *He is so good looking, and I am really horny.*

❧ Jamie and Marc walked to the pond. Marc decided that he would drive the truck to Jamie's house later. He wanted to be alone with Jamie now.

Jamie was feeling the same way, and for some reason he was nervous. *Is he going to kiss me again?* Jamie wondered. His palms were sweaty, and his groin was crying. He had never been attracted to anyone like he was to this man. He would never just jump into bed with someone so easily, but he would do whatever this cowboy wanted and not worry about the consequences.

They continued the walk to the pond in silence. When they got there, Jamie stopped and told Marc that it was his favorite place in the world.

Marc watched Jamie's face in the moonlight, with his blond hair shining in its glow. He had never seen anyone more beautiful. *God, I want to do this right, but I am not sure I can keep myself under control being around him.*

"Marc? Why are you not talking?"

Marc couldn't stand it any longer. He moved very swiftly and took Jamie in his arms. He kissed his most kissable lips, with all the passion that he had been thinking about doing ever since he sent him away. Marc groaned out loud as Jamie responded, opening his mouth for Marc's tongue to enter. Marc licked him everywhere inside his warm mouth. Their tongues were dancing together, and one was no more demanding than the other. Their breathing became erratic, and both men were consumed with the other. The outside world no longer existed. Finally, they came up for air. Neither one knew who broke the kiss. When they separated their lips, they stood in silence, staring at each other.

"Jamie, I have no idea what's happened to me since I met you, but you have taken over my entire life. I can't think of anything else but you. I had to bring the horse so that I could do this."

He took possession of Jamie's lips again, and Jamie melted into a heap of mush, making small, faint sounds that made Marc crazy.

Against Jamie's lips, Marc whispered, "I want you so much, and this is so hard for me because I have never felt this way for any other man. I can't get you out of my mind." He broke the kiss again and held Jamie firmly in his arms, moving his head back so he could see Jamie's eyes. "Do you feel anything even remotely close to what I feel for you?"

"Yes, Marc. I haven't thought of anyone but you since you sent me away. Why did you do that? You could have had me then if you had entered my room that night when you were outside the door. I would not have been able to deny you anything."

"Okay, Jamie. I'm knocking at your bedroom door. Will you let me in now?"

Jamie answered by once more kissing him, and then taking this very handsome cowboy by the hand and leading him to his house with the promise of heaven on Earth.

Heaven on Earth

Jamie led Marc to the house. When they got inside, Marc pulled Jamie back into an embrace. "Jamie, I want you to know something before we go any further."

"What? What is it?" Jamie asked, a little worried. *Is he going to tell me that this is going to be a one-time thing and, when he goes back to Cheyenne, it will be done?*

Marc saw the look of concern on Jamie's face and quickly spoke. "I have never been with a man before because I didn't want to unless it was for a real relationship. I can't just sleep with you, and then be pushed aside. I don't want meaningless sex. That is not me. If we do this, you will be mine and I will be yours and only yours."

Jamie was moved by Marc's words and relieved that Marc wasn't going to leave him after. Jamie put both hands on Marc's cheeks and pulled him down into a sweet but emotional kiss as tears formed in Marc's eyes. At that moment, he knew he loved this wonderful, handsome cowboy, and he was going to show him how much. "Marc, come knock on my bedroom door like you asked me if you could. I want to let you into my bedroom, my heart, and my life." Jamie led him to the master bedroom. The room was huge, and the bed was a four-poster king.

Marc stopped outside and smiled at Jamie. "You go in and shut the door. I'll give you a minute or so, and then I'm going to knock." He knew this was silly, but he wanted to do it anyway.

Jamie did as he asked. When he shut the door, he raced to take off his clothes. He wanted to be standing, waiting, when Marc knocked. He lit some candles and dimmed the lights in the room. He was ready.

Marc figured he had waited long enough, so he tapped on the door. Both of them knew this was laughable, but it was sort of symbolic too.

Jamie told Marc to come in. Marc opened the door and stopped dead still. The picture before him was unbelievable. Jamie was standing in the candlelit room with nothing on. Marc didn't think he could move; the site mesmerized him. Jamie's skin and hair were glowing in this light. He was absolutely the most exquisite thing he had ever laid eyes on. He looked like a Greek god, only with blond hair.

Marc took a couple of steps into the room and stared at Jamie. "I have never seen anything in my life that I wanted more than you at this moment."

"Come here, Marc. Come close to me."

Marc closed the distance between them in two steps. He touched Jamie's face, and then moved his hands down Jamie's magnificent body. Jamie started unbuttoning Marc's shirt and pulled it off. When he slipped Marc's jeans and briefs down and off, he exposed Marc's manhood. Jamie uttered a sound that Marc had never heard before. Jamie had to touch Marc. He brushed his hand against Marc's hip and groin, causing Marc to grab Jamie and pull him against him.

"God, Jamie. Your touch sets me on fire. I have never felt this before. Please show me how to make you happy."

Jamie knelt in front of Marc and took him into his hands. He kissed the head and all the way down the shaft with tiny kisses. He handled Marc's balls gently and licked them.

Marc started moaning, and his breath was coming faster. "Oh, my god!"

Jamie took him in his mouth and gently, with his teeth, moved very slowly up the shaft to the tip. This was driving Marc insane. Jamie licked up the back of his cock, and then took him again into his mouth. Marc thought there could be no better feeling in the world than this sensation that Jamie was causing with his mouth. Jamie moved up and down with a smooth, rhythmic motion that sent Marc over the top. He came in Jamie's mouth, pulsating with so many waves, and Jamie took it all. He licked Marc clean and stood up to face him. Marc kissed him and ran his tongue into Jamie's warm, wet mouth — the mouth that had given him so much pleasure.

Jamie was starting to ache from his own need to come. Marc noticed and took Jamie to the bed. They climbed in, and Marc laid Jamie on his back. Marc moved down to give Jamie the same pleasure he had just given him. With his mouth wrapped around Jamie's cock, he moved up and down. He was not practiced at this, so he stumbled a little but caught on quickly when he heard sounds of pleasure coming out of Jamie. As aroused as Jamie was, it didn't take long before he started to come. Marc was unsure about swallowing Jamie's cum, but when he tasted it he wanted it all. They were wrapped in each other's arms, and neither wanted to leave the other.

"Jamie, are you happy right now?"

"Yes, Marc. I couldn't be happier. Why do you ask? Don't you think we were good together?"

"Of course. I think we were great! Since I'm not experienced, I had my concerns," Marc said.

Jamie was amazed that a personality as strong as Marc — a man who owned a 750-acre ranch — could be so vulnerable and unsure when it came to making love, but Jamie was willing to teach him.

Jamie wrapped his arms tightly around Marc and snuggled against him. "You are good enough for me. I want to sleep in your arms and wake up in them in the morning. Just hold me, and don't let me go."

They slept. Tomorrow was another day.

Coming Together

Derek and Keith talked most of the night. They felt the need to get to know each other. They would be working together, at least until the horse was settled in.

"Keith, how do you like the farm — what little you've seen of it?"

"I like it fine, but what I like most about it is meeting you. What are your duties here?"

"We can talk about that tomorrow. How long have you been with Mr. Morgan? Have you two ever …?"

Keith cut him off. "No — heavens, no. He's been waiting for just the right man to come along, and it looks like he's found him. It was quite obvious the way he reacted in Cheyenne when your boss came to visit us. Also, what gave it away was when he said that he was going to bring the horse himself. I knew then that this guy was special. The final thing was that we had to drive nonstop to get here."

"Well, I'm glad you came with him."

"Me too."

"We'd better get some sleep. I have a feeling that we're going to have an early day tomorrow. Do you remember where your bedroom is?"

"Yes, but aren't you going to escort me up there?" Keith asked with a smile on his face.

"I think you're a big boy and can find your own way. I have to shut everything down and lock up. You'll be fine alone." Derek grinned at the hurt look on Keith's face, but he was feeling playful.

Keith went upstairs, and Derek started locking up and turning lights off.

As Derek walked up the stairs to his bedroom, he ran straight into Keith. "What do you think you're doing? You scared me to *death*! I wasn't expecting to run into you in the hall."

Keith moved closer and put his hands on Derek's cheeks. "I have wanted to do this ever since you walked out of the barn this evening." He kissed Derek very softly.

Derek responded very quickly. He opened his mouth to let Keith in and kissed him deeply, matching kiss for kiss, lick for lick.

"I want to spend the night with you, Derek. I want to show you how much being with me would do for you."

Derek pushed him away. "What? Do you think you're that hot? That no one can resist you? With an ego like that, you can forget about getting me into bed with you. I don't need you to show me how to … Oh, hell. Get out of my way." Derek pushed past Keith and headed to his bedroom. When he got there, he made sure the door was locked. *How dare he?* Derek thought. *He is good looking, but not that damn good looking. God, what an ego!*

Derek got undressed and went to bed. At about 4 a.m., he was awakened by a knock on his door. He knew it was Keith. He got up and went to the door. "What do you want?"

"I want to come in and talk to you. I don't want us to get off on the wrong foot, and I couldn't sleep until I apologized for what I said to you. Please, Derek. Open the door and let me in."

"Keith, it's 4 a.m. We can talk tomorrow." Derek went back to bed.

Keith knocked again. "Please, Derek, let me in. I promise I won't attack you."

Derek knew that he was not going to get any more sleep if he didn't let him say what he wanted. He went over to the door and unlocked it. Keith heard the lock move, and he opened the door. He stood there, unsure of what do to.

Derek lost his patience. "Okay, Keith. What do you want to say? Let's get this over with, so I can get some sleep. I have a lot of chores to do in the morning."

"I'll help you with them. Just listen to me. I am sorry for being so crude. I didn't mean to come off like some Casanova. I'm not that experienced with men … but I wanted you and just didn't handle it well."

"Apology accepted. Now, can I get some sleep? Go away." Derek turned to go back to the bed when Keith grabbed his arm, pulling him close.

"I want you," Keith said as he moved his hand down to Derek's cock. He touched him and got a response almost immediately.

Derek had pajama bottoms on and nothing else. He groaned a little when Keith touched him and wanted him to continue. Keith knew that his hand was not rejected, and he kept getting braver. He reached in the front of Derek's pajamas and took him into his hand. He moved up and down a couple of times until Derek leaked some precum.

"Derek, I want to continue but not unless you say that you want me to. Do you want me to keep going?"

"Yes," he whispered. Derek was feeling good under Keith's expert touch.

Keith took both hands and worked Derek up and down. Derek was moving his hips forward, wanting more. Keith pulled off Derek's pants, and Derek was standing completely naked. He pulled Keith to the bed and lay down, pulling Keith on top of him. Keith stripped off his pajama bottoms too, and both men lay naked with their bodies touching in every way.

Keith moved down and took Derek in his mouth while holding his balls and gently massaging them. He licked up the back of his cock and then down to the sensitive spot between his cock and his balls. He licked around his balls and then between his rectum and the base of his balls. Derek was moaning for Keith to move faster. Keith took him back in his mouth and moved rapidly until Derek came. They both came down from the throws of passion and stayed very still in each other's arms.

"I can't believe I let you do that. I had no intention of having any more to do with you. God, can you persuade a guy to change his mind!"

"I wanted you, and I knew, regardless of what you said, you wanted me too — until I opened my big mouth and inserted my foot."

"That is a colorful description, but I can think of something else that's much better inserted in your big mouth than your foot."

Both men laughed and hugged.

Keith smiled. "You owe me, Derek."

Derek shook his head. "Let's get some sleep, okay?"

They both closed their eyes and drifted off.

◅ Marc woke up first with Jamie still lying in his arms. He smiled and remembered the previous night. *God, Jamie was so easy on the eyes and so wonderful to be with!* Marc was glad that he had waited for Jamie to come into his life. He pulled him closer and kissed him on the forehead. Jamie stirred and looked up at Marc.

Marc whispered in Jamie's ear, "I am falling in love with you."

Jamie heard the words and sat up, wiping the sleep from his eyes. "Did you say what I *think* you said?"

"Yes, Jamie. I am falling in love with you."

Jamie fell back into Marc's arms and said, "I think I'm falling in love with you too, but how can this be? We just met. We don't even know anything about each other. I do know that I can't get you off my mind. You have occupied every waking hour of my days since I met you. I just want to be with you."

Marc hugged him with all the strength he had and told Jamie that he wanted to be with him also. Marc claimed Jamie's lips, his mouth, and his tongue. Their kisses got deeper and more urgent. When they stopped kissing, Jamie tried to get his breath under control.

"Do you know how you make my heart, my body, and my mind want you *totally*, Marc? I want to crawl into your skin. It's as though I can't get close enough to you. God, you have totally possessed my soul."

Marc caught his breath and listened to Jamie describe his feelings for him. All he could say was that he felt the same way.

Jamie wanted to lighten the mood. He thought they needed to talk about the heavy stuff later tonight, perhaps over dinner, wine, and candlelight. Right now, he wanted to ride with Marc and show him the grounds. "Marc, let's get up and shower and take a ride before breakfast. What do you say? I want to show you my home."

"Okay," Marc said reluctantly. "I guess I can wait until tonight to have you all to myself. I want to make love to you, Jamie."

Jamie knew what he was trying to say, and he knew that, even though he had never given himself completely to another man, he was ready to do so with Marc. He also knew that Marc had also never been with a man before, and they would learn together.

"Let's get up, Marc," Jamie said as he pulled him out of bed and guided him to the shower. "I'll use the one off the other bedroom down the hall."

"Ah, Jamie. Why don't you shower with me? It would be so much more fun!"

"I know — that's the *exact* reason why I am not going there with you. We would never get out of this bedroom!"

Marc was feeling playful. "So? What's wrong with *that*?"

"Get in there," he said as he pushed him toward the bathroom. "I'm outta here."

Jamie waited until Marc was in the bathroom. All of a sudden, he ran over to Marc and grabbed him, spun him around, kissed him quickly on the mouth, and then ran out before Marc could react.

He heard Marc holler as he left the room, "You're in trouble now, Walker!"

Walker's Pond

Jamie and Marc got ready for their ride. Jamie came downstairs first and waited anxiously for Marc to come down. When he spotted Marc on the stairs, he almost fainted. Marc was wearing black jeans, a black Western shirt, black cowboy boots, and a black cowboy hat. With his flowing black hair and blue eyes, he was the most stunning-looking man Jamie had ever seen. *Wow, this gorgeous man is going to be totally mine soon*, Jamie thought. *Thank you, Lord, for sending me to Cheyenne to buy a horse!*

At the bottom of the stairs, Marc walked up to Jamie and noticed his expression. "You like what you see, Jamie?"

"Oh, I don't know. I guess you'll do," he said as he closed the small distance between them and put his lips on Marc's wonderful mouth.

Marc reacted by pulling Jamie into his arms and opening Jamie's mouth with his insistent tongue. Jamie started moaning, wanting more.

Marc finally released Jamie's luscious lips and stood smiling at him. "Now, will I *just* do?"

Jamie was still trying to get his breath back. "Yep, you will *more* than do. I think I'll keep you around."

"You bet your sweet ass you will!" Marc laughed.

He walked past Jamie and headed to the barn to get their horses ready. Jamie had already asked Derek to get two horses saddled for their ride. When they got down to the barn, Marc and Jamie noticed that Derek and Keith were quite friendly. They were standing close and had shit-eating grins on their faces.

"What have *you* two been up to?" Marc asked. "You both look like you've been up all night. Hmm … let me see … been in bed with each other all night?"

"Maybe," Keith said as he smiled at Derek.

Derek walked past Keith and smacked him on the butt.

❧ Jamie and Marc got on their horses and set off on a morning ride around the property. Jamie was anxious to show Marc what he owned and how beautiful it was. They rode hard and even challenged each other to a race. In full gallop across the fields, Marc noticed how beautiful Jamie was on the horse with the wind blowing his blond tresses from his face. He looked as if he were one with the horse. Jamie was also watching Marc. It was obvious that he rode all the time and was extremely comfortable in the saddle.

They finally pulled the horses to a stop and got off to walk around the pond. They walked for a while, leading their horses to a tree and tying them to it.

"Let's go sit by the pond," Jamie suggested.

Marc moved beside him and sat down. He thought it was a pretty and peaceful place. The water in the pond was so clear that you could almost see the bottom, and the area was surrounded by trees — huge, beautiful oaks, which had obviously been around for several hundred years.

This place must be steeped in history, Marc observed. *Probably dating back to the early 1800s.* He could see why Jamie thought this place was so special. "Jamie, come sit closer to me," he motioned as he patted the spot next to him.

Jamie did as he was asked. Marc put his arm around Jamie's shoulder and pulled him down on the ground, laying him flat. He moved onto Jamie and pinned him under his body. He started at his lips and kissed him lightly, and then moved to his ear and neck. Jamie melted under Marc's lips. Marc kept moving down Jamie's neck to the area exposed by the open collar. As he did so, he started unbuttoning Jamie's shirt. When he got all the buttons undone, he opened the shirt to expose his beautiful chest and abs.

"God, Jamie. You are so beautiful."

Marc put his hands on Jamie's chest and gently touched his nipple with his fingers. Jamie moaned. After hearing that sound come out of Jamie,

Marc kissed his nipple and licked around it, flicking it with his tongue. This was driving Jamie crazy.

Jamie whispered Marc's name and begged, "Please ..."

Marc was so turned on that he moved his hands across Jamie's chest and fondled him all the way down to his belt buckle. Jamie was breathing heavily and moving under Marc. He whispered Marc's name again, and Marc almost came in his jeans at the sound of his name softly coming from Jamie's lips. He had never felt like this before, and he didn't want this feeling to end. As he kissed Jamie again on his soft lips, he put his hand on Jamie's crotch. Jamie let out a moan and moved his hips forward, pushing his hard cock into Marc's hand.

"Marc ... Marc ..." Jamie muttered, moving his head from side to side. "Please, take me in your mouth. You are driving me *crazy!*"

That was all Marc needed to hear. He immediately pulled off Jamie's jeans and briefs. He went down on Jamie and took him into his mouth. He started moving up and down while sucking at the same time.

Jamie was almost screaming in ecstasy. *I want to stop this because I want Marc in my mouth also,* he thought. He suddenly pulled Marc's head up and told him to please take his pants off. "I want to take you in my mouth. I want to do this together."

"What do you mean, Jamie? I don't understand ..."

"Just take off your jeans and I'll show you."

Marc did as he was asked.

"Lie down. I promise you won't regret it."

Marc lay on the ground, and Jamie took his position over Marc with his head at Marc's feet. Marc looked up and had Jamie's cock in his face. Jamie took Marc in his mouth and started moving up and down. Marc was getting the idea and took Jamie back in his mouth. They worked together until they both came. They were in heaven with each one tasting the other. It was so powerful. Marc had learned something new again with Jamie.

"That was amazing, Jamie. I *love* being with you. It's like I can't get enough of you! Let's get out of the rest of our clothes and have a swim before we go back to the house for breakfast. The water looks so inviting."

"Okay, Marc. Whatever you want. Last one in is a rotten egg!"

Jamie ran to the pond with Marc on his heels. They swam and played and kissed. When they had almost worn themselves out, they climbed out of the water and got dressed.

As they mounted their horses, Jamie looked at Marc and said, "I want to be yours forever."

Marc shook his head as if to say, "Me too."

Dinner for Two

Marc and Jamie rode back to the barn and turned the horses over to Derek to brush down. Keith was in the exercise ring, riding Shadow around.

Jamie approached Derek and asked him about last night. "Are you and Keith getting along okay? It looks to me and Marc that you did more than chat last night."

"You could say that. We did have a good time. You'll have to thank Marc for me. I'm so glad that he brought Keith with him. Speaking of Marc, how are you two getting along? I could tell that he was important to you when he called and you heard his voice. I knew then that I didn't have a chance with you. I really care about you, Jamie, and I want you to be happy. I knew when I saw that constant grin on your face since he got here that you are. I just hope he doesn't hurt you. What's going to happen with the two of you when he goes back to Cheyenne?"

"He'll move here, I'm sure. Maybe Keith will come here to live with Marc. You'd like that, wouldn't you?"

"I wouldn't be too sure about that! I don't think Marc's going to give up his ranch."

"Yes, he will. He loves me."

About that time, Marc came into the stable. As he came up behind Jamie, he asked, "*Who* loves you?"

"Who do you *think*?"

They both laughed and headed to the house. Derek did not laugh because he felt that Jamie was in for some heartbreak.

Keith brought Shadow into the stall and brushed him down, put some oats in the feeder, and came out to stand with Derek.

"Keith, do you think Marc will ever leave Cheyenne and move here with Jamie?"

"Heavens, no," Keith answered. "Jamie will have to move to Wyoming if he wants to be with Marc. Why do you ask? Did he say he would?"

"No. Jamie just thinks that Marc will be willing to stay here."

"Never happen. I assure you."

⋘ The day went by very quickly, and Jamie was getting anxious to have dinner with Marc. He had a lot of things planned for tonight, and he wanted everything to be just so. Jamie gave all the instructions to Betsy, the African American cook, and his butler Maurice and went up to take a shower and get ready. Marc had already gone up to his room. When he heard Jamie come up the stairs, he stuck his head out of the door and grabbed Jamie as he passed.

"Marc, what are you doing?" Jamie asked as he was dragged into the room.

Marc didn't answer. He pulled Jamie close, put both hands on his cheeks, and claimed his lips. "God, I love kissing you. I can never get enough!"

"I enjoy it too, Marc, but you're going to have to let me go and get ready for our dinner."

"Okay, okay. I'll let you go for now, but tonight I'm not going to let you slip away. You're going to be mine. I want to possess you — body and soul!"

"You'll get your chance later, I promise."

⋘ Marc and Jamie had spent the entire day together, talking and working with Derek, Keith, and Shadow. Jamie told Marc of his plans for Shadow. He shared the bestselling books he had written — none of which Marc had read, he confessed, as they just weren't his "cup of tea." They were fictional stories of historical time travel, with the main character falling in love with someone from another time. Marc said he preferred reading nonfiction, such as books about Indians and their interactions with white settlers. Jamie told Marc that his next book would take place in Cheyenne, with a very handsome Indian warrior, written just for him.

They laughed about that, and Marc said, "You write it, and I'll read it!"

❧ Marc came down to dinner first. He had struggled with what to wear but finally decided on starched jeans, cowboy boots, and a red Western shirt that looked incredibly good on him with his black hair and blue eyes.

Maurice asked Marc what he would like to drink. Marc settled on a beer and waited in the lounge for Jamie to come down. When Marc turned around and saw Jamie coming into the lounge, his heart skipped a beat and he gasped. *Thank you, Lord, for giving him to me.*

Jamie wore a pair of jeans and a gold, button-down shirt, which was the same color as his hair and showed off his golden-brown eyes. Jamie was so pleased that his looks got that kind of response from Marc. Marc immediately closed the distance across the room and took Jamie into his arms, kissing him passionately, sliding his tongue into Jamie's warm mouth, and smothering him with kisses all over his face and neck.

"You know that you are knock-down gorgeous, and I want to do all kinds of great-but-naughty things to you! I'm not sure I can wait until after dinner to take you completely and make you a part of me."

Jamie teasingly said, "Well, I guess you will *have* to wait because we are going to eat first."

"Oh, okay, but then ..."

They walked hand in hand into the dining room. The lights were out, and candles were lit all around the room. The table was set and ready for a very intimate dinner. Wine was poured, soft music played in the background, and the first course was served.

Marc kept staring at Jamie because he was absolutely the most beautiful thing he had ever seen with the candlelight dancing in his eyes. Marc couldn't help himself. He leaned over the table and briefly kissed Jamie, whispering, "I'm lost every time I look at you. I can't think straight, so you'll have to lead me through this night!"

Jamie was so taken with Marc's words that tears formed in his eyes. "I know this is very soon since we've only known each other a couple of weeks, but I want you to know that I do love you, Marc."

Marc was so happy to hear those words. He was not the only one feeling the draw between them. He had never encountered anyone like Jamie and, as soon as he saw him, he knew he was hooked. "Jamie, I am in love with you too. Let's finish dinner so we can go on with our wonderful, exciting evening. That is, if you want to finish dinner!"

Jamie got up, walked around the table, and pulled Marc to his feet. "You want me to lead you through the night? Well, let's go on that journey."

ᴥ Jamie led, and Marc followed. He took Marc to his bedroom suite and opened the door. Marc couldn't believe his eyes. There were candles everywhere and all lit. It looked like hundreds, but Marc knew that it couldn't be that many. There was a fire in the fireplace and a beautiful, thick, plush, white bearskin rug on the floor in front of the fire. Jamie had exceptionally soft music playing, and the whole room smelled of jasmine. He had planned it to be perfect for their first time together.

Jamie pulled Marc into the room and shut the door behind them. "Marc, I want to take this slow and savor every moment of our lovemaking." He pulled Marc in front of the fireplace and moved in close, so he could start undoing his shirt. "God, Marc, you look so good in red. Well, for that matter, you look good in anything you put on, but now I want you without any clothes." He began to push off Marc's shirt from his shoulders and moved his hands down his arms until it hit the floor. Then he put his hands on Marc's chest and felt his pecs, moving his hands very softly across his chest.

Marc was in heaven. He loved feeling Jamie's hands on him. When Jamie licked his nipple and gently sucked on it, Marc thought that he had never felt anything so erotic and wonderful. He responded by trying to kiss Jamie's neck.

Jamie let him kiss his neck for a short time, but he wanted to be in control for a while. He put his hands on Marc's belt buckle and started to undo it. Marc sighed and closed his eyes. Jamie ran his hand down the front of Marc's jeans and found his target. Marc made a small sound and opened his eyes. He looked straight into Jamie's golden-brown eyes and saw the lust and love that was shining back at him.

Marc's cock was very hard, but he agreed with Jamie — he wanted this to last. He started undoing Jamie's shirt, one button at a time. He ran his hands under Jamie's shirt and around to his back, pulling him against his bare skin. The sensation of Jamie's skin touching his was very addicting.

They held each other, bare chest to bare chest, wrapped together. Jamie kissed Marc's lips slowly, licking his lips and putting his tongue on his lower lip so that Marc would let him in. Marc's mouth opened, and Jamie moved in. He kept kissing Marc and licking all around his wonderful mouth. He could feel Marc's hard cock against his, and it was driving him crazy.

They pulled themselves apart and stared at each other for a second, and then started rubbing chest to chest, mouth to mouth, tongues dancing together in perfect unison. Marc started undoing Jamie's jeans and pushing them down. He stepped out of his own jeans and Jamie followed suit. Neither one had worn underwear, anticipating this very thing. They didn't want anything between them. Marc wanted to feel Jamie all over. They rubbed their groins together, feeling the want between them. Jamie moved away from Marc and lay on the rug in front of the fire, reaching up for Marc to join him. When he looked down at Jamie, Marc thought that he had never wanted anything this much before.

He knelt down and kissed Jamie again. "Jamie, I want you so much. I hope I can last long enough!"

"It will be wonderful, Marc. You'll see."

Jamie encouraged Marc to lie down beside him. They wrapped their arms around each other and pressed their bodies close enough to know that each one could come anytime. Marc leaned up and positioned himself to be able to taste Jamie's cock. He ran his tongue down Jamie's cock and up and around the head. He put his tongue in the slit at the top and heard the most wonderful sound come out of Jamie. Jamie breathed heavily, his chest moving up and down, faster and faster. Marc could taste the precum, and it was delicious. He put his mouth over the head and took it entirely in his mouth. Moving up and down, he ran his hand down and around Jamie's balls.

Jamie cried out in ecstasy. He was moving his hips up and down. "Marc … Marc … stop or I'm going to come!"

"Yes, you are." Marc moved up and down again, and Jamie filled his mouth with cum. It tasted so good, and Marc licked him completely until Jamie came down from his orgasm.

"Marc, I want you deep inside of me. I have never given myself to another man, and I want you to be my first and last. I have saved myself for you — the man I love."

"Jamie, I'm not sure what to do since I've never done this."

Jamie shifted himself, spread his legs, and said, "Do whatever you feel is the right way."

Marc watched and got the idea. He rubbed his hand over Jamie's cock to his butt. He loved the feel of Jamie in his hands. He moved farther back and touched Jamie's love spot. He paused and looked at Jamie. "Jamie, are you sure you want to do this? We can stop if you want — I don't want you to feel you have to." Marc's real fear was that he was afraid he would hurt Jamie and disappoint him. He was so nervous that he was visibly shaking.

"Marc — I want this, please. Don't worry. You love me, right?"

"You know I do. I came all the way from Cheyenne just so I could be near you again. I have never done that for anyone else. If I was unsure about it before, it went away when I saw you again."

"You are not going to hurt me, Marc, and I know you are not going to disappoint me. I've got some things that I'm told we need. They're in that drawer over there."

Marc got up and went to the drawer. Jamie had gotten a tube of lube and some condoms. He came back to the rug and lay down again with Jamie. He was still hard, so there wasn't much need for more foreplay. Jamie spread himself again and told Marc what he should do with the lube. Marc put some on his fingers and started toward his goal. Using one finger, Jamie started to move around. Marc could feel how tight he was and worried again about hurting him. Jamie was becoming breathless while Marc moved his finger in and out. Marc added another finger and spread both fingers inside of Jamie, going around in circles and in and out. By this time, Jamie was really squirming underneath Marc. Marc saw his facial expressions and was getting turned on just watching Jamie. He knew he was making him happy.

"Marc … please … I want you inside me."

Marc was ready, and he reached for the condom. He placed himself at the entrance to Jamie. Jamie raised his hips and stuffed one of the fireplace hearth pillows under him. He put his legs around Marc's waist and opened them wider. Marc instinctively knew what to do. Both guys were so turned on and had raging hard-ons. He pushed forward and saw Jamie wince.

"Please, Marc — make me yours," Jamie moaned.

Just hearing Jamie say his name while he was moaning was such a turn-on to Marc. He moved in a little closer and was amazed at how tight and hot Jamie felt around his cock. *God, he is everything!* Marc moved back and forth and, the more he moved, the more Jamie moaned his name.

Finally, Jamie couldn't take it anymore. He put his hands on the hearth above his head and pushed toward Marc as hard as he could, shoving Marc all the way into him. Marc let out a cry, grabbed Jamie's hips, and pounded into him at a rapid pace. Jamie was working himself and Marc kept coming into him hard.

"Jamie … Jamie, my love. You're mine, and I'm yours, and I am coming! Oh, god!"

"I'm coming too!" Jamie shouted.

They were both so loud that it was hard to know what was going on.

With waves of pleasure, Marc was spent and lay down on Jamie's chest with his head in Jamie's cum. He licked some of it, and then ran his fingers in it and put them in Jamie's mouth.

"Oh — *so* good," Jamie moaned.

They lay there for a few minutes, and then Marc was soft and slipped out of Jamie. Jamie hated him leaving his body. He had never felt anything like that before. He had given his virginity to Marc and now he belonged to him. Marc was coming down from cloud nine. He wrapped his arms around Jamie and held him. Jamie put little kisses on Marc's face and nose.

"Jamie, I love you with all my heart. Please stay with me for always. Promise me."

"I promise, my wonderful, handsome cowboy! I am yours, and I will always be with you."

They cuddled and watched the logs crackle in the fireplace. After a while, the embers got lower.

"Do you want to get up and shower and go back down to finish our meal?" Jamie asked.

"No. I want to shower and put some more logs on the fire and lie on this rug and maybe have another taste of you. That's all the eating I need to do right now."

"Well, I led you through tonight. You can lead me through our life together."

The Separation

Jamie and Marc spent every day together, working with Shadow during the day and making love at night. They could not get enough. It was the end of the week, and Marc and Keith had to get ready to go home. That night, Jamie and Marc knew they were going to have to make some decisions about where to go from here. Neither wanted to be separated from the other. At dinner that night, they talked about the future.

"Marc, how long will it take you to settle the sale of your ranch in Cheyenne and move the horses and everything here?"

Marc looked at Jamie in disbelief. "What are you *talking* about? I'm not selling my ranch. I thought you would move to Cheyenne with me. You can write your novels anywhere, and I certainly have more room for both stables of horses at my ranch than you do here."

Jamie was shocked. He never thought about leaving his homestead. "Excuse me, Marc, but why do you think I can give up the only home I have ever known and just pick up and move to Cheyenne?"

Both men were starting to raise their voices a little.

Maurice came in to see if all was okay. He also thought that his presence would calm things down a little. "Sir, can I get you and Mr. Morgan anything else to drink or eat?"

"No, Maurice. That will be all. I think Mr. Morgan and I are done here," Jamie said with anger in his voice as he walked out of the room.

"Jamie, wait! Okay, right. That is really mature. Run out at the first hint of trouble."

Jamie came back into the room, raising his voice even more. "What is there left to say? You won't sell your ranch, and I won't sell my family farm."

"Jamie, do you love me, or was this just about sex?"

"How can you say that after what we promised each other?" Jamie was angry and hurt at the same time. "I'm going to ask this one more time, Marc: Do you love me enough to come here and live with me or not?"

"You aren't being reasonable, Jamie. The ranch is my life!"

"Well, the farm is mine, so I guess that answers the question of whether love is enough. It's not! I'll have Maurice help get your stuff ready for you and Keith to leave in the morning." With tears in his eyes, he added, "Goodnight and goodbye, Marc!" Jamie turned and left the room. He didn't look back, and Marc didn't stop him.

Marc called Keith at the farmhouse and told him that they would be leaving before daybreak. He and Jamie had completed the sale of Shadow the first night they arrived, so there was nothing else to do but pack and leave.

୬ "Keith, what's going on with our bosses?" Derek asked.

"They're fighting, and the breakup looks permanent."

"Does that mean that you and I aren't going to be able to see each other when you go back to Cheyenne?"

"Of course not, Derek. Who cares what *they* do? We'll stay in touch and visit on holidays and vacations."

"We had better make the most of tonight because it will be a while before I can come to Cheyenne to see you." They moved in close and hugged each other. "I loved having you here with me, Keith. Let's go up to my room and make love the rest of the night. Let our bosses fight if they want!"

"I told you that Marc would never sell his ranch and move here. Jamie was fooling himself if he thought that."

"I know, but he loves Marc, and he thought that Marc loved him too."

"He does — but he will never leave Cheyenne."

୬ Jamie watched from the bedroom window as Marc and Keith got their stuff into the truck. He had not seen or spoken to Marc since last night's conversation. *Why is he doing this? I thought he loved me.* Tears rolled down his face. His heart was breaking, and there was no changing Marc's mind. *I can't leave my grandmother's farm. I was born here. There are too many memories. Why can't Marc understand that?* Jamie knew that the only way they could be together was if he gave up everything and moved to Cheyenne. *This is not fair, damn it! Why or how can he just walk away from me?* Jamie asked the room. *God, I love that man. I will always love him.*

Marc looked up and saw Jamie watching from his bedroom. He could tell that he was crying, but he could not give in and move here. With tears in his eyes, he looked one more time at Jamie, and then climbed into the truck. Keith gave Derek a hug and a kiss and told him that he would call when he got back to Cheyenne. Just as they were about to pull away, Marc got out of the truck and ran into the house and up to Jamie's bedroom, bursting in the door. Jamie turned around and stood still, staring at Marc. He couldn't take his eyes off of Marc's lips.

Marc crossed the room, took Jamie into his arms, and begged, "Please don't let this be the end of us. I love you and want you to be with me, always."

They were both crying now.

"I can't leave my home, Marc, and you can't leave your ranch, so …" He couldn't stop crying long enough to say anything else. It seemed hopeless. "If we love each other, we should try to work it out."

"Are you willing to move to Cheyenne for me?"

"No. I can't do it!"

Marc kissed Jamie and told him, "I will never ask you again. If you ever change your mind, you know where I'll be." He let go of Jamie and walked out of the room. He got in the truck and pulled away, glancing back one last time. Jamie was not in the window.

Keith looked at Marc's sad but stern face and asked, "Can't you two work this out?"

A teardrop fell onto Marc's cheek as he shook his head. "No."

The Book

Jamie tried to get back to life as usual. When he went to the stables to see Shadow and talk to Derek about how things were progressing with the horse, he always knew that, if he asked about Marc, Derek would know. He and Keith were in touch every day. The problem was that he couldn't bring himself to ask; it still hurt too much.

Maurice watched his boss with sadness in his heart because he knew that Jamie was hurting inside. Maurice wished he could talk to Jamie because he knew how heartbreak felt. He remembered when Jamie hired him. He was on extended service from England and didn't want to go back because his love had left him and never came back. He met Jamie and was hired immediately.

That was three years ago. Jamie had become a successful and famous writer and needed a staff to manage his home. Maurice needed a place where he could work so he could stay in the States, and it worked out perfectly. Maurice's beloved wife of 28 years had left him for another man, and he had to get away from England. Working for Jamie had been the easiest job he had ever had. Maurice was given a staff of three to manage: Betsy, the cook; Hildegard, the maid; and John, the driver. Maurice loved taking care of Jamie and his house. He had always been a generous and approachable boss. Living in Jamie's house had lessened the sadness and heartache after his wife left him, but every so often he would think about how much he loved her and still did.

Everyone on the Three M Ranch knew that Marc was terribly upset. It had been only three months since he and Keith had left Berea, and he barely spoke to anyone other than to give the staff orders. He and Keith, on the other hand, talked often about Jamie, but Keith never told him what Derek reported to him.

Neither of the men had gone out with any other since the breakup. After what they had together, nothing else could compare. Marc had waited all those years for the right guy to come along, and now that he had, no one else would do. Keith and Derek often discussed ways to get the two men to give in and talk. So far, no luck. As each day and month passed, Marc and Jamie suffered but remained very stubborn men.

Finally, Jamie finished the book he was writing about the beautiful, hunky Indian warrior named White Eagle. When he wrote about this Indian, he patterned his looks after Marc. He kept his word to his true love and wrote the story about the Cheyenne warrior who fell in love but could never have his love.

All of the sadness that Jamie felt for losing his love came out in the story of White Eagle. On many nights when Jamie wrote, tears flowed down his face. He missed Marc so much that his whole body ached for him. Writing the novel, *Cheyenne Love*, somehow helped ease the pain of his loss. When he sent it to his agent and publisher, they both read it. This book was different than anything he had written, and they loved it. Jamie's agent asked about the inspiration for the book.

Jamie merely said, "Someone I will always love but can never have."

Six months later, Jamie's book became a bestseller, and he did book signings and talk-show interviews. He also met with movie producers about making *Cheyenne Love* into a movie. All the traveling made him happy. He didn't dwell on Marc so much and what might have been. He would always love Marc, but it didn't hurt so much anymore. *Time heals all wounds, and that is somewhat true*, Jamie thought. He could pour all his love for Marc into making the book a movie. It somehow brought him closer but with less pain.

⮥ Keith bounded into the house with a book in his hand. "Marc! Have you seen or heard about this?"

"What is it?"

"It's called *Cheyenne Love* — and guess who wrote it?"

Marc's heart went into his throat, and he couldn't breathe. He looked at the gorgeous Indian on the cover and saw the text at the bottom of the page: "Written by Jamie Walker." He opened the first page and read, "Dedicated to the man I love, always and forever."

Marc couldn't put the book down. As he read it, he cried and thought, *God, Jamie. Why do I have to love you? Why can't I get you out of my head and out of my heart? Is this ever going to pass, Lord?*

Two weeks later, Marc was watching the news. An announcement came on for the celebrities who would appear on David Letterman, and he heard Jamie's name. He started to turn the channel but couldn't stand not to watch it. When Jamie came out, Marc could have died right there from lack of oxygen because he was holding his breath. *God, he looks more beautiful than before.* All Marc could do was stare at the television. *I want him so much. He needs to be with me. This is where he belongs — in my arms.*

Marc picked up the phone and dialed Jamie's number. He knew that David Letterman was taped many days ahead.

Jamie answered. "Hello?" He knew someone was there. "Hello? *Hello!* Marc, is that you? Please answer me!" Jamie heard a click, and the line went dead. All the emotions he was trying to bury resurfaced in one moment. He knew it was Marc, and he broke down, sobbing, "Please, God, let me get over this!" He prayed and cried, but he knew he would never be free of Marc.

A Chance

It had been a full year since the day Marc walked out of Jamie's life. They had not seen or talked to each other in all that time. *Cheyenne Love*, the movie, was nearly finished. The last scenes were being filmed on location in Cheyenne. Jamie was apprehensive about going to that location, but they needed him as a technical advisor. Also, he had to assist the scriptwriter in transferring his book to the big screen.

He turned to Derek and said, "You're in charge here. I'll have to go to Cheyenne for the filming of the last part of the movie. The Hawthorns will be here to help you with the other chores around the farm. I don't know how long I'll be gone … probably a month. If you need anything, call me."

"Are you going to see Marc while you're there?"

"No. I haven't planned on it. I'll be so busy on the movie set and, besides, I'm sure he's moved on with someone else."

"No, he hasn't, according to Keith. He's still carrying a torch for you. You know, he called you one time about three months ago but said that, when he heard your voice, he couldn't speak. You both are such fools."

"Excuse me? *What* did you say?"

"You heard me! Why would you let geography keep you two apart? Both of these places are just houses … material possessions. What you two shared in your brief time together is worth more than a hundred farms or ranches. Like I said … fools!"

"You don't understand, Derek. This farm has been in my family since the pioneer times in the early 1800s."

"SO WHAT?" Derek said loudly. "Do you think your grandmother would want you to lose the love of your life — your soul mate — for a piece of *property*? I think not! Keith says the same thing to Marc. You two are throwing a love of a lifetime away, and it's a crime."

❧ "Marc, did you know that they're going to be filming *Cheyenne Love* here in Cheyenne and, according to Derek, Jamie will be here for about a month as a technical advisor?"

"Are you *serious*? Do you know this to be a fact?"

"Yes. Derek wouldn't tell me this if Jamie weren't coming. I wish Derek was coming also, but he says he has to take care of the place. He'll have a nice, elderly couple — Mr. and Mrs. Hiram Hawthorn — living at the farm and helping him with chores while he takes care of the horses. I really miss him. We communicate every day on email and sometimes on the phone, but that's no substitute for holding him in my arms and making love to him."

This whole conversation was driving Marc crazy. The thought of having Jamie that close and not being able to hold him would kill him. *How am I going to stay away from Jamie if he's here in Cheyenne? I need him so much. He's part of me now. He must be feeling the same way. Can he really come to Cheyenne and not want to see me?* Marc couldn't shut off his mind. He decided that he had to know.

❧ The first day of shooting took place by the train station in town. As they were running the scenes, Jamie sensed that Marc was there. He scanned the crowd of onlookers and spotted him. His heart stopped. He stood a distance away in the same black cowboy hat, black jeans, and red shirt that he wore to dinner the night they first made love by candlelight on the bearskin rug in front of the fire. They stared at each other with love, lust, and many other emotions.

Jamie couldn't stand it. *No! No! I won't let him do this to me again.* He had to turn around and try to concentrate on the scene. *Why is he here? I can't concentrate with him here. Please go!* Jamie's thoughts were filled with sadness.

Marc watched Jamie turn his back to him. He stood there a minute longer, and then came to a decision. He walked toward Jamie. When he got right up behind him, he leaned in and whispered in his ear, "Not this time."

Jamie felt Marc's breath on his cheek and the heat coming from his body.

"I want you," Marc whispered, "and I am not going to take no for an answer."

Jamie slowly turned around to face Marc. He looked into those beautiful sapphire eyes and swayed. He felt faint.

Marc instinctively grabbed hold of him and pulled him the last few inches into him. "You are mine, Jamie Walker, and you will always be." He took possession of Jamie's soft, kissable lips and forced his mouth open with his persistent tongue. They were both lost to the fact that they were in the middle of a crowd of actors, cameramen, a director, and onlookers. They didn't care. It had been a year since they kissed or even spoke to each other.

When they came up for air, Marc said, "Please, Jamie, come home with me. I need you so much. You are the missing part of me. Please … I am begging you."

Jamie wanted this as much as Marc did, but would it change things? "Marc, I don't think we should do this."

"Then stop thinking and for once just *be*. I want you in my bed. I want to love you and come inside you and be with you. Please don't make me beg any more than I already have."

Jamie grabbed Marc on both sides of his cheeks and kissed him with so much passion that their audience hollered, "Get a room!"

Marc swept up Jamie in his arms and carried him to the truck. He yelled back at the crew, "Mr. Walker will not be back for the rest of the day — and maybe not tomorrow either!"

Everyone watched in astonishment with smiles on their faces. Jamie wrapped his arms around Marc's neck and tingled all over. He was back in his true love's arms, and he was going to stay there. He had yearned to be right here for the past year.

Marc leaned down and kissed him quickly and softly. "I love you, Jamie. Are you still in love with me? I have to know."

"Marc, I have never stopped loving you. I will always be yours, but you already know that if you search your heart. I gave myself to you completely, and there will never be another man for me. *Ever!*"

Marc smiled his wonderful smile at Jamie, and Jamie was in heaven.

The Reunion

When they were in the truck, Marc said to Jamie, "Please slide over and sit next to me."

Jamie did as he was asked. Marc put his right arm around Jamie's shoulder, pulled him close, and kissed him again with fire and lust. Their need was too overwhelming. Jamie moved his hand to Marc's leg toward his groin.

"Oh, my god, Jamie! Touching me again will make me come. I have built this up for a whole year, waiting for you."

That was all Jamie needed to hear. He unzipped Marc's jeans and reached for his target. Marc was hard and leaking precum. Jamie took Marc in his mouth. Marc moaned and moved forward for him to go deeper. Jamie licked and sucked and ran his tongue on the back of the shaft, driving Marc crazy.

"I am not going to last much longer," Marc moaned.

Jamie ignored him. He moved up and down for a few strokes, and then went lower, licking him at the base of his cock.

Marc moved and groaned, making sounds that Jamie had not heard from him before. "Please, Jamie … more … more. Suck me hard and fast. I need you."

Jamie complied. With one more time down to the base and back up, Marc shot into Jamie's mouth. He didn't think he would ever stop, and Jamie never missed a drop.

As Marc was coming down from this amazing blow job, he told Jamie, "You wait until I get you home. I am going to slam so hard into you that you'll beg for more and more!"

Jamie zipped up Marc's jeans and stayed next to him in the seat. He didn't want to leave Marc's side for a moment. Marc had his right arm around Jamie, and he held him tightly. He was determined not to let Jamie go again. Jamie laid his head on Marc's shoulder. He was content. When Marc made the decision to claim Jamie, he knew that, if Jamie came with him, he did not plan to let him go away again. Jamie was very quiet, and Marc thought he might have fallen asleep in his arms.

All of a sudden, Jamie spoke. "What are we doing, Marc? I still want you as much as ever, but us being together and making love again … will it solve anything?"

"Jamie, let's not talk about that right now. Let's just enjoy being together again. I've been aching to be next to you and hold you tightly. I love you more than life itself, and I know you still feel the same about me too. You just demonstrated that quite nicely, I might add," Marc said with a grin on his face.

Jamie looked at Marc's face and melted when he saw his grin and those sapphire eyes dancing and twinkling at him.

"God, Marc, I love you so much! Sometimes I think my heart will burst." He nuzzled close to Marc's chest again and stayed there.

Marc drove the short 14 miles to his ranch. Both men were noticeably quiet but content. Marc pulled up to the long driveway and stopped in front of the house. Jamie started to get out, but Marc stopped him. He bent down and claimed Jamie's lips once more. When they separated, Marc told Jamie to let him get the door on Jamie's side. Jamie watched Marc walk around to his side of the truck and open the door. Jamie climbed out and immediately fell into Marc's arms.

"I love being in your arms again, Marc."

"Yeah, this is where you belong for always. We will work out everything else later. For now, I just want to hold you and make love to you and show you how much I've missed doing this." He claimed Jamie's lips once more.

&s Keith saw Marc and Jamie pull up, and he couldn't wait to tell Derek what was going on. It was a good sign that they might be able to finally all be together. Jamie started toward the door, but Marc stopped him. Once again, he swept up Jamie in his arms and carried him into the house.

Jamie loved this possessive side of Marc. Once inside, Marc put him down.

"Please, Jamie, come up to my bedroom, and let's make mad, passionate love. I don't intend for us to come out for a long, long time."

"Marc, I have missed you every minute of every day."

"Me too! We belong together, not apart. This past year has been a waste and so sad. Come on, Jamie. Enough talking for now. I have other things that I want to do with you, and talking doesn't figure in unless you tell me what you want me to do to you and the wonderful sounds that you make when I am inside of you. I have not been able to get those sounds out of my head for a whole year."

Love for Always

Jamie and Marc went upstairs and locked the door. Marc had given his staff strict orders that he and Jamie did not want to be disturbed unless they asked for something. He had already called the staff from his truck and asked them to send champagne to his room. He planned to celebrate their reunion before they made love. The champagne was chilling in his room when they arrived.

Marc poured two glasses and proposed a toast. "To us — together for always."

Before they could finish the drink, they were in each other's arms, kissing, feeling, and responding. Marc pulled Jamie into a full-body hug. Every inch of their bodies was in contact with the other. They could both feel the need between them.

"God, Jamie, I have missed you more than you will ever know."

"Me too, Marc. You are all I've thought about every day for an entire year."

Marc kissed Jamie with great love and desire, and Jamie opened his mouth to receive him.

"I can't wait any longer, Jamie," he whispered against his lips. He pulled Jamie over to his bed and started undressing him: first the shoes and socks, and then the shirt. Once that was done, he kissed Jamie on the neck, licking him down to his shoulder and back up. "You are so beautiful."

Marc took off his own shoes, socks, and shirt, and then moved right up against Jamie — chest to chest. He ran his hands over every inch, touching and kissing every spot, sucking and licking on his nipples, and watching them get hard and erect. He loved running his tongue over and around them and watching Jamie's face. He could see how much Jamie loved it. Jamie started to breathe heavily and moaned with small, faint sounds from deep inside. Marc always loved the sounds that Jamie made during their lovemaking. He sat Jamie on the bed and asked him to lie back. He unbuckled Jamie's belt and unbuttoned his jeans, pulling them down and off along with his boxers. He stood at the foot of the bed and just stared. *God, he is so gorgeous! He has the perfect body.*

Jamie watched Marc, and then finally asked, "Are you going to stare at me all day, or are you going to get undressed and join me?"

"I am not rushing this. I've waited to be with you again for an entire year."

Marc undressed the rest of the way and climbed in bed beside Jamie, pulling him into his arms. Lying on their sides, their whole bodies were touching. The need for each other was so evident with both sporting full hard-ons. They pushed their groins together and rubbed up and down. Both were breathing heavily. Marc kissed Jamie all over his neck, and then moved to his chest, making sure to stop long enough to give both of his nipples attention on the way down to his waist. He knew he would elicit those wonderful sounds from Jamie when he touched his tongue to his nipples.

Jamie responded the way Marc knew he would. Marc sucked and licked, enjoying the feel in his mouth. Jamie moved and bucked toward him, begging him to take him in his mouth. Marc moved on, following the line of hair down to his groin. He wanted to taste Jamie too. He took his cock in his mouth and tasted his precum.

"Jamie, you taste so good!"

Marc sucked him, ran his tongue down the back of his cock, and then down to the space between his shaft and his balls. He kissed and licked until he heard Jamie groan. He moved back up and took him into his mouth, moving up and down with a slow movement. Jamie begged him to stop or he was going to come. Marc ignored him the way Jamie had done in the truck. He wanted to taste every bit Jamie could give him. It had been so long, and he remembered and craved his wonderful taste.

"Marc, please stop or I won't be able to stop. Oh, my god … too late. Marc … Marc!" Jamie moaned in a deep, sexy voice that almost made Marc come — and he hadn't even gotten inside of Jamie yet!

"Jamie, give me all of it. I want this first." He moved a couple more times and received what he had been asking for and wanted. Jamie kept coming like he had never had an orgasm before. Marc took all of it and licked Jamie clean. Jamie was still coming down when Marc reached for some lube on the nightstand. "Jamie, I'm going to get you ready. I can hardly wait until I can be inside of you. Please spread your legs for me."

"No, Marc. I want to be on top with you."

"Okay, but I want to get you ready." He put lots of lube on his fingers and inserted them into Jamie. First one finger; then, as he felt Jamie relax, he put in another. He was moving his fingers in and out and finally felt that Jamie was ready.

Marc started to put on a condom, but Jamie asked, "I haven't been with anyone since you, and you said you hadn't either. Do we have to use that? I want to feel you inside me without any barriers."

"I'd much rather not use one either," Marc said as he prepped his cock with lube.

Jamie stopped him and asked, "I get to be on top, remember?"

Jamie straddled Marc and impaled himself onto him. He planned to go slowly but couldn't control himself. He sat down with a force that shocked both of them. He sat still for a moment, and then started moving up and down. Jamie was the one in control, and he loved having power over Marc. He got a good rhythm going and drove both of them nuts.

"Oh, my god, Jamie! You feel so good," was all Marc could get out. He was trying his best to not come too early, but Jamie was making him crazy.

Jamie was hard again also, and Marc grabbed him and started working him up and down. He got into the same rhythm with Jamie, and they were in heaven.

"Marc! Oh, Marc … I'm coming!"

At the same time, Jamie stopped moving on Marc. Marc couldn't stand it. He bucked up his hips, slamming into Jamie. Two strokes like that, and he shot his wad deep into Jamie. As he was coming, he told him that he had been going crazy without him. Jamie could barely speak, but he managed to tell Marc that it was the same for him.

Jamie felt spent. He laid his head on Marc with him still inside. Marc's abdomen and chest were covered with Jamie's sweet love juice, but neither seemed to mind. They were together again and neither wanted to let the other one go. A year is a long time to be apart, but neither seemed to forget how the other felt during their lovemaking. It was like they had never been apart. Jamie was content to lie like this forever, but Marc was getting soft and starting to fall out of Jamie. Marc lifted up Jamie and rolled him onto his side. Cum was oozing out of Jamie, and both were sticky and getting uncomfortable.

"What do you say we take a nice, hot shower and get something to eat?"

"Okay, Marc. Whatever you want."

When Jamie got off the bed to go to the shower, he had remnants of Marc running down his inner thighs. Marc loved seeing that. He had his man back and, if he could help it, he would never let him go again.

∽ Marc and Jamie showered and played with each other. Marc took Jamie in his arms and hugged him while the water ran over them. He grabbed some shower gel and started washing Jamie. When he got to his groin, Jamie moved and groaned, making those sounds that only Jamie could make. He was turning Marc on again by just listening to him.

Marc grabbed Jamie by the waist and turned him around to face the shower wall. He fingered him again, but he didn't have to do much because Jamie was already wide open and ready. Marc placed his cock against Jamie and slid in easily. He pushed in and out, closing his eyes and feeling the tightness around him.

He whispered in Jamie's ear, "You feel so wonderful! I could do this all day and never get tired."

Jamie just moaned. It was all he could do. He was so turned on that he couldn't put two words together. Every time Marc pushed in and hit his prostate, he would moan. As Marc was doing these wonderful things behind him, Jamie was stroking himself. Marc reached around, found Jamie's hand, and put his on top. He worked with Jamie up and down, and together they made Jamie spray the shower walls. Marc kept moving in and out, hitting Jamie's prostate with each stroke. He was driving Jamie crazy. Marc couldn't stop.

All of a sudden, he pushed into Jamie as hard as he could, harder than he had ever pushed before, and caused Jamie to come again spontaneously and without any warning. That had never happened to Jamie or Marc before.

At the same time, Marc shouted, "I'm there, Jamie, my love … I'm giving you my love!" He came deep inside, and he was so spent that he could barely stand.

Jamie held onto the shower wall and swayed. His legs were like rubber. Neither had experienced anything this strong before. The hot water was making them weak in the knees. Marc turned Jamie around and kissed him softly, and then helped him out of the shower. Jamie grabbed a towel, but Marc had other ideas.

"Jamie, please let me do that."

Marc took the towel and started drying him. When he got to his groin, he knelt in front of Jamie and tenderly lifted his balls to dry them. The minute he did that, Jamie started getting another raging hard-on — exactly what Marc had *hoped* would happen! He took Jamie in his mouth and licked and sucked and kissed him up and down until Jamie gave him what he was so hungry for. Marc swallowed all of Jamie's wonderful love juice and licked him clean again. After this last bout of lovemaking, Jamie was unable to stand. Marc picked him up and carried him to the bed.

"Wow, I feel so weak, Marc. You have to let me rest for a while."

"I know, but it's hard for me to keep my hands and mouth off of you."

"You have to give me time to rest. I feel like such a weakling right now. What you do to me drives me nuts!"

"I know, but I feel that I can't get enough of you! And I'm making up for all the time we missed this past year."

"Just lie with me for a while," Jamie said.

They got under the covers and held each other. Soon, both men drifted off to sleep, locked in each other's arms.

Lost Love

The next morning, Jamie woke up first. He looked at Marc, who was still sound asleep, and thought, *God, he is so handsome! How did I get this lucky? We are compatible in everything we do, but how are we ever going to make this work? One of us will have to give up their home … but which one?*

As he pondered this, Marc opened his eyes and looked straight into Jamie's beautiful chestnut eyes. "How long have you been awake?"

"Not too long. I was just studying your face, so I can burn it into my memory forever."

"What are you jabbering about? You don't need to memorize my face. You'll see it every day for the rest of our lives."

"You don't know that, Marc! We still have a big problem to work out."

"What problem is that?"

"Oh, come on. You aren't dense. The problem of who gives up their home for the other."

"Are we back to *that* again? I don't want to talk about that. I just want us to be together right now. We can work out the details of you selling your place and moving here later … much later."

As Marc pulled Jamie close to him again, Jamie balked and pulled away. "What are you saying? That I have to move here? What about *you* moving?"

"That is out of the question."

"You're telling me that you won't even entertain the idea?"

"No, Jamie. I thought you understood when I brought you here that this is where you and I belong. I cannot leave Cheyenne."

That did it for Jamie. He got up and started getting dressed.

73

"Where are you going? Don't tell me that after what we shared last night you're leaving me again."

Jamie didn't say a word. He just kept getting dressed.

"Jamie, STOP! Talk to me. Don't do this to us again!"

Not a word out of Jamie.

Marc bolted from the bed and grabbed Jamie's arms. "STOP! What are you *doing*? Talk to me."

Jamie jerked his arms free and left the bedroom. He rushed down the steps and out of the house, running right into Keith.

"Where are you going in such a hurry?"

"I have to get out of here, Keith. He did it again."

"He did *what* again?"

"Marc just assumed that I would give up all I have and live here with him."

"Jamie, don't do this to him again. It will kill him. He loves you more than anything!"

"Well, obviously not. He loves this ranch more," Jamie said in tears.

Keith pleaded with Jamie. "You are such a fool. You'll never find a love like his again. If you leave him this time, I'm not sure you'll ever be able to come back."

"Well, so be it," Jamie said. His heart was breaking.

"May I ask you a question?"

"Sure, I guess so."

"Do you love him as much as he loves you?"

"Yes, Keith. But I can't be dictated to and told where to live."

"You and he are both unworthy of such a love. Derek and I would give anything to have a love half as good as what you two have, and you're throwing it away."

Jamie didn't want to listen anymore. He had to leave. "Keith, will you drive me to town? I need to get back on the set and get far away from here."

"As you wish. I certainly will because you don't deserve his love. You're always running away. That's what you do best."

"How *dare* you talk to me like that!"

"Why shouldn't I? What I said is the truth. You don't deserve him, and after today I'm sure that you won't be welcome here again. He deserves to be with someone who wants him over everything and everyone else. That person is not you."

Jamie didn't look back at the house because it would have killed him to see Marc again. Keith dropped him off at the movie trailer, and neither spoke the whole way. Keith phoned Derek and told him what was going on with the "two idiots," as they called them.

ᴖ The next day, Jamie was on the set and knew that Marc was nearby. He could feel him, but when he scanned the crowd, he could not find him. The month went by quickly and filming was done. Jamie never ran into Marc again but always knew that he was close by, watching him.

I know I'm being stubborn, Jamie thought, but for some reason he couldn't give in. It had become obvious that Marc was not going to change his mind either.

ᴖ Jamie flew home. When he got there, Derek came to pick him up instead of John.

"Why are you here to get me, Derek? Where is John?"

"I told him that I wanted to pick you up because I'm going to try to wake you up and put you back on a plane to Marc."

"I am not going back."

"Do you love him, Jamie, or do you just want sex with him?"

Jamie swung back and punched Derek. The punch knocked him down, and right away Jamie felt bad for doing it. He reached out a hand to help him up. Derek was rubbing his cheek.

"I am so sorry for that, Derek. I didn't mean it."

Derek laughed. "Well, at least I got my answer. You would not have hit me if I was right, so it's obvious that you are truly in love with Marc."

"Yes, Derek. I love him with all my heart."

"Well, he doesn't believe that. He told Keith that you obviously were *not* in love with him or you would not have left him again. He says he's done. He says it hurts too much, and he told Keith that he couldn't wait for you any longer. He's going to try and get on with his life. Keith says he doesn't buy it, but that's what he passed on to me. Like Keith and I said, you're both fools. You have a love that anyone would do anything to have, and you guys just toss it away, like it means nothing. Such a shame!"

Jamie couldn't talk about it anymore. He rode to the farm in silence. *Marc is through waiting for me. He's going to move on. So be it. I guess Keith was right when he said that I would not be welcome there again.*

❧ The movie debut was a great success. The picture was up for an Academy Award for Best Picture, Best Screenplay, and Best Actor. Family, friends, and everyone at the farm were so excited for Jamie, but he could care less. It had been months since he left Marc's bed, and he was still dreaming about being in his arms, remembering how he carried him off and made love to him in the shower until his legs wouldn't hold him; how he dried him off and put him to bed; how he woke up in his arms after a night of pure bliss. Here he was — alone and miserable. Keith had stopped reporting to Derek about Marc, so that made Jamie very anxious. *Is he with someone else now? Is that why Keith stopped reporting to Derek?*

About eight months after Jamie left Cheyenne, he got word from Derek, who got it from Keith, that Marc was coming to the awards. This news made Jamie nervous. *What will I say to him if I see him?*

❧ Academy night arrived. As Jamie walked down the red carpet, he spotted Marc along the rope. He looked handsome in a cowboy tux, all black. The sight of him took Jamie's breath away. Jamie started to move toward Marc and saw a handsome man approach and put his arm around him. Marc turned and smiled at his male friend. Jamie couldn't breathe. The two men looked very cozy, like they were definitely more than just friends. Marc saw Jamie watching them and smiled. Jamie decided that the right thing to do was to go over to the ropes and say hello.

He walked up to Marc, smiled, and held out his hand. "Hello, Marc."

"Hello, Jamie," he said as he took his hand.

The electricity went right through Jamie.

"I want you to meet my friend Gary. Gary, this is Jamie Walker, the man who wrote *Cheyenne Love*."

"Hi, Jamie. It's nice to meet you. I'm excited to meet a real celebrity." He smiled at Jamie with a smile that brightened up his whole face.

Jamie thought that he couldn't be any more perfect: blond hair, baby-blue eyes, and a long, lean body. Gary immediately put his arm around Marc, almost possessive of him.

Jamie looked at Marc and said, "I am happy for you, Marc." He looked back at Gary and added, "Very nice to meet you."

Jamie moved down the red carpet and was ushered to his place with the cast and staff of *Cheyenne Love*.

"Good luck, Jamie!" Gary hollered after him. "We hope you win!"

Jamie looked back and met dark blue eyes staring at him. Marc was watching him intently. *Why is he looking at me like that? God, I can't stand this. I never really believed he would move on, but I guess he has.*

Jamie had a hard time concentrating on the ceremony, so when they called the movie as the winner, someone had to nudge him. He was deep in thought, feeling like someone had punched him in the gut. He could barely breathe. He went up to receive his Oscar for Best Screenplay and didn't know what to say. He thanked everyone having anything to do with the movie.

Then, just as he was about to leave the stage, he said, "I would like to thank the man I love, who inspired me to write this story. He had never read any of my books, so I asked him what he would read, and he told me 'stories about Indians.' Therefore, the idea for *Cheyenne Love* was born. I should be sharing this win with him, but that's not possible. I just wanted him to know that he had a lot to do with this story."

Jamie left the stage, and Marc watched for Jamie to come back to his seat, but he didn't return. The ceremony was over, and Jamie was nowhere to be seen. The crew had cornered Jamie backstage and made sure that he was going to the post-Oscar party. He didn't feel like celebrating but knew he should show up.

∽ Jamie stood by himself at the party and felt someone behind him. He turned, and there stood Marc. All Jamie could think to say was, "How did you get into this party?"

"One of the cameramen invited me because he remembered me from that day during filming when I carried you away. I just wanted to congratulate you on your win and thank you for what you said up there — even though I'm not that man anymore."

"Where's Gary?"

"He's in the men's room. Well, anyway, congrats!" Marc walked away.

A few minutes later, Gary rejoined him.

I have got to get out of here, Jamie thought as he headed to the door.

Marc watched him leave and felt like screaming, "STOP! YOU KNOW YOU STILL LOVE ME!" Instead, he stood silently.

Jamie caught the next plane out of LAX and was never so glad to be back home. Derek met him at the airport and asked how it went. Jamie told him about seeing Marc and his date.

Derek gasped, "Are you *sure* they were a couple?"

"Oh, yeah. He had his arm around Marc, and they seemed close."

"What did he look like?"

"He was gorgeous with blond hair and baby-blue eyes and a body that wouldn't quit."

"Could you tell if they were lovers?"

"No, but what else *would* they be? They sure didn't act like casual friends!"

"I don't know, but Keith never mentioned anyone like that to me."

Heartbreak

Things went back to normal pretty quickly. Horses needed tending, and Jamie was busy writing. He seemed really lonely, and Maurice, Betsy, and Hildegard were more than a little worried about him because he was becoming a recluse, hardly ever going out or having any company.

"How can we help him, Hildegard?" Maurice asked. He talked with Hildegard a lot because he felt comfortable around her and, if truth be known, he liked her a little more than he felt he should.

Betsy spoke up. "I think we should try to talk Mr. Walker into letting the Hawthorns come back to help Derek with the farm, and then Mr. Walker can visit his friend in Cheyenne."

"We could try, Betsy," Maurice said, "but I don't think he would go. You know how stubborn he is. He thinks Mr. Morgan should come here."

"I know, but I don't think he will leave Cheyenne," Betsy answered.

Hildegard chimed in. "Well, if he loves Mr. Walker, then he should give in and come here. Maybe he doesn't love him like he says he does. I'm not sure he is good enough for Jamie!"

"Hildegard, what are you saying? You do not call Mr. Walker by his first name!" Maurice reprimanded her. "Don't forget your place in the house."

"I know. It just makes me mad that the man Mr. Walker is in love with doesn't care enough to make him happy."

"You know, I think we should stay out of it, now that I think about it," Betsy said with fervor. "We should let them work it out. It's really not our place to even be discussing it."

Maurice and Hildegard knew that Betsy was right.

ॐ Derek had been so busy with Shadow that he didn't come up to the mansion much anymore. Jamie tried to keep busy with his new book, but all he could think of was Marc. He couldn't get the picture of him with the blond out of his mind. *I have got to stop this! He has moved on, and I should do the same.*

Jamie stopped writing for a while and went down to the stables to see Shadow. He didn't do this often because seeing the horse made him feel worse, bringing back so many memories. Derek was working with the horses when he came in.

"Hey, Derek."

"Hi, Jamie. It's nice to see you down here. It's been almost three weeks."

"Well, you know why, I'm sure. The horse brings back too many memories that I want to forget. I need to move on with my life."

"Have you heard from Marc, Jamie?"

"No. Why do you think I would hear from him? He has a new love in his life."

"And who would *that* be?"

"You mean Keith hasn't told you about the gorgeous blond, blue-eyed guy I told you I saw Marc with? I believe his name was Gary."

"No. He hasn't mentioned him at all, and we talk every day." Derek knew who Gary was but couldn't tell Jamie because Keith said that it would just hurt him more.

ॐ Another month went by, and Derek had some news that Keith wanted him to pass on to Jamie. Marc and Gary were going to have a ceremony to seal their relationship, even though they couldn't get married in Wyoming. Gary was going to move in with Marc at the ranch. Derek didn't want to tell Jamie this, but he felt that he had to, so Jamie would finally move on as well.

"Jamie, I have some news to tell you about Marc."

"What? Is he hurt? Worse?" Jamie started to panic.

"No. Sit down with me, please."

"What's going on, Derek? You're scaring me."

"Marc is going to sort of 'marry' Gary."

"NO! NO! Please tell me that this is a joke." Jamie sunk into the sofa with tears rolling down his cheeks. "Oh, god, no ... this can't be. Please tell me it is not so, Derek."

"Jamie, do you really think I would tell you something like this if it weren't true?" Derek saw that Jamie was crumbling into a sobbing mess. He sat down and put his arms around him.

Maurice came in and saw Jamie crying. He looked at Derek and asked if there was anything he could do. Derek shook his head. Derek and Jamie sat together until Jamie stopped sobbing and started getting control of his emotions.

"I never believed Marc would do this," Jamie said. "I know he loves me, but I guess love isn't enough. You told me that I was a fool, and you were so right. I had the love of my life, and I threw him away. Now someone else will spend the days and nights with him. At some point, I'll just be a distant memory of someone he once loved."

Derek first thought that there was nothing he could say to ease Jamie's pain, but then he reconsidered. "Jamie, have you thought about fighting for Marc? You know you could go there and try to reason with him. He would listen to you because I know that he still loves you. He just thinks that you don't love him enough to come to him, so prove him wrong and go to him."

"It wouldn't change anything because I am still not willing to give him what he wants of me — giving up the only place I have ever known. Maybe this is for the best. He will have someone to love who wants to live with him in Cheyenne."

Jamie walked out of the room, went up to his bedroom, and shut the door. When he was alone, he cried for the love he would never have. *God, my heart is ripped from my chest, and I'll never be well again.*

Deception

Marc pulled Keith aside and asked, "Keith, did you tell Derek the story about Gary?"

"Yes. I told him exactly what you told me, and he said he'd tell Jamie."

"I hate to deceive him, but I know that this is the only way he'll move forward and hopefully find happiness."

"You must love him more than I thought — to forgo your own happiness so Jamie can be happy."

Marc had asked his best friend from high school to pose as his new love. Gary said he wasn't sure he could pull it off since he was straight, but he wanted to help Marc, and Marc had told him to follow his lead. Gary laughed and told him he would do it — but no kissing.

"Don't worry, Gary. I don't want to kiss you either!"

They both laughed at how ridiculous this was going to be. After Gary met Jamie, he told Marc that he was foolish for not telling him the truth. He said that Jamie could almost make him want to be gay.

"Yeah, he is gorgeous, isn't he?"

"Marc, why don't you just go to him?"

"You know why. You've always known since we were in school."

᪥ Jamie was still not talking to anyone at the house. He was basically staying in his room. He could not talk about Marc because, every time he did, he would lose it and start to cry. He kept telling himself that he had to move on but couldn't bring himself to do it. He would always love Marc until he drew his last breath on Earth!

Derek told Keith how badly Jamie took the news.

❦ The cold weather came. Advisories were out, and winter had arrived at the farm in Berea. All crops were turned over in the fields for planting in the spring. Derek was still busy with the horses but was unable to work them the way he wanted due to the snow and ice. This was definitely a quiet time for the farm.

Winter had also come to Cheyenne. There was lots of snow on the ground at the Three M Ranch. Since last spring, Marc yearned for Jamie each day. He knew he did the right thing by having Keith lie to Derek about Gary. He just wished that he could have gotten Jamie to move here. They would have been so happy. *Oh, well. I've laid down the path for us to follow, and it can't be changed now.*

Time passed, and Keith had to keep lying to Derek about Gary. He hated it, but that was the way Marc wanted it.

"Keith, can you get away for a week and come stay with me at the farm?" Derek asked. "I miss you so much. Please ask Marc for the time off."

Keith asked Marc, and he told him to go. Things were slow at the ranch, and he really wanted news about Jamie. Keith took the next plane out and arrived in Lexington, which was the closest airport to Berea, and then called Derek. Derek had already driven to Lexington and was waiting in the baggage-claim area. Keith raced to get to Derek. He saw him first and snuck up behind him, wrapped his arms around his middle, and kissed him on the neck.

"Hi, my love," Keith whispered.

Derek turned around in his arms and kissed him longingly. "I have missed you *so much*, Keith."

"Me too."

They got Keith's bag and went to the truck. Inside the truck they kissed again, and then headed out. "How is the farm and Shadow?"

"All is well there."

"How's Jamie?"

"He's not good. He's not eating well, and he hardly ever comes out of his room. He just stays up there, writing his novel and pining for Marc. Speaking of Marc, how are he and Gary doing? Are they happy?"

"Derek, pull over a minute. I want to talk to you, and I want your full attention."

Derek was worried when Keith said this, but he did what he was told to do. "Okay. What? You have my attention."

"Gary and Marc are not together, married or otherwise."

"But, you said …"

"I know what I told you, but it was all a lie, so Jamie would move on and find someone else to love and make him happy."

"That isn't going to happen because he hardly ever comes out, and I know that Marc is the only one he'll ever want to be with. When you love someone like Jamie loves Marc, no one else will ever take his place. Why did Marc do this, and who is this Gary?"

"Gary is a friend of Marc's from high school. He agreed to this charade even though he's straight. He cares about Marc, so he agreed."

"Well, that answers that question, but why? Did he really want to kill Jamie?"

"No. It was totally selfless. After all this time, he knew that Jamie was never going to change his mind about moving, and Marc can't move. So nothing else could be done. He hoped that, if Jamie thought he had moved on, then he would too and finally be happy."

"God, these two are killing me!" Keith said as he pulled Derek into his arms. "Aren't you glad that we don't have these problems?"

"Don't we? We aren't living together either, and we should be."

Keith listened to what Derek was saying and was curious as to what he was feeling, so he asked him to spell it out. "Do you think we should be living together, Derek?" Keith held his breath while he waited for the answer.

"Yes because I … uh … I … I'm in love with you." It was the first time Derek had ever said this to Keith.

Keith caught his breath. "You are in *love* with me?"

"Yes, you fool! How could you not know?"

Keith leaned in and gave Derek a long and sultry kiss. When he pulled away, he looked softly into Derek's hazel eyes and said, "I'm in love with you too. So what are we going to do about it?"

"Well, first, when we get to the farm, I'll show you how much I love you, and then we should talk about our plans. I want to be with you, and I am not going to be stubborn like Jamie and Marc."

When they got to the farm, they disappeared into Derek's bedroom and locked the door. They spent the rest of the day and night making love and making plans. Derek was going to have to tell Jamie that, at some point soon, he would be moving to Cheyenne to live with Keith.

⮌ The next day, Derek and Keith were in the stables to check on Shadow. Jamie couldn't stand it. He wanted to hear any information about Marc. When Jamie walked into the stables, Keith whispered to Derek to keep the secret.

"Hi, Keith," Jamie said. "How are you doing? I know that Derek is very glad to have you here. How is Marc?"

"He's really good. Not terribly busy right now, so he has a lot of time on his hands."

Jamie didn't want to ask the next question, but he couldn't stop himself. "Is he happy with Gary?"

"Yes, Jamie. He seems to be." Derek wanted to scream that it was a lie, but he knew what Marc had done for Jamie was the best for him, given the situation.

The whole week that Keith was there, Jamie tried to come to the stables every day. Maybe Marc would call Keith about something, and then he could ask to talk to him. *This is crazy,* Jamie thought. *I'll call Marc.*

Jamie picked up the phone and dialed Marc's number. He didn't know why he felt the need to talk to him all of a sudden, but he chalked it up to seeing Keith again. The phone rang three times.

"Hello?"

"Hi, Marc."

When Marc heard Jamie's voice, tears formed in his eyes, and he was a little choked up. "Hi, Jamie. How are you?"

"I've been fine, Marc. Thanks for asking." This small talk was hurting both of them. Finally, Jamie had to ask, "How's married life treating you and Gary?"

Marc wanted to tell Jamie the truth but knew that nothing had changed. "It's been fine, Jamie."

Jamie listened to the way Marc sounded when he answered him. "Just *fine*, Marc? Not great?"

Marc was silent. This lying was too hard. "Yes. Just fine. After all, Gary is not my first love, and they say you never get over your first. Look, I'm sorry to cut this short, but Gary and I have a dinner engagement. It was nice talking to you. Tell Keith to come home soon." Marc hung up and sat on the floor and sobbed. *I love him more than life. How can I go on like this? I need him with me. Why did he have to call? I was good until I heard his voice.*

Jamie listened to the dial tone for what seemed like minutes. *Why did I call him? I didn't want to hear that he's happy with Gary. There's nothing to be done.*

Keith had to go back because his vacation was over, but they made plans for Derek to come to Cheyenne after the spring crops were planted. Derek was not going to tell Jamie for a while yet. He noticed that Jamie was even more withdrawn after talking to Marc. Jamie and Marc were definitely star-crossed lovers.

The Accident

Keith told Marc how bad Jamie was. "He is not moving on like you thought he would. This lie is destroying him slowly, one day at a time. Please, Marc. Tell him the truth. Your plan did not work. He isn't eating or sleeping well, and he looks gaunt. He literally is grieving himself into an early grave. You have to help him."

"It's only been a few months. He will get better."

"You're not much better."

Marc thought, *Keith is right, but how can I do it?*

❧ Keith was riding one of the stallions that Marc was going to sell to a buyer from Texas. Things were fine at first, but the path was a little icy and snow-covered, and he didn't see the rise in the ice. His horse lost his footing and fell with Keith still on his back. Keith's head hit a rock and knocked him out. The horse was lying on Keith's right leg and couldn't get up.

When Keith didn't come back, Marc got worried and went to look for him. He found them on the trail. He checked Keith, and he was still breathing but not conscious. He immediately called 911, and then tried to get the horse off Keith.

As the horse flailed about while trying to get up, Marc noticed that the horse's leg was badly broken. He would have to be euthanized because the break was severe. He got on the phone again and called the vet who takes care of his horses. The EMTs got there fast and attended to Keith. One of them helped Marc get the horse off Keith. When they finally got the horse up, he couldn't stand and went back down again. This time, though, the EMTs had pulled Keith free.

"Take him to the hospital," Marc instructed, "and I'll wait here with the horse for the vet. Then I'll come. Please take good care of him."

Marc's vet came and agreed that the horse could not be saved. "Go to the hospital and check on Keith. I will take care of this."

"Okay. I'll call you later to make arrangements for the horse."

Marc sped to the hospital. When he got there, they had Keith in the nuclear medicine department for a CT scan and an MRI of his skull to assess the damage. They were sure he had a skull fracture but were worried about pressure to the brain. He had not come to yet, which also worried them. They put Keith in the ICU and hooked him to a heart monitor and an IV. He was exhibiting signs of hypothermia, so they had him under a warming blanket to bring up his body temperature.

Marc looked at all the equipment hooked to Keith and got really scared. He sat next to his bed and held his hand. "Keith, please open your eyes."

Several hours had passed since he was admitted, and the doctors said that the longer he went without waking up, the worse it could be.

Suddenly Keith's eyes flickered, and he spoke one name: "Derek." He spoke the name again and then slipped into a coma. The doctors raced in and asked Marc to leave the room because they wanted to assess him. Keith's doctor came out and told Marc that, if he had any family, he should call them to come at once. They weren't very hopeful. Marc knew that Keith didn't have any living relatives, so he called Derek.

"Derek, this is Marc."

"Hi, Marc. What is it? Do you want to talk to Jamie?"

"No. I need you to listen. Keith had a bad accident, and he's in bad shape. You need to get here as soon as you can."

"What do you *mean*? He is going to be okay, right?"

"No, Derek. They don't hold out much hope. He called your name twice, and then slipped into a coma. Please get here as soon as you can."

Tears rolled down Derek's cheeks. "How did this *happen*?"

"I'll tell you when you get here. Just please come now. He needs you here."

Derek got off the phone, called the airport, and booked the first flight to Cheyenne. He ran up to Jamie's house and told him what was going on.

"How bad is he, Derek?"

"I don't know, but Marc says I need to come now. He's in a coma, and the doctors are not giving much hope."

"What? Well, go. I will figure out something here. When you get there, let me know what is going on please."

Derek packed, and John drove him to the airport. Jamie called the Hawthorns to see if they could take over the duties at the farm.

≪ Derek arrived at the hospital within five hours of Marc's call. When he walked into the ICU and saw Keith, he almost passed out. He was so pale and swollen and bruised, with IVs and lines all over his body. One side of his head was disfigured where it hit the rock.

Derek started crying and sat down beside Keith, took his hand, and leaned over to kiss his lips. "I'm here, baby. Please wake up and talk to me." He stayed there, holding his hand and crying for hours. There was no change in his condition.

Marc came in the room and asked Derek to come out for a while, so he could tell him what happened. "The horse slipped on the ice and went down, trapping Keith under him. They got the horse up and off him, but they had to put the horse down. Keith was conscious some of that time and was calling your name. The doctors told me that, when he slipped into a coma, it was a bad sign. Possibly the pressure on the brain had increased, so they were monitoring him very closely. They had hopes that he would come out of it, but as time went on it was looking very grim."

Derek called Jamie to fill him in. Jamie felt so sorry for Derek. He knew that Derek loved Keith. Derek sat day after day, holding Keith's hand and talking to him, telling him to please wake up and love him.

Finally, after two weeks of being in a coma, Keith blinked his eyes. When he opened them completely, he saw Derek and squeezed his hand.

"Oh, my god, Keith! You scared me. I thought I was going to lose you!"

Keith was very weak, but he smiled at Derek and whispered, "I love you too."

Marc came in the room when he heard the nurse say that Keith was awake. When Marc got to Keith's bed, he leaned down and hugged him slightly. "You had us all worried sick! We can't run this ranch without you."

Keith started to say something but couldn't get it out. Alarms went off, his heart rate climbed, and the doctors and nurses ran into the room and ordered everyone out, calling a "Code Blue." Keith was crashing. Marc and Derek were pushed out of the room. Keith was nonresponsive. Derek was screaming his name, and Marc had his arm around him, trying to stop him from running back into the room. The staff worked on Keith for a few minutes. Finally, his doctor came out and told them that they had stabilized Keith but needed to take him to surgery to relieve the pressure on his brain. The doctor told them to wait in the surgery waiting area, and he would come out when they were done.

Derek was very scared. He couldn't lose Keith. While Keith was in surgery, Marc and Derek talked about the future. Derek told him that he and Keith had decided that he would move to Cheyenne to live with Keith.

"Have you told Jamie this news?"

"No, not yet, Marc. We were waiting until all the necessary arrangements were made. Of course, I'll need to give Jamie plenty of notice to replace me."

Marc had to ask, "How is Jamie? Does he have someone to love him now?"

"You're *kidding*, right? He will never have anyone because he's too much in love with you. He's told me that he intends to spend the rest of his life alone."

"He shouldn't do that. He should find someone who can love him and stay with him in Berea to make a life."

"Marc, you're kidding yourself. He will never get over you like I'm sure you've gotten over him." Derek was angry now. Keith was fighting for his life, and he and Derek wanted to be together. Marc and Jamie were throwing away what they had. This whole situation was not fair.

Derek started to say something else to Marc, but the surgeon came into the waiting area. The look on his face was heavy.

Derek didn't wait for him to speak. He screamed and fell to the floor, sobbing, "NO! NO! NO! PLEASE, GOD, NO ..."

Deception Never Pays

The surgeon helped Derek sit on the sofa in the waiting room. "He is not gone. He is still alive."

"But your face — you looked so sad, I thought …"

"I'm sorry. We relieved the pressure on his brain, but he's in critical condition. His vitals are way too high, and he remains in a coma. I am not going to sugar coat this. He is still in danger of not making it. We need his vitals to stabilize and for him to wake up. I am going back into recovery. He will be in his room in an hour."

"Derek, let's go down and get something to eat," Marc said as he led him to the cafeteria.

After they ate, Derek felt better. They returned to the ICU just as they were bringing Keith to his room. Derek grabbed Keith's hand and kissed it and begged him to come back to him.

❧ Derek spent the next eight hours sitting by Keith's bed. He kept talking to him about what they were going to do when he moved there. Marc stayed with Derek at the hospital. The next morning, things started to look better. Keith's vitals had returned to normal. He was still not awake, but Derek was encouraged that he may make it after all.

Marc came in to relieve Derek for a while. Derek went to the ranch and showered. He told Marc that he would be back in an hour. Marc went to the nurse's station to get some water and ran straight into Jamie. Marc was speechless.

Jamie found his voice first. "Marc! How is Keith? Is Derek in his room? I'll go in, if that is okay."

Marc was still having trouble finding his voice. He couldn't stop his heart from racing at the sight of Jamie, and his mouth was very dry.

"Well, the *least* you can do is say hello, Marc." Jamie was hurt and mad because Marc wouldn't even speak to him, and he brushed past him on the way to Keith's room. Marc grabbed Jamie's arm to stop him. Jamie jerked his arm away from Marc's touch, which brought back many memories.

"Jamie, I'm sorry. It just took me by surprise when I saw you! Derek is at my ranch, taking a shower. He'll be back soon. Keith is still in a coma. Please come into his room." That was all he could manage to say. Being this close to Jamie without pulling him into his arms was killing him. Even though he couldn't, he wanted to shout, "I love you still and forever!"

Jamie went into Keith's room. He sat next to the bed and took Keith's hand. He bowed his head and said a silent prayer for him to wake up. Marc stood at the door and watched Jamie. He still couldn't believe that he was here.

Derek came up behind Marc and touched him on the shoulder. "Why are you standing at the door?"

Marc nodded his head toward Jamie.

"Oh, my god! Hi, Jamie," he said as he ran into the room.

"Hello, Derek. How are you holding up?" He gave Derek a big hug. A wave of want and jealousy ran over Marc as he watched them hug. "He didn't wake up while you were gone. I am so sorry, Derek."

Jamie and Derek walked into the hall to talk. "The doctors say that, the longer he stays in a coma, the worse it could be. God, Jamie, I can't lose him. I love him so much."

"You need to have faith that God won't take him away from you."

Derek went back into Keith's room. Jamie stayed outside to give Derek his privacy with Keith. He sat in the waiting area; Marc followed him and sat down.

"How have you been, Jamie? I heard that you're writing another book. What is this one about?"

Jamie looked Marc in the eyes and said matter-of-factly, "It's about a lost love."

That statement really hurt Marc because he knew that it was probably about them. He felt that he had been kicked in the gut, and the nonchalant way Jamie said it caused him to hurt even more.

"How is Gary?" Jamie asked, even though he really didn't want to hear that they were happy.

"He's doing fine," Marc lied. He knew he had to keep up this sham.

"Where is he? I would have thought that he would be here to support you."

"He has to work, so he gets the updates when I go home at night and when Derek goes back to take a shower and sleep for a little while."

Something seemed off with Marc's manner. He was too vague with his answers. Jamie felt that he wasn't telling him the truth, but how could he find out what was going on with Marc? He wondered why he even cared, but he *did* care and wanted to know. He came to a decision.

"Marc, I was wondering if I can stay at the ranch with Derek, so we can catch up. It would be easier if I were there … if you don't have a reason why I shouldn't," he added when he saw Marc's face, which looked like he was going to jump out of his skin.

"Uh … no … there is no reason why you can't stay at the ranch."

Jamie knew by Marc's actions and the scared look on his face that he was hiding something. *Maybe he and Gary are not as happy as he would want me to believe.* "I promise that I'll stay out of your and Gary's way. You won't even know I'm there."

Marc was in a panic. *Now what? Was Jamie kidding when he said that I wouldn't even know he was there? I feel him even if he is not next to me. Gary isn't in town right now, so he can't come over and pretend. What am I going to do?* He stood up and paced back and forth.

Jamie knew that Marc's antsy behavior was suspicious. *I will find out what's going on before I leave,* he promised himself.

❧ Derek came out of the hospital room and walked straight up to Jamie. "Did you book a hotel room before you came to the hospital?"

"No, Derek. I just asked Marc if I could bunk at the ranch with you."

Derek jerked his head around to look at Marc. They exchanged a weird look, giving Jamie even more to go on.

Something is definitely off here. What are they hiding? Jamie vowed to find out before he went back home. He got up and asked Derek if he could go back in and see Keith.

"Sure."

Jamie walked directly in front of Marc, coming close on purpose. Marc sucked in a breath and Jamie heard it. *Marc's still bothered by me when I get close. Why is that? If Marc is happy with Gary, why am I still able to get this reaction from him?* Jamie disappeared into Keith's room.

"What are you thinking, Marc?" Derek asked. "Jamie can't stay at the ranch. He'll find out your secret regarding Gary. Then what? You never should have made up this sham. It never pays to lie. It will come back to bite you in the ass, and it looks like that's exactly what's going to happen here."

"I know, but what was I going to give as a reason why he couldn't stay with us? He knows I have a big house." Marc sat down and put his head in his hands. "God, this is going to blow up in my face, isn't it?"

Derek shook his head and said, "If you're going to continue with this façade, you'd better call Gary to see if he can come back or Jamie is going to find out the truth!"

Marc knew he was right, so he made the call.

Gary answered right away with concern in his voice. He knew that Keith was in the hospital and was afraid that it was bad news. "Hello, Marc. Please tell me that Keith isn't gone."

"No. He's still in a coma, but his vital signs are improving."

"Well, how is everyone else doing?"

"Gary, can you make a quick trip? Jamie's here, and I told him that he could stay at the ranch."

"What? Are you *nuts*? Why did you tell him that? Never mind. You're going to have to come clean, Marc, because I can't get back for a few more days. I'm sorry."

"I can't tell Jamie the truth!"

"Well, you'll have to come up with something then. You know, he's going to find out sooner or later, so just get it over with and tell him."

"Some friend *you* are! Just kidding, Gary. I know you'd help if you could. I'll see you in a few days."

"Tell him, Marc!"

ᕚ Jamie sat down next to Keith. He took his hand and started talking to him. Keith moved his fingers in Jamie's hand, which got Jamie's attention.

"Keith, open your eyes please. Can you hear me? If you can, squeeze my hand."

Keith squeezed his hand! Jamie jumped up and yelled for Derek to come at once.

Derek ran into the room and asked, "What? What *is* it?"

"He's coming to. I was talking to him, and he moved his fingers."

Derek took the seat from Jamie and begged Keith to open his eyes. Derek bent forward, kissing his lips and softly whispering, "I love you."

Keith slowly opened his eyes and was having trouble adjusting to the brightness. Jamie turned off the overhead lights, so they wouldn't bother him. That helped, and Keith tried to open his eyes again. He looked at Derek and told him in a whisper that he loved him too.

Marc went to get the doctor, and they came back into the room.

"Well, Keith, welcome back from your long sleep! I need to check you, and then you can spend time with your friends." The doctor listened to his chest and performed a complete neurological exam. All was good, he reported to the room.

Keith was trying to say something but was having trouble verbalizing, so Derek put his ear to Keith's lips.

"I am very hungry, my love," Keith said.

Derek laughed and hugged him.

"What did he say?" Jamie asked.

"He says he's very hungry!"

The doctor explained that they would have to start him on clear liquids, and then they would see. Keith made a face. Everyone in the room laughed.

Derek leaned over and kissed him again. "We are glad that you came back to us, and I am *so* glad that you came back to me! I could not have gone on without you."

Keith was very weak, but he smiled at Derek and whispered, "I love you so much."

Jamie and Marc left the room, so they could have their time together.

"Well, I guess Derek will stay here with Keith tonight, so I'll check into a hotel," Jamie told Marc. "I only wanted to stay at your ranch to catch up with Derek, but I'll do it later."

Jamie went to the nurse's station to get a phone book. He was going to stay at the Plains Hotel, which he remembered was the great historical hotel they stayed in while filming *Cheyenne Love*. He wrote down the number, sat on the sofa, and made calls to get a room and a cab.

"Stop, Jamie. I told you that you could stay at the ranch. It's silly for you to stay at a hotel when my house is so big." Marc had no idea what he was doing. He should have let him go to the hotel because that would solve his problem about not letting Jamie know that he'd lied, but he wanted him close.

Jamie was hoping that Marc would stop him. He took a chance by saying that he would go to a hotel, but he was determined to find out what was wrong. "Okay, Marc, if you are sure that I won't be in the way with you and Gary."

"No. It will be okay. Gary won't mind."

When Marc said this, Jamie felt like he had been stabbed in the heart all over again. *I don't know if I can do this.*

Discovery

Jamie climbed into the truck with Marc and leaned against the passenger door. He couldn't stand to be this close to Marc. He wanted to scoot over and wrap his arms around him, but he knew he was not his anymore, and he would not welcome this gesture.

Marc was very aware of the turmoil that was going through Jamie. He too wanted to get close to him and pull him into his arms and never let him go, but he knew that Jamie was no longer in his life and, with the deception he had started, he had no right to take this step. Marc's biggest concern was how he was going to cover up the lie about Gary. *Why did I do this to both of us? Just being this close to Jamie is driving me crazy! I am so in love with him.*

They rode to the ranch in silence.

When they pulled into the driveway, Jamie's heart started to pound, and he felt that he couldn't breathe. He never thought he would be back here again. *How am I going to do this?*

When the truck stopped, Jamie jumped out right away. You would have thought that the seat was on fire with the way Jamie got out. He knew that he was acting stupidly, but he couldn't stand to be in close proximity with Marc.

Marc got out of the truck and went to the back to get Jamie's suitcase. Jamie reached for it at the same time, running headlong into Marc. They were so close that they could feel each other's breath on their cheeks. Marc looked into Jamie's eyes and held his gaze. He moved one step closer and was right up against Jamie. Their bodies were touching.

What is Marc doing? Jamie thought. *He looks like he's ready to kiss me. I'm not moving … he'll have to move first.* Jamie knew it was stupid to stand his ground, but, if truth were known, he loved being this close to Marc again.

Marc leaned his head down and barely touched his lips to Jamie's.

Jamie met Marc's lips and kissed him back but then pulled away quickly. "What are you *doing*, Marc? Don't you care about Gary seeing you kissing me, or do you have that little respect for me to do this when you're a married man?"

"I'm sorry, Jamie. I have no excuse. I guess old habits die hard," Marc said as he turned away and walked into the house.

Jamie grabbed his bag and followed him. When they got inside, Marc told his housekeeper to put Jamie's suitcase in one of the guest rooms and told Jamie to follow him into the parlor. Marc's manservant Chase came in and asked if they would like something to eat and drink. Marc told him to bring two beers and fix a steak dinner for two. They would eat in a little while.

Marc turned to Jamie and said, "Please make yourself comfortable on the couch. I'll check on your room and be back in a second."

"Marc, are you going to tell Gary that I am here? Why did you say, 'dinner for two'? Isn't Gary eating with us?"

Marc stopped dead in his tracks. His mind was racing, but he stumbled about what to say. "Yes. He'll eat with us. I guess I'm so used to saying, 'two for dinner.' I'll correct it with my cook and go find him. Be right back."

Jamie still thought that Marc was acting oddly. *Why would he forget that it would be three for dinner? Something is just not right. I guess I'll know more when I see Gary again and watch them together.*

Outside of the parlor, Marc thought, *What do I do now? I'm going to have to come clean, I think, but he will really hate me then. I just can't tell him now. I'll think of something.* He went upstairs to his bedroom and paced around for a few minutes, trying to kill time.

Meanwhile, Jamie was walking around the parlor and silently muttering, *What's the big mystery, and why did Marc kiss me? I saw the want and desire in his eyes when we were standing against each other. God, how I wanted him to take me in his arms and hold me! Jamie, you have to stop this! Marc is not yours anymore.*

Marc came back into the parlor and said, "Jamie, Gary sends his regrets, but he's really sick and in bed. He thinks he has the flu, so he won't join us for dinner. I told him to stay in bed and that I would be up later if he needed me."

"Oh, I am so sorry he's not feeling well. Tell him that I hope he's better tomorrow." Jamie was glad that Gary was not going to join them. He was looking forward to being alone with Marc.

∽ Jamie and Marc sat across from each other, drinking their beers. The tension was so thick that you could cut it with a knife. Neither knew what to say. Jamie wanted to get up, pull Marc out of his seat, and beg him to take him in his arms. Meanwhile, Marc was wishing that he had not told Jamie the lie about Gary.

Finally, Jamie asked, "What is the next step with Keith? Now that Keith is awake, when will they let him come home?"

"I don't know, but I am sure that Derek will keep us informed. What are your plans, Jamie? How long are you staying?" His mind told him that he should hope that Jamie would not stay long, but his heart screamed, "Stay with me, Jamie, always. I love you and always will!"

Jamie didn't know if Marc wanted him to leave by asking this question, but he would not stay any longer than he needed to. He could hardly stand the stress of being around Marc. "I'm leaving in the morning. I'll go to the hospital to see Keith and to tell Derek that I am going home."

Marc felt like someone had punched him in the gut. *God, why did I make up this lie? Well, now you're paying the price for your deception. Jamie is in arm's reach, and you can't touch him.*

Chase came in and told them that dinner was ready. Jamie followed Marc into the dining room. Marc sat at the head of the table, and Chase guided Jamie to sit in the first place to Marc's right. Chase brought them two more beers and served the steaks. Marc and Jamie sat in silence as they ate. Jamie was wondering why it felt so strained being with Marc. They were acting like total strangers instead of ex-lovers.

All of a sudden, Jamie brushed against Marc's leg with his leg, and both men froze. The connection instantly caused problems for Jamie, and his jeans got very tight and uncomfortable. Marc did not make a move to pull his leg away. He let the connection last. He wanted more contact with Jamie than just this. Jamie didn't move either. Marc stopped eating and sat back and looked at Jamie, watching the expression in his eyes change with every second their knees were together. Jamie stared back with the same longing and intensity that was in Marc's eyes.

Chase came into the room to see if they wanted more beer, which broke the spell.

Jamie moved his knee and asked, "Aren't you going to send up some food to Gary?"

Marc felt the emptiness right away. He wanted that contact back. "I'm sure that he doesn't feel like eating anything right now."

Chase looked at Marc with a questioning look.

Something is just not right here, Jamie thought. Then it hit him that maybe Marc was lying. He would not stop until he found out what was going on.

⁓ They finished their meals and took their drinks to the parlor. Jamie sat on the couch, close to the fire. Marc noticed how beautiful Jamie was, with the glow of the fire dancing on his face. Marc stood with his foot on the hearth, watching Jamie out of the corner of his eye.

Jamie noticed how sexy Marc looked and wanted him even more than before. *I have got to stop this. He is not mine anymore.* "Marc, I'm going to go up and say hello to Gary. I'm not afraid of getting the flu — I've had my flu shot." And, with that statement, he headed toward the door.

"NO ...," Marc said more loudly that he meant to. "You can't go up there."

Jamie kept walking. Marc closed the distance between them and grabbed Jamie's arm.

"Why don't you want me to say hello to Gary?"

"I just don't want him disturbed. Maybe he'll feel better in the morning, and you can see him then."

Jamie could see the panic in Marc's eyes, so he stopped and tried to remove his arm from Marc's grasp, but Marc didn't let go; instead, he moved closer. Jamie could feel the body heat, and his heart beat faster. *What is he up to now? Oh, my god. He's going to kiss me again! I want this … I want this, but I shouldn't let him.*

Marc moved swiftly before Jamie could pull away and kissed him with the passion of a starving lover. He moaned against Jamie's mouth and forced him to open it and let him in. He was no longer holding back. He wanted Jamie, and he couldn't stop. Jamie melted into Marc. They both felt the want and the need between them, and the bulges in their jeans left little to the imagination. They were both ready to strip and fall on the floor to satisfy their longing and love for each other. It was abundantly clear to Jamie that, regardless of Marc's situation, they were still very much in love. Nothing had changed. They couldn't keep their hands off each other.

Marc led Jamie to the couch and had all intentions of making love to him right there. He pushed Jamie down and fell on top of him. "I want you now, Jamie. I can't go another minute without having you as my own." He kissed him on the mouth, neck, and ears.

Jamie suddenly came to his senses and pushed Marc off, causing him to fall to the floor. Jamie jumped up and headed for the door. "God, Marc! How can you be so crass and unfaithful to your marriage? You are a bastard, and I am glad we didn't marry. You'd probably be unfaithful to me too."

Marc was stunned at Jamie's words, but he knew why he was saying these hurtful things. *He really believes my lie.*

Jamie stormed up the stairs to his room and closed the door. *It was a bad mistake to stay here with Marc. I can't control myself, and he obviously can't either.* He decided to go to Marc and Gary's room and tell Gary how sorry he was and that he hoped he would be able to forgive Marc this small mistake.

Jamie knocked on the door to Marc's room and waited. No response! He opened the door and went in to talk to Gary. He expected to find him in bed, but the bed was made with no sign of Gary. He walked into the bathroom to see if he was in the shower, but he found no one. *What is going on here?*

He sat on the bed to try and sort this out. Being there brought back so many wonderful memories of their lovemaking. He couldn't help lying on the pillow with his eyes closed, remembering. *Oh, how I love Marc and still do! What is he trying to do to me by making me want him again? And where is Gary? Why did he lie to me about Gary being sick up here?* Jamie was deep in thought with his eyes still closed. He didn't hear Marc come in.

Marc moved very quietly to the bed and watched Jamie. *He knows that Gary is not here. I'm going to have to tell him the whole story, but will he listen to me or run away — the way he has always done?*

Time for Truth

Marc sat on the side of the bed, and Jamie's eyes flew open, but he didn't move.

"What's going on here, Marc? Where is Gary?"

Marc put his finger on Jamie's lips to stop him from talking. "I have to tell you the truth now, Jamie. I never expected you to come here again, so I never thought I would have to tell you. Are you willing to listen and not say anything until I am done?"

Jamie nodded his head.

"The first thing you need to know is that I am still in love with you, Jamie. There has never been anyone else and never will be."

"But ..."

Marc stopped him again and continued. "You agreed to listen until I was done. There was never a Gary, and I am not married."

Jamie started to protest and move, but Marc stopped him.

"Please, Jamie, listen to me. I made up the whole story and made Keith and Derek go along with it. I wanted you to be able to move on and find someone who could be happy living with you in Berea. That person is not me. I thought that, if you thought I had moved on, then so would you.

"Gary is my best friend. We grew up together all the way through high school and college, and he is straight. He agreed to do this for me because I convinced him that this was for you. He always thought I was crazy, especially after he met you at the awards. He thinks we belong together, and no one else will ever satisfy us.

"He is so right. I will never be with anyone else. I love you more than this ranch, my life, everything — but I cannot move away from here. I have good reasons that I have not shared with you. I did this because I want you to be happy and live a full life with love. I don't want you to be alone for the rest of your life like I intend to do. I had not been with anyone before you, and I will never be with anyone after you, so you were wrong when you accused me of being unfaithful. I will always be faithful to you until my last breath on Earth."

Jamie was crying at this point and could not even see Marc's face for the tears.

"Well, Jamie, now you know the truth, and I'm sure you will never forgive me for putting you through this heartache. I heard from Derek how much you were suffering, but I still felt that it was for the best since neither of us can give in to the other." Marc got off the bed and left the room. He could not stay another moment with Jamie on his bed.

Jamie stayed in Marc's bed for a long time, trying to take it all in. He was feeling so many emotions: anger, relief, heartache, love, sadness, yearning, anger again, and understanding. He asked himself, *What should I do? Can I forgive him for all these months of heartache and longing for something that I thought was gone? Jamie, what do you want? Are you willing to let Marc go away from you again?* As he thought and felt all these things, he closed his eyes and fell asleep.

◈ Hours passed. Marc waited for Jamie to come downstairs, but he didn't. Marc decided to check on him. He first looked in Jamie's room, but he was not there, so he went to his room and quietly opened the door. He found Jamie in his bed, asleep on top of the bedspread. He walked over and thought that he was by far the most gorgeous man he had ever seen. He watched him sleep for a few more minutes, and then decided that he should wake him up so that he could sleep in his own bed. He was fairly sure that Jamie would not want to share a bed with him. He shook him a little, and Jamie opened his eyes. Marc could have lost his soul in those eyes staring back at him.

"Jamie, you've been asleep for a while, so I think you should wake up now and go to your own room. I promise I will not bother you."

Jamie stared at him for the longest time and then asked, "Marc, is that what you want me to do — go to my own bed?"

Marc almost lost his composure. *What is Jamie doing? Is he trying to drive me crazy and make me suffer the way I caused him to suffer?* When he got over the shock of what Jamie was asking him, he responded, "No. You know that is not what I want. I want you to stay in my bed with me, but I know how you must feel about me now, so I would never ask you to stay. Tomorrow you will be back at your farm, and that will be the end of it."

Jamie ignored Marc's response and asked the same question. "Marc, is that what you want me to do — go to my own bed?"

Marc sat on the side of his bed, pulled Jamie into his arms, and kissed him passionately and completely. Jamie responded by kissing him like he could not get enough of him either. Marc pulled off Jamie's shirt and kissed him on his neck, ears, and chest. Jamie was in heaven and had no intention of stopping him. Marc stood up and pulled off his clothes, and then unbuckled Jamie's pants. With one movement, he had them off, and both men were completely naked. Marc moved to the other side of the bed and lay down, pulling Jamie's naked body close to him. Jamie was hard and ready to have Marc make love to him. He had come to the decision to let the hurt go and let the love come back between them. He wanted Marc and no one else.

They kissed and kissed until both of them had swollen lips, and they wanted it all. Marc took Jamie into his mouth first to give him the pleasure that he had been storing up.

Jamie moaned and bucked and was not too far from coming. "Please, Marc, make me come."

Marc went all the way down and sucked and hummed against Jamie's hard cock until he couldn't hold back anymore. Jamie shot his load into Marc's willing mouth. Marc had been craving the wonderful taste of Jamie for so long and took every drop. It was quick, but it had been so long since they were together. Marc was hurting at this point, so he grabbed his cock and started working himself.

Jamie stopped his hands and pushed Marc on his back. He moved quickly and positioned himself between Marc's legs. "Now it's my turn." He teased Marc a little by licking down his shaft and back up, putting his tongue on the slit at the top and, getting a good taste of Marc's wonderful juices. He loved the taste of his love and missed it so much. He had yearned for it so many nights alone in the dark.

Marc moaned and begged Jamie to take him all the way in. Jamie opened his mouth wide and went down on Marc, at the same time caressing his balls and moving his hand back to Marc's opening. He came off Marc's cock and moved between his legs, licking him around his opening. Marc was making noises that Jamie had never heard. He could tell that Marc was going to shoot his load, and he didn't want to miss that, so he took him back in his mouth.

Marc grabbed Jamie's head and fucked his mouth until he screamed, "I'm coming!"

Jamie sucked and swallowed and licked him clean.

As Marc came down, he pulled up Jamie to kiss him. "Oh, my god, Jamie. I always thought our lovemaking was great — but this was *unbelievable!*" Marc held Jamie in his arms until they both came down and were quiet again.

"Jamie, I want you to know that I love you and will always love you, no matter what happens from here."

Jamie listened quietly to Marc and tried to decide what he wanted to say. Finally, he responded. "Marc, I have to say this just once, and then I will not say it again. You really hurt me when you let me think that you had moved on with Gary. And then when I heard you were married, I wanted to die. I even thought about ending it all. I now know the truth, and I do understand your motive. I had to tell myself that the important thing in all of this is that you *are* still mine and I love you — so I cannot hold this hurt any longer. I forgive you, but please don't hurt me like that again. I wanted to wait for a while before we made love again, but when you come near me I can't stop myself. I will always want you — and *only* you — to make love to me and grow old with me."

Marc couldn't stand it any longer. He pulled Jamie to him and kissed those kissable lips until neither one could breathe.

"Marc, I want you to come inside of me and make me yours again for the rest of our lives."

Marc didn't need to be asked twice. He wanted this too. It seemed so important to both of them. He got some lube and started preparing Jamie.

It was like starting all over again, which was okay with both of them: slow and easy. When Marc pushed, Jamie cried, causing Marc to stop. He was frightened that he had hurt him. "Jamie? What's wrong? Did I hurt you?"

"No, Marc. Please don't stop. These are tears of happiness."

Marc leaned down and kissed Jamie tenderly and whispered against his lips, "I love you, Jamie Walker, for always." He pushed all the way in and started moving slowly at first, but Jamie wanted him hard and fast. Jamie bucked into him, causing Marc to lose control and pound Jamie into the mattress. Both came at the same time with Jamie spurting spontaneously from the whole lovemaking session and Marc exploding deeply into Jamie.

When they separated, they lay in each other's arms — mess and all. They didn't care. If they moved, it might end the happiness, so they clung to each other and fell asleep totally exhausted.

The Secret

The next morning, Marc woke up first and stared at Jamie in his arms. He thought about what Jamie said last night, particularly about how Jamie was tempted to end it all when he heard about Marc marrying Gary. *God, if my lie caused him to do that, how would I ever be able to live another minute? You are so stupid and selfish. You really don't deserve his love.*

About that time, Jamie opened his eyes and saw that Marc was crying. "What's wrong? Aren't you happy that we're together again?"

"Oh, Jamie, yes! But I was thinking how close I could have come to losing you forever."

"What are you talking about?"

"You told me that you thought about ending your life over my stupid lie."

"Hush, Marc. It's over, and I am still here."

"How can you be so forgiving of what I did?"

"I told you — I decided to give up the hurt and let the love come back. I am so happy that you're still mine and belong to no one else. So stop talking and kiss me!"

Marc pulled him in and kissed him over and over.

"We should get up and shower, eat some breakfast, and go see Derek and Keith," Jamie suggested.

After they got cleaned up and ate, they agreed to talk about the future later. When they got to the hospital, they found Derek lying in bed with Keith, and both were asleep. Jamie went to the nurse's station and asked if Keith was still doing okay. The nurse told Jamie that he had a good night and would probably be able to go home in a few days.

Jamie went back and told Marc. They went to the waiting room to wait until Derek and Keith woke up.

While they were there, Marc decided that he should finally tell Jamie why he couldn't move away from his ranch. "Jamie, I want to tell you something else that I have not been able to share with you."

Jamie got a worried look on his face but didn't say anything and let Marc talk.

"I know you've always thought that I was being stubborn by refusing to move to Berea with you. The fact is that I *cannot* move — not that I didn't *want* to. What I'm going to tell you is very private, and the only ones who know are my best friend Gary, Keith, and my house staff. I have a twin sister who lives in a separate wing in the house."

Jamie interrupted Marc and asked, "Why didn't you tell me that you have a twin, and why haven't I met her? Why do you keep her a secret, especially from me?"

"Hush, Jamie, and I will tell you. When Mary and I were 18 years old, we were out riding. It was slippery, and her horse went down, pretty much like Keith's did, only she wasn't as lucky. She cracked her skull on a rock and never came out of the coma — even after all these years. Our father brought her home when the doctors said that they could do no more for her. They said she might stay in this coma until her body quit and shut down, or she might wake up anytime without warning.

"Before my dad passed away, he made me promise that I would never sell the ranch, and he wanted me to always keep her here with me and to never put her in a nursing home. So you see why I can't come to live with you. I want to be with you more than you know, but I can't sell the ranch and break my deathbed promise to my dad."

"Marc, I'm speechless. Why didn't you tell me this? Why would you hide her from me? You have to know that I would never hurt her."

"I know that, but my pride kept me from telling you. I thought that you should want to be with me enough to leave your place, and I didn't want Mary to be the reason. My ego — or pride, or whatever — was driving me to stay silent about her."

"Are you ashamed of her? I don't understand why you kept this from me. Did you ever think that, if I had known sooner, it might have saved us from all this separation?"

"You were so set on staying at the farm for your own family reasons that I didn't think it would make a difference."

Just as Jamie was about to say something, Derek walked into the waiting area. "Hi, guys. I am happy to report that Keith is going to be fine! They did another neurological test last night, and he still has no deficits. His memory is intact, and he should be able to come home in a few days. I can hardly wait to get him all to myself!"

"That is great, Derek!" Jamie said.

Marc looked at Derek. "What are your plans when Keith comes home?"

"Well, I guess this is as good a time as any. Jamie, I'm moving to Cheyenne to be with Keith as soon as the spring crop is planted. So you will have to hire a new farmhand and groom. We're in love, and we're not going to be as stupid as you and Marc are about not being together."

"Well, Derek," Jamie announced, "you should know that I'm aware of the deception, and I also know the reason that's been keeping Marc here, so I have some decisions to make myself." Jamie smiled at Marc, who had a shocked look on his face, the same as Derek's. "What? Why are you two looking at me like that?"

"Soooo! Does this mean what I *think* it means?" Marc asked. "Do I dare hope what you are planning?"

Derek chimed in at that point, looking from Jamie to Marc and back. "You two have gotten back together, haven't you?"

Marc walked over to Jamie and pulled him close. "Yes. We are back together, and I might add *better than ever.*" He noticed Jamie blushing and tightened the grip on his waist.

"Wow! Wait until I tell Keith. He'll be so happy!" Derek went back into Keith's room.

Marc turned Jamie to face him. "Are you really thinking about coming to live here with me?"

Jamie reached up and kissed Marc and just shook his head. Marc pulled Jamie close to him and told him that he was going to love him and hold him and never let him go. They stood and hugged, wrapped in each other's arms.

"You know, Marc, there is a lot to do," Jamie said, "and I want to see Mary. God, she must be beautiful — a female version of you. Wow!"

"She won't know you're there, but if you want to, we will do that later today."

"You don't know what she hears. She may have been hearing you talk to her all these years."

"I sat for hours after you left me, telling her how sad I was. For some reason, it made me feel better."

"With meeting Mary, bringing Keith home, and going back to the farm to decide what needs to be done there, it's going to be a busy few weeks or maybe months. I know that I don't need to ask you this, Marc, but I will anyway just to hear you say it. Will you wait for me to get my personal affairs in order?"

Marc took Jamie in his arms again and whispered against his lips, "No way."

Jamie pulled back and looked at Marc sadly. "What? You won't wait for me?"

"No. I am not letting you go away from me for any amount of time."

"But …?"

Marc silenced him with a kiss. "I am going with you. You will never get too far from me again — *ever!*"

Sweet Mary

Marc and Jamie left Derek with Keith at the hospital and told him that they would be back later. Marc wanted to take Jamie home to meet his sister. They went to Mary's wing of the mansion, and Marc told her nurse that she could take a break while he and Jamie were there.

When they walked into her bedroom, Jamie's breath caught in his throat. Looking at her face was like looking into Marc's; their features were identical. She looked so peaceful, like she was sleeping. Jamie thought of fairy tales he used to read to his little niece. She was definitely a sleeping beauty.

Marc went to her side and leaned down to kiss her on the forehead. "Mary, I want to introduce you to someone. This is Jamie. I told you about him. He is my love, my future."

Jamie sat down in the chair by her bedside and took her hand in his. "Hi, Mary. I am so glad to meet you. I want you to know that I love your brother more than life itself, and I promise to make him happy until we both leave this Earth. I would love to come talk to you every day, if that is okay with you. I'm going to my farm in Kentucky and arrange to move here with your brother, so I'll be away for a short while. When I come back, we'll get to know each other." He bent forward and kissed her on the head, just like Marc did. T

As they were leaving, Jamie said, "Marc, she is so beautiful. It's like looking at you, only with feminine, softer features."

"Now do you fully understand my not being able to leave Wyoming? I can't send her away from here. This is the only home she has ever known."

"Yes, Marc. I do get it. I still have a little trouble understanding why you didn't tell me your reason. Your silence on this matter has caused us a lot of wasted time. Your reason for staying here is far more important than mine is for staying at my farm. My farm is important to me because it's been in my family for generations, but that's a silly reason compared to yours."

"I told you that my ego wouldn't let me tell you. I thought that, if you loved me enough, then there shouldn't even be a question."

"Well, I felt the same about you. I felt that if you loved me enough, you would move in with me. We were both very stupid, but enough said about this. We need to make plans now. Keith is not going to be able to take care of things here, so Derek can stay here to help you with the ranch and horses. I will go home and settle the farm and ship my horses here. I also need to figure out …"

"Whoa, Kentucky boy. I told you: I am not letting you out of my sight! We'll go back to Kentucky and work on the arrangements together as a couple."

"But what about Derek and Keith? They probably could use your help."

"No. I talked to Keith's doctor this morning, and he said that, except for some cuts and bruises, he should be able to resume his work slowly in a day or so. He said that Keith was incredibly lucky to have no problems after all he had been through. Derek said not to worry because he would take care of things. So, as soon as we get Keith home and settled, we'll leave for Kentucky."

Jamie just stood there, looking at Marc and thinking, *I never thought I could love this man any more than I already do, but I do!*

Marc looked at Jamie and asked, "What?"

Jamie moved up to Marc and wrapped his arms around his neck. "I love you more than words can say, Marc Montgomery Morgan," he said as he softly kissed him.

"Stop or we won't get to the hospital!"

᠅ "Keith, do you believe that Jamie and Marc are done being stubborn and that Jamie is moving here?"

"I am so glad that Marc finally told Jamie why he couldn't leave Cheyenne."

"What do you mean 'told him'? What is there to tell? Jamie had to finally give in to Marc because Marc was not about to give …"

"No, hon. You're wrong. I can tell you why now, because Jamie knows the whole truth."

As Keith told Derek about Mary, Derek felt so bad about what he had been thinking about Marc. "Wow! No wonder Jamie decided to sell and move here."

❧ For the next two days, Marc and Jamie made love every night and planned their future every day. They would leave for Kentucky on Friday.

Keith was coming home, and Derek was walking on cloud nine. He was finally going to be able to hold Keith in his arms, naked, with no nurses looking at them. "Keith, when I get you home, we are going to my bed, and I promise I will be gentle with you, but I need to have you in my arms."

"That is where I want to be more than anywhere I can think of."

Derek, Marc, and Jamie brought Keith home, and Derek immediately kept his promise by taking him up to his bed. Jamie and Marc knew they would not see them for the rest of the day. Around dinnertime, they came down to join Jamie and Marc. As they ate their dinner, they talked about what was going to happen in the immediate future.

Derek and Keith were so happy that Jamie and Marc were finally together. They talked about what needed to be done at the ranch. Most of the work would have to be done by Derek because Keith was still not up to par, but he could supervise him as to what he did with the horses.

Derek told him that he was used to working with horses and Keith laughed. "I know you are, but let me boss you around a little." They bantered back and forth playfully, loving being together again.

Jamie and Marc made arrangements to fly to Kentucky in the morning and told the other two to call immediately if they needed them. All four retired to their rooms … well, not quite. Keith went to Derek's room, and Jamie went to Marc's.

Derek wanted to give Keith some rest since he kept him busy all day. "You go to sleep, my love, and I will be with you when you wake in the morning."

"I am pretty tired. I love you Derek," Keith said as he drifted off to sleep.

Derek whispered in his ear, "I love you back."

❧ Chase came up to Marc's room to announce that Gary was downstairs.

"Great! Tell him that we will be right down."

"Are you sure that I should go down with you, Marc? Maybe you should talk to Gary alone." Jamie wasn't sure how he felt about Gary. He knew the deception was Marc's idea, but how could Gary do this to someone, knowing it could be hurtful?

"No, Jamie. You are coming with me."

They both went downstairs. Gary was in the den, waiting. When they walked in, Gary turned around and Jamie again thought that he was gorgeous.

"Hey, Marc, Jamie! I heard the news from Chase. I'm glad you finally know about Marc's deception, and I'm truly sorry about my part in it, Jamie. I hope you can forgive me as well. I told Marc all along that he was being foolish, but he felt that it would help you move on."

Jamie stood still for a moment and sized up Gary. He seemed sincere. Marc and Gary did not know what Jamie's silence meant, and they were hesitant to say anything else. Jamie finally moved toward Gary and held out his hand. Gary shook it.

Jamie smiled at Gary and said, "I am glad to see you again, and this time I would like to be your friend too."

Gary smiled back. "Marc, you are a very lucky man!"

"That I do know, Gary," Marc said as he pulled Jamie to his side.

Jamie continued. "I thought I was angry at you, Gary, but like I told Marc, I'm letting the hurt go. If he had to pick anyone to be 'married' to, I am glad that it was a straight guy and not a gay one!"

All three burst into laughter.

"I would love to be your friend, Jamie," Gary said, smiling from ear to ear.

When Gary left them about an hour later, Marc and Jamie retired to their room.

"It is so good to have Keith home and well," Marc said. "Those two will be happy together, and so will we."

Jamie and Marc made love until they could hardly move.

"Marc, I love you, but you are going to have to stop because I am very tired — and sore, by the way!"

"What? Can't take too much of a good thing?"

"Go to sleep. I love you," Jamie said. "Night."

They fell asleep, holding each other.

Selling the Farm

Early the next morning, all four met for breakfast and talked about the next couple of weeks. Keith told Marc not to worry about anything at the ranch. With Derek there and Gary back in town, he knew that they would be fine.

Jamie and Marc were driven to the airport to settle things in Berea. When they arrived at the farm, the Hawthorns greeted them.

"How is Keith?" Mrs. Hawthorn asked Jamie.

"He's great! Thanks for asking. I want you guys to be the first to know that I am selling the farm and both houses and moving to Cheyenne with Marc. Oh, by the way, let me introduce you. Mr. and Mrs. Hawthorn, this is my boyfriend and love, Marc Montgomery Morgan."

"It is a pleasure to meet you, Mr. Morgan. We have heard a lot about you from Maurice, Hildegard, and Betsy," Mrs. Hawthorn explained. "They were kind of mad at you for not moving here with our Jamie."

"Please call me Marc, and I can just imagine how they felt. Nice to meet you."

"Yeah, well, Marc had a really good reason for not moving here, so I am moving to be with him," Jamie told them. "I will contact a real estate agent. In the meantime, if you know anyone who might be in the market for a farm, let me know. Derek is not coming back, so can you guys stay until I get this place sold?"

"Sure, Jamie. We love it here," Mr. Hawthorn said.

With that, Marc and Jamie went to the barn to see about the horses and how Shadow was holding up without anyone walking him on a daily basis. He was fine, so they went to the main house where Maurice was waiting for them.

Hildegard stepped forward and said, "Hi, Mr. Walker." She and Betsy were waiting for their cue to go back to work.

"Betsy, please cook us a homemade, fried-chicken dinner with all the works. Mr. Morgan eats way too much beef. Oh, and before you all go back to your duties, let me tell you what's going to happen. I'm selling the farm and moving to Cheyenne with Marc. Now, before you start worrying about your jobs, Marc and I talked about how we could keep everyone on staff from both households. Maurice, you would be in charge of the whole staff; Hildegard, you will work alongside Marc's two maids as equals; Betsy, we want you to run the kitchen and help feed the ranch hands in the bunk house. Marc's cook will work for you because you are more experienced. Are there any questions?"

Maurice spoke up. "Mr. Morgan, don't you already have a manservant?"

"Yes, Maurice, but he would rather drive for me and not be in charge of the house. He says the maids give him headaches."

"I know how that feels," Maurice said as he looked over at Hildegard.

"I am sure you do," Marc said. "My man's name is Chase, by the way. You will be in charge at double your salary. That goes for you also, Betsy. Hildegard, you will get a sizable pay raise."

"Oh, my god. Yes, yes, YES," yelled Hildegard. "That sounds great!" She was so happy that she hugged Jamie.

"Hildegard!" Maurice yelled at her. "What do you think you are *doing*?"

"It's okay, Maurice. She's just happy."

Betsy shook her head at Hildegard in disgust. *She is a loose cannon*, Betsy thought, but she loved her all the same. They were all extremely excited.

"Well, guys, I haven't heard a 'yes' from anyone but Hildegard. Do you accept our offer to come with me to Cheyenne?"

Maurice was trying to stay dignified when he spoke. "Yes, sir. I would love to come with you, and thank you, Mr. Morgan."

Hildegard and Betsy agreed. "We second that!"

"Okay, then! That part is solved. Now, to deal with the hard part: selling the farm. How am I going to do this? I've lived on this farm my entire life."

Marc watched the pain come across Jamie's face because this farm was all he had ever known. *It's breaking my heart, watching him give up his homestead,* Marc thought, *but I don't know how else we can do this. I feel like I am being selfish.* "Jamie, can I talk to you privately?"

"Sure, Marc. What's the problem?"

"Are you sure about leaving your farm and all that you have known here? If you're not sure, then we need to decide what to do."

"Yes, Marc. It is going to be very painful to leave this place, but now that I know you can't come to me, there is no choice. I want to be with you for the rest of my life and, like Derek told me a long time ago, my grandmother would not want me to choose a house over my true love. She would want me to be happy, and I can hear her say, 'Jamie, you should never give up the love of a lifetime just because of a house. There are a lot of memories here, but you will always remember them, and now you are supposed to make new memories with your true love.' My grandmother was a very smart woman, so I need to listen to her voice in my head."

Marc walked over to Jamie and took him in his arms. "I just want to hold you and tell you that I will always love you and will do all that is humanly possible to make you happy."

"I know that, Marc. That's why, even though this is hard for me, it's the way it's supposed to be. I want to spend the rest of my life showing you how much I love you."

◢ It was late when they finally retired to the den to drink some coffee and plan what they had to do the next day. Jamie stood in front of the fireplace, sipping his coffee.

Marc stood back and watched him. He knew that Jamie was sad, and he understood. He walked behind him, put his arms around his waist, and pulled him close. He kissed him on the back of the neck and whispered in his ear, "Jamie, I am so in love with you. I know that you are sad. I hate that this is hurting you."

"Stop, Marc. What would hurt me more is not having you with me for the rest of my life. There are a lot of memories here, but we will make our own memories together. That is more important."

"I do know what you are sacrificing for me."

"Now that I know you are mine and always have been, it is no sacrifice."

"Jamie, I have something for you that I wanted to give you that time I came to see you at the movie filming in Cheyenne. But the way things ended, I never gave it to you. I want you to have it now." He pulled out a jewelry box and handed it to Jamie.

"What is it?"

"Open it and see."

Jamie opened the box. Inside was an ID bracelet in 18-carat gold with "Jamie and Marc" engraved on the front. Inscribed on the back was, "I am yours and you are mine, forever. Love, Marc."

Big tears rolled down Jamie's face. "Oh, Marc. How *beautiful*! You have kept it all this time?"

"Yes, Jamie. I couldn't bear to get rid of it. God, how I love you."

He picked up Jamie and carried him upstairs to Jamie's room where they first made love. They undressed each other carefully and, when they were naked in each other's arms, they took things slowly and tenderly. They wanted this night of lovemaking to be even more special, like their first time in this room. Marc lifted up Jamie again and carried him to the bed.

"No, Marc. Stop."

Marc froze. "What is *this* now? Oh, god, no!"

"No … no … it's not bad," Jamie assured him. "There's a fire going, and the bearskin rug is still here." Jamie gave Marc a sweet, innocent look that melted Marc into submission.

Marc got the hint. He moved them both to the rug and pulled Jamie down beside him. "Is this what you want, my love?" Marc kissed Jamie with all the longing of a man who had been without his love for a long time. Even though they had made love over and over since the night Jamie forgave him, they had not made love here where they first consummated it. "Jamie, have I told you how much I love you and thank God every day for bringing you to Cheyenne to check on Keith and Derek? If you had not come to see them, we may never have come back together, and we would have lost the only love that either of us could ever want."

"I know, Marc. I love you too and feel like the luckiest man in the world because I have your love to be with me always."

They spent most of the night making passionate love until both were satisfied and surrendered to sleep.

❧ "Marc ... Marc! Wake up! I just had a perfect solution for the farm!"

Marc rubbed his eyes, still half asleep, and looked at Jamie's animated face. "What are you so excited about this early in the morning? You know you kept me up most of the night making love to you, and then you wake me up at the crack of dawn."

"Oh, hush your bellyaching. You know that you wanted to make love to me most of the night," Jamie grinned. "I didn't have to twist your arm."

That was all it took. Marc pulled Jamie into his arms and gave him a very thorough kiss. "Now, what were you saying?" He smiled at how disoriented Jamie was after that powerful kiss. "What's the matter? Can't you *talk* now?" He puffed up his chest at Jamie.

Jamie wrestled him to the rug and sat on top of him. "*Now* who has control, Mr. Morgan?"

Marc noticed the satisfied look on Jamie's face because he knew that he had him right where he wanted him. "I think you had better get off me, or I will not be responsible for what I do to you next."

"Promises, promises," Jamie said as he got up and ran to the bathroom.

Marc was hot on his trail. He grabbed him and pushed him against the bathroom door. "Do you want to surrender now or after I have my way with you?"

"How about *after* you have your way with me?"

They were having fun playing but, when Jamie said this, Marc could not stop himself and kissed Jamie's lips and forced him to open up for him.

Jamie opened his mouth to let in Marc's luscious tongue and moaned when their groins rubbed together. "Marc, please take me now."

Jamie was Marc's to do as he pleased, and he pleased a lot. Marc wanted to take him right where they stood. He lifted up Jamie, and Jamie wrapped his legs around Marc's waist. He put his fingers in Jamie's mouth to lubricate them. Jamie was wide open and ready for Marc. Marc entered Jamie hard and fast, but both were so hot at this point that Jamie didn't even protest the roughness; in fact, he was getting hotter by the rough way he was being taken.

Both worked to satisfy their need for each other. Marc moved faster and faster until he came deep inside Jamie. He was breathing so hard that he could barely catch his breath. He slowly slipped out of Jamie, and Jamie took his legs from Marc's waist. He was a little shaky, but Marc held him tightly as he got his balance.

Marc kissed Jamie again and licked down his neck, around his rock-hard nipples, sucking and flicking his tongue against them. As he moved farther down, he noticed that Jamie was so hard that it looked like he might break. Jamie moaned and tried to move his hips toward Marc but was a little too shaky. Marc held him still and moved down to take Jamie into his mouth. He worked him gently at first, but Jamie moved with him and wanted it faster. Marc sucked and licked up and down his shaft until he heard Jamie's breathing catch, and he knew that he was going to taste his wonderful love juice. Jamie came and filled Marc's mouth, and Marc never lost a drop. He came back up and held Jamie tightly.

"Wow, I didn't wake you up for this," Jamie said, "but I am sure glad you thought I did! When we get cleaned up, I would like to tell you what came to me in the night."

Both got in the shower and washed to get ready for the day.

"What did you want to tell me, Jamie?"

"I'll tell you at breakfast. Let's go eat."

"I already had a little morsel this morning," Marc said with a wicked smile as he walked Jamie downstairs.

"Oh, you think you are so cute, don't you?"

"What? And you *don't*?" Marc asked as he patted Jamie on his cute ass.

The Solution

They sat down for breakfast, and Marc turned to Jamie. "So what was the brilliant idea that you wanted to tell me?"

"What would you think if I didn't sell the farm?"

Marc started to get nervous and wondered where this conversation was leading. *Was Jamie having second thoughts about moving?* He knew that he shouldn't feel this insecure, but after all the times they had separated, he couldn't help it.

Jamie noticed the change coming over Marc. "Now don't start thinking bad things. Just listen to my idea."

"Okay. Let me hear it."

"What if I kept the farm and found out if Keith and Derek wanted it to be their home? They could live here for free and raise horses for us. We could have the farm strictly for breeding horses, and your ranch would be for racing and selling them."

"What do you propose I do without a groom for my horses if Keith was here?"

"You and I can take care of them for a while until we find someone. We could let Keith and Derek live here free, like I said, and pay them a salary to help with the groceries and normal household expenses. Well, what do you think?"

"I don't know. I am not sure what to think. What makes you think that Keith will want to come here to live? He is a Wyoming boy, born and raised."

"That may be, but I can't believe they wouldn't jump at this offer. I'm sorry, Marc, but I can't see four gay men living under the same roof, so they would have to find a place anyway, and their funds might be tighter that way than what I am proposing. I mean, come on ... a free house instead of one they would have to shell out money for? They would be foolish to turn it down. And, besides, Keith has always acted like he was comfortable here, and I know that Derek loves this farm."

"Well, okay, but what about the main house? What are you going to do with that?"

"I thought we could hire someone to live there and take care of it, and we would have a place of our own when we come to visit Derek and Keith and check on the new foals."

"What kind of people?"

"Like a husband-and-wife team. Whenever we come here, they could take care of us."

"Wouldn't they need a staff to help them? Maybe a couple could manage the house, but they could have a cook and a maid, at least. You and I certainly have the money to maintain three houses."

"It sounds like you're getting on board with this idea," Jamie said with a big smile on his face.

Marc couldn't resist that smile. He leaned over and kissed him lightly. "I am beginning to see how this might work. If we did this, you would be able to keep your place that you love so much. That's the best part of your idea because I know how much this was hurting you."

"Don't think like that, Marc. I want to be with you no matter what I have to do to get there. Sell my home or not. But, if I can have the best of both worlds, why not?"

"Okay, Jamie. That part is done. Now, how do we convince Derek and Keith? Also, who are you going to get to live in the mansion?"

"Here is my idea: I will ask the Hawthorns to move into the house and take care of it. That way, Mr. Hawthorn can help Derek plant the crops. I will pay them a salary to maintain things here, and then hopefully we can visit often. I can still enjoy my property with the farm and Walker's Pond. When you brought Shadow, do you remember when I took you to the pond for our first time and how romantic that was?"

"And very hot, if I recall," Marc chimed in.

"Yes, I do recall. That was the first lesson I taught you."

"Oh, yes, you surely did! I might need a refresher course though."

"Oh, you *think* so, huh?" Jamie teased Marc.

"Yes. I think we should revisit that before we go home," Marc teased back.

"Home ... what a nice sound that has," Jamie said.

Marc was tired of talking. He got up from the table and pulled Jamie into his arms. "I just needed to hug you tightly, hearing you say that about our home — and it *is* our home now." He whispered in Jamie's ear as he took possession of his lips. "You know, I don't think I will ever get tired of kissing you. When we get so old and feeble that we can hardly stand, I will still need to kiss those wonderful lips of yours."

"Do you know how great that sounds?"

"What part?"

"The 'old together' part," Jamie said as he hugged Marc again.

"Do you want to call Keith and Derek? How do you want to go about this?" Marc asked.

"I am going to ask the Hawthorns if they can stay in the farmhouse a little longer, and then you and I will go home and talk to Keith and Derek in person."

"Okay. Let's get started. The sooner we do this, the quicker we can get you moved in with me."

Jamie instructed the house staff to get his clothes packed and shipped. He talked to the Hawthorns about staying at the farm until he had a chance to talk to Derek and Keith. Marc made the arrangements to fly to Cheyenne later that night. When they got on the airplane, they planned their life together, and both men could not believe that it was finally happening.

"Weren't we stupid to waste all that time?" Jamie asked. "But it's over now, and we need to move on. Do you think Derek and Keith will agree to my plan?"

"I think they will. It's a good deal." *I hope they will,* he thought. *If not, Jamie and I will be right back where we started.*

❧ Chase met Jamie and Marc at the Cheyenne airport and drove them to the ranch. Keith and Derek were waiting for them and were eager to hear what had happened in Kentucky.

"Keith, how are you doing?" Marc asked.

"I am great and so happy to be alive. Derek told me what a close call I had. He told me that the doctors were not sure I was going to make it, and that's why you called Derek here."

Derek was getting antsy. He and Keith were both waiting for Jamie's news. "Well, come on! Don't keep us in suspense! What happened with the sale of the farm? I know it was really hard for you, Jamie, but it is the right thing to do."

"Okay. Let's all go into the parlor and get comfortable, and we'll let you in on what's happening."

Derek went to the fridge, got four beers, and sat down next to Keith.

"I am not selling anything!" Jamie announced.

"Oh, no!" Derek said. "Don't tell me that we are doing that dance again! I thought you two were together this time." His face showed anger and disappointment.

"Calm down and let me tell you. Marc and I are still together …"

"And we're going to stay that way!" Marc chimed in.

"Please, all of you, let me finish. I want to ask the two of you if you would consider moving to the farm. Now, before you answer, listen to what Marc and I propose."

Marc moved closer to Jamie and put his arm around his shoulder, showing his support. Jamie went into all the details about both houses. Keith and Derek sat quietly, listening. As Jamie was talking, they both turned to look at each other and tried to think what the other was thinking. Finally, Jamie was done.

Keith's mind was going in all directions. *I don't want to leave Cheyenne. Why does it have to be this way? Derek was already agreeing to go back to Cheyenne with me. Will Derek be angry if I don't agree to this?*

Derek could see the pain in Keith's eyes. He knew that Keith did not want to live in Berea. *I will let him make the decision, and I'll do whatever he wants.*

Keith spoke up first. "You are okay with this, Marc?"

Marc shook his head "yes" and said that, in his opinion, it was a good deal.

Derek spoke up. "Did you guys even take into consideration that Keith would be leaving his home if we did this? Why would you think that it would be easier for him to leave any more than it was for you to leave the farm, Jamie? Do you think his home is not as important as yours?" It was obvious that Derek was angry.

Keith grabbed Derek's arm and looked at Marc and Jamie. "Well, we have all the information. Derek and I will discuss this privately and give you our answer tomorrow."

Both men got up and left the room.

"Wow, Marc. I guess I didn't consider that they would not jump at this offer."

"I think they are in shock and are having trouble taking it all in. Let's wait and see what they say tomorrow. If they say no, then we will look at it again and figure out who could take it over, so you won't have to sell."

"I love you so much, Marc."

"How about taking me to bed and showing me how much you love me?"

Jamie grabbed Marc's hand and pulled him up to their room.

Hard Decision

Keith and Derek went upstairs and shut the door. They needed to have a serious discussion regarding how this would change their original plans.

"What do you think of this, Derek? Do you want to go back to Berea and live on the farm?"

"No, not necessarily. I want you to do what you want to do because I have already planned to live here with you. I can imagine how hard this is for you since this is your home. It's not so important for me to leave Kentucky because I'm not from there anyway."

"I didn't know that, Derek. Where are you from? I can't believe I've never asked you this before. I just figured that you were from Berea, I guess."

"I'm from Indiana. I grew up on a farm there, so that's why I know so much about farming, and Jamie taught me about the horses."

Keith walked over to Derek and put his arms around him. "There is so much that we don't know about each other, but we have a lifetime to explore it. I really want to know what you think."

"Well, it would be a lot cheaper if we did this because, like Jamie said, we would live there free, and they would pay us a salary on top of that. We certainly aren't going to get a better deal. We would have to move from here anyway because I agree that I can't see four gay men living in the same house. So we would have to pay rent and utilities and have money for gas to go to and from the ranch. The salary would be the same either way, but we could certainly have more money in Kentucky since we wouldn't have all the other expenses. That's my two cents! But again, I'll do whatever you want."

"Let me think about it for a while, okay?"

"Sure. Take all the time you need."

Keith had so many thoughts going through his head, and he was having a hard time thinking about living somewhere else.

Derek told him that he was going downstairs to get a beer. "Do you want me to bring you one?"

"Sure, Derek. I'll take one too."

"Are you okay, Keith? You look really tired, and you know it hasn't been that long since you came home from the hospital. I don't want you stressing out over this decision and making yourself sick."

"I won't, Derek. Please don't worry. I'm fine."

⌇ Derek went downstairs to get the beers. He thought he would leave Keith alone for a little while.

Keith paced the floor, trying to decide what to do. He looked in the mirror when he went to wash his face. *What is my problem?* All of a sudden, it came to him what they should do. It would be so much better financially if they went to Kentucky. *I need to tell Derek what I've decided.* He came down to the kitchen to find Derek.

Derek heard Keith come in and turned to look at him. He handed him a beer and told him to sit for a moment and just relax.

Keith sat back and drank from his beer bottle. After a moment, he said, "Derek, I've come to a decision."

"Well, are you going to keep me in suspense or …?"

"I think we should try it for financial reasons, but I want to leave the door open to come back here if I'm not happy in Berea."

"Do you think you won't be happy with me?" Derek asked. He was a little hurt, but he was trying not to show it.

Keith noticed anyway. "Derek, I'm sorry you thought that I meant I wouldn't be happy with you. I *will* be happy with you. I'm just not sure I will be happy in *Kentucky*. I think we should try it though. I want to tell Jamie that, if we are going there, they need to leave his horses with us because I'm not a farmer. I can take care of the horses, and you can take care of the fields, since that's what you know. Would that work for you?"

Derek walked over to Keith and said, "That works for me! Do you want to tell Jamie and Marc tonight or in the morning?"

"No. They can wait. I need to rest. Let's go up to our room and start making plans for our future."

The Big Move

Marc and Jamie were waiting patiently at breakfast to hear what Keith and Derek were going to do.

"Do you think they'll except my offer to live in Kentucky on the farm, Marc?"

"I think they will, but we'll just have to wait and see what they decide."

Keith came down first and told Chase what he and Derek wanted for breakfast. Then he turned to Marc and Jamie and said, "Derek will be down in a few minutes."

"What have you guys decided?" Marc asked. He knew that Jamie was dying, inch by inch, with the wait.

"When Derek comes down, then we'll talk to you about it."

Marc and Jamie felt that Keith was a bit agitated, which made them very uneasy.

This is not going to go well, I fear, Jamie thought.

Marc noticed Jamie's uneasiness and came over to put his arm around him for support.

Jamie leaned in and whispered to Marc, "I am not getting good vibes from Keith, and Derek is taking his good ole time getting down here!"

Marc tried to be positive for Jamie. "Don't worry before we know that we have something to worry about." He was getting a little upset with Keith for all the drama and suspense.

Derek sauntered into the dining area and sat down next to Keith.

"Well?" Jamie asked, directing his question to Keith. "What have you decided?"

Keith took Derek's hand and said, "We have talked about this proposition and decided to move to Kentucky with some conditions."

Jamie visibly relaxed and let out his breath, which he was unconsciously holding. "Well, good! You won't be sorry. This is going to be the best for you financially."

"Not so fast!" Derek said to Jamie. "Keith told you that we have a couple conditions."

Marc spoke up. "Okay. Let's hear the conditions."

Chase brought in Keith's and Derek's food and served coffee to everyone. They all started talking while they ate.

"The first one," Keith explained, "is that I want an out if I don't like living there. I would like to be free to say if it isn't working for me."

"Do you mean that you don't think you would like to live with Derek in Kentucky?" Marc asked.

"No, I did not say that. It has nothing to do with living with Derek. We love each other and are going to be together, but I've never lived anywhere but Cheyenne, and I just need to know that, if I am not happy in Kentucky, we — and I mean *we* — can come back here to Cheyenne."

Derek remained quiet and watched Keith negotiate their lives. He was so proud of him. *God, I love this man, and I am so glad that Marc brought him to Kentucky over two years ago!*

Marc and Jamie looked at each other and both came to the same answer: "Okay!"

Jamie added, "We can agree to that. What's the second condition?"

Keith took another bite of his food. "Okay. Here is the deal. I am not a farmer. I have worked with horses practically my whole life, so we want you to leave your horses at the farm, Jamie, so that I can do what I know, and Derek will handle planting the crops. In other words, he will handle the farm side because he was raised on a farm, and that's what he knows."

Marc and Jamie looked at each other again and paused for a moment. "We'll have to talk about this for a few minutes because we have made arrangements to move most of my horses here. Excuse us, please!"

Marc and Jamie left the dining room and went to the library. Keith and Derek smiled at each other.

"What do you think they'll say, Derek?"

"I think Jamie will agree to leave the horses there. He'd be crazy to move them if it meant us not taking the offer."

◈ In the library, Jamie asked Marc what he thought about this second condition.

"I think we should leave your horses at the farm. Keith will run that part of your business. It sounds like Derek wants it that way too. He agreed with the conditions, and maybe he's more comfortable with doing the farming side and letting Keith run the horse breeding. We can also visit as often as you feel it's necessary."

Jamie walked over to Marc and put his arms around his neck. "Have I told you today how happy I am to be moving here with you and how much I love you?" He gave Marc a small peck on the mouth. "It's also really cool that you're willing to go along with me about keeping my farm."

"I know how much of a sacrifice you're making for me, and I know you love your home as much as I do mine. Besides, you wouldn't be the Jamie I fell in love with if this was easy for you."

"Okay. Let's go tell them that we agree to their terms."

Marc followed Jamie into the dining room.

"Guys, we agree to both conditions!" Jamie announced. "We need to make this move happen soon because the Hawthorns are still living there. How soon can you be packed and ready to go?"

"We can be ready to go tomorrow," Derek said.

"Good! Marc and I will fly to Kentucky tonight, and you can start driving back in the morning."

Marc went to make flight reservations, and Keith and Derek went to pack. They would drive Keith's truck back to the farm. They decided to take just what they needed for now and have Jamie and Marc ship the rest to them. Marc arranged for one of the ranch hands to take care of the horses for a few days while they were gone. He told Jamie that he would advertise Keith's position when they got back from Kentucky.

◈ The day went by fast. Marc and Jamie flew to Kentucky at 6 p.m. When they got to the farmhouse, Jamie asked the Hawthorns if he and Marc could talk with them. They all sat down together.

"I'm wondering if you two would be willing to come to my house and live permanently?" Jamie asked them. "Keith and Derek are coming tomorrow, and they will be living in the farmhouse."

"What do you mean?" Mr. Hawthorn asked.

"I want a couple to move into my house and maintain it, so when Marc and I come to visit the farm we will have a house to stay in. I will hire a small staff to help you, and I will pay you a handsome salary. My thinking is that you would be here to help Derek with planting and maintaining the fields."

"It sounds good to us because we love staying on the farm. You know I've missed it so much since I sold my farm and moved into the tiny apartment that we have."

Mrs. Hawthorn put her arms around her husband's shoulders. "He really *has* missed it."

"Well, does that mean that you want to do this?"

"Yes! Yes! We'll do it," she said.

Mr. Hawthorn grabbed his wife and gave her a big hug. "When should we move in? It's still a little while before we need to start planting the fields."

"Move in as soon as you have all your arrangements made."

"We have not really seen much of your house, Jamie. Can we take a tour later?"

"Sure. We would love you to do that!"

Marc and Jamie went up to the main house. Hildegard, Betsy, and Maurice were almost done packing and getting ready to go to Cheyenne.

"Maurice, make sure that you get Chase to introduce you to your new staff there and get everyone settled in. There's a separate wing at the ranch to accommodate the three of you. Have you got your airline tickets squared away yet?"

"Yes, sir. All of that is done. We leave for Cheyenne in the morning. Thank you, sir!"

Jamie and Marc were quite pleased with the way this move was going. Keith and Derek would be here tomorrow, and Maurice, Hildegard, and Betsy would be off to Cheyenne as well. The only thing left to do was to show Mr. and Mrs. Hawthorn around the house. Jamie talked with the

Hawthorns and decided to let them hire the cook and the maid. After all, they should hire whomever they felt comfortable with.

ઝ Keith and Derek arrived in Berea late in the day. They had left Cheyenne in the middle of the night and drove straight through because they wanted to get to Kentucky and get settled. Marc and Jamie met them at the farm.

"Hi, guys! How was the trip?" Jamie asked.

"It was tiring but good. Have Maurice, Hildegard, and Betsy left yet? We'd like to say goodbye to them, and then we'll unload the truck and get settled in."

Keith and Derek went to the main house and said their goodbyes, and then came back to start unloading the truck.

"Maurice, John will drive you three to the airport, and Chase will meet you in Cheyenne. He'll drive you to the house and help get you settled. Jamie and I will be back in a day or so. We have to get everything done here before we can head back."

ઝ The Hawthorns told their landlord that they would be leaving. The apartment was furnished, so all they had to pack were their clothes.

"We'll move a little at a time until it's done," he told his wife.

Jamie and Marc helped them move, and then went out to the barn to meet with Keith about Jamie's horses. Derek already knew them, but they wanted to give Keith a little knowledge about how Jamie's horses are cared for differently than Marc's.

"I'll help him until it's time to plant the field. Then Mr. Hawthorn and I will be busy out there," Derek said.

Mr. and Mrs. Hawthorn told Jamie that they were sure they knew what needed to be done. Jamie gave them their first month's wages, so they would have money to stock the kitchen the way they wanted. He did the same for Keith and Derek. At this point, Marc and Jamie felt ready to leave all of them to their own devices, and they could go home to Cheyenne in a couple of days. They made the arrangements, and then went up to Jamie's room.

"Finally, we're alone," Marc said as he pulled Jamie into his arms. "Are you still okay with this move, Jamie?"

Jamie kissed Marc and rested his head on his shoulder. "I have never been surer of anything in my life."

"Home. It truly is going to be home with you there. I love you so much, Jamie."

"Do you know how good that word 'home' sounds flowing off your lips? You are my home, Marc, and I love you with all my being."

They spent most of the night talking and making love.

Settling In

Jamie and Marc helped everyone get settled and decided to go back to Cheyenne later in the day. Marc changed their reservations and took Jamie on a walk down to Walker's Pond. They wanted to reminisce about their first time making love by the pond before they went away. Jamie got quiet while they were sitting by the water.

"What are you thinking about, Jamie? You have a sad look on your face. Are you having second thoughts about leaving here?"

"No. It's just hard to leave this special place. I have been coming to this pond to think ever since I was young. It'll be strange not having it close by when I need it, but I don't want you to worry. I am not sorry that I made this decision. I still wish you would have told me about Mary a long time ago."

"I know, but I told you my reasons."

"Speaking of Mary, I would like to spend some time with her when we get home. I haven't had much time with her yet. I want to remedy that today. Is that okay with you, Marc?"

"Sure, we can do that as soon as we get back."

ॐ The flight to Cheyenne went fine, and Chase was waiting for them. On the drive to the ranch, Chase told Marc that Maurice, Betsy, and Hildegard were all settled in, and he was extremely glad not to have the responsibility of the house. He was much happier driving for Marc.

When they got to the house, Maurice was waiting at the door. "Hello, sir," he said to Marc.

"Maurice, please call me Marc. I can't stand to hear 'sir.' We're going to be one, big, happy family here. Okay?"

"Yes, sir — I mean, Marc."

All three laughed.

"Where are Hildegard and Betsy?" Jamie asked.

"Oh, they're up in their quarters, trying to get settled in. You know how women are, Jamie."

"Yes, I do!"

"I will take your bags to your rooms."

"Maurice, take our bags up to Marc's room. I'll be sleeping in there from now on," Jamie said with a wink to Marc.

Marc put his arm around Jamie. "Yes — he will be by my side forever. I am never letting him get too far from me again. I have waited a long time for this day to finally be here. Maurice, we're going to see my sister in a little while. Can you arrange for Betsy to get some sandwiches ready first?"

"Sure, Marc."

Marc smiled at hearing his name coming from Maurice. "Jamie, let's go down to the stables while the sandwiches are being made and check on the horses."

"Okay!"

They went down and met with the ranch hand, who had been taking care of things.

"I need to get a groom hired soon," Marc said to Jamie.

"I can do the duties until we get someone. You know I love working with the horses."

"Yes, I know. But you'll have your hands full making love to me and writing your novel."

"Oh, yeah? And who said I will be making love to *you*, Mr. Morgan? Maybe I have other plans." Jamie felt playful because he was so happy.

"Oh, is that *so*, Mr. Walker?" Marc teased. He grabbed Jamie around the waist, pushed him toward the house, and pulled him up the stairs to their bedroom. When he got Jamie inside and shut the door, he pulled his shirt over his head and, within seconds, had Jamie completely undressed. He backed away to take in the full view. "I love looking at you, Jamie. I have been mesmerized by the sight of you from the first day we met, and I still cannot get enough of you."

"Same here," Jamie said as he unbuttoned Marc's shirt. When he got it off, he grabbed the front of Marc's jeans and pulled him in close. He kissed Marc on his ear and whispered, "Make love to me."

Marc let out a groan and pulled Jamie to the bed. Jamie lay down and watched as Marc finished getting undressed. Marc climbed in, and Jamie immediately pulled him on top, kissing Marc passionately and exploring his mouth with his tongue.

Marc was ready to take Jamie but wanted to go slower. He kissed him down his beautiful body and took each nipple in his mouth, sucking very softly. Jamie moaned and thrust his hips toward Marc. He was so hard and ready. Marc loved it when Jamie moved his hips like he couldn't get close enough. Marc rubbed his cock against Jamie's, causing both of them to almost lose it. Marc put his hands around both of their cocks and started stroking them up and down, up and down. Both were going wild.

"Marc, if you don't stop ..."

Marc didn't want Jamie to come until he had him where he could taste him. He took him in and put his tongue on the slit, tasting Jamie's precum. *God, he tastes wonderful,* Marc thought as he went down on him completely to the bottom of the shaft. He grabbed Jamie's balls and fondled them as he moved up and down, sucking on Jamie's beautiful cock.

Jamie was squirming and bucking and going crazy. As he came in Marc's mouth, he yelled, "Marc! Marc! Oh, god!"

Marc took every drop. He loved tasting his love. He knew he would never get tired of his taste. Jamie was coming down, and Marc needed to be inside of him. He grabbed the lube and spread Jamie's legs. He put some on his fingers and moved in and out of Jamie. Jamie moaned again with each finger that Marc inserted. Marc pushed his fingers in and out, working Jamie and getting him ready. Jamie put his legs on Marc's shoulders and spread them wide. Marc entered slowly at first, but then pushed in all the way when Jamie moaned for more.

"Harder, Marc — take me harder."

That was all Marc needed to hear from his love. He pounded him hard and fast. Every time he plunged in deep, he hit Jamie's prostate, which would set Jamie off.

"Fuck me, Marc … fuck me harder and harder."

Marc fucked him hard, hitting his prostate.

Jamie was like a crazed animal. "Oh, god! Fuck me … fuck me … all the way … harder, deeper!"

The last time Jamie yelled, "FUCK ME HARD! NOW!" Marc grabbed Jamie's ass, plunged two more times, and came with tremendous force. He groaned and released all he had inside Jamie.

"I felt you shooting deep inside of me. Oh … that was *hot*! I love that feeling, Marc. I love it when you really fuck me hard like that."

"Me too, Jamie. I love fucking you hard and having you beg me for more," Marc said breathlessly. Marc loved it when Jamie talked dirty while he plunged deep inside him. Jamie always loved getting fucked in the ass ever since the first time they tried it, and Marc had no problem giving him what he wanted. They lay in each other's arms until both were quiet again.

"I think we should go down and eat the sandwiches Betsy prepared, and then go visit Mary," Marc suggested.

Jamie started to get up to go and take a shower and said, "We'll spend as much time with Mary as you want."

"Whoa! Where do you think *you're* going? Did I say you could leave me just now?"

"What? What do you want me to do?" Jamie asked as he reached for Marc's luscious-looking cock and stroked it up and down. "Is *this* what you want?"

"You know it is!"

Jamie already had Marc hard again. He bent down and licked his shaft up to the tip and back down again, all the while caressing the area between Marc's rectum and his scrotum. As he listened to Marc's groans getting louder, he asked, "You love this. Don't you?"

"God, Jamie, you are driving me crazy," he said, barely above a whisper.

Jamie loved it when he could elicit these sounds from Marc. He knew that their lovemaking was incredible and always would be. It was as if they were made for each other, and no one else would ever be able to satisfy them. Jamie moved back up and put his tongue in the slit at the head.

Marc let out another moan. "Jamie! Jamie!"

Jamie released Marc's cock from his mouth and kissed him on each side of his groin, following the line of hair from the groin to his navel. He kissed him all over his abdomen and chest and then back down to his scrotum. Jamie wanted him so hot that he would beg for release. He kissed him all around his cock and balls without actually taking him into his mouth.

"Jamie, you are driving me crazy ... please take me in your beautiful mouth."

When Jamie took Marc's hard, engorged cock and balls into his mouth and gently sucked, Marc could take no more and begged Jamie to finish him off.

"Not yet!" Jamie moved to Marc's rectum and rimmed him with his tongue.

When Jamie stuck the tip of his tongue inside of Marc, he gasped and cried out, "Oh, my god, Jamie. Finish me off ... please!"

Jamie obliged by swallowing Marc's cock whole and letting Marc fuck his mouth until he gave Jamie what he worked so hard to get. Jamie swallowed it all, and then licked him clean.

Marc pulled Jamie in close and kissed his lips, tasting himself on them. "Jamie, you are so good at giving head. I don't think I will ever grow tired of you taking me into your wonderful mouth."

"You don't have to worry ... I love the taste of you and love it when you start fucking my mouth."

Marc pulled Jamie in close and was content just to hold him. They lay quietly again for a little while.

"Marc, may I ask you something?"

"Sure. You know you can ask me anything."

"May I come inside of you just once? I want to feel what it's like."

"Well, since I have only been with you, I guess I'm willing. I would like to see what it feels like to have you come in me. That way, I'll know what you feel. Okay, Jamie. Anything to please you."

"You know, we'd better get up and go eat or Betsy will never forgive us. We'll pick up this conversation later."

They got cleaned up and went down to eat.

"Betsy, tonight we will have steaks for dinner."

"Yes, sir, Marc. I love my new kitchen. I will make you a fine meal."

"I'm glad you like it, Betsy, and I'm glad that you all have agreed to come here with Jamie. It helps to make him feel at home. Jamie, do you want to go see Mary now?"

A Sister's Love

Marc and Jamie went to see Mary after they ate. Marc told the nurse that she could take a break and that they would probably be with Mary for a couple of hours. They went into Mary's room and sat down on each side of her bed. Jamie could not get over how beautiful she was, lying there like she was just sleeping. Jamie took her hand and held it with both of his.

"Hi, Mary, I'm Jamie. I hope you remember me. I've come back to see you. I've moved here permanently, so you will be seeing me every day from now on. I would love it if you would wake up and let me see your beautiful eyes. I'm sure they're like Marc's and, you know, I love to look at his all the time. I want you to know that I love your brother so much, and I'm going to spend the rest of my life making him happy."

"Hey, sis, I am sitting here holding your other hand, listening to my love talking to you. Can you believe it? I finally got him to live here with you and me. It was a great struggle, but now that's over," Marc said as he winked at Jamie. "You know how sad I've been these last couple of years, trying to get him here? But that doesn't matter anymore. I finally succeeded. He's here now, so our conversations from now on will be happy ones."

ᦉ Mary was listening to Jamie and Marc, trapped in silent thoughts:

Over the years, Marc, you've been telling me how you wished that you could find someone to love. But, since you were gay, you never thought you would find that person. Now you have!

Right after I fell, I remember when you sat beside my bed and told me that you were gay. I was not surprised because I always noticed how girls flocked to you — my own friends too — but I never saw you respond to any of them. I wondered then but decided to wait until you felt like coming out to me.

Then, when Marc met you, Jamie, for the first time he could not stop talking about love. Sometimes I hated you because you kept hurting him. I figured that you two would never be together, and I wished that Marc would forget you and find someone else who would want to genuinely love him. Every time Marc would come to me and talk about you, he would cry and lay his head on my chest. Jamie, I never thought you would come here, and I really didn't want you to, especially since you didn't seem to love Marc the way I felt he should be loved. But now, hearing the love expressed by you both, you have my love too.

Marc, I wish you could hear my thoughts. You have been such a faithful brother, coming here every day to talk with me and share your innermost thoughts. I've held on because I felt you needed me here to listen to you, but now you don't need me anymore. You have Jamie, and I know you'll be happy with him for the rest of your life. Dad has been calling and waiting for me, so I think it is time for me to go. You will have my love with you forever. I want you to love Jamie — and Jamie, please stay with Marc — for the rest of your lives. Someday we will meet face to face when I come back for you and Marc.

Mary squeezed both of their hands and took her last breath. Marc looked at Jamie, and Jamie looked up at Marc. Both noticed that she was no longer breathing.

Marc screamed her name and kept shouting, "No! No! Mary! Please don't leave me!"

Jamie was also crying. His heart was breaking for Marc, seeing the pain he was in. Jamie thought sadly, *How can this be happening now? After all these years?*

Marc looked up at Jamie and spoke through his tears. "Jamie, she squeezed my hand. What do you think that meant?"

"She squeezed mine too. I think it was her way of telling us that she heard what we said to her. She held on for you because she felt that you needed her here. But now that you're happy with me, she knows that I love you and will take care of you. She felt free to move on to her new life with God." Jamie reached over and kissed Mary on the cheek, and then walked around to Marc. He leaned over and put his arms around Marc's shoulders, kissing him on the cheek. "Do you want to be alone with Mary for a little while, Marc?"

Marc could barely speak as the tears ran down his face. "Thank you, Jamie. Do … you … mind?"

"Of course not. I'll let the nurse and caregiver know what's happened. Take all the time you need. I love you, Marc."

Marc once again laid his head on Mary's chest and let it all out. "Mary, why did you leave me now? Jamie says it was because you knew I'm happy. I want to believe that. I *have* to believe that."

An hour went by and Marc still had not come out of Mary's room. Jamie decided to leave him alone and went to call Derek at the farm to let him and Keith know.

Keith got on the phone. "How is Marc doing, Jamie?"

"He's very sad and is still with her."

"Did she ever wake up?"

"No, not exactly. The strangest thing is that she must've been in some kind of conscious state because she squeezed both of our hands before she took her last breath."

"Wow, that is really profound! I know Marc is going to be lost without her. Thank God he has you with him now. He went in every day to talk with her. He always believed that one day she would wake up. Thanks for calling, Jamie. Derek and I will come back to Cheyenne for the service. Have you made any arrangements yet?"

"No. I'll help Marc with whatever he wants to do."

"We'll see you two sometime tomorrow."

Marc finally left Mary's side and found Jamie at the stables. Jamie had been on the phone with Gary, letting him know that Mary was gone. Gary told him that he would be right over and would help make the necessary arrangements.

"Alright, Gary. See you in a few."

Marc walked up to Jamie, and they embraced.

"Jamie, I talked with Mary's nurse. She said that you had talked to her and Mary's caregiver about how peaceful Mary passed and how much we appreciated all that they had done for her. They really appreciated hearing that. She told me that she had called Dr. Alwood, who's been taking care of Mary and me since childhood. He's also been taking care of Mary for the last 18 years since her accident. He's coming to the ranch to prepare the death certificate. Mary's nurse will stay until then. I told both of them that I would cut a final check for their services and then some. They both will be moving out tomorrow."

"Do you have a funeral home that you want me to call? Gary is coming, and we'll take care of any necessary arrangements."

"That would be great, Jamie. I'm going to have her cremated and her ashes spread on the ranch. She always loved the ranch and riding horses, so it seems only fitting to scatter her ashes along her favorite trail."

Jamie took Marc into his arms and held him tightly. Marc started crying again and clung to Jamie.

"Let it all out, Marc. I'm here for you — whatever you need."

Marc pulled himself together and gave Jamie a very loving kiss, and then they walked back to the house.

∽ Gary had arrived and greeted Marc, giving him a long hug. They sobbed for their loss, quietly consoling each other.

When Dr. Alwood arrived a few minutes later, he went to Mary's room. He actually felt relief for Mary. She was now free of her broken body. He wrote the death certificate and came down to talk with Marc. "I'll call the funeral home to come get her, if that's okay with you."

"I suppose it's time. Jamie was going to call, but that would help, Dr. Alwood."

Dr. Alwood walked up to Marc and told him that Mary was finally home with her mother and father. "I am sure she is happy."

"Yes, I know. I am going to have her cremated and will spread her ashes on the ranch."

"Oh, that would be exactly what she would've wanted! She always loved it here. Let me know when you are going to have the memorial service and the spreading of her ashes."

"We will."

The funeral director came and talked with Marc and Jamie. He got his instructions from Marc and then went up to get Mary.

Marc did not sleep much that night. Jamie held him and let him talk or cry or sleep. He knew that Derek and Keith would arrive the next day and talking with Keith would probably help him too. Jamie knew that it would take Marc a while to completely come to terms with Mary not being with him anymore. Jamie sent a prayer to God and asked him to take care of Mary and Marc.

"Jamie, are you awake?" Marc asked.

"Yes. What is it?"

"I thought I heard you talking."

"I was just saying a prayer for Mary."

"Do you think she's happy now, Jamie?"

"Yes, I do. I think she's riding her horse again and has her eyes open with a smile on her lovely face. As she gallops with her horse, her raven hair is blowing in the wind. She's happy and free of her bed."

"Oh, Jamie, that last statement is so great! I'm glad you said that because I felt very selfish keeping her here, tied to her bed. Now she's free. I love you even more — if that's possible — for helping me see this." He cuddled up to Jamie and fell fast asleep.

⊰ Keith and Derek arrived at 1 p.m. the next day and both held Marc, telling him how sorry they were.

"It's okay now. Jamie made me see how great this is for Mary. She's no longer a prisoner in her bed. She's riding with the angels."

Three days later, the funeral director brought Mary's ashes to the house, and Jamie called Dr. Alwood and told him that they were going to ride out to Mary's favorite place on the ranch at sunset. "We will say a few words, and then give Mary her freedom by spreading her ashes."

Everyone gathered at the stables to ride out to Mary's special place. Gary, Keith, Derek, Marc, Jamie, and Dr. Alwood rode horses. Chase brought Mary's nurse and caregiver, and Hildegard, Betsy, and Maurice followed behind those on horseback. When they arrived, prayers were said, and Marc talked about his sweet sister. At that point, he and Jamie galloped the horses, holding hands and spreading her ashes as they rode. The sun was going down. As they looked up, streaks of light shone from the heavens down to the trail — at least that was how it looked to everyone.

"Goodbye, Mary. I love you," Marc said as he blew a kiss to the heavens.

Happiness is Love

Five years passed. Jamie and Marc sat on the porch, watching their little four-year-old play with her toy horses.

"Mary, Uncle Keith and Uncle Derek are coming for a visit today. Do you want to show them what a good rider you are?"

Mary beamed from ear to ear. "Oh, may I, Daddy Marc? You know I am *really* good!"

"No modesty here!" Jamie said, laughing with Marc. "Don't you think that's for Uncle Keith to say?"

"He *will* say that I am the best rider. You know he will."

Marc couldn't get over how much Little Mary reminded him of his sister. When he and Jamie found her in the orphanage, she was only one year old, and she had raven hair — just like their Mary. They had to make the adoption happen. It was as if Mary guided them to her. These past three years had been incredibly fulfilling, and their daughter was perfect and loving. She always called them Daddy Marc and Daddy J, which suited them fine. Keith and Derek also fell in love with her as soon as they saw her.

Over the years, Jamie and Marc had traveled back to Kentucky several times a year, and Keith and Derek had visited them in Cheyenne even more. Mr. and Mrs. Hawthorn loved to spoil Mary each time Marc and Jamie took her back to the farm. They considered themselves her grandparents, and she called them Nana and Papa.

"Okay, sweetie," Jamie said. "I'll go down and saddle Patches, so when Uncle Keith and Uncle Derek get here, we can go to the stables and watch you ride."

Jamie taught her to ride when she turned two, so Marc bought her the paint horse and she named him Patches.

"Can I help you, Daddy J?"

"Sure, sweetheart! Hey, Marc, we'll be back in a little while, okay?"

"I'll have Betsy get things ready for a cookout, so we can eat when everyone gets here. Chase has already left for the airport to pick up Keith and Derek." Then Marc took Mary's little face in his hands and added, "Uncle Gary is also coming to watch you ride, Mary."

Mary giggled with excitement and jumped up to hug Marc around the neck. "Oh, I love Uncle Gary so much! He always tells me how *beautiful* I am!"

ᴔ Jamie let Mary help him by getting down the blanket that went under the saddle. When she reached for the saddle, Jamie stopped her.

"Daddy J, I can do it! I am a big girl."

"Mary, you are too little to pick up the saddle. It is way too heavy, even though you are a big girl. I will show you how to do it. Then, when you get a little bigger, you'll know what to do. Okay?"

Mary stuck out her lower lip and said in a sad voice, "Okay, Daddy J."

When Gary, Keith, and Derek arrived, Mary wouldn't let them rest until they all went to the stables to see her ride. She was so cute on Patches, with her little cowgirl outfit and hat. The two proud daddies snapped pictures left and right.

Marc put his arm around Jamie and hugged him tightly. "Jamie, I can't believe how complete our lives are today."

Jamie kissed him. "I thought I couldn't be happier when I came here with you, but now that we have Mary, I feel like my heart is bursting with joy."

"You know, every time I look at our Mary, I think about Sis when we were that age. She would be so proud of our little one. Karen has done a really good job teaching her."

"Yes, she has. Hiring Karen was a good call on your part, Marc. She's been a great influence on Mary."

As soon as they brought Mary home, they had hired Karen to be her nanny. They needed Karen to help teach Mary how a little girl should act, which neither knew anything about.

When Mary was done showing everyone how great she was —
according to her — they all applauded as Jamie helped her off Patches.
She was so proud of herself! While she was basking in all the attention,
Betsy called them. The barbecue ribs were ready.

"Maurice, gather your staff. We'll all eat together as one, big, happy
family."

"But Marc, I don't think that would be proper."

"I think we've been together long enough that we can sit down at the
table and break bread together. Right, Jamie?"

"Absolutely, Marc. We are all family and always will be. Now, Maurice,
go get Hildegard and the rest."

They all drank, ate, and talked until darkness fell. Karen announced
that it was Mary's bedtime, so she said goodnight to everyone. Karen
loved her little charge. She was such a joy to teach. Mary jumped into
Uncle Keith's arms, and Derek moved in to join the hug.

"Don't you think that I am the best rider you have ever *seen*?"

"Yes, Mary," they both chimed in. "You certainly are!"

"I told Daddy Marc that you would say that."

"May I get a hug too, beautiful girl?"

"Of course, Uncle Gary! I have lots of hugs for you!"

Jamie patted her on the behind. "Okay, little one. Go with Karen and
dream of riding Patches until tomorrow."

Jamie and Marc kissed her, promising to come up and tuck her in.
Karen took her by the hand and led her into the house.

After giving Karen time to get Mary ready for bed, Marc and Jamie
went up for their nighttime ritual of reading her a story and saying her
prayers before tucking her in snuggly. They loved this part of the day,
saying sweet dreams to their sweet Little Mary.

❧ Keith and Derek had spent the week with Marc and Jamie but needed
to get back to Kentucky. They said their goodbyes, and Chase drove them
to the airport.

"That was a nice visit. They have the perfect family now with Little Mary. She is such a joy to be around," Keith said with a smile, "but I am ready to get back home. Aren't you, Derek?"

"You never cease to amaze me, Keith, calling our farm in Kentucky 'home.' I was always worried in the beginning whether you could be happy there. I had convinced myself that we would be moving back to Cheyenne after a couple of months. Now, here it is, five years later and we're still there!"

"I love our home because we are there together," Keith said as he took Derek in his arms and kissed him passionately.

"You'd better stop that right now, Keith, or we won't be allowed in the airport!"

Chase shook his head as he watched in the rearview mirror.

"I love you so much, Derek, and I couldn't be happier. The farm is very relaxing and wonderful, and I have never been sorry I made the move with you. I think my favorite place on the farm is Walker's Pond, and I am sure you know why."

"Oh, let me think ... could it be the incredible lovemaking we have there after a hard day's work? I know — it's the *swimming!*"

Keith grabbed him again. "Don't make me hurt you," he said jokingly.

⮑ Marc and Jamie were finally alone ... *really* alone ... after the week of riding with Mary and having fun with Keith and Derek. They always enjoyed their visits, but they also loved their privacy.

Marc pulled Jamie into his arms and took possession of his wonderful lips. He kissed him with so much love and passion that it took Jamie's breath away. He wanted to melt into him.

Marc pulled back and took in every feature on Jamie's face. "Jamie, I want you to make love to me."

Jamie pulled Marc into an embrace and said, "Marc, I want you so much." He grabbed Marc's hand and pulled him to the bed.

Jamie lay on top of Marc's muscular body, and they made love for hours. Finally, as they relaxed in each other's arms, they talked about how they got to this wonderful time in their lives, especially about the first time they met.

"You scared me, Jamie, because I had never had anyone affect me like you did from the first site of you. I couldn't stand to even be next to you! You stirred emotions that were foreign to me."

"Is that why, when you kissed me, you pushed me away?"

"I didn't know what to do, so I sent you away. But then, I couldn't get you off my mind."

"And now look at us, Marc. How happy and fulfilled we are! We were stupid to let so much time go by that we could have been together."

"My sweet love, that is all water under the bridge. We have had a great life for the past five years, so the two years we were foolish doesn't really matter anymore." Marc pulled Jamie close and kissed him again and again. "I will never get tired of kissing you, Jamie."

"I feel the same."

They held each other tightly, almost afraid to let this special moment go. Marc got quiet, and Jamie wondered what was going on in his mind.

"Marc, where are your thoughts right now?" Jamie saw tears rolling down Marc's cheeks. He wiped them away with his thumbs, leaning in and whispering into Marc's hair, "You're thinking about Mary, aren't you?"

Marc nodded. "I miss her so much, Jamie."

"Of course, you do. Twins always have a deeper connection than regular siblings."

"You know that Little Mary has helped a lot with the loss, but I still think of Mary almost every day. Today really got to me when I saw our Mary riding Patches. I could see Sis on her horse at that same age."

Jamie hugged Marc; no words were needed. After a while, he asked, "Don't Keith and Derek seem happy?" He was trying to take Marc's mind off Mary.

"Yes. I am so glad that it all worked out with them living in Kentucky."

"Marc, did you know that they are talking about adopting a little boy? Derek shared that with me on this trip."

"I didn't know that! I hope they do because a child completes your life as we surely know. Did you say a *boy*? Does that mean that they have one in mind? Oh, my! This is good. That means Little Mary will have a

159

playmate when we visit them and when they come here. She would love that! Sometimes she seems lonely. Hmm … maybe we should think about adopting another child ourselves."

Jamie smiled at Marc. "I don't think so just yet. Mary keeps us pretty busy."

"Let's get in the shower and clean up a little," Marc said as he gave Jamie a quick peck on the lips.

Marc opened the shower door and climbed in after Jamie. He moved against Jamie's back and pushed up against Jamie's cute ass.

"Do you want more, Marc? You are unbelievable!"

"Yes, I am. I'm going to spend the rest of my life showing you just *how* unbelievable." He put his hand on Jamie's back and stroked his muscles and the soft indentation along his spine. He thought lovingly at how amazingly beautiful Jamie's skin was. He soaped Jamie down and then himself. Marc turned Jamie around and said, "I have a surprise for you, so let's get rinsed and dried off."

"What? What *is* it?"

"You'll see!"

Jamie's curiosity was peaked, wondering what kind of surprise Marc had in store. He couldn't imagine what it could be. When they finally came out of the bathroom in their robes, Marc took Jamie's hand and sat him down on the bed. He told Jamie to stay there as he went over to the bureau and opened the drawer. He walked back to the bed and got down on one knee in front of Jamie.

"Marc, what are you doing?"

Marc reached up and took Jamie's face in his hands, pulling him forward to kiss him tenderly. "Jamie Walker, I love you and want to share the rest of my life with you. Will you marry me?"

"*What*? We can't get married in Wyoming!"

"You haven't answered me yet. Jamie, will you marry me?"

"Of course I will marry you! But how? Where?"

"That doesn't matter right now … we'll find a place that will marry us. I want you to be mine forever, and I want to be yours. You came into my life and turned it upside down and upright again. I don't ever want to be without you. I've waited for you all my life, and you are everything to me."

He slipped a gold band on Jamie's finger. "This is a symbol of our love. I have one for you to put on me." He handed Jamie the other ring, which was identical to his.

Jamie smiled and put the ring on Marc's finger.

About that time, Little Mary bounded into their room and jumped up on the bed beside Jamie.

"What are you doing up, Mary?" Jamie asked as he hugged her.

"I wasn't sleepy, and I am still so excited about today."

"It's fine to be excited, honey, but you need to go to sleep." Marc picked her up and kissed her cheek.

Jamie got up and hugged both of them. "I am so happy, and I love both of you so much!"

Mary smiled her sweet smile and kissed them. "I love my two daddies this much!" She stretched out her arms as far as they would go.

Marc smiled at Jamie. "How did we ever get so lucky?"

Karen came looking for Mary in Marc and Jamie's room. "I am so sorry about this, sir. I went to do a final check and found her missing from her bed."

"It's okay, Karen. She was just too excited to sleep. She's ready now," as Jamie noticed her yawning.

"Goodnight, sweet one," they both said as Karen took Little Mary in her arms and carried her back to bed.

Marc pulled Jamie back into his arms when they were alone again. "You once told me that you led me through the night when we made love for the first time, and I had to lead you through the rest of our lives together. Well, the rest of our life starts now with these rings and the promise of marriage. I promise to love you and take care of you forever." He kissed Jamie thoroughly, with all the love that was possible for one to give another.

When they broke their kiss, Jamie whispered softly, "I will love you forever, my Cheyenne Love."

The Past

Derek and Keith arrived home after their visit with Jamie and Marc. They had lots of fun in Cheyenne but were glad to be back at the farm. They checked on the horses and checked in with Mr. Hawthorn before going to the farmhouse to settle in for the night. It had been a long day with the goodbyes in Cheyenne and the flights from Cheyenne to Lexington.

"Derek, I am really tired and want to go to bed. Are you coming up soon?"

"I'll be up in a little while. I am still running on Wyoming time and not quite ready for bed."

Keith kissed Derek tenderly and went upstairs.

Derek sat down to write in his journal, which he kept every day since he first came to Kentucky from Indiana over 20 years ago. He read back to the beginning and noticed a name: Kyle Douglas. *Oh, my god! I haven't thought about him in years and years.*

Kyle was a straight guy who broke Derek's heart when he was 18 years old. They were friends, and Derek had a crush on him. When he told Kyle that he was gay, Kyle walked away from him and never talked to him again.

God, just reading his name brings that hurt back like it was yesterday! I wonder what made me go back to this time again, Derek thought as he fell asleep. He laid his head on the desk and started to dream that Kyle was saying, "Derek, I was so wrong! I want you with me. I just didn't know how to handle it before when you told me that you were gay. I am straight and shouldn't be having these feelings, but I am. Please come with me!" He felt Kyle pull on his arm.

"Derek … Derek! You are dreaming."

Derek looked up from the desk and saw that Keith was pulling on his arm. "What?"

"You were calling out some guy's name."

"Who's name?"

"Kyle. Who is Kyle?"

"He isn't important, Keith. He is someone I used to know when I first came to Kentucky. It's just not important."

"Okay. Well, come to bed. I don't want you sleeping down here."

Derek closed his journal and followed Keith upstairs. The guys got into bed and held each other, both falling back to sleep.

৵ Derek woke up first and got showered and dressed. He let Keith sleep. He wrote a note that he was going to town for supplies and would be back shortly.

While driving to town, Derek thought about the dream with Keith. *Whatever made me dream about him? Why was Kyle acting like he wanted me?*

Derek parked the pickup truck in front of the store and went in with his list. As he rounded the aisle with the meats, he ran right into a very handsome guy with auburn hair and blue eyes. He looked right at him and noticed that he was nice looking, but that was the extent of his thoughts about the stranger. He excused himself and started to walk away.

"Derek? Is that you?"

Derek stopped and turned around. "Yes," he answered as he looked at the auburn-haired stranger. "Do I *know* you?"

"Don't you recognize me? I know I am a little taller and definitely heavier than the last time we saw each other."

Derek still looked a little puzzled.

The stranger came up to him now and held out his hand. "I am Kyle. Kyle Douglas."

"Oh, my god, Kyle! I didn't recognize you," he said as he took his hand. "Sorry. Your hair is darker, and you are taller than I remember."

"Yes. It's been … what, 20 years or so?"

Derek noticed that Kyle still held his hand. He pulled his hand away. "What are you doing here in Berea?"

"I just moved back. I am a doctor and have taken a job at the hospital as chief of staff. What are you doing now?"

"I am running a horse-breeding farm. I live at the Walker homestead."

"Oh, I see … you always did love farming and such as I remember."

"Yes, I do."

"I am buying a farmhouse close to where you live," Kyle said. "It used to be the Shaffer homestead. Do you remember it? We used to sell Mr. Shaffer lumber from the lumber yard where we worked when we first came out of high school."

"Yes, I remember. We worked there that whole summer, and then you went away to college."

"Did you go to college, Derek?"

"No. I stayed at the lumber yard for several years, and then got the job with Jamie Walker on his farm, learning the horse-breeding trade. I have been there ever since. Do you have a wife and kids now, Kyle?"

"No. I am not married."

Derek found this hard to believe because he was handsome and a doctor — the kind of guy every girl dreams about marrying.

"Well, it was great seeing you again, Kyle, but I have to go and get the supplies that I came for."

"Oh, okay. Sorry to hold you up. Can we have dinner some night?"

"I will check with Keith and get back to you." As soon as Derek said this, he saw Kyle's face change. *What is that look about?*

"Who is Keith?"

"He is my partner whom I live with at the farm. Well, see you," Derek said as he turned and walked away to finish his shopping. He did not want to relive Kyle turning his back and walking away from him again.

Kyle stood and watched Derek walk away. *God, he is so handsome! I was such a naïve jerk back then. How could I just walk away from Derek like I did? Thank god, I grew up!*

Derek wondered why Kyle had dropped back into his life. *Last night, I dreamed about him, and today I ran smack into him at the store! What does this mean?*

When Derek got home, Keith was up, dressed, and in the stables with Shadow. Derek went straight to the stables and gave Keith a hello hug from behind.

"How is Shadow doing, Keith?"

"He is doing well," he asked as he turned to embrace Derek. "Not to change the subject, but did you get us stocked up again?" He gave him a strong hug and told Derek that he missed him when he got up and found him gone.

"Yes, Keith. I got everything on my list, so we are set for a while."

"Good."

"How are the rest of the horses?"

"They are great, Derek. Mr. Hawthorn took good care of them while we were gone. I know that was hard for him because he is more comfortable with plowing and planting the fields."

Shadow came up behind Keith and nudged him. They both laughed. Shadow always did that when he wanted oats added to his feeding bag.

"Derek, do you remember the first time Marc and I brought Shadow to Jamie? I remember it like it was yesterday because, when you came out of the stables, my heart stopped. I couldn't believe how great you looked. I wanted you then and couldn't take my eyes off you."

"I knew that was going on with you. But, if you remember, we didn't start off on a good footing that night," Derek reminded him with a smile. "You were *way* too arrogant for me."

"Yeah, I knew that I had come on stronger than I wanted to, but that was how much I wanted you."

Derek gave Keith another quick hug. "I am sure glad that Jamie bought Shadow from Marc because he has been a great stud for us, don't you think? Over the years, we've gotten 10 beautiful horses from his loins, and three mares are pregnant with his foals." Derek was trying to find the right words to tell Keith about running into Kyle and said, "I met someone in town whom I haven't seen in 20 years."

Keith led Shadow into his stall and asked, "Who?"

Derek followed him and timidly answered, "Kyle Douglas!"

Keith noticed a change in Derek's voice. "What did *he* have to say?" Keith was getting some very strange vibes from Derek's reaction to seeing this guy. "It is clear by your body language that this meeting bothered you. Who is he to you? Isn't that the name of the guy you mentioned last night in your dream?"

"Yes," Derek said as he turned and left the stables for the house. Derek did not want to talk about him right now. He had to figure out why Kyle affected him this much after so many years.

Keith let it drop but was determined to find out who Kyle was. They spent the day getting things done around the farm. Jamie called around dinnertime to check how their trip went and how the horses were. Keith saw his chance to get some information from Jamie on this guy Kyle since Derek had gone up to the main house to talk with Mr. Hawthorn.

"Jamie, do you know anything about a guy named Kyle Douglas?"

"Wow! I haven't heard that name in years. Why do you ask about him?"

"Derek was calling out Kyle's name in his sleep. Then, this morning, Derek ran into him at the store."

"Really!"

Keith noticed that Jamie seemed surprised. "Yeah, and when he ran into him, it had a weird effect on him. What is this guy to Derek?"

"Did you ask him?"

"Yes. He said that he was not important, but his body language said something else."

"He was a really close friend to Derek when he first moved to Berea from Indiana. He told me that he came out to him, and Kyle never spoke to him again. It broke Derek's heart because he had fallen for him. The problem was that he was straight and didn't want any more to do with Derek after that. He even called him a faggot."

Keith took this all in but had to process it later. "Thanks for telling me, Jamie. I will have Derek call you when he gets back." Keith hung up the phone and was wondering why this bothered him so much. *What is your problem? Derek is in love with you, not this guy Kyle. Let it drop.*

⤜ Marc came in the room to see how Derek and Keith were doing.

"Keith just told me that Derek's first love has come back to town," Jamie shared.

"Who is that?"

"His name is Kyle Douglas, and he really upset Derek back in high school when he called him a faggot and then never spoke to him again. Derek was in love with him. When he came out to Kyle and told him how he felt, Kyle was cruel."

"Derek doesn't still care for Kyle, does he?"

"I am sure he doesn't. It was a good 20 years ago. But Keith seems to be a little concerned. I hope Derek has enough sense to stay away from this guy. It could open up old wounds and only cause him heartache again," Jamie said with a worried look.

◈ Kyle walked into the hospital to meet the administrator, take a tour of his new post, and meet some of the staff. He was eager to get started as chief of staff. He had studied and worked long and hard to reach this level in his career and, when this opportunity opened up, he jumped at it.

His reason was twofold: He could come back to a town that he always loved, and he might have a chance to get back in touch with Derek. He had been so cruel to him before, and he later regretted his behavior but never had the chance to make amends. Now that he had seen him again, it was really hard. He didn't know how to get back in Derek's good graces. Many things had changed since they were stupid and naïve young men. He wanted to keep busy, so he would not think of Derek. He needed to focus on other things; after all, he was just someone from his past.

The administrator showed Kyle to his office and then around the hospital. The nurses were buzzing about how good looking their new chief of staff was. Someone even told them that he was single. He knew what they were all talking about, but he couldn't be bothered with hospital grapevines. When he got settled, he would plan a meeting with the staff to give them his feelings on hospital gossip. His private life was private, and he intended to keep it that way.

It was a long day but a good one. He liked the hospital and some of his colleagues. This place was going to be a good fit for him. Five o'clock finally came, and he had to get out and meet the real estate agent to finalize the sale of Mr. Shaffer's farmhouse. Kyle always loved that house when he was there in his youth and always hoped to someday live there. Mr. Shaffer had passed away, and his children were eager to sell it. Now he was going to realize his dream.

After the meeting with the real estate agent, Kyle realized that he was just down the road from the Walker farm. "I think I will go by and pay my respects." He wanted to see this Keith person, who was living with Derek. His curiosity was driving him to go there. When he pulled up, Keith was coming out of the stable.

"May I help you?" Keith asked.

Kyle got out of the car and held out his hand. "You must be Keith."

"Yes. Do I know you?"

"No. I ran into Derek this morning at the store, and he told me your name. I am Kyle Douglas."

"Oh, nice to meet you," Keith said as he shook Kyle's hand. He also noticed how handsome this guy was. *Derek left out that fact. I wonder why?*

Derek came down the lane from the main house and saw Kyle talking with Keith. *Oh, my god! What is he doing here?* He approached the two of them.

"Kyle, what are you doing here?"

"I was at the Shaffer farm and thought I would come by and set up the dinner I invited you both to."

"That was nice of you, but I think we have to pass. We have a lot of work to catch up on around here."

"Of course we can go … Kyle, is it?" Keith asked, looking right at Derek.

"We have a lot to do around here, Keith. Going out now is out of the question. Maybe at a later time."

"I don't agree, Derek. I think we can take off one evening to have a little dinner and conversation," Keith said as he walked over and put his arm around Derek's waist. "We work pretty hard around here, and this could be a good way to relax for a little while. When do you want us to have dinner together, Kyle?"

Kyle flinched a little bit while watching Keith with his arm around Derek. "Uh … how about tomorrow evening?"

"That will work. Where?" Keith asked.

Derek was getting madder by the minute. He wondered what Keith was trying to do. *I do not want to go to dinner or to any place else with Kyle. Keith can see that, so what is he doing?*

"Let's meet at R&J Steakhouse at 7 p.m."

"We will be there. Won't we, Derek?"

"If you want to that much …" he mumbled under his breath.

Both Keith and Kyle noticed how reluctant Derek was. Keith was getting suspicious as to what this hesitation was all about.

Kyle said his goodbyes and walked away, adding, "See you there at seven then!"

Keith turned to Derek and said, "Do you want to tell me what is up with you? What are you afraid of? I know the story about him."

"*How* do you know? Did you read my journal?"

"I would never do that. I asked Jamie when he called earlier. I know you thought you were in love with him, but he is straight, isn't he?"

"Yes, and I am *not* in love with him!" Derek said angrily.

"Well, I would hope not since you say that you are in love with me. So what is your problem? He seems nice enough."

"Nothing. I just don't want to get involved with him again."

"I don't think that one dinner would make us involved."

"*Okay!*" Derek said and stormed into the house. He knew that his actions were too extreme, but all the hurt came flooding back when he saw Kyle.

Keith followed him into the house, walked up to Derek, and took him in his arms. "Derek, maybe we can fix him up with Chrystel. If they hit it off, we would have some friends to hang out with here in Berea. Marc and Jamie are too far away. She is a veterinarian, and he is our new chief of staff. How perfect is that? They would have so much in common and an added plus: She's single and beautiful with long, dark hair and green eyes. What is not to like about her? That is, if you are into women."

They both laughed at that last statement. Keith and Derek had gotten to know Chrystel when she came to check out the horses, and they always thought she was too wonderful to be alone.

Derek was feeling a little better now. "Let's invite her to dinner with us and see what happens. Keith, you always know how to get me out of being angry with you." As he pulled him toward the bedroom, he asked, "Want to make me feel even better?"

"Oh, yes. I very much want to make you feel better," Keith said as he moved his hand down to feel the bulge in Derek's jeans.

"God, how I love when you touch me," Derek said as he kissed Keith passionately. When they came up for air, Derek took Keith's hand and led him to their bedroom. "I need you so much, Keith."

Keith could take no more. Derek could always get him to do whatever he wanted by talking seductively to him. In the bedroom, he pulled off Derek's shirt and undressed him very quickly. "You are mine, Derek. Always remember that," Keith told him as he kissed him, tasting Derek's wonderful mouth with his tongue. He made love to Derek, taking his time so there was no doubt that he belonged to him. Afterwards, they lay satisfied in each other's arms. "Derek, we had better get up and make that call to Chrystel. Let's hope she can go to dinner with us."

"Okay. I will get dinner started. You come down when you are ready, and we will make that call," Derek said as he kissed Keith one more time.

≪ Later that evening, after they had dinner, Derek called Chrystel to talk about going to dinner with them and Kyle the following night.

"Chrystel, Keith and I have been asked out to dinner by the new chief of staff and wondered if you would join us."

"You are not trying to fix me up, are you?"

"No."

"You don't sound very convincing, Derek!"

Chrystel was leery because people were always trying to fix her up. She came to Berea 10 years ago to set up her veterinary office, and she had been taking care of Jamie's horses almost as soon as she arrived. She liked Jamie instantly. Derek was taking care of the breeding of the horses because Jamie was a famous author and spent most of his time writing. Jamie would come to the stables to ride and help Derek with the births, but mostly she worked with Derek.

Derek never knew that Chrystel was attracted to him, and she always hoped they could get together someday. Then she heard that he was gay. No other man interested her, so she stayed single and did not date. She knew there was no hope, but still wondered about it. When Derek brought Keith home to live, it was hard for her. Keith coming to live with Derek squelched the last threads of hope that she had to get close to Derek. She tried to dislike Keith, but it was hard because he was so nice. Even so, there was some resentment about Keith.

"Okay. I will go with you guys. What time?"

"Seven p.m. We will pick you up on our way."

Introductions

The next day, Keith and Derek worked in the stables. Several of the mares were pregnant and needed close attention. Shadow had done his job well. Jamie and Marc were pleased with his success over the past five years. He had sired 10 new foals, and now the mares were pregnant again. Derek was having a hard time concentrating because he was worried about the dinner with Kyle. He really didn't want to get involved with Kyle again because he still carried the emotional scars from 20 years ago.

∽ Kyle was busy at the hospital, getting to know the staff. He wanted to stay busy and not think about the dinner. He looked forward to being with Derek — and Keith too — but he needed to concentrate on his work. Berea Hospital was a tiny hospital but had acquired some exceptionally good surgeons and up-to-date equipment. Kyle was impressed. Several of the nurses flirted with him shamelessly, but he tried not to notice. He observed several general surgeries and went on rounds to meet the patients in the hospital. He really liked his staff.

The day went by quickly. His house would not be ready for a week, so he went to a hotel in town to get cleaned up.

∽ "Derek!" Keith yelled. "What is *wrong* with you? Pay attention!"

Derek was drifting, remembering the bad times with Kyle. He couldn't get them off his mind. "Sorry, Keith. Just deep in thought."

"What is the problem?"

"Keith, you have no idea how it felt when Kyle turned on me. I still feel it sometimes like it was yesterday. I really don't want to be involved with him again."

"Do you still have feelings for him?"

"NO!" Derek yelled. "I have already *told* you, but the hurt is still there."

"Well, I think this dinner will help you get over that. Also, I will be right by your side the whole time."

"I know I am acting foolishly, and I will try to get past it." He was a little ashamed about yelling at Keith.

Keith was secretly worried. Even though Derek cared about Kyle many years ago, just the sound of his name elicited strong reactions. Keith couldn't let it get to him. *It will be fine,* he thought. *Chrystel will help.*

Derek got dressed for dinner. He didn't care how he looked because he was not trying to impress Kyle. *I don't care what he thinks of me anymore. I am over him completely.*

Keith returned from the stables to get ready. He noticed that Derek had on an old pair of jeans and a flannel shirt. "What are you wearing? You can't go out with me like *that.* You look like you are going to muck the stalls in the stable instead of going to dinner."

"I just don't think this dinner with Kyle is important enough to dress for."

"Derek, you are making me crazy over your attitude about Kyle. It makes me think that there are still some feelings there."

"There isn't! I just don't *like* him, and I don't get why you insist on getting to know him. You should respect my feelings in this matter. He is a homophobe, and I know what I am talking about."

"He may have been that way when you came out, but I don't think that is true now. You guys were young then, and he didn't understand how he really felt about gays. He has matured. He is a doctor now and understands the genetics of it." Keith came close to Derek and put his arms around him. "I love you, Derek, and I think you are the best-looking guy I have ever seen. I want to show you off because I am immensely proud that you are mine. Will you please change into something really cool and let me show everyone in town how lucky I am?"

"Okay, but only for you." Derek leaned in and kissed Keith, and then went upstairs to change his clothes. Keith started up after him, but Derek stopped him. "Oh, no! We will be late for dinner if you come up with me. You know that I can't keep my hands off you!"

"Oh, okay, Derek. I will wait down here against my will, I want you to know."

Derek came down the steps and walked into the living room. When Keith saw Derek, it took his breath away. He had on pale-green dress pants and a green-and-tan sweater with a brown corduroy blazer over the top.

"Wow, I didn't mean for you to look good enough to eat. You look amazing!" Keith kissed him passionately and didn't want to let him go. "Maybe we should cancel dinner."

"Keith, you need to back off, or we will not get to dinner. You wanted this so much, so we are going. Besides, we are already late picking up Chrystel."

"Okay. I will run up and get dressed. It won't take me long. Be right back down."

◈ They picked up Chrystel and then went to R&J Steakhouse. When they got out of the truck, Chrystel commented on how great Derek looked. She felt a little pang of longing by looking at him.

"Thanks, Chrystel, for that nice compliment."

They walked into the restaurant and immediately saw Kyle, who was standing by the bar. Kyle turned around when Keith touched his arm and just about lost his composure when he saw Derek.

"Kyle, I want you to meet Chrystel. Chrystel, this is Kyle Douglas." Chrystel held out her small hand.

Kyle took it, swallowing it up in his large hands and saying. "Nice to meet you."

"Same here. All the buzz in town is about our new chief of staff."

"Are you a nurse at the hospital?"

"No. I am the veterinarian here in Berea."

"Oh, so you take care of Derek and Keith's horses?"

"Yes, among others."

The whole time Kyle and Chrystel were talking, Derek was standing off to the side. A flashback — about how badly he was treated when he came out — caused him to once again be deep in thought.

Keith noticed and came over to him, putting his arm around his waist. "Come on, Derek. Stay with us, okay?"

"Just bad memories surfacing again."

"It will be okay. That was 20 years ago."

"Then why are you making me go out with my past?"

"I feel that you need this to finally get past it. Please do this for me."

⤚ The hostess told them that their table was ready. Keith led the way with Chrystel behind him, and Derek and Kyle followed. Derek could feel Kyle's presence and didn't like how uncomfortable it made him feel. He could feel Kyle's eyes on him.

All of a sudden, Derek turned around and got right in Kyle's face. "Do not think that we are going to be socializing after tonight. *You got that?*" He turned around and continued walking toward the table with Kyle on his heels.

Kyle was really thrown by the hostility and venom coming from Derek. Keith noticed immediately that something was wrong when Derek and Kyle got to the table. Derek sat next to Keith, and Kyle sat next to Chrystel. You could cut the atmosphere with a knife.

Keith leaned in to whisper in Derek's ear. "What just happened with you two?"

"Nothing. I just told him not to expect this again."

As they ordered drinks and food, Chrystel asked, "So, Kyle, how do you like the hospital staff?"

"They are all great. Everyone in Berea has been so welcoming. I always loved living here before, but I think it is going to be even more wonderful this time. What about you? How do you like it here? Do you have a husband or a boyfriend?"

Keith thought it was a good sign that he liked Chrystel and was trying to find out her situation.

"I think it is a great town. I have only been here 10 years, but I really do love it. I do not have a husband or a boyfriend. I have only wanted one man, and he is not available to me, so I plan to be single for the rest of my life."

"That is too sad. You should not feel that way. There is bound to be someone out there for you," Kyle said.

As Derek shifted in his seat to pick up his napkin that dropped on the floor, he bumped knees with Kyle. When he sat up, he saw something cross over Kyle's face. *What was that look about?*

Keith noticed it too and thought at first that it was sexual tension. *Now why would a straight man react that way?*

Kyle couldn't explain the reaction to Derek's knee touching him. He had to get his emotions under control. He looked at both of them and asked, "Derek, how long have you guys been together?"

"Keith moved here with me five years ago," he said as he leaned over and grabbed Keith's hand. Both smiled at each other.

"Yup! It has been five glorious and wonderful years," Keith answered with love in his voice as he squeezed Derek's hand.

Kyle noticed the gesture.

So did Chrystel. *God, I have got to get past this! They have been happy for years now. I know it is hopeless, but it kills me every time I see them show affection toward each other.*

Kyle remained quiet, deep in thought. The waiter came back to see if anyone wanted more coffee and dessert.

"I would like a glass of merlot … the best you have," Kyle requested. He needed something to calm his nerves. This was harder than he thought it would be. He didn't like watching the affection between the two men. *Why did I push so hard for this?*

"Keith, ask the waiter for our check," Jamie said. "It is 9:30, and we need to get back to the farm and check on the mares. You know how nervous Mr. Hawthorn is about being alone with the horses."

"Don't worry about the check. I will take care of it," Kyle offered.

"NO! I don't want you paying for anything for Keith and me," Derek said hatefully.

"Whoa, Derek! There's no need to be rude. Sorry about that, Kyle," Keith said, glaring at Derek. "You ready to go, Chrystel?"

"I think I will stay and have a glass of wine with Kyle. I'll take a cab."

"No, Chrystel. I will be happy to take you home," Kyle added. "Derek, I am sorry if I offended you in some way. I never meant to do that."

Derek glared at him, and then said goodbye to Chrystel and left. Keith grabbed the waiter and paid the check, and then said his goodbyes.

Keith went to the car and climbed in the driver's side. He looked at Derek, who was pouting and terribly angry, and asked, "What the hell was *that*? I have never seen you act so badly to others. Your behavior was embarrassing, to say the least. What got into you?"

Derek sat quietly, not saying a word.

Keith kept after him. "Well? What have you got to say?"

All of a sudden, Derek let all the hostility he was feeling fall on Keith. "You had no right! You made me sit through a difficult dinner, and now you are mad because I didn't behave so nicely. I told you that I didn't want to go, but no … you wouldn't take no for an answer. You forced me to sit for over two hours with someone who treated me with such loathing, and I am supposed to play nice? How many times do I have to tell you that I don't want anything to do with him … EVER!"

Keith started the car and drove home. Both men rode all the way in silence. When Keith pulled into the farm, Derek jumped out and stomped into the house. He went up to the guest room and slammed the door. Keith followed him upstairs and went to their room, but Derek was not there.

"Okay, Derek," he said as he tried the door to the guest room, but it was locked. "Let me in. You are being foolish. We need to talk."

"What is there to talk about? I told you what I thought about having anything to do with Kyle, and it didn't matter to you. You did what you wanted to do, and now I have nothing else to say."

"Fine. You can stay in there and pout or whatever, but I am going to check on the horses like you said we needed to do back at R&J Steakhouse."

There was no answer from inside the room, so Keith went down to the stables. He needed some time alone to figure out exactly what was going on with Derek.

⋰ "Chrystel, do you like old movies? I have a great collection."

"Yes, I do, Kyle. As a matter of fact, I would like to see what you have some time."

The two talked about their collections, music, their careers, and some of the strange cases that Chrystel had seen in her practice. Both enjoyed the other's company very much. When Kyle stopped at Chrystel's house, she invited him in for coffee.

"Sure, I would love to. It is still early."

Chrystel was anxious to show Kyle some of her old classic movies. Two hours passed, and both looked at the clock. It was getting late, and Kyle had to be at the hospital early, but they were so lost in conversation that they didn't notice how late it was.

"I have to go, Chrystel. It has been a lot of fun hanging out with you. Thank you so much for coming tonight. I am glad that Keith and Derek introduced us. I feel that I have met a friend whom I can have fun with, if you are willing." As he walked to the door, he added, "When I get my house, you will have to come over and watch a movie with me."

Chrystel followed him to the door. "Kyle, why did Derek act so rudely to you? I have never seen him act that way toward anyone. He is always so easygoing and friendly."

"I guess he has not forgiven me for what I did to him 20 years ago. I was hoping that he had gotten past it, but I guess not."

"What did you do to him?"

"It's a long story for another time. Thanks again!"

Chrystel closed the door and went to get things cleaned up, so that she could get ready for bed. She knew that she was not going to let it drop. Her curiosity was killing her. *If Kyle won't tell, maybe Derek will.*

∞ Keith walked into the stable and found one of the pregnant mares on the ground, obviously in severe pain, with blood everywhere. *Oh, my god! Something is very wrong.* He had seen this before and knew that it was not good. He ran to the phone and called Chrystel.

"Chrystel, one of the mares is down and in trouble. Come quickly!" He then called the house, and Derek answered the phone.

"What do you want, Keith?"

"Get over yourself and get your ass down to the stables. One of the mares is down, and something is very wrong."

Derek went to the barn and saw that the mare was in a lot of distress.

Chrystel ran to the door after Kyle left. She called him, and he stopped the car and came up to her. "Keith just called and has trouble at the stables. Will you take me over there, so I don't have to get out my car?"

"Sure. Hop in!"

Chrystel and Kyle arrived at the Walker farm within minutes. She found the mare down with Keith and Derek beside her. Chrystel knew that it was way too early to have the foal. The water sac had already broken, and she was bleeding badly. Chrystel took over. Derek looked at Kyle and asked why he was here.

"Chrystel needed me to drive her. Sorry if that is a problem for you."

"It's not. I would have to care for it to bother me."

Kyle looked at Derek and shrugged it off. Derek was just going to have to get past this resentment. Kyle knew why Derek felt this way but kept hoping it would pass. Right now, he was more concerned about helping Chrystel. Blood was everywhere.

Chrystel examined the mare. "She has ripped herself open with the foal in a bad position. I am not going to be able to save the foal, but I will try to save the mare."

Keith and Derek were quite upset.

"What can we do to help?" Keith asked.

"Nothing. Just try to keep her calm. Kyle, can you help me? You are a surgeon, and this is not a whole lot different. I need to do a C-section to get the foal out. He is sideways. Okay? We will need to sedate her."

Chrystel and Kyle worked for over an hour, trying to save the mare. The foal was gone. Finally, Chrystel gave Keith and Derek the bad news: The mare could not be saved. She had lost too much blood.

ঙ Mr. and Mrs. Hawthorn had been out for the evening. Upon returning home, they saw the lights in the stable, so they came down to see what was wrong. Keith told them that they lost both mare and foal. The Hawthorns were devastated. That mare was Mrs. Hawthorn's favorite.

"What happened?"

"Not sure, but the foal moved into a bad position sideways and ripped the mare inside," Chrystel explained.

Derek went up to Keith and hugged him tightly. His anger was gone, and both guys just needed each other right then, forgetting that anyone else was in the stable. Kyle watched intently, and Chrystel noticed but went back to the task at hand.

Mr. Hawthorn spoke. "I will have some hands from town come and bury the mare and foal. You guys go on. We will take care of this."

Keith and Derek thanked Chrystel and Kyle for their help and left the stable arm in arm. Both were so sad with the turn of events.

"I will call Jamie and Marc in the morning," Keith said. "For now, let's just go to bed. I am exhausted mentally and physically."

They retired for the night, and nothing more was said.

ᴥ The next morning, Keith called Marc and told him what happened. "Chrystel did an amazing job with the help of Dr. Kyle Douglas, but they couldn't save her."

Marc had the phone on speaker and Jamie asked, "What was Kyle doing there, Keith?"

"Chrystel was with him when we called, and she had him come to help. He is a surgeon, you know."

"Yes, I heard. I just can't figure out why he is so much in your lives now."

"Don't worry about it, Jamie. You know that Derek and I are committed to each other, so it is not a problem. Derek doesn't want him in his life, but he is here again, and it is a small town. Chrystel seems to like him, so maybe they will hook up."

"Well, as long as you guys are okay. Do you need us to come there to help?" Marc asked.

"It is all under control. Sad, but we are handling it."

Renewal

Kyle got an unexpected call on his cell phone: It was David Jenkins. He had not thought about David since residency. They were boyfriends then but had broken up. David said in the voice mail that he was at the Lexington airport and asked if Kyle would pick him up.

What is he coming here for? Kyle thought. *We have not been together for nine years.*

David was excited at the prospect of seeing Kyle again. He was still in love with him and had not been able to get him out of his mind or his heart. He applied for a position at Berea Hospital to see if there was anything left between them. The hospital was advertising for a chief of surgery, and he took the opportunity.

Kyle ignored the buzzing of the phone when David called again. He refused to talk to him, let alone pick him up at the airport. *I am not going after him. He will have to find his own way here.* Kyle went to the CEO's office to find out why David was coming to Berea. Kyle knocked on the door to Dr. Mitchell's office.

"Come in ... oh, Kyle, please sit. I have been meaning to call you. We have a new chief of surgery coming today. The board just hired him. I believe you know him. He told us that you were in residency together. His name is ..."

Kyle interrupted. "David Jenkins, right? That is why I am here. How could you hire him without letting me have a say about who is picked to work on my staff? I am the chief of staff, and I should have been notified." He got up to leave.

Dr. Mitchell was taken aback by how angry Dr. Douglas was. "Please sit. Let's talk about this. You sound like you are against him being here. I got the impression that you are friends."

"We were but not anymore. That doesn't matter though. Are you saying that he was the best candidate for the job?"

"Yes. Out of all the applicants, he is the most qualified."

Kyle sat quietly, thinking about how he felt. He and David didn't part well, and he was very hurt when he caught David with another guy. It was a bitter parting because he loved him so much and couldn't believe he would do that. This was nine years ago, and he was sure that he was over it, but he didn't want to revisit that part of his past.

Kyle had taken this job to be near Derek. He realized a year ago that Derek kept coming into his mind, and he couldn't shake it. He had to see him and figure out what it all meant. When he was a teenager and friends with Derek, he was in denial about his sexuality and couldn't imagine being with a man — nor did he want to be! Derek broke their bond of friendship when he came out to him. It scared him, so he did the only thing he could do: Deny it, pull away, and be cruel. He later regretted how he treated Derek.

When Kyle got to med school and residency, he allowed himself to accept that he was attracted to men. David was his first, and they stayed together the whole four years of residency. He was happy until David cheated. Kyle walked away from him and never looked back. David tried to contact him over the years, but he refused to let him back in. Now here he was!

Dr. Mitchell shook Kyle out of his thoughts. "Kyle, let's give David a chance and see how it goes. Okay?"

"I guess I will *have* to since you hired him already."

🙠 David rented a car when he realized that Kyle was not returning his calls. He arrived at Jean's B&B and checked in. He needed to get to the hospital to meet with the CEO and Kyle. He could not wait to see Kyle!

David arrived at Berea Hospital as Kyle headed out to his car. They ran into each other on the steps.

"Kyle, I am so happy to see you again! How have you been? I know that you are the chief of staff, and that fact made me apply to Berea."

"Why do you want to be in Berea? You know that there is no reason to see each other. I have moved on, and I hope you have also. I am not happy that you were hired without the board telling me. I just found out when you called me. By the way, forget my phone number."

"I know I screwed up all those years ago, Kyle, but I have never forgotten you. Please … can't we go for a drink later and at least talk to each other about what has been going on the last nine years? I have to go in and talk with Dr. Mitchell and get the lay of the land, and then I will be free."

"Who do you think you *are*? You also have to meet with me since I will be your immediate boss. I am going to get something out of my car, and then I will talk to you in Dr. Mitchell's office." Kyle pushed past David, almost knocking him down.

He will get over this as soon as the shock wears off and he gets used to me being here, David thought as he went into the hospital. *I can't give up on this. I will win him over.*

Dr. Mitchell greeted David with a handshake and a friendly smile. Ten minutes later, Kyle walked into the office. The tension could have cut the air with a knife. It was obvious to Dr. Mitchell that Kyle wanted no part of this guy.

∞ As they were leaving Dr. Mitchell's office, Kyle grabbed David's arm. "You are really arrogant to think that I would let you back into my life! Just because you will be a part of my professional life does not give you the right to involve yourself in my personal life. Two professionals at the hospital will be the extent of our contact. I am not interested in anything more with you. Do I make myself clear, David?" He pushed past David and went to the parking lot.

David ran after him and grabbed his arm. He spun Kyle around and kissed him in front of the hospital. "You will change your mind. You will remember how good we were together … how great the sex was between us. You will want me to take you to bed again. I know you will because you just responded to this kiss." David walked away, leaving Kyle astonished about what had just happened and the raging hard-on that he left him with.

Kyle could not deny feelings that he thought were buried nine years ago. He was very confused.

Exposed

David came to work the next day and was introduced to the surgery staff. He settled in nicely and knew that he was going to like it. The hospital was small by the standards he was used to, but the winning point was that Kyle was there. The other plus was that he liked the staff and his personal scrub nurse.

Kyle tried to stay out of the surgery area for a few days. He was not ready to address what happened in the parking lot and the fact that the whole hospital was abuzz. Hospital grapevines are horrible for any kind of gossip, and David sure gave them something to talk about.

Great! How am I supposed to deal with all the gossip and looks? Kyle thought as he walked into his office. *I did not want my personal life out there for all to see. Thanks, David!*

 ❦ Chrystel stopped by the Walker farm to check on the rest of the horses and their prized possession Shadow.

Keith came around the corner and into the stables. "Hey, Chrystel. How are you today?"

"Have you heard the news that everyone in town is talking about?"

"No. About what?"

"Someone from the hospital staff told someone at R&J Steakhouse last night about what the whole hospital is talking about."

"Well … *what*?" Keith asked, a little agitated.

"You are not going to believe this! The new chief of surgery arrived a few days ago and is gay!"

"Well, good for him. Is that the news?"

"No. Guess who he was seen kissing in front of the hospital?"

"Good lord, Chrystel. Just *tell* me!"

"Kyle Douglas!"

"*What?* Can't be, Chrystel. You know that Kyle is straight."

"Well, I guess we were all wrong."

"No way! This can't be true. You know how he treated Derek 20 years ago."

"Well, I don't know, but they said that Kyle didn't fight him."

"Oh, Chrystel, I am so sorry. You have been seeing him, haven't you?" Keith felt so bad for her if it was true.

"Yes. He has been coming over and watching movies, but that is all. We are just friends. Don't worry about me. Wait until Derek hears about this. He will freak out!"

"You are right. I don't think I will tell him just yet. He may not hear it for a while. He doesn't go into town that often, and maybe by the time he does they will be done talking about it."

⮦ Kyle spent the next week trying to figure out what he should do about the situation in which he found himself. He and David had run into each other several times. Avoiding him proved not to be a viable option, so he had to come to terms with the whole mess.

Every time he saw David, he remembered what it was like when they were happy together, and those bad memories weren't as painful anymore. He was torn because he was lonely and very horny. He wanted Derek, but he knew that Derek could not stand to be around him and would never forgive him. He also knew that Derek was very much in love with Keith. It was obvious, so he decided to give in. Besides, the whole hospital knew now that he and David had been a couple. That kiss spread like wildfire, so there was no way he could keep his sexual orientation private.

He found David in post-op and asked, "May I see you in my office when you are done here?"

"Sure, Dr. Douglas." David was hopeful at this turn of events as he walked to Kyle's office and knocked on the door.

"Come in."

"You wanted to see me?"

"David, I have decided that trying to avoid you is going to be impossible and stupid, especially after what we once meant to each other. I would like to know if you would agree to have dinner with me tonight, so we can talk about where we will go or not go from here."

"Sure, I would *love* that! You know that I hope we can get back together. That was my main reason for coming here." He walked toward Kyle to take him in his arms.

Kyle backed away. "I am not ready to commit to anything permanent, but we should talk. After all, we will be working together. I will pick you up at the hotel around 7 p.m."

"Okay, Kyle. I will be waiting." As he left the office, David felt particularly good about this turn of events. *Maybe there is a chance for us after all, and I can get Kyle back in my life and my bed,* he thought as he practically danced back to surgery.

∽ "Derek, we have had a busy week, and I think we deserve a break," Keith announced. "What do you say to a nice dinner and possibly a late movie? Tomorrow is Saturday, and we can sleep in. Well, maybe not *sleep* in, but …" He came up close to Derek and took him in his arms. "We could come home and make love all night."

"I am all for that!" Derek said as he kissed Keith. "We haven't been able to spend quality time together with all the work at the stables."

"I will make it up to you tonight, Derek. I promise."

"That is one promise I will insist you keep! I have missed our lovemaking. We should not let our work take us away from each other." Derek kissed Keith again very passionately.

"Do you want to go to dinner, Derek, or finish what you seem to be starting?" Keith asked playfully.

"That was just to give you a small sample of what you'll get later."

"I will change and be ready in 10 minutes," Keith said as he bounced up the steps. He was excited because it had been a while since they went out just to have fun.

⚘ At 7 p.m., Kyle pulled up to Jean's B&B where David was staying. David had not looked for a place of his own yet because he was hoping that he and Kyle would reunite and that he could move in with him. He wasn't sure that he could make that happen. But, if he couldn't, he was going to check out renting a room temporarily. He didn't want to be tied to a lease in case Kyle wanted him back.

"You look nice, David," Kyle said as David got in the car. Kyle always liked the way David looked with his brown hair and very dark eyes. He acknowledged that he was still attracted to him, but he really didn't want to have a serious relationship with him again. Unfortunately, the man he wanted didn't want any part of him.

"Thanks, Kyle. I dressed for you. I know you like this color on me."

"Please, David. Don't read too much into this. I just felt that we should talk about how we can make this work … us working together."

David slid over to Kyle and put his hand between Kyle's legs. "Oh, I think we can work *something* out." He moved his hand back and forth. "Oh, yeah, I think we can."

"David, STOP! I don't know that I want this!"

"I know!" David said with confidence, but he stopped. He didn't want Kyle to kick him out of the car before the evening got started. He slid back to his side of the car.

Kyle was relieved because, for a second, he did want him to continue. They arrived at R&J Steakhouse and waited at the bar for a table to open up.

"I am extremely excited about tonight, Kyle. I am hoping that you will forgive me and give us a second chance."

"It is pretty hard to forgive seeing you in our bed with another man."

"That was nine years ago. Surely you can let it go."

"We will talk about this when we get seated. Not here at the bar," Kyle whispered. He didn't want the whole town to know his business. They already knew too much as far as he was concerned.

⚘ Keith and Derek walked into R&J Steakhouse just as Kyle turned around to check on their table. He and Derek ran right into each other.

"I am so sorry, Derek. I didn't see you!"

Derek mumbled something under his breath.

Keith spoke for both of them. "It is fine, Kyle. How have you been?" He held out his hand. He didn't want to have this conversation but didn't want to be rude either. He also didn't want Derek to sense anything wrong. "Are you here with Chrystel?"

Derek stood behind Keith. He did not want any part of this conversation.

Kyle hesitated for a second when David came up behind him. "No. This is David Jenkins. He is our new chief of surgery."

David held out his hand to Keith. "Hi. I am Kyle's ex."

Kyle wanted to kill David right there, but what was he going to do? David didn't lie, but he didn't want Derek to find out this way. He wanted the chance to tell him in his own time.

Derek stepped forward and could hardly get the words out. "Kyle … is this some kind of a sick joke?"

"No, Derek. It is true. David is my ex-boyfriend."

"How can this *be*? You are straight — not a faggot, remember? Isn't that the word you used when addressing me? Keith, let's get out of here. I have suddenly lost my appetite."

They started for the door when Kyle grabbed Derek's arm. He looked right into Derek's eyes. "Don't do this, Derek. I have wanted to tell you about me but could never form the right words."

Keith stepped between Kyle and Derek and said, a little harsher than he had intended, "Take your hands off my boyfriend."

David got in the middle of them and asked what the problem was.

"The problem," Derek explained, "is that this piece of trash has hurt me for the last time!" He stormed out, leaving all three men speechless. Kyle was trying to digest what Derek had just blurted out. Keith was stunned by hearing those words.

David realized that Derek was his rival for Kyle's love. *This may be harder than I imagined*, he thought.

What did Derek mean by "hurt me for the last time"? Kyle pondered. *Does this mean that he still carries some feelings for me buried deep inside?*

Keith ran after Derek. "Whoa! What just happened back there?"

"How can Kyle be gay? He is straight!" Derek asked Keith, obviously very shaken.

"The better question is what you meant by 'hurt me for the last time.' It sounds like you still have feelings for him; otherwise, he could no longer hurt you."

"Keith, I don't have feeling like that for him now. I just meant that I have endured enough hurt from him when he acted straight, and now … NOW he says that he is gay!"

"God, Derek. I could hate Kyle for the fact that he was your first love and treated you so badly. Let's don't think about him anymore. We had plans for tonight, right? Let's go home and get some good use out of our wonderful bed." Keith pulled Derek into a very loving kiss and opened the door for him to get in the truck.

They headed for home … *their* home!

Love at Walker's Pond

Because Derek was quiet on the drive home, Keith was quite concerned and asked, "Derek, are you alright? You have not said a word since we got in the truck."

"I am fine … just have a lot on my mind. I can't get over the fact that Kyle is gay."

"I know it was a shock, but why do you care so much? You say that you have no feelings for him anymore, but your whole demeanor says something else."

Derek took Keith's hand and told him that he loved him and only him. "I love you so much, and I am happy with you, so please don't worry."

"If you say so. I can't wait to get you home and make love in our wonderful, new, king-sized bed."

"I was thinking of making love at the pond. Don't you remember the nights we made love down there? Even during the week when I first met you, we snuck down to the pond and made love several times. I love making love to you there — the two of us lying in the grass, naked, with the moon shining on the water and the ripples coming in very slowly to the shore." Derek leaned in to kiss Keith. "How about Walker's Pond tonight?"

"God, Derek. I am ready, and you haven't even touched me yet! I love making love at the pond. I remember too the first night I met you when Marc and I pulled up to the Walker farm, and you came out of the stable to help with Shadow. I just about creamed my jeans just looking at you! I knew I had to have you, and I prayed that you were gay."

Derek laughed at that last statement. Keith was happy to hear that laugh again.

193

"Yes, Keith. As I remember, you were a little too anxious and arrogant for me. But I was also flattered that you wanted me so much." A frown came over Derek's face after he said that.

"What? What is that frown for?"

"Sorry. It just made me realize that no one until you came along had ever acted like they wanted me. I even tried to come on to Jamie one time, but he didn't want me either. Kyle definitely didn't want me when I told him that I was in love with him."

This revelation hurt Keith, but he didn't want Derek to know. Instead, he wanted to put the emphasis on their relationship and love. "Well, that is nothing to frown about because I want you and have since the first second I laid eyes on you. You are mine, Derek, and I am yours, and no one is going to come between us." Keith was desperate to make sure Derek believed that all he would ever need was him. He did not want Derek to keep thinking about Kyle and the love that was lost because of Kyle's ignorance.

"I love you too, Keith, so much. Don't worry. I know that we are together for always. You are the only man I want. Please believe that." Derek said the words but even he wondered why this revelation about Kyle had bothered him so much. For that matter, why did he have him on his mind ever since they came back from Cheyenne? *What is wrong with me? I have to get this off my mind. I do love Keith and want to spend my life with him. But I can't deny that this has really thrown me — Kyle coming back into my life and now finding out that he is gay.*

They pulled up to the farm and immediately Derek said, "Let's go to the pond, Keith. I want to make love to you there tonight."

"Okay," Keith said as he grabbed a blanket from the back of the truck. "Let's go!"

⮝ They walked hand in hand, anticipating how wonderful it would be to make love at the pond. It had been a while. They didn't realize how much they missed it. It was a balmy night, and the moon was full — perfect make-out weather!

194

"Let's go skinny dipping first," Derek said as he shed his clothes and ran to the edge of the water. It was a little cold, but it would feel great with Keith's naked body in the water with him. "Come on, old man!"

"Oh, yeah? Who are you calling *old*?" Keith teased as he stripped off the last piece of clothing and ran straight for Derek.

Derek looked him up and down as if seeing him for the first time naked. "You are so handsome, Keith. You take my breath away."

Keith took Derek in his arms. "You are more than handsome to me. You are beautiful with your light brown hair and hazel eyes, which turn a vivid green when you are in the throes of passion. And I love to make them change colors," he said as he took possession of Derek's full lips.

Their bodies responded in mutual want and need. Derek took Keith's tongue in his mouth and trapped it there. He wanted to taste Keith. He wasn't satisfied with that, so he kissed Keith down his neck and onto his chest, stopping to suck on each nipple on his way down to his destination.

"I thought we were going …" Keith couldn't mouth the words because Derek was making him moan instead. He started pushing his extremely hard cock into Derek's.

Derek continued to kiss Keith down his abdomen to his groin. Keith was ready for Derek to swallow him whole. Derek was in no hurry. He licked up the back of Keith's cock and played with the head, twirling his tongue around and around.

"Please …," Keith begged. He was going crazy.

Derek opened his mouth wider, so he could take in Keith totally. He moved up and down and held Keith's balls. When Keith started pushing toward Derek's throat, he came with such a force that Derek couldn't swallow it all. *God, Keith tastes so good!*

When Keith finished, Derek stood up with cum all over his mouth and kissed Keith on the lips. Keith could taste himself in Derek's mouth, and it was so hot that he was already starting to recover.

Keith grabbed Derek's hand and pulled him into the water. He needed a chance to get control of himself before they went much farther. "Derek, I want to swim with you and then make love on the blanket under that beautiful, full moon. What do you say?"

"Okay! The water feels good, doesn't it?"

They swam for a while, and then lay on the blanket under the moonlight and made love over and over. Both were happy and satisfied, and soon they were asleep — all curled up in each other's arms.

Little did they know that they had an audience.

~ Kyle had told David that he would come back to R&J Steakhouse in a while, but he needed to talk to Keith and Derek first. David didn't like it but felt that, if he challenged him, he would lose.

Kyle left David and followed Keith and Derek to the farm. When he got there, he saw them go down to the pond, hand in hand. David followed but ended up witnessing the whole scene. Watching Derek make love to Keith, and then watching Keith take Derek completely, was so hard to watch, but he couldn't tear himself away. He could not believe how it upset him. It was obvious that they were really in love, and it bothered him. *What is your problem? Why are you surprised that they love each other? You have known that from the first time you saw them together.* It hit Kyle like a ton of bricks. *You want to be the man whom Derek is making love to, but you have no chance with him … EVER … so leave him alone.*

Kyle quietly left the two alone, asleep in each other's arms, and went back to his car without being noticed. He couldn't stay there anymore, and he didn't want them to find out that he had seen them making love. It would be too humiliating and one more reason for Derek to hate him.

~ Kyle drove back to R&J Steakhouse to see if David waited for him. When he walked in, he saw him sitting at the bar with a beer in his hand. "David, I am glad you waited for me."

David gave him a glaring look and asked if he got to talk to Keith and Derek. He figured that he should ask, even though he could care less about the answer.

"Yes. I saw them but didn't get to talk to them."

"What? Then why were you gone so long?" As soon as he said that, he wished he could take it back because he did not want to give Kyle any reason to leave their date that night. "I mean, why didn't you talk to them?"

"I couldn't find them at first and then, when I did, I decided that it was not the right time."

David decided to leave it at that. "Well, do you still want to have dinner and talk, or what?"

"No. Let's go back to your hotel. We can have a nightcap there."

David could hardly contain his excitement. "Let's go!"

❧ David and Kyle drove to the hotel, and Kyle followed David to his room. As soon as the door was closed, he grabbed David and started unbuttoning his shirt. He couldn't get it off fast enough. Kyle unbuckled his belt and undid his slacks. Before long, David was standing naked in front of Kyle.

David came closer and helped Kyle with his clothes. Kyle pushed David against the door and started kissing and touching him all over. David was on fire. He had waited nine long years for this to happen. He wanted Kyle so much. He kissed him and stuck his tongue deep into his open mouth. The kissing got hotter and more urgent.

"David, suck me off now."

David spun Kyle around and pinned him against the door, immediately doing as he was asked. Whatever Kyle wanted, he would do.

Kyle had his head against the door and his eyes closed. His breathing got heavier and faster with each up-and-down stroke of David's mouth. "Oh, Derek, I am coming … I am coming." He shot his cum into David's mouth as he called out Derek's name.

David heard what he said but still did not want to confront him. He wanted Kyle back so much that he would ignore what he said, even though he hurt inside. *I can't say anything to him because I am so in love with him. What else can I do but be silent and hope that he comes back to me and forgets Derek?*

Kyle never realized that he had called out Derek's name at the time of climax.

They got dressed and decided to talk later; it just wasn't the right time. David did not push either.

"I have to go, David, but thanks for what just happened. I will see you at the hospital tomorrow."

As Kyle drove home, he thought about the whole evening. He had just used David for his own needs and felt sorry for that, but he could not help or stop himself. He had gotten so turned on while watching Derek and Keith. He also knew that it was not a good move on his part. He was sending David mixed messages, which he did not want to do because he did not know what to do about him.

Revelation

The next day, Kyle didn't feel like going directly to the hospital. He didn't want to see David, and he knew that he would run into him if he went there. He decided to take a walk around town and familiarize himself again. It had been 20 years since he lived here. Many things had changed, and so much had stayed the same. He kept denying who he was.

Derek was on his way to the feed-and-grain store and was daydreaming about the lovemaking down at the pond. It had been amazing! Making love was always good between him and Keith, but this time was really special.

He didn't see Kyle coming up in front of him and ran smack into him. Kyle grabbed Derek around his shoulders to keep him from falling.

"Let me go! Why do you think you can put your hands on me?"

"I am sorry, Derek, but I didn't want you to fall. You obviously weren't thinking about where you were walking."

"You arrogant son of a bitch! Implying that I don't know how to walk down the street." Derek knew that he was being ridiculous, but he couldn't stop the words. He tried to get past Kyle. It was making him extremely nervous to be so close to the first man he fell in love with, and he didn't like the feelings that it was bringing back to him. "What kind of game is this, Kyle? You are not gay, so why are you pretending to be gay with this guy David?"

"Derek, you don't know what you are talking about. I *am* gay and have been all along. I just didn't know it for a long time … or rather didn't want to admit it." Kyle couldn't take his eyes off Derek's mouth. He wanted to kiss him so much and make Derek remember how he use to feel about him when they were back in high school, but he knew how Derek would react. He thought he would wait for him to adjust to the fact that he was gay.

Derek was aware that Kyle was looking at his mouth, and he had a good idea what was on his mind, but he was determined that it would never happen. He had hurt him so badly when they were back in school. Besides, he was in love with Keith and didn't want anyone else. *Let David have his fill of Kyle. I want no part of him … not anymore.*

"I have to get to the feed store," Derek said with a sneer on his face. "You have a great day." He walked past Kyle and moved down the street.

About that time, Derek's phone rang, and it was Keith. "I just called to tell you that I love you, Derek. Last night was amazing, and I can't wait to make love to you again tonight."

"I love you too, Keith. You are right. Last night was amazing making love to you. God, Keith, I am so in love with you."

Derek did not know that Kyle could hear his side of the conversation. Kyle felt his heart break a little, knowing what he had witnessed at the pond. He wanted to be in Keith's place. *Why didn't I act on my feelings way back when I wanted to touch Derek and couldn't admit that I wanted him?*

⤳ Derek finished his business at the feed store. He got some coffee and sat on a bench at the campus to get control of his emotions after bumping into Kyle. He knew that Kyle wanted to kiss him. If he were honest, he also knew that he wanted him to do it. *What is this about?*

David walked by on his way to the hospital.

Derek decided to take this opportunity to find out about Kyle. "Hi, David. Do you remember me? I am Derek. Can you sit with me a minute? I want to ask you something."

David sat next to Derek.

Derek blurted out, "How can Kyle be gay?"

"We met in med school. One night, we were both at the same gay bar. He was trying to do the gay scene but didn't know what to do. We hung out until the place closed, and then I took him home with me and taught him how to make love to a man. Derek, he was a fast learner and an exceptionally good sex partner. I can't get enough of him."

Derek sat in silence, taking it all in.

David looked at Derek and could see why Kyle wanted him. "God, Derek, he gives the best blow jobs I have ever had! He is always so willing once I introduced him to all of it. He loves making love. Our first time together was amazing. He took to it like a duck takes to water. I can't stay away from him. That is why I followed him here."

Derek was getting hot and bothered just listening to David's description about being with Kyle. *Why couldn't he have been willing for me? Wow, what is wrong with you? You have Keith, and he is amazing and in love with you.* Derek had heard enough. He had to get away.

"Bye, David. Thanks for the talk."

David smiled at Derek. He knew what had just happened. He saw that Derek had a bulge in his jeans, which needed to be taken care of because he had gotten Derek worked up while telling him about Kyle. David would have obliged Derek in a minute if he would have let him. It was the reason Kyle left him. He couldn't be faithful, and here he was again, thinking about another man! As David walked to the hospital, he saw Kyle and couldn't stop himself from telling him about Derek.

Kyle saw David coming toward him and thought, *Oh, my god! I do not want to talk to him right now.* "What are you doing on campus, David?"

"I was walking to the hospital on the scenic route, and I ran into Derek. He stopped me and was asking a lot of questions about you. He wanted to know how you decided to be gay. I told him a little about our love life, and he got a raging hard-on just listening about you. I am not sure that he is completely over you. But he has Keith, and they are very much in love, so I think we should basically have as little contact with them as we can."

Kyle could not believe what he was hearing! *Is it possible that Derek still has feelings for me? God, I want that so much! I would love to be able to get Derek completely alone and see. Derek is all I can think of, even after I was with David last night.*

❧ Derek drove home immediately. He needed Keith! When he got there, Keith was outside getting ready to go in the house. Derek pushed Keith into their home, stripped him in no time, and smashed him onto the bed. He got naked and looked at his lover. Keith's face was all shock. He knew he had to slow down, but he wanted Keith to take him so hard that he wouldn't be able to sit down the next day.

"Derek, are you okay? What are you doing?" Keith had never seen Derek like this. It was a little scary. His Derek was so sweet and relaxed; this Derek seemed bewildered.

Derek saw Keith's face and came to his senses. "Sorry, Keith. I was just so horny that I had to have you, or I would explode. Last night was great. Finally, we had time to be together. I loved the night we shared at the pond, and it awakened my sex drive, I think. Sorry!"

Derek couldn't tell Keith the whole truth ... that the story about Kyle made him hot ... that the things David told him were like a movie in his head. Kyle and David — he knew it was stupid and wrong, but he wanted to be with Kyle in that moment.

Keith pulled him in bed and started to stroke him. No foreplay was needed; precum was streaming over his hand already.

Derek kissed him hard on his mouth. All he could say was, "Keith ... Keith ... Keith ..."

Keith's touch was tight and rough. He could see that was what Derek needed now. Part of him wanted to stop there because it had nothing to do with lovemaking, but it was arousing to see how horny Derek was.

Derek couldn't form sentences anymore. He tried to calm down with everything he had. He had no right to act like this with Keith — the man he lived with and loved — but he couldn't stop. Much later he regretted it, but Keith assured him not to worry.

✃ Keith was asleep, his arms wrapped around Derek. He talked a little in his sleep, but Derek couldn't understand what he said. Derek moved out of Keith's arms and put his arms under his head. He and Keith had sex, but he wasn't satisfied.

He knew that Keith had done this for him. Keith was the kind of man who loved foreplay, caressing, and kissing. Derek had been way too impatient. The most embarrassing thing was that it wasn't Keith who made him act like an animal. Visions of Kyle and David made his cock get hard in an instant.

Confusion made Derek shiver. He and Keith were happy, and no one was going to disturb their happiness. *So why am I having fantasies about Kyle more than ever before? Keith is my love, my life. The way Keith makes me feel is unique. Kyle never came close to that! Kyle never acted like he wanted me. Why had David told me so much about their sex life? If Kyle had feelings for me, why didn't he show me?*

The idea was wrong, but his cock grew harder thinking about it. Stroking his cock, he thought about Kyle. He suppressed a moan because he didn't want to wake up Keith. His breathing became irregular as he moved his hand faster. "Shit!" His cum messed up their bed. He needed to clean it up before Keith could see it. He didn't want him to know that their lovemaking had not satisfied him. Keith should be all he needed, but he couldn't get the vision of Kyle out of his head. *Oh, my god. You have gone off the deep end, Derek. Get a grip!*

Derek was up early. He took a shower and made Keith breakfast. He had made up his mind: He was with Keith, and he wanted it to work. He loved him, and that should be enough. He felt guilty for his fantasies, so he decided to focus on Keith.

He kissed Keith's cheek and whispered in his ear, "Wake up, baby. I have coffee for you. … Keith, wake up! We have to take care of the horses."

No reaction. Derek caressed his face, planting tiny kisses on his nose, and pushed his cock into Keith's. He heard a moan.

&ᔛ Much later, Keith went into town after he and Derek had attended to the horses. He wanted to stop by Chrystel's house to talk about the horse that had a lump on the lower part of the leg. After their visit, he sat on a bench to enjoy the sunshine. He closed his eyes and reflected on what had happened earlier. The way Derek had woken him up was great. Derek made him feel special.

"Hi," Keith heard someone say.

He didn't want to open his eyes. He just wanted to daydream about his perfect lover.

"Are you sleeping?"

"No. I'm just enjoying the sun and the silence," Keith said, hoping the voice would go away. He looked up and saw a tall guy whom he had seen sitting in Chrystel's office. "Sorry. Do I know you? My name is Keith."

"I know. I'm Galen," the tall guy responded. "I am Chrystel's cousin. I saw you at her office a little while ago and asked who you were. I am visiting from out of town and don't know anyone." He held out his hand.

"Nice to meet you … Galen, is it? That is a very strange name but nice. Chrystel doesn't talk much about her family. Where are you from?"

"I am from Chicago, but I'm thinking of relocating to a quieter, smaller place. I can work just about anywhere. I work for a computer company from my home. I have been talking to Chrystel about maybe settling in Berea. It seems like a genuinely nice community. Gay friendly, so Chrystel tells me, which surprises me since it is sort of redneck country."

"Are you gay?"

"Yes. Chrystel told me that you are too, and you have a partner named Derek. I am hoping that we can become friends. If I move here, it would be nice to have friends who think and feel like I do about things. Chrystel says that she is going to plan a party for this weekend, so I am hoping that you and Derek will come. We can get to know each other."

"That would be okay with us. Have Chrystel let us know what time, and we will be there. Sorry to cut this short, but I have to get back to the farm. It was nice meeting you." Keith walked away, headed toward the truck, and thought, *What a nice, pleasant, and very nice-looking guy. It would be great to have a friend who did not upset Derek the way Kyle and David do.*

∽ Chrystel prepared for her cookout party on Saturday. She went to the hospital and put up a notice on the bulletin board and let Kyle and David know about it. She wanted to have some fun, and it would be a way for everyone to get to know her cousin Galen. She was hoping that he would move here. She loved her friends — especially Derek — but it would be nice to have family around. She planned to confide in Galen about her feelings for Derek sometime when the subject presented itself, but not yet.

Chrystel ran into Kyle in the hall of the hospital. "Are you going to be able to make the party on Saturday, Kyle? I am inviting anyone who wants to come. My cousin Galen just came to visit and is thinking about moving here, so I want to introduce him to all my friends."

"Sure, you can count me in. Is Derek coming? Oh, I mean Keith too, of course."

Chrystel noticed that he added Keith as an afterthought. She knew that he did not have a chance with Derek because he and Keith were very solid. She knew that all too well. "Yes. They are both coming. Should be a fun time. Are you bringing David?"

"No! We are not together, Chrystel. I know that he wants to be, but we had our time and it is over, as far as I am concerned."

"Well, I did invite him. I hope that is not a problem for you."

"I don't care. He lives here unfortunately, but we are not a couple."

"Good. Maybe I can fix you up with Galen. He is gay and doesn't know anyone here but Keith."

"How does he know Keith?"

"He met him the other day when Keith came to the office with a question about one of their horses."

The loudspeaker blared, "DR. DOUGLAS TO THE OR, STAT! DR. DOUGLAS TO THE OR, STAT!"

"I've got to go, Chrystel. See you Saturday. Thanks for the invite."

⋙ "Derek, Chrystel is having a party on Saturday, and half the town is going. I told her that we would come too. Mr. and Mrs. Hawthorn will be here to oversee the horses, so let's go and have some fun."

"Sure, Keith. I would like to go to Chrystel's. When you say, 'half the town is coming,' what does that mean?"

"She put up a notice at the hospital."

"Oh, great! That means that we once again have to deal with Kyle and David. I can't believe that, no matter what we do, we can't get away from them. The party does not sound like so much fun anymore."

"You know, Derek, I am getting tired of this same conversation. Kyle and David are friends of Chrystel's, and she is our friend, so you have to figure out how to get over this thing you have about Kyle … whatever that might be," Keith said as he stormed out of the house. He was so over this. He thought that Derek was being juvenile and needed to grow up. After all, he was 38 years old, and it was 20 years ago that Kyle shunned him.

Derek thought about Keith's reaction. *What is my problem? I can't seem to get past this, and I know it is wearing thin with Keith. I don't want to lose him. I will talk to Kyle and try to resolve the feelings I am having. Keith is too important to me. Maybe I will call Jamie and talk to him. He knows the whole story, and he knew Kyle. That's what I will do!*

❧ The next morning, Derek called the Three M Ranch. Keith had gone out to exercise Shadow, and this was a good time to talk candidly with Jamie.

"Hello?"

"Jamie, it's Derek. I need to talk to you about Kyle. Can you talk now?"

"What's up, Derek? Is Kyle giving you a hard time?"

"No. He is really not doing anything, but I can't get him off my mind. It is terrible, now that I know he is gay. You know how much I loved him, and I know that he wants me. I love Keith, but I cannot deny that I am attracted to Kyle. I even imagined being with him while I was making love with Keith. That is the worst thing I have done. It is like cheating on Keith. He deserves better from me."

"Wait a minute … Kyle is *gay*? How do you know this?"

"Long story. I will tell you some other time."

"What makes you think that he wants you now? Has he made a move toward you to give you that impression?"

"I bumped into him the other day, literally. He had his arms around me to keep me from falling, and the feelings that stirred in me were devastating. He kept looking at my lips, and I knew that he wanted to kiss me ... and I wanted him to. I had to get away from him. It made me so angry, but then I went home and fantasized about him. I seem to be so angry all the time, and it is really affecting Keith and me. What should I do?"

"I think you should have a long talk with Kyle and try to sort out what this is all about. You are right. It is not fair to Keith if you still have feelings for Kyle. I am not sure about this, but I don't really think that you still care for Kyle. I believe that you love Keith, but these are just unresolved feelings that don't have much validity. After you have this talk with Kyle, then you can move forward. You may never be able to be good friends with Kyle, but you would not be so angry all the time when you were around him. Don't you agree that this might help?"

"Yes. I knew that you could help me. Changing the subject, how are you and Marc? How is Cheyenne? I miss you guys. The horses here are good. Mr. Hawthorn is such a great help to us. Shadow is doing well. He is such a magnificent horse. I bet you thank God every day that you bought him from Marc. Look how that all turned out! You guys were meant for each other and would never have met had it not been for that wonderful horse. Keith and I thought that you would never figure it out. Also, because of that horse, Keith and I found each other."

"I am an incredibly lucky man to have found my soul mate," Jamie agreed. "I am happy here. Little Mary is such a gem, and life could not be better. You and Keith will get back to that good place once you resolve this issue with Kyle. How is Kyle, by the way? How does he look? Is he a good doctor? Do you know anything about him now? Maybe he is a wonderful man and nothing like the jerk of 20 years ago. Have you even tried to get to know him?"

"No, I have not. Too much hurt and anger. Everyone here likes him a lot, and they say that he is a fantastic doctor. He is also really handsome. Do you remember his red hair when we were in school and that he was very thin? His hair has turned a darker auburn color, and he has filled out — heavier but not fat. His eyes are still an amazing piercing blue. God, listen to me, gushing over his looks. He is very attractive, but I have no idea how he is as a man."

"Derek, you have to deal with this, or it will eat you alive. I have to wonder myself, listening to you talk about him, if you are still in love with him. Maybe he is the love that you will never get over —the one that only happens once in a lifetime, like Marc and me. If that turns out to be the case, then you need to be honest with yourself, with Kyle, and with Keith. No one wins this way. Have you talked to Keith about him? Does he think you still have residual feelings for Kyle?"

"I think he did in the beginning, and probably still does if I was honest about it. I will have a talk with Kyle. Should I tell Keith that I am going to do this or just do it?"

"I think you should be honest and upfront with Keith that you want to talk with Kyle."

"Thanks, Jamie. I needed this talk. Give Mary a hug for me and tell Marc that we love you guys. Bye!"

Derek thought about his talk with Jamie and went to the stable to talk with Keith. Keith was riding Shadow, so Derek decided to wait until after Chrystel's party. He would arrange to meet with Kyle and have a talk.

The Party

On Saturday morning, Derek woke up after a difficult night's sleep. He had chills, and he felt like he had a fever.

Keith saw his face when he came down to breakfast. "Derek, you are pale as a ghost! What is wrong?"

"I don't know, but it seems to be some kind of a bug. You'd better stay away, or I will make you sick too. I really think that I should go back and lie down. Can you handle the chores today?"

"Sure. You go back to bed. Maybe you will feel better later. I will check on you in a while."

Derek went back upstairs. He was all bundled up in bed, drifting in and out of a restless sleep. He kept dreaming of Kyle kissing him and how good it felt to have his lips on his.

When Keith came up to check on him, Derek was covered up to his neck, murmuring something that he could not understand. He did, however, hear one word: Kyle. Keith stood still for a minute, feeling hurt and wanting to see if Derek would say anything else. Total silence! *Why is he calling Kyle's name? When he gets over this sickness, we are going to have a long talk and figure this out.*

❧ Derek came downstairs and was feeling better. His fever had broken, and he was not chilled anymore. Keith was sitting at the kitchen table, and Derek noticed that he was deep in thought.

Keith looked up and saw Derek standing there. "How are you feeling?"

"I am still not feeling well but certainly not as bad as this morning."

"I am going to call Chrystel to tell her that we cannot come to the party tonight."

Derek noticed that Keith was a little off but couldn't figure out why. "What is wrong with you? Are you getting sick too?"

"No. I am fine. We just need to call Chrystel," Keith said abruptly.

"No. You go for us. I will stay here and try to get over whatever this is. Chrystel will be so upset if both of us don't come. At least one can go."

"Okay. I will go. You stay here and get well."

When Keith left to go to Chrystel's, Derek was asleep again. He was still troubled by hearing Derek call out for Kyle but decided to deal with it later. Derek was too sick to talk about anything this important.

⇜ Keith arrived at Chrystel's house. The first person he ran into was Kyle. *I don't want to talk with him right now.* He walked over to a face he remembered and said, "Hi, Galen."

"Hi, Keith. I am so glad you came. Where is Derek? I was looking forward to meeting him."

Kyle was close by and heard Derek's name. He noticed that he was not with Keith.

"He is sick at home," Keith said. "I didn't want to leave him alone, but he told me to come and have some fun. I am going to get a beer."

"I will get you a beer," Galen offered. "How about sitting with me and talking? I would like to get to know you better. I will be right back."

As Galen went to get Keith a beer, Chrystel came over and sat down. "Where is Derek?"

"He is home sick."

She was so disappointed that he did not come. "Is it anything serious? Has he seen a doctor? Maybe Kyle should go check on him."

"No! He is fine. It is just a bug of some kind. He does not need a doctor." *Especially not Kyle,* he thought.

"Well, I am so glad that you came. I see that Galen is getting you something to drink. Food will be ready in a while. Maybe you can take some home to Derek later."

Galen came back with two beers and sat down beside Keith. "Can I tell you something without you freaking out?"

"Sure. I don't freak out easily. What?"

210

"I am attracted to you! I told Chrystel that I thought you were great looking and to introduce me to you when I saw you in her office the other day. She proceeded to tell me that you are spoken for. It was so strong of an attraction that I followed you, so I could introduce myself. I hate that you are with someone, but I still wanted to tell you. I have not been attracted to anyone like I was instantly with you."

Keith felt a little uncomfortable about what Galen said, but he was also flattered — especially with his bruised ego about knowing that Derek was thinking about another man. *Why shouldn't I be flattered? Maybe I will flirt a little, just to get even with Derek for making me think this way.*

Galen followed Keith to get another beer and thought, *Wow, what a great ass! Oh, yes, I want to get to know this gorgeous man better.* Galen's remark was out before he could think, but Keith hadn't responded. Keith was with Derek, and Galen had no reason to try anything with him.

After a few beers, Keith relaxed a little; in fact, he was kind of drunk. *I haven't eaten enough,* he thought, *but I like it.* Talking with Galen was easy, and he was really nice on the eyes. In his dizzy state of mind, Keith dared to talk about what Galen had said earlier. "Uh, Galen … what did you mean when you said that you were attracted to me?" A stupid question, he knew, but Galen was very willing to explain.

"Like I told you, I was very attracted to you from the moment I saw you. You have such calming, warm brown eyes that gleam with flecks of gold when the sun catches them. I wanted to kiss you on the spot the day I met you. You are very handsome, Keith." He caressed Keith's cheek lightly.

Without thinking, Keith leaned toward Galen, and Galen pulled him closer. After drinking so much, Keith didn't care or think about what he was doing, and he kissed Galen.

Galen didn't think either and opened his lips to touch Keith's tongue, very lightly. *God, this is so much better than I ever dreamed about! Keith is such a great kisser.* A shock went through Galen's body and, at that moment, Keith could have had him if he wanted.

❧ David walked over to Kyle. "Are you avoiding me tonight, Kyle?"

"No. I just don't want to talk right now. You need to find some other way of entertaining yourself and stay away from me socially. I do not want a relationship with you outside of work. I think I have made that clear."

"Oh, *really*? What about the night that you let me suck your cock?" David said, louder than he intended.

"That was just a lapse in judgment, and I needed sex. You were willing. That is the problem. You are always willing for anyone who wants to make the mistake of getting involved with you."

"You are only saying these things because you want Derek and can't have him. He does not want you, and he will never make you happy. When are you going to see that? You could have me all the time if you just remember how good we were together."

Kyle walked closer to David and grabbed him by the collar. He doubled up his fist and said, "Stay away from me! I don't want you now or ever again. Go hook up with someone else!"

Everyone at the party could hear their raised voices.

Chrystel immediately went over and pleaded, "Guys, please! No fighting here. This is a party. David, have you met my cousin Galen?"

"No, Chrystel. I have not." He gave Kyle a look that could kill, and then followed Chrystel to where Galen and Keith were getting drunk together.

Kyle had heard Keith say that Derek was at home sick. He thought that it might be the perfect opportunity to get Derek alone and find out if he had feelings left for him. Knowing how much Derek loved him back in school, his ego was big enough to hold onto the possibility that Derek wasn't over him completely.

Kyle watched Galen get Keith drunk. Maybe he would keep him occupied for a while, so he could have a chance to get Derek alone. This was what he had been hoping for! Kyle ducked out of the party without anyone noticing. David was talking and drinking with some other guys from the hospital, and Chrystel was busy entertaining her guests.

᳖ Kyle arrived at Keith and Derek's farmhouse and knocked on the door.

Derek yelled, "Did you forget your key again, Keith?" There was no answer, so he got up and went to let him in. When he opened the door, his mouth dropped open, and he was speechless for a second.

"Well, aren't you going to let me in, or do I have to talk to you out here in the dark?"

"What are you doing here? Where is David?" Derek's voice rose to a higher pitch. "Kyle, what are you *doing* here?"

Kyle moved swiftly before Derek had time to react and grabbed him. "I came for this," he answered, pulling Derek against his body with his face inches away from Derek. He moved in closer, all the while focusing on Derek's very kissable lips.

Derek felt that everything was moving in slow motion; in reality, it was amazingly fast when Kyle claimed his lips. Derek tried to turn his head to break the contact, but Kyle put his hands on each side of Derek's face and was not going to give up the fight.

Derek felt the reaction all the way down to his toes and back up to his groin. *God, how long have I waited for this moment?* He returned the kiss. He wrapped his arms around Kyle's neck and tried to get closer, even though there was no room between them.

Kyle moved from Derek's mouth to his ear and neck. "God, Derek! I want you so much that I can hardly stand it," he whispered.

Kyle's hot breath drove Derek crazy. He was totally lost in this moment. Kyle moved to Derek's chest, kissing his neck all the way down. Derek's breathing was becoming heavier with each touch of Kyle's lips on his skin.

Kyle could tell that Derek was getting very turned on. He looked into Derek's beautiful hazel eyes, which were shining green with passion. "I want you, Derek. I want you now. Let's go up to the bedroom."

This statement brought Derek to his senses. *Bedroom ... oh, my god ... OUR bedroom! Keith's and mine.* He pulled away from Kyle. "I can't do this with you. I am in love with Keith."

"Don't try to tell me that you are in love with Keith and that you no longer have feelings for me. I know better. Your cock tells a whole other story. You want me as much as I want you. Hard cocks don't lie. You want me to take you as much as I want to. You can deny it until doomsday, but you still want me after all this time."

Derek felt defeated. He knew there was some truth to what Kyle said. He hung his head and very quietly asked Kyle to leave.

Kyle stood there, looking at Derek and watching all the emotions pass across his face.

"Please. Please leave, Kyle."

◈ Galen looked at Keith with seduction in his eyes. He grabbed Keith and took him outside, past the garage where they could have some privacy. He couldn't believe that Keith had kissed him like that. He didn't want to think about the fact that Keith was with Derek. He could only think about his own needs right now, and he needed Keith.

Keith was a little dizzy. He had to sit. He grabbed Galen's hand and walked him over to a bench behind the garage. He sat down, opened his legs, and pulled Galen between them. Galen laid his hands on Keith's legs and started to caress them. Keith had a hard time concentrating, and his cock twitched in his pants. Galen's touch was tender but determined. As his hands slid to his thighs, Keith breathed in.

Keith looked at Galen, his eyes half closed and his mouth slightly open. Galen closed his eyes and bent down, searching for Keith's lips with his tongue. Galen knew that he was going to get what he wanted. Keith was his, at least for the night.

They went inside the house and walked to Galen's room. Galen could do with him what he wanted, and it was obvious that Keith wanted him. He did not care that Keith was drunk and really didn't know what he was doing, but something was driving Keith to continue, and Galen didn't think it was the beer.

Keith couldn't think anymore. He roughly touched Galen and needed to get him naked. His skin was soft, and his hands were driving Keith crazy when they slipped into his boxers. Keith shivered as his hands stoked him.

Galen didn't waste a minute. He grabbed Keith and put him on the bed, opened his pants, and pulled them down with his boxers in one move. He fell on his knees and took Keith's cock in his hand. He looked up one more time to be sure that Keith wanted this, and he did. Before he knew what happened, Galen licked his cock and his balls and took him in his mouth.

৶ Kyle looked at Derek. "You really want me to leave?"

Derek nodded.

Kyle took his face in his hands and forced Derek to look at him. "I only want to tell you that I love you, Derek. I do now, and I did in school. I'm sorry that I gave you such a hard time. I couldn't face it then, but now I'm ready, and you have a partner. It sucks!"

Derek looked at Kyle. "Yes, it does. I loved you so much, but now I'm happy with Keith. Please don't do this to me again."

Kyle caressed Derek's cheeks with his thumbs and kissed him softly on his lips. "I won't, Derek," he whispered. "You can trust me about that. But, if you ever need me, I will always be here."

Kyle went back to the party, wandering around with his mind full of thoughts about Derek. He went upstairs to find a bathroom when suddenly he stopped, shocked by the sight of a kissing and very aroused couple lying naked on a bed in one of the bedrooms. He reached for the phone in his pocket and took a picture of them.

৶ Derek sat on his couch, confused and sick. He could still feel Kyle's body touching his, and his hard cock aroused Derek almost to a point of no return. But he couldn't. He had Keith. Lost in thought, he was startled by the noise of his cell phone. He saw a text message and opened it, almost fainting when he realized what he saw in the picture.

After Kyle sent the text, he was sick that he did it. He hated the fact that he had hurt Derek like this. Once again, he was the cause of his pain and hurt.

Derek felt terrible. He had a headache and the fever made him shiver. Lying in bed, he tried to do some deep thinking as to what had happened. The picture that Kyle sent him was printed in his brain: Keith and this strange man having sex.

*Why did Kyle send this to me? Why does he always have to hurt me …
and now Keith too?* He texted Kyle, "You win. Once again, you have shown
me that I am not worthy of love. You turned on me when we were young,
and now Keith is in another man's arms. Who is this guy anyway? I guess
it doesn't matter. You win!"

Derek's self-confidence diminished by the minute. If he was honest
with himself, he thought too much about Kyle. He had been strong
tonight, but Kyle was right. His touch and kiss got Derek's body on fire.

Why wasn't Keith home yet? What did "home" mean? It was a place to
be safe and wanted. He wanted Keith; he had chosen to be with him. But
the devil had settled in his brain. It was not only Keith. He wanted Kyle
also, and Keith obviously felt the same way, or he would not have been
with this other guy.

He heard Keith unlock the door. Keith stumbled to the bathroom and
brushed his teeth for a long time, trying to hide the scent of another man.
He slipped into bed and whispered, "Are you awake, Derek?"

Derek didn't answer because he didn't know what to say. The smell of
sex hung in the air as tears dropped on his pillow. *So this is it. It happened.
Now what?*

Confrontation

The next morning, Derek got up first. He glanced at Keith and started to tear up all over again. *I can't look at him right now. I have to get out of here and think.* He jumped in the shower to wash off the sickness from the last 24 hours and got dressed. As he was leaving, he heard Keith stir. *I have to leave before he wakes up.*

Derek went to the main house and talked with Mr. Hawthorn to see if he would take care of his chores that day, and then left the farm. He wasn't sure where he was headed, but he knew that he needed to get away from Keith. He found himself at Kyle's farm, and Kyle's car was still there. *What should I do? Should I knock or just drive away? Why did I even think to come here?*

Kyle could not believe his eyes when he looked out of the kitchen window and saw Derek sitting in his truck. Before Derek could decide, Kyle ran out of the house and opened the door to the truck. "What are you doing here, Derek? Are you going to just sit there, or are you coming in?"

"I guess I just needed to have a cup of coffee and ended up here." Derek knew this sounded stupid, but that was all he could think to say. "As you know, Keith slept with some guy last night, and I don't know what I am doing. I can't figure out why except that you once again showed me that I am not someone whom anyone can really love. Why did he do this? I would never have been unfaithful to him."

"Get out of the truck and come in the house. You need to talk to someone. I can't think of a better person to talk to. I can prove to you that you are not at fault."

"Don't you have to be at the hospital this morning?"

"It is Sunday. I am off today unless they need me for an emergency. Come inside."

Derek followed Kyle inside and sat down on the couch.

"Do you want some coffee? Make yourself comfortable." He brought Derek a cup of coffee and sat down beside him. "I am so sorry for sending you that picture last night. I was upset that I wanted you, and he has you, and there he was having sex with someone else. I should never have done that. You did not deserve to find out that way, and you are wrong about not being worthy of someone loving you. *I love you* … always have. I did not win as you said in your text. I don't have the one thing I want more than anything in this world … you!"

"Kyle, what are you doing today? Do you have plans?"

"I was supposed to meet David for lunch, but I really don't want to do that. I hate being with him because he won't give up trying to start something again. I am sure that he is not planning on the lunch though because we got in a fight over you last night at Chrystel's party. I wanted to slug him, but Chrystel stopped me. What do you have in mind?"

"Well, I need to get away before Keith comes to find me. He will see my truck and know that I am here. I don't want to talk to him today. Not yet. Where can we go? We also need to talk about unresolved issues, so we may as well do that while we are talking through all this trouble." Then, it finally sunk in what Kyle said about David. "What do you mean that you almost fought over me last night?"

"That doesn't matter right now. I know a place that has a spa where we can go and relax and take all the tension away. It would be an incredibly quiet and peaceful place to talk, and Keith would never find you there. We will put your truck in my barn and drive my car."

"That sounds great. Let's go. You and I need to have a good, long talk. That was Jamie's advice."

"You talked to Jamie, and he told you to have a talk with me?" Kyle thought that this was a good sign. Derek obviously had been thinking about him if he needed to get advice from Jamie. He knew that Jamie hated him, so Kyle thought it was probably a very strange conversation.

"Yes. I am trying to get past the anger I have for being around you again."

"Okay. That is what we will do. Go and talk alone." It had such a great sound to Kyle. *Alone with Derek, far away from Berea, where no one can find us.*

◈ Kyle and Derek drove for about an hour. Kyle registered them into a private cabin in the mountains with a spa inside.

"This is a very private and peaceful place, so we can get into the hot tub and relax. I have ordered food to be delivered later along with wine and cheese. I want you to relax and talk to me."

They walked into a beautiful log home in a very heavily wooded area. It had a hot tub on the porch and one inside with a fireplace close by. Derek saw how romantic this place was and became worried.

"Why did you bring me here? Did you think that you would seduce me?" He was once again angry with Kyle.

"No, Derek. That was not my plan. Why do you always think the worst of me? I wanted to do something nice for you, so we could talk and sort out our relationship and your relationship with Keith." Kyle had good intentions where Derek was concerned and just wanted to help him.

"Okay. I am sorry."

"What do you say we get into the hot tub? There should be some bathing suits somewhere. Let's look and see if we can find them."

They found some suits in the closet by the hot tub. They changed in separate areas of the house. Derek was a little embarrassed about being so scantily clothed in front of Kyle. Kyle noticed how great he looked in the bathing suit and brought him back to the day at the pond when he watched him and Keith make love. Just thinking about it again gave him a hard-on. He needed to put some other vision in his mind. He was determined not to come on to Derek. He had promised him that this was a good talking session and nothing more. Kyle went to put on some music, thinking that it might help Derek relax.

Derek got in the hot tub and watched Kyle come back into the room, seeing him for the first time. He had never seen him in so few clothes since they had never been intimate. Derek noticed that he was really sexy and didn't want to take his eyes off what he was seeing. He noticed that Kyle's butt was perfect and his legs muscular.

Kyle noticed that Derek was looking at him. He climbed into the water opposite Derek. "Wow! This feels really nice, doesn't it?"

"Yes. Thank you for this. Kyle, will you answer a question?"

"Sure. Anything you want."

"Why did you turn on me so cruelly when we were in school? If you were gay, why couldn't you have just told me that you were not interested? Why did you have to call me a faggot? That hurt me to the very depth of my soul."

Kyle could see the emotion on Derek's face and knew that he could never make this right. He had hurt him more than he ever dreamed, and there was nothing left to do. After a long pause, he started to get out of the tub and said, "Derek, you should go back to Keith and forgive him for this one indiscretion. He made a mistake, but he loves you and deserves you."

"Stop! You still did not answer me."

"There is no answer. I was young and unsure of my own sexuality. It scared me that I was gay, and I thought I hated you for making me feel things that I thought I shouldn't be feeling."

"What were those feelings?"

"Derek, I told you … I wanted to make love to you. When you came near me, I got this urge to take you in my arms and kiss you, and I was not supposed to want a guy like that. I was supposed to want a girl. So I hated you for that … or I *thought* I hated you. To keep you away from me, I called you cruel names."

Derek moved across the tub toward Kyle. "Do you want me now?"

"God, Derek. Please move back to where you were. This is not fair."

Derek moved against Kyle, and Kyle moved away. Derek moved against him again.

"Derek, quit it! You don't know what you are doing. You are angry with Keith, and you are overreacting."

Derek got out of the tub, took off his bathing suit, and turned around to face Kyle.

Kyle lost his breath and whispered, "Derek, what are you doing?"

"Take your suit off, Kyle. What's that look? Haven't you ever seen a man naked before? Get out of your suit. Isn't it confining?"

"What are you doing, Derek? You can't do this!"

"Oh, yes I can. This is something that I have fantasized about for years. I have you here now, and I am not going to let this pass."

Keith had no idea what he did last night, thought Kyle, but he knew in his heart that Derek was just reacting and not thinking rationally. "No, Derek. You are reacting to a mistake on Keith's part, and you will regret this later. I will not take off my suit. You need to stay over there on that side of the hot tub, and we need to have that talk we came here for."

Derek moved over to Kyle and reached under the water for the top of his suit, pulling it down. "I want you, Kyle. Please make me yours."

Kyle couldn't stop the impulse to comply with Derek's wish. He stripped off his suit under the water and stayed right next to Derek.

Derek moved in even closer and begged, "Please put your arm around me and hold me for a while."

Kyle was dying at this point. "Derek, do you know what you are doing to me? I want you to be mine, and now you are offering me what I have wanted for 20 years. I am not sure what to do. I don't want to be your experiment or because you are mad at Keith."

Derek moved quickly onto Kyle's lap, facing him, and started to kiss him on his neck. Their cocks were touching under the water, and Kyle thought he had died and gone to heaven.

"Derek? You had better stop, or there will be no stopping me. Is this what you really want?"

Derek ignored him and kept his assault going with his lips and tongue. He licked a path from Kyle's ear to his lips, and then kissed him deeply. Then he licked down his neck, across his shoulder, and down to his nipple. He sucked it gently, and then went to the other one.

Kyle was losing control fast. "Derek, please!"

There was no stopping Derek. He wanted this.

Kyle put his arms around Derek's waist and moved his hips forward. He started moving his groin against Derek and reached under the water and put his hand around Derek's cock. He stroked him a couple of times, and Derek started moaning deep, guttural sounds. This set a fire in Kyle, and he could no longer control himself nor did he want to anymore. He put one finger inside of Derek and moved it in and out.

Derek loved this. He arched backward toward Kyle's finger. "Please, Kyle … more."

Kyle added a second and third finger and got Derek ready to receive him. When he thought he was ready, he raised Derek up, positioned himself at his opening, and then sat Derek down. The water helped Derek open up. Derek wanted and needed to go down on Kyle all the way, but Kyle wouldn't let him hurt himself. He wanted to go slowly with Derek.

Kyle moved a little farther in and then heard Derek say, "The hell with slow, Kyle. Take me all the way. I want you inside me. I want to feel each stroke as you move in and out."

Kyle pushed all the way in, and Derek bounced up and down on Kyle's cock. Kyle took hold of Derek and started stroking him again.

"Oh, god, Kyle. I am going to explode!" As Derek came down on Kyle's cock one more time, he came all over Kyle and in the water.

Kyle grabbed Derek's ass and moved in and out a few more times, and then came so strong inside of Derek. Derek fell forward against Kyle's chest and stayed there until he could breathe normally again.

Kyle held on to Derek. He had thought of this moment for so long and wanted to savor it. He had always loved Derek, but Derek was never his. Now, at this moment, he was. *Even if he doesn't stay with me, I have had my dream.*

They held each other and let the hot water soothe them. Derek was still sitting on Kyle's lap and lying against his chest. He was drifting off to sleep because he was very satisfied.

"Derek, what are you thinking and feeling right now?"

Derek was in heaven. "I am thinking that I am finally home." He knew that he should feel guilty, but that was the last feeling he had. He wanted to get himself together and start all over again. He wanted to show Kyle how much he wanted to please him too.

Kyle could not believe what he was hearing. *This can't be happening. I have wanted Derek for 20 years, and now I have him. What am I going to do next? I don't want to ruin this and lose him again.* "Derek, I think we really need to have that talk."

"No, Kyle. I want to keep making love. I don't want to talk."

"Come on. Let's get out of here and get dressed. I want to talk."

Derek had other plans, and they didn't include talking. He was going to make love with Kyle all day. It felt right. He knew that he would be able to persuade Kyle pretty easily. He knew that he had total control, and he loved it.

❧ When Keith woke up, he had a terrible headache, and it was not just because of the booze. His memory started to work. He reached out for Derek. He didn't have a strategy and didn't know if he was going to tell him right away what had happened last night. He didn't understand where the urge to be with Galen came from. He was cute all right, but he didn't love him nor would he ever. It was just pure sex. It was just physical. He had been horny and angry at Derek. He drank too much, and then it was all about need.

Derek was not there when he went downstairs. He went into the living room to see if Derek had left a note. There was nothing. He went to the barn to look for him and ran into Mr. Hawthorn, who was doing Derek's chores. Keith asked him if he had seen Derek. Mr. Hawthorn told him that Derek said he was going out for a drive and wanted him to do his chores.

Keith looked at his cell phone, and there were no messages. Suddenly, he saw Derek's phone on the table. He looked at the screen and saw the picture. It made him stop breathing. *God, no! Derek knows. He has left me.*

Keith fell on his knees. His brain was exploding with many thoughts. He knew that he had hurt Derek. He thought about last night. He tried to figure out at what point he had stopped thinking. It was not the beer; he couldn't use that as an excuse. He wasn't that drunk, at least not so much that it could explain what he did.

Kissing Galen was the moment. It felt so good. He didn't kiss any man like that except Derek. Kissing Galen was what he wanted to do, and he just wanted to have sex with the man he was kissing. Galen told him that he was sexy and how hot he was, and that turned him on, so he just went for it. And now he had to face the consequences. He had to think about what this meant to his relationship with Derek. Maybe they weren't as right for each other as they first thought. If they were, how could this have happened? He loved Derek, no question about that … but at this point, it didn't seem to be enough.

⮬ Derek did not want to stop making love with Kyle. He was doing something that he had always wanted to do, and it just seemed right. Kyle, on the other hand, was very worried. He let Derek have his way the rest of the afternoon, and then they had dinner sent in with wine.

"We need to have a talk, Derek. I don't want you to go back and feel guilty about what we did, and I don't want you to start hating me again. I could not bear that. I love you too much. Please let me be a part of your life. Let's get you home. It is almost 7 p.m. We have been here all day long with nonstop sex. I just hope that you won't regret today after you go back to reality. I love you, Derek, and I always have. Just remember that."

⮬ Derek and Kyle drove back to Kyle's farm. As they walked to the barn to get Derek's truck, they saw Keith come down the driveway. Keith took one look at Derek and Kyle and knew what had happened between them.

Keith got out of the car and walked over to Derek. "What have you been doing with Kyle all day, Derek?"

"What do *you* care? You had your fun with some stranger last night. Who was he anyway? Not that I care. Never mind. I am going to go home and take a shower. Kyle, we will talk tomorrow. Thank you for today." Derek got in his truck and drove home.

Keith took another step toward Kyle and told him to stay away from Derek.

"I will stay away from him if that is what Derek wants, not you," Kyle said as he walked into the house.

⮬ Keith followed Derek home. When he got there, Derek was already in the shower. He was sore and needed to rest. Keith went into the bathroom, opened the shower door, and turned off the water. Derek stood there, soaking wet and extremely uncomfortable.

Keith handed him a towel and told him that he could take a shower in a minute. "I want to talk to you, Derek. I *do* care. Tell me what you did with Kyle. I know that I hurt you, and you saw that picture of me and Galen."

"So that is his name. Galen! Galen *what*? Who is he?"

"Let me finish what I was saying, Derek. I don't know why it happened; it just did. I have to know. What did you do with Kyle?"

For some reason, Derek wanted to hurt and shock Keith. "We made love in every position imaginable. I let him have me, and I started it. He didn't want to make love to me at first, but I let him know that I wanted him inside me and every way. Because he loves me, he gave in, and I loved every minute. We did it over and over, and I am very sore. Are you satisfied now? I don't know what else to say. I know that we are going to have to talk about this and about where we will go from here, but right now I need to lie down."

Keith followed Derek into the bedroom. "You can't drop a bomb on me like that and then say, 'I have to lie down.' I don't *care* how sore you are, which, by the way, I am sure you deserve. We are going to talk," Keith said with venom in his voice.

"What is there to say right now, Keith? We both have been bad in the last 24 hours. Do you want me to say that I am sorry for what I did with Kyle? Well, I can't. Are you sorry for what you did with Galen?"

Keith stood there, not saying a word.

"That's what I thought. You are no sorrier than I am, so what do you think *that* means?"

"Derek, do you love me?"

"Yes, Keith. I love you more than you will ever know. Do you love me?"

"God, yes, Derek. I don't know why I had sex with Galen. I love you. I had some drinks, but that is not what I am using as an excuse. I really have none. I know why you slept with Kyle. I think you had to know if you were still in love with him. Are you?" Keith waited for Derek's response.

"I was so hurt when I saw the picture of you and Galen. I couldn't get it out of my mind. Then, when you came home, I could smell him on you.

You reeked of sex. I had to get out of here and away from you. I never intended to go to Kyle, but I ended up there because I didn't know where else to go. We went away to talk about our residual feelings because I did not want to be angry around him. Then, one thing led to another. I was all about the loss of us. The pain of seeing you with another, and then it was all about him and me. I can't say that I don't still have feelings for him, but I don't know what I want to do about them. He was my first love, and you never get over your first. I need some time to figure this all out."

"Did you enjoy him making love to you?"

"I can't say that I didn't. It would be a lie. I did love every minute. I know that hurts you, but it needs to be said. Did you enjoy being with Galen?"

"I did enjoy it. He is a really good lay, but that is all he is to me. You are what I want, so where do we go from here? Do you still want me, Derek, or are you not going to be satisfied with just me?" Keith waited for Derek's answer again. He hoped that he would be enough for Derek.

"Keith, would you lie in bed with me please? I can't talk to you about this when you are standing there all angry, with your arms crossed." Keith didn't know what he wanted to do. He didn't want to lie next to Derek. He knew that he couldn't resist those hazel eyes. He would have forgiven him without talking it out if it had been anyone but Kyle.

Keith hadn't realized that his body language had been so defensive. He wanted them to get over this. He wanted Derek, but why was he so aroused by the first man who came on to him? He didn't have special feelings for Galen; he hardly knew him. He was just Chrystel's cousin. But, when Galen seduced him, he was very willing.

"Keith … let's talk about all this tomorrow. I love you, but I also have extraordinarily strong feelings for Kyle. I have to figure this all out, but not now."

Reality and Truth

Kyle arrived at the hospital with a new outlook on life. He had just spent the entire Sunday with the man he loved and wanted to be with, and that man might want him too! As he was going down the hall, David yelled for him to stop, but he kept walking. He did not want to have a conversation with David and ruin his mood.

David followed him into his office anyway. "Can't you even give me the courtesy of talking to me about Saturday? We were supposed to have lunch yesterday, but you blew me off."

"What is there to say, David? I think I was pretty clear about how I feel about you. I do not want to have anything else to do with you, so you should have gotten the message about lunch. I will not let you mess up what I may have going now, so why don't you start looking for another relationship … or maybe even a new hospital and state."

David was terribly upset and hurt at how cold Kyle was behaving toward him. "So what is this good stuff happening to you? Please tell me that it has nothing to do with that damn Derek." After he said these words, he saw Kyle's face. "Oh, my god! It *is* about him, isn't it? Well, you need to get over him because he will never let you touch him. He hates you, and I love that he hates you. Besides, he is totally into Keith."

"Oh, is that *so*, Mr. Know-It-All? As a matter of fact, I …" Kyle stopped himself just in time. He did not want to share what he and Derek shared yesterday. It was none of David's business and very private. He gathered his papers and walked down to the surgery suite.

David would not give up and followed right on his heels. "Were you about to tell me that you fucked Mr. Perfect?"

Kyle turned around and slugged David in the jaw, knocking him onto the floor. Kyle was on top of him, getting ready to hit him again. The whole staff saw what had happened and came to break it up. They pulled Kyle off David. Kyle grabbed his fist and rubbed it because it hurt hitting him, but it felt good too.

"You are a piece of trash, David, and not worth any further thought," Kyle said as he walked into the surgery area to have his weekly meeting with the surgery staff, leaving David lying on the floor.

Everyone was shocked and helped David get up. He grabbed his jaw, and his nose was bleeding. One of the nurses told him that he should go to the ER to have someone look at his nose because it might be broken. Of course, the whole hospital was buzzing with the news within the hour.

David left the hospital after getting his nose set in the ER. It was broken, and his eyes were already turning black and blue. His jaw was also bruising and a little swollen. He looked like he had been in a bar brawl. Kyle landed a rather good punch, and David was very angry. He drove directly to the Walker farm and, as he drove up, Derek was coming out of the stables, leading a horse out to one of the fields. Derek stopped when he saw David get out of the car. He couldn't believe how badly he looked.

Derek was about to ask David what had happened. Before he got it out, David walked up to him and told him that Kyle was bragging all over the hospital that he had fucked Derek … that he was an easy lay … that anyone could have him. As a matter of fact, maybe David would try him because Kyle said he was so good. Maybe they would invite him for a threesome …

Derek wasted no time. It was all he could do to keep from punching David in his already broken nose. "What happened to your face, David? Did Kyle punch you? I don't know if he said those things or not, but your face tells me that something more than what you have said happened. I will find out the truth." With that, Derek tried to push him back into his car.

David got right into Derek's face and said, "You did let him fuck you, didn't you? You will never have him. I will never let him have you."

Derek pushed David into the car and told him to get off the property and never come back. If he did, he would call the police. David left. Derek decided that he would confront Kyle about what was or was not said.

◈ When Derek found Keith, he said, "I have to talk to Kyle. David was just here and said some vile things, and I need to know if Kyle said them or not."

"Surely you don't believe anything that David says. Why do you care? You know how he feels about you and Kyle. It is certainly obvious, to me at least, that he thinks of Kyle as his, and he hates you because he knows that Kyle wants you." It hurt Keith to say this, but it was true; he knew that Kyle wanted Derek. Did Derek want Kyle?

"I have to protect my reputation. David says that Kyle was bragging about me, and I need to know if it is true. I will be back as soon as I am done talking to him."

Derek got into the truck and drove to the hospital. When he pulled into the parking lot, Kyle was leaving. Derek got out, and Kyle came over, happy to see him. When he got closer, he saw that something was not right.

"Derek, what are you doing here? What is wrong? I can see that you're upset."

Derek just blurted it out. "Did you tell people at the hospital that you fucked me?"

"What? How can you *ask* me that? You know that I would never say something like that about you. I wouldn't and don't share my private life with anyone. My private life is my business and no one else's. Where did you hear this? It is a lie!" He grabbed Derek by the shoulders. "I would *never* do that."

Derek shook Kyle's hands off him.

"Derek, please don't do this. I would never do something as bad as this. I love you."

"Your boyfriend paid me a visit a little while ago and said that you were bragging all over the hospital that you fucked me, that I was easy, and that anyone could have me. As a matter of fact, David invited me to a threesome with the two of you. He wants to try me now that you say I am so good." Derek knew while he was saying these words that they weren't true because he could see the shock and confusion and hurt … yes, hurt … on Kyle's face, but he couldn't stop. The old anger was back. He was ready to believe the worst of Kyle. He had to get out of there before he said anything else. He turned to go back to the truck, but Kyle grabbed his arm.

"Don't do this, Derek. You can't do this. You should know me better than this."

Derek shook out of his grip and kept walking away.

"God, you are a hateful man! Why do I keep trying to make you understand how I feel about you when you truly don't want to see it? Go back to Keith and stay away from me. Anyone who could think that I am that evil is someone I don't need in my life." Kyle got in his car and drove off, leaving Derek standing by his truck.

Derek knew that he let his venom and anger resurface and started thinking irrational thoughts about Kyle. He knew from the way David looked when he came over that Kyle had not said those things and probably punched him out when he said something bad about him. *Why can't I let this anger go when it comes to Kyle? I do have feelings for him. Strong feelings. I may even still love him, yet I hurt him and think the worst automatically. Jamie was right. I really don't know what kind of man Kyle is today. I only think of him as the cruel teenager 20 years ago. I need to get away for a while. I will call Jamie and take a trip to Cheyenne.*

Derek drove back to the farm and looked for Keith. He found him in the bedroom, lying on the bed. "What is wrong with you? Did you catch the bug that I had the other night?"

"No. I'm just lying here, wondering what you and Kyle were doing again. I can't get that image out of my head. You and Kyle in bed or wherever."

"You know what? I can't get the image out of my head of you and the guy you were fucking, so I need to get away for a while. I am going to take a trip to Cheyenne to visit Jamie and talk to him about this whole ugly mess. He knew Kyle when we were in school. He is the only one who will understand right now. I am going to make reservations to Cheyenne, and then call Jamie to tell him that I am coming."

He left Keith lying on the bed with his thoughts. He really didn't care right now what Keith was thinking. If they had a chance to be together, he had to do this.

He called Jamie and made plans to fly to Cheyenne in the morning. Jamie told him to come, and they would talk as much and as long as he needed. Mr. Hawthorn said that he would help Keith with the work. Everything was arranged.

Derek went back upstairs and started packing; Keith just watched from the bed. Finally, he asked Derek what happened when he went to see Kyle at the hospital.

"I told him off and told him to take his hands off me. I could not let myself believe that he did not say those things. I knew that he didn't say them because David had a broken nose and a swollen jaw, so it was obvious that Kyle had punched him out, but I still couldn't let the anger go. It came back. He finally told me that basically he was done with me."

That scared Keith because it might make Derek want Kyle even more. "And what was your reaction to that?"

"I didn't get a chance to react because he stormed off. I guess he has had enough of my anger, just like you." He finished packing and got into his side of the bed, turning his back on Keith.

Keith did not know what else to say either, so they slept next to each other without touching for the first time — not even kissing goodnight.

Back to Cheyenne

The next morning, Keith drove Derek to Lexington to catch a plane to Cheyenne. They both were pretty quiet in the truck on the way to the airport. Finally, when they got there, Keith took Derek in his arms and told him that he loved him. "Hurry back to me."

Derek told Keith that he loved him too, but he needed to do this. "I will call you when I get settled and check in every day."

During the plane ride, Derek thought about the last weekend. *What happened? In the course of 48 hours, Keith had been unfaithful, and I gave into my feelings and yearnings for Kyle. Then there was the fight with Keith, and the fact that Kyle walked away from me permanently — or so it seems. Let's not forget David and his cruel words and threats. Do I need to worry about his threats?* He was brought out of his thoughts when they announced the preparation for landing.

Jamie was waiting for him at the baggage claim. They hugged. It was so good to see him again.

"Where are Marc and Mary?"

"Mary is in school," Jamie explained. "Karen is going to pick her up, and Marc is on a short business trip to get another horse for our stables."

"Wow, Little Mary is old enough for school now?"

"Well, yes. She is in kindergarten. She loves it too. She will be extremely excited to see you. She misses you guys. So tell me what is going on with you. Are you and Keith okay?"

"No, we are not. He is upset because I have all this anger over Kyle and can't seem to let it go. So he cheated on me with some man he just met, and then I turned to Kyle and we made love all day the next day. What a mess."

Jamie was in shock. "Derek, what in the *world* is going on with you two?" He knew there were some problems concerning Kyle but nothing this serious.

"Can we talk about it later when we get to the ranch?"

"Sure, whatever you want. I am here for you to vent with and talk with and hopefully help you understand your feelings."

⋙ Kyle had gone home after his confrontation with Derek in the hospital parking lot. He had no idea why he said what he said to Derek. He could never walk away from him, but he couldn't believe how hurt he was that Derek believed the vile things that David had told him — especially after the amazing day that he and Derek had spent on Sunday. Then it dawned on him that he was right about Derek using him to get back at Keith for cheating, which hurt even more. He decided to stay away from Derek. It was too hard to be around him.

The next day, Kyle went to Chrystel's house after his rounds at the hospital. He had also avoided David most of the day. David didn't seem to want to run into him either. Kyle wanted to talk about the whole mess with Chrystel and tell her that he could not be friends with Keith and Derek anymore.

"Come in, Kyle. How have you been? I didn't get to see much of you at the party on Saturday night. Did you have fun?"

Galen walked downstairs to get a cup of coffee. "Kyle, do you remember Galen?"

"Yes, I do. How are you, Galen?"

"I am fine. I just told Chrystel that I have arranged to move here from Chicago. I will find an apartment and then move my stuff. It should be easy because I don't have any furniture, just my clothes and a computer. I am renting a furnished apartment in Chicago now. Chrystel says I can live here, but I feel that we both need our own space and privacy. I met a guy at the party who is looking for a roommate, so I think I may do that. His name is David Jenkins. Do you know him?"

Kyle just about fell off his chair! "Yeah, you could say that. He is not a nice person, but he is well thought of around here. He is a doctor with me at the hospital."

Chrystel had forgotten to tell Galen that David and Kyle used to be a couple.

"How do you know him? He seems really nice, and he is gay, which makes it easier for me. We think the same way about some things, if you know what I mean."

"Yes, I certainly do, and you have more in common than you know." Kyle was thinking about seeing Galen in bed with Keith. He knew that Keith was with someone but did not care. "David and I were together for a few years, and then he cheated on me. I came home early one day and caught him in bed with a friend of ours. Needless to say, that was the end. That was nine years ago. He followed me here, thinking that he could win me back, but there is absolutely no chance of that ever happening. I will give you a word to the wise: Don't get involved with him in a personal way. He will cheat on you too. He does not know how to be faithful, but maybe that is not a problem for you like it is for me."

"It is for me too," said Galen. "I don't believe in people who are in a relationship and then cheat on their partner."

Kyle doubted these words but, after all, he didn't really know this guy other than seeing him naked with Keith.

"Galen, can you leave Kyle and me alone?" Chrystel asked. "We would like to catch up. Aren't you supposed to meet David to talk about the apartment?"

"Yes, and I am going to be late. It was nice to see you again, Kyle. Hope we will see each other again."

"I am sure we will. It is a small town, and Chrystel is a good friend of mine."

Galen left the house and drove off.

"Okay. What is *wrong* with you, Kyle?"

"Chrystel, have you seen Derek or been to the Walker farm since your party?"

"Yes. I was just there a little while ago to check on the horse that has a growth on his lower leg. Why?"

"How was he?"

"I don't know, Kyle. He is gone! Keith said he left today for Cheyenne indefinitely. He has no idea when he is coming back. He even said that he may never be back, but I don't believe that because this is where he is from. Keith wouldn't tell me what was going on, but I know that something is very wrong over there. Do you know what it is about?"

Kyle was suddenly sick to his stomach. "Yes, I know what is wrong. It is a long story. Do you have time to talk?"

"You are scaring me, so you'd better spit it out. I know that you are somehow involved because I have seen Derek's reaction to you from the first day, and we have talked. I know you are in love with him the same as me. I know I can never have him, but you do have a possibility of that since he is gay. I think it is a slim chance though because of his feelings for Keith, but still …"

"Yes, I am in love with him, and he is in love with me. I honestly believe that. He just can't accept it yet. But now it doesn't matter because I told him that I was done with him. I am tired of being hurt by his rejection and his anger, and the hatred that he shows when he is around me. He also let me make love to him all day on Sunday, and then turned on me. I was happy, and I know he was too. He told me that he felt like he was home. Then David and his venom ruined it, and once again Derek went back to hating me."

"Oh, my god, Kyle! You made love to Derek? How did that happen? What about Keith? How could Derek do that? How could *you*? Especially after the way David treated you. How could you be a part of Derek cheating on Keith?" Chrystel was appalled. These were her friends. She was also very jealous that Kyle had Derek and she could never have him.

"Well, let me tell you what happened at your party on Saturday. Galen took Keith upstairs and had sex with him until extremely late while Derek was home sick. I'm not sure how they got up to the bedroom without you seeing them, but there is a picture of the two of them in a bed, going at it like rabbits, and Derek saw that picture."

Kyle didn't want to tell Chrystel that he had taken the picture of Keith and Galen because he loved her very much and didn't want her to think badly of him.

He continued. "Derek came to me the next day and wanted to talk. We had already arranged to talk out all the anger and such from years ago, so that we could somehow be friends. Derek wanted to go somewhere that Keith would not find him because he was not ready to talk with Keith about what he saw. I took him to a cabin in the woods, so we could be totally alone and talk out all this mess. I promise you that was all I planned to do. I just wanted him to feel safe, so that we could really bare our souls and clear the air, and maybe somehow end up with some kind of relationship."

"So how did it change?" Chrystel asked. "I guess Derek shared with you what Keith had done. I still can't believe that! I knew Galen was attracted to Keith but never dreamed he would do this. I know they both had a little bit too much to drink, and I did see them close together and talking but really didn't think anything was wrong with it. So how did this go from you guys talking to making love?"

"Well, believe it or not, I did not start it. Derek did. I really tried to get him to stop, but he was just feeling pain because of what Keith had done. He said that, when Keith came home early Sunday morning, he reeked of sex. He could smell it on him. He knew what he had been doing. I tried to talk with him about this whole situation.

"All of a sudden, he took off his clothes and wanted me to make love to him. Even then, I tried to stop him, but he would not take no for an answer, and I am only human. I love him and wanted him very much for 20 years. He was ready to give me what I wanted, and I finally gave in.

"After we made love, I told him that we should get dressed and talk, but he refused. He said that he felt like he was finally home and wanted to make love all day. I took him back to my house at 7 p.m. Just as we got there, Keith was coming down the driveway. I don't know what happened between them after that, but they went home.

"The next day at the hospital, David confronted me about Derek, saying really foul things about him, and I knocked him to the floor. I broke his nose, and his jaw was swollen. It felt good too. Now the whole hospital knows that we came to blows outside of surgery.

"The next thing I know, Derek arrived at the hospital to see me. I was so happy to see him when I came out of the building, but then he laid it on me. Derek said that David had told him that I was bragging at the hospital that I fucked him, that he was easy, and that anyone could have him. David also told Derek that, since I had said that he was so good, he decided he would try him. He even invited Derek to a threesome with David and me.

"I was shocked that Derek could believe that of me and very hurt. I would *never* do that. My private life is very private, as you know. It is no one's business what I do. I finally had what I have wanted for so long. Why would I throw that away by saying things like that? Derek should have known I would never do that, but he was not hearing me.

"So I finally had enough of Derek's anger and hatred, and I told him that I was done. I did not want someone in my life who could think I was that evil. I walked away from him and left him standing there. I have not seen him since." Kyle hung his head at this point and just let it all out. The tears flowed, and he felt like he was at the end of a long road. He was totally exhausted. His emotions had been all over the place since Saturday.

Chrystel came around the table and put her arms around Kyle. "Let it out, Kyle. You need to release all of this pent-up emotion. Thank you for telling me. You know that I will keep it private and will never share this with anyone."

"I know that, Chrystel. You are the only one I could talk to about this. With both of us loving Derek, you know how hard it is. I love him so much. I would give my life for him if I had to. It hurt me so deeply when he thought that I would say those things about him. I know now how much I hurt him 20 years ago when I called him a faggot. I feel that deep pain now.

"There isn't anything I wouldn't do for him. I would even walk away if he wanted to be with Keith. I did not want him to cheat on him with me, but I couldn't stop him once he was determined. I wanted him too much. I know that is a cop-out, but it is the truth. I was not strong enough to resist him. But it really doesn't matter because I can't go back with him now. I can't deal with his anger and hatred anymore. Now that we made love and were as close as two human beings can be, I can't go back to that. He will sort this out with Jamie and then come back to Keith. I will keep my distance and, if it gets too hard to avoid him, then I will start looking for another job at another hospital and put lots of distance between us."

Chrystel's heart was breaking for Kyle. She knew that she could never leave Berea as long as Derek was here. She did not know how Kyle would be able to leave for the same reason, but she felt that it was a little different for her because she could still remain close to Derek by being his friend, but Kyle would never be able to do that. "What are you going to do about David? I hope Galen will not rent with him now, but he is a grown man, and I can't tell him why he shouldn't be around David."

"I know that Galen is your cousin, but I think he and David will get along very well because they are the same ... just wanting to satisfy their primal needs and not worry about what consequences could come from their actions or who gets hurt. Wow ... I just thought of something. Maybe that would be an answer to my prayer. If Galen and David got together, then David will stay out of my life. It is bad enough that I have to work with him, but I don't want anything to do with him. And trust me, I will get him out of Berea Hospital as soon as I can. I will find a way to get rid of him. Let them go fuck each other all day, every day ... that would be a beautiful thing."

It hurt Chrystel a little because she loved her cousin, but she totally understood Kyle's position. "What does Keith say about all of this? I assume he knows about you and Derek."

"Oh, yes, he knows. Derek didn't mince words about telling him. Keith told me to stay away from Derek. I told him I would do that when Derek told me to, not him. But that is a moot point now. I made the decision to stay away on my own. Remember, Keith is not innocent in any of this either. He slept with Galen, and I am sure he told Derek about that too."

~§ Galen came back and told Chrystel and Kyle that he and David were going to rent a place on campus, close to the hospital. They looked at it and signed the lease. David was going to check out of Jean's B&B where he had been staying and move into the new place right away. Then, he would head back to Chicago to get his stuff packed and be back as soon as he got it all wrapped up.

Kyle and Chrystel looked at each other and then at Galen as he bounded upstairs. "Okay. This should be interesting," Kyle said, shrugging his shoulders.

Galen came back down and stuck his head in the door again. "Oh, by the way, you should see David's face! He said that he ran into a door in the dark and broke his nose. He looks awful … like he had been in a bar fight with some rednecks."

Chrystel and Kyle laughed as Kyle rubbed his knuckles again. Galen missed that.

∽ In Cheyenne, Derek unpacked and came downstairs. He saw Jamie and went over to him.

Jamie said, "I will have Maurice get Betsy to fix us some lunch, and we can sit down and talk."

"Okay. I am so confused. I just had to come here to see if you could help me sort all this out."

They sat down to eat and talked about casual things: what was going on with the horses and Shadow; how Mr. and Mrs. Hawthorn were doing; the farm and the wonderful pond that Jamie missed so much now that he was in Cheyenne. It was always his favorite place on the farm. It was also Derek's favorite place, and he loved making love to Keith down there.

After lunch, Jamie and Derek retired to the den and told Maurice to make sure they were not disturbed. Karen was to take care of Mary until they had time to get some of the talking done. Of course, they knew that they would not be able to settle anything in just one talk, but they were going to get the recent information on the table.

"Why don't you start by telling me why you felt the need to leave Berea and come here so suddenly?" Jamie began. "I know that it is all about Kyle, so let us start there. How are you feeling about him? What do you think this is all about?"

"Well, I don't know where to start really, but I will try to give you an overview. When Kyle came to town, all the hurt and anger rushed back like it was yesterday. I had not been able to deal with him in any capacity. He tried to be friends with Chrystel, Keith, and me, but I could not stand to be in the same room with him. As time passed, I realized that part of it is because I still have feelings for him, and I'm not sure how to deal with them. Everyone in town loves him … I hear that he is a particularly good doctor and chief of staff. The staff is always saying good things, but I can't get over this memory of him calling me a faggot. So I have been fighting these feelings about him and my attraction to him. I even started dreaming and fantasizing about him when Keith was making love to me. I think that was the worst feeling."

"Does Keith know that you were doing this?"

"No, at least not at first. Now he does though."

"What do you mean? Did you tell him or call out his name, or something like that?"

"No … you haven't heard the worst of it yet. Keith had been quite upset with me over Kyle. He was convinced that I still had feelings for him, and he was right. He was also tired of my anger and hatred for Kyle. Then, the other night — Saturday to be exact — Keith went to a party that Chrystel held at her house, and then went to bed with her cousin in one of her upstairs bedrooms!"

"He *what*? Where were you?"

"I was sick in bed with some kind of bug. I told him to go because I was just too sick. So he went."

"But what made him have sex with this guy? Did he know him?"

"No. He had just met him a few days before the party, but he fucked him over and over that night. He came home reeking of sex. I could smell the guy all over him."

"How did you find this out? Did Keith tell you when he got home?"

"No. When Kyle heard that I was sick, he came over to see if I still had feelings for him, but I shut him down. I have to admit that I wanted him when he kissed me, but I couldn't do it when he mentioned going up to the bedroom. That brought me to my senses, and I asked him to leave, which he did without giving me any trouble. Before he left, he told me that he was in love with me and always had been. That was all there was to it until he went back to the party and walked by the bedroom where Keith and this guy were going at it. Kyle took a picture and sent it to me on my phone."

"Oh, my god, Derek! That was horrible to find out that way and for Kyle to send it to you."

"Yes, and he was so sorry after he did it. The next day, I had to get away from Keith, so I got in the truck and started driving, unsure of where I was going. I ended up at Kyle's farm and told him that I didn't know why I was there, but I really wanted to talk to him. He agreed that we needed to talk.

"I told him that I had talked to you, and he agreed that you and I should talk more about the situation. He said that he would take me somewhere where Keith would not find me because I told him that was what I wanted. We put my truck in his barn and left in his car. He took me to a cabin in the mountains. It was beautiful and had a hot tub. I noticed how romantic it was, but that was not why we were there. Kyle also told me that he was sorry that he had hurt me again for sending that picture. For some reason, I believed him and was glad that he had sent it to me."

"So what happened then? You had sex with him, didn't you?"

"No. Don't say that. We made love; it wasn't just sex. I wanted to be with him. He made me feel like it was where I belonged. I felt like I had come home. I also want you to know that he didn't start it either. I did. He tried to get me to stop, but I didn't want to. He even begged me to stop because he was only human, but I wanted him. I WANTED HIM! Oh, wow! What have I done? I do want him … always have … and now he doesn't want me."

"What do you mean he doesn't want you? He has *always* wanted you from what I can tell, even 20 years ago when he was afraid to admit it. I don't understand you."

"He has finally had enough of my anger and hatred. He says he doesn't want me in his life anymore. He wants to be rid of me once and for all."

"*Who* wants to be rid of you?" Marc asked as he walked into the room. "No one could ever want to be rid of *you*!"

Jamie and Derek jumped up to hug Marc. Jamie was still like a love-struck schoolboy when he looked at Marc.

Derek noticed how cute they were around each other. They couldn't seem to get enough. "It is so good to see you, Marc!" Derek said as they all sat down.

"What are you doing home, Marc?" Jamie asked. "Not that I am complaining!" He leaned in and kissed him.

"The deal for the horse fell through, so I decided to come back home to my love." Marc squeezed Jamie's knee. "So what is going on? Where is Keith? Is he out at the stables?"

"He is not with me. I came on my own because I wanted to talk with Jamie about a problem I have about some unresolved feelings. Keith stayed home. I need to be away from him right now."

Marc turned to Jamie with a concerned look. "Please tell me that you two are not having trouble. You guys are perfect together and so much in love, like Jamie and I are."

"Well, I am not so sure of that now. I can't imagine that you would cheat on Jamie or Jamie would cheat on you. That is exactly what happened to Keith and me. He slept with a total stranger whom he had just met a few days before a party that Chrystel gave at her house. I didn't go to the party because I was sick in bed. When he came home, I could smell sex all over him. I could not even talk to him, so I pretended to be asleep."

Marc was speechless. He did not know what to say. How could that be? He knew that Keith was in love with Derek. He had told him so many times when they talked on the phone. "I don't know what to say, Derek. What does Keith use for an excuse? I guess nothing because there is no excuse. I am extremely disappointed in him. I never thought he was like that."

"Please don't judge him too harshly because I am sure it was my fault. He knew that I had feelings for another man, and it finally drove him to it. I am not innocent either because now I have been unfaithful too. So we are both messed up right now, but I take full responsibility for this because I do have feelings for someone else." Derek looked over at Jamie. "Have you told Marc about my history with Kyle Douglas?"

"Yes. I have told him the story of when you two were in high school."

"So this is about Kyle? Are you involved with him?"

"No. I am not really involved, Marc. It's just that he has come back into my life, and I have never really gotten over him after 20 years. He has returned to Berea, and we run into each other all the time because he is friends with Chrystel and the whole town loves him. But I have slept with him now, and I am more confused than ever."

"Boy, when you guys screw up, you *really* do it good, don't you? This is going to be more in Jamie's area, especially since he knows this guy. But I will tell you this: I don't approve of being unfaithful, but I do know that Keith loves you more than anything. So I guess you have to decide what you want and, if it is Keith, if you can forgive him and if he can forgive you. We love you both, so I am hoping that you guys work this out. We will support you in whatever decision you make. Right, Jamie?"

Jamie nodded.

Marc got up to head for the stables and added, "I will see you later."

"You guys are so lucky to have each other. You make me wish that I could have this same kind of love and relationship, and I thought I had it with Keith. But now …"

"You will figure this out. You don't have to do it in one day. Let's find Karen and play with Mary. It'll take your mind off this for a while."

"Good idea. I can't wait to see that sweet angel again!"

᪐ The next day, Keith awoke after hearing a car in the driveway He jumped up, thinking it might be Derek coming back to him already. When he looked out the window, he saw that it was Kyle. *Why is that bastard here?*

Kyle knocked on the door.

Keith went downstairs to see what he wanted. "What are you doing here? Derek is not home."

"I came to talk with you, Keith. I know that Derek is not here."

"Of *course*, you do! I am sure that Derek told you his plans," he said sarcastically.

"He did not call me nor would he after Monday. Chrystel told me that he was gone. I need to clear up something with you, Keith. Derek and I are not going to be together. He will talk things out with Jamie, and then come back to you. He made it abundantly clear that he will never get past his anger and hatred toward me, and I can't deal with it anymore. So I have told him that I am done."

"Wow, you finally broke him down and got him to sleep with you!
You got what you wanted, and now you are throwing him away. I have
never really liked you because of the way you affected Derek when he was
around you, but I knew that you were in love with him … or so I thought.
It was all about just wanting him. You cad!"

"Excuse me? That is like the pot calling the kettle black! Who cheated
on Derek with the first guy who came along? NOT ME! You are wrong
too. I am in love with Derek, and I believe that he is in love with me, but
that doesn't matter anymore. He is yours! I have walked away.

"When he believed the foul words that I was supposed to have said to
David about him, I realized that there was no future for Derek and me.
I can't do anything to get him past this hurt, and he now has hurt me too.
So that is the way it is. You can't build on a foundation that has no trust,
regardless of how much you love each other. I do hope that you two can
figure it out and start building the trust again. You can depend that I will
avoid Derek as much as possible in a small town like this. If I find that it
can't be done, then I will look for another hospital to go to." Kyle turned
and left before Keith had a chance to react.

Keith was taken aback by this turn of events and realized the depth
of Kyle's love for Derek. He was not sure that he could walk away from
Derek and be happy with someone else. He hated to admit it, but he
gained new respect for Kyle.

⚘ On this beautiful morning, Derek decided to take a long ride on one
of the horses. His mind was all over the place. He wanted the feel of the
wind in his hair as he rode as one with the horse. He thought it would
clear his head and help him think better.

He and Jamie had talked late into the night after putting Little Mary
to bed and having dinner and wine with Marc. He loved being back here.
The Three M Ranch was three times the size of Jamie's farm. There were
plenty of acres to run a horse free, at full gallop.

As Derek rode, Jamie noted how great Derek looked on the palomino
that Marc had picked for him. His hair was almost the same color as the
horse. Jamie took a picture without Derek knowing and sent it to Kyle. He

did not know why he needed to do this, but he felt in his heart that Derek would return to Berea and be with Kyle, not Keith. This broke Jamie's heart a little because he and Marc loved Keith and he never liked Kyle very much, but Derek loved him; he was sure of that. Jamie knew this was true because Derek would not have slept with Kyle if he didn't.

Derek rode for hours, stopping once to rest the horse by a stream that ran through the property. While the horse drank, Derek sat under a tree. He closed his eyes and relived the events of the last few days. He could feel Kyle next to him and remembered the words David had said. He also remembered what Keith had done. *How did all this get so messed up so quickly? I am in love with Kyle, and I need to go back and tell him, and then tell Keith my decision. He will be devastated, but it is unfair of me to keep him hanging on to the hope that I will stay with him. I have always been in love with Kyle and will never get over him. I know that now. When we made love, it felt so right. It was where I belonged for over 20 years.*

Derek fell asleep under the tree, thinking about all this. While he was sleeping, he dreamed about Kyle walking away and telling him that he was done. He said out loud, "No! No!" He woke up just as another rider appeared.

Jamie had come looking for him because he was gone so long. He remembered when Keith was thrown off the horse and had almost died. Derek had been gone since breakfast, and it was past lunch and heading to dinnertime. He did not realize that he had slept so long. His horse was grazing close by when Jamie got there.

"You had us worried, so I came looking for you."

"I am sorry I worried you, Jamie. I have been thinking, and then I fell asleep."

"When I rode up, you were yelling in your sleep, 'No! No!' What was *that* about?"

"I was remembering Kyle walking away from me and telling me that he was done. What am I going to do, Jamie? I am in love with him and want to go back to him, but now he doesn't want me. How am I going to get him to take me back?"

"I knew this was going to be your final decision about Kyle. You have always loved him, and that is a love you never get over. I am sorry for

Keith though. He loves you so much, and he deserves to be happy. I don't know how Kyle is going to react to this news. I think he will be so happy that you chose him and forget what he said about being done. You know that he is not my favorite person because of the way he hurt you, but if he is what you want, then Marc and I will support you all the way. Come on. Let's go back to the house and clean up before dinner."

"Can we stop by Mary's memorial stone where we spread her ashes? I want to visit with her for a while, and I know her spirit is still around her favorite spot on the ranch."

"Sure! You ride over there, and I will head home and tell Marc that you are okay. He will be waiting to hear. Take all the time you need, Derek. There is still plenty of time before dinner."

Jamie rode back to the ranch house while Derek rode to the area where Mary's stone was placed in memory of her. He tied the horse to the gate that Jamie and Marc had put around her stone. They wanted some permanent place to visit with Mary. It always made them feel close to her.

Derek walked over to the stone and sat down. He always felt such peace talking to Mary, even though he never knew her. Every time he and Keith came to visit, they would all ride out there to pay their respects. He also used to come by himself sometimes after Jamie talked about how he loved to sit and talk with her and how much it helped him when he was having all the problems and separations with Marc. Derek had seen pictures, and she was identical to Marc. She was so beautiful with her long, flowing black hair. He felt it was such a waste that God took her so young.

"Mary, it is me, Derek ... remember? I wanted to come and talk with you for a while. I need your help with something. I have told you so many times how happy I was and how much I loved Keith, but now things have changed. I do still love Keith, but I am not in love with him. I love another man whom I have loved almost my whole adult life and finally have come to terms with that. But he doesn't want me, and I am hurting Keith. I can't help that I love this other man ... the heart wants what the heart wants." Derek knew that Mary could not answer him, but it helped him by saying it out loud to her. He stayed there for a long time, and then said his goodbyes and rode back to the house.

༄ Kyle was sitting in his office at the hospital when he received a text message on his cell phone. *It had better not be David,* he thought as he picked up the phone. He was stunned! He could not believe the vision on his phone: Derek was sitting on a beautiful horse, looking like he was getting ready to ride off. He was magnificent with his light brown hair almost the same color as the horse. What a site! He also could not believe who sent the picture or why.

It broke Kyle's heart to look at it, knowing that he would never be with Derek. It was almost cruel of Jamie to have sent it, but he could not bring himself to delete the picture. He decided that, since he would not have Derek anymore, he would have his picture blown up and framed to keep with him always.

He sent a text back to Jamie: "Thank you!"

Staying away from Derek was going to be the hardest thing Kyle ever had to do, and he knew it.

Home Is Where the Heart Is

Derek had a nice final evening with Jamie, Marc, and Little Mary, and he decided that it was time to go home and straighten out everyone's life. His talks with Jamie had really helped. He was ready.

He made arrangement to fly home the next day but did not tell Keith. He wanted to see Kyle first and convince him that he was past the anger and that he never believed what David said. He needed Kyle to take him back.

Once he was back in Berea, Derek arranged for a car service to take him to Kyle's house. They dropped him off and left. Derek put his suitcase on the ground, walked up to the front door, and knocked, but there was no answer. Kyle's car was there, so he knew that he was home. When Kyle didn't answer the door the second time, Derek went to the barn. He found Kyle working on a woodworking project, so he walked in and called his name.

Kyle turned around and looked straight at him. "Derek, you need to leave now. I have nothing to say to you."

Derek ignored him and came close. "Please listen to me, Kyle. I am in love with you and have come back to tell you that I want to be with you. I will tell Keith later."

Kyle almost took him in his arms but then remembered his vow. "How can you be in love with someone as evil as me? I told you when you decided to believe David — a liar — over me that we had no future. I meant what I said."

"Kyle, you can't really mean it. You know that it was just my anger coming out again. I really do not believe what David said."

"You don't get it, do you? I can't deal with the anger and hatred that you show around me. You hurt me deeply when you thought that I could do what I was accused of doing. I know now for sure how deep your hurt about me was because you made me feel it."

Derek grabbed Kyle on both sides of his face and claimed his lips. He made Kyle kiss him back by putting his tongue to his lips. Kyle could not stop his reaction. He grabbed Derek around the waist and pulled him close like a man possessed. He opened his mouth with his tongue in response to Derek's advances.

Suddenly, Kyle pushed Derek away so hard that he almost fell. "Stay away from me! Go back to Keith. He needs you. I will try to avoid you in the future, and I would appreciate the same from you. This is a small town, but we need to make this work. Go home!"

"Kyle, no, I want to be with you." Derek was desperate for Kyle to hear him, but he wouldn't.

"You only slept with me to get even with Keith. I should have known that when I gave into you at the cabin, but I wanted to believe that you were finally mine. How can you be mine when you really don't love me? Those are just words. If you loved me, you would never have said what you said in the parking lot the very next day after we made love. I don't want you. You can't build a relationship without trust, and you truly don't trust me. Leave! *Leave!* GET OUT!"

Kyle did not mean half of what he said, but he had to do it to make Derek want to avoid him. It would make it easier to get over his wanting Derek. The cruel way that he treated Derek and the things he said would make Derek's anger and hatred of him come back, and then he would stay away.

Kyle turned around and continued working on what he was building. Derek stayed for a minute longer, just staring at Kyle's back. Kyle knew that Derek was still there, so he turned around again and yelled, "GET OUT!"

Derek went outside, picked up his suitcase, and walked down the driveway. He thought of calling Keith to come and get him, but he called Chrystel instead. She picked him up at the end of the driveway, and neither saw Kyle watching from the other end. It broke Kyle's heart to watch this, but it was for the best. The anger that Derek felt would never go away, and it would eventually destroy them both.

❧ "Derek, why didn't you have Keith pick you up at the airport, and what were you doing at Kyle's?"

"I had a car service drive me here because I needed to talk to Kyle before going home."

Chrystel could tell that something was very wrong with Derek. "Why didn't Kyle drive you home?"

"Why all the questions? It doesn't matter. *Nothing* matters anymore. Just please take me home. I called you because I needed a little more time before seeing Keith, and I knew that he would hate picking me up at Kyle's."

"Derek, are you leaving Keith? Are you in love with Kyle?"

"I don't know *what* I am doing right now. Kyle came back to town and made me love him again, and Keith cheated on me with Galen and now our trust is broken. Keith knows about Kyle, so I just don't know if any of it can be salvaged."

"Well, you have two men who want you. Now you have to choose. Someone is going to get hurt for sure."

"No. Only one man wants me, but who knows? Maybe he doesn't want me either."

"If you are talking about Kyle, he wants you but doesn't trust that you won't turn on him again."

"Great. Did Kyle talk to you about this? So I guess you know that I slept with him?"

"Yes, he told me, and he told me what David said to you and that you believed it. You were foolish there. You should have known Kyle better than that. He is a very private person and would never talk about anything so private to anyone."

"Well, he told you!" Derek said hurtfully.

"That is because we are close friends, and we both have something in common. We are both in love with you." There ... she *said* it. She knew that it would throw Derek, and it did.

"Chrystel, you can't mean that! You know there will never be a 'you and me.' I love you but not that way."

"I know that, silly, but when I first came to town, I fell for you and did not know that you were gay. I found out later, and then you brought Keith

251

back to live with you. I am under no illusions but, because of that, Kyle and I are close."

"Please tell me that this is not the reason you are uninterested in any man. You never date."

"It is what it is! You can't help whom you fall in love with. It is okay though … I love you and Keith as friends too, so I am happy. Kyle and I will hang out and commiserate together. He says that he walked away from you, so what were you doing there?"

"I went there to tell him that I had decided to be with him, but he wouldn't hear me and told me that he wanted no part of me. So nothing matters now."

"Don't give up if he is what you want."

"I got the message loud and clear. I will leave Kyle alone."

Chrystel pulled up to the farm to drop off Derek. He took his suitcase in the house, and he and Chrystel went down to the stable. She had decided to check on the horse she had been treating. They found Keith with Shadow.

Keith turned around, shocked to see Derek home. He came up to Derek and put his arms around him. "How did you get here? Why didn't you call and let me know that you were coming home?"

"Chrystel brought me."

"How was Cheyenne?" Keith was trying to be lighthearted but knew from Derek's demeanor that things weren't good.

"We can talk about that later. Chrystel, why don't you stay and have supper with us? You haven't eaten yet, have you, Keith?" Keith knew that Derek was stalling.

"No. I haven't eaten yet. Yes, Chrystel. Please stay."

"Okay!" She knew what was going on. It seemed that both of them didn't want to have this talk, and she stayed for several hours.

⌁ "Derek, we need to talk now that Chrystel is gone," Keith said. "With the lack of reaction or warmth that I got from our hug in the stable, I know that you do not have good news for me. You want Kyle, don't you? Should I leave and go back to Cheyenne, or what?"

"No. You should stay. We should try to work this out if we can, but it is not going to be easy. I don't trust you anymore, and you don't trust me after all that I have done. But if you want to try, then I will too. I will say this: I don't want to sleep with you right now. Sex is not going to solve our problems, so I will move into the other bedroom for now. I think we need to start over slowly. Are you willing to do this?"

"Okay, Derek. I will take you any way I can. I don't want to lose you. What about Kyle?"

"That is not an issue anymore. He will be just someone I knew once. Nothing more." Saying those words cut deeply into Derek's heart, but he knew that Kyle meant what he said.

Derek moved his clothes to the other room and unpacked. He called Jamie and told him what happened when he went to Kyle's.

Keith heard him from the other bedroom and knew that he had gone to Kyle first before coming home. *So Kyle rejected Derek. He must have meant what he said the other day about being done and staying away from him.* Keith felt bad for Derek because he knew it probably hurt him a lot, but he was also thankful to Kyle for turning Derek back to him. He wanted him even if he loved Kyle. *Derek loves me too. I believe that, with time, I can make him fall in love with me again.* Keith noticed how lonely it was in that big bed without Derek. *I will get him back in our bed again, and it won't take that long,* he thought as he drifted off to sleep.

Derek lay most of the night and thought about Kyle. *How am I going to do this? I don't want anyone but Kyle making love to me. How do I go back to Keith's bed?* He finally drifted off too.

The next morning, Derek and Keith got up and worked in the stables without talking too much. Two mares were ready to deliver, so there was a lot to do to keep busy. Keith hugged Derek a couple of times, and Derek hugged back, more like a friend than a lover. For now, that was going to have to be okay with Keith.

⊰ Kyle could not sleep at all. He paced the floor all night. He wanted to take Derek right there in the barn when he came in but could not let himself give in again. For his own well-being, he had to keep Derek away and try to forget him.

He arrived at the hospital, biting off everyone's head from the lack of sleep and his unhappiness. The staff was busy with gossip, wondering why the chief of staff was acting like an ass. They thought it had to be a lover's quarrel between him and David. They were still talking about the big fight in the hall, and David still looked like he had been in a bar brawl.

Life's Adjustments

After one month, Derek still did not want to go back to Keith's bed. He couldn't get Kyle off his mind, even though Kyle had kept his distance.

Keith was miserable. He was trying to be patient with Derek, but it was wearing thin. Finally, one evening while they were eating dinner, he looked at Derek and asked , "Are we *ever* going to be like we were before all this happened? You said that you were willing to give us another chance, but we are still as far apart as when you came back from Cheyenne. I love you and want you back in my arms and in my bed where you belong. Can't you at least try?"

"I know this is hurting you, Keith, but I am just not ready."

Keith came up to Derek and pulled him into an embrace.

As he pushed him away, he said, "Keith, what are you *doing*?"

"Damn it, Derek! Either you want me or you don't, but this limbo is not easy to deal with. I think I should just leave and go back to Cheyenne."

Derek grabbed his arm as he turned to walk away. "No, Keith. Don't … that is not what I want. Oh, hell! I don't know *what* I want you to do. I know this is hard for you, but I don't think you want me in your bed while I am thinking of someone else. Do you?"

"Of course not, but I don't know how much more of this separation I can take while living under the same roof. I want you so much, and it is killing me that you are in the other room, so close, and I can't be with you. You are here but not with me." Keith turned and walked to the stables.

Derek did not stop him.

ᖇ Chrystel was heartbroken as she watched all of her friends being so unhappy. Kyle was at her house more than he was home, and Keith always confided in her. She knew that Keith was hurting, but so was Derek. *Good lord, what a mess!* Kyle had told her that he was going to try and have some kind of relationship with David, just to take his mind off Derek. She told Kyle that she thought it was a mistake and would end badly.

ᖇ Mr. Hawthorn called the house and told Keith that Jamie had called him because he got no answer at the farmhouse.

Keith told Mr. Hawthorn that Derek was out in the field, working one of the horses, and he had just returned from town. "What did Jamie say?"

"Jamie and Marc are coming to Berea for a sale of some of the horses. Marc has buyers for four of your one-year-olds."

"Okay. I will tell Derek when he gets back to the stables. It will be great to see them. I hope they can stay for a little while."

Derek rode in just as Keith hung up from talking to Mr. Hawthorn.

"Great news, Derek! Jamie and Marc are coming to Berea to take some horses to a couple of buyers who want our one-year-olds."

"Oh, good. It will be great to see them and have some of the stock taken off our hands. The stable is getting a little overcrowded. I sent Jamie a text about this a few weeks back. I guess that is why they are selling some. Do we know how many?"

"Yes. They are selling four of the one-year-olds to several buyers, as I understand."

"When are they coming?" Derek asked.

"I think next week, but I am sure they will call back with more details. You know what that means, don't you?"

"No. What do *you* think it means? If you are going to say that I should sleep in the same room with you while they are here, forget it. There are plenty of bedrooms at the farm, but they will stay at the big house anyway."

"But they don't know that we are still not a couple," Keith reminded Derek.

"I am sure Jamie knows because he knows how I feel."

"Oh, that's right. I forgot that you are still having a hard-on for Kyle," Keith said angrily and stormed off.

Derek didn't care that Keith was angry. It was the truth. He still yearned for Kyle every night when he was alone in his bedroom. He even imagined Kyle making love to him over and over. Jamie knew that Kyle wouldn't take Derek back, but he also knew that Derek had not been able to give himself to Keith either.

I need to talk with Jamie again, Derek thought. *Maybe he can help me adjust to losing Kyle and being with Keith again. He is very smart and has a way of making me see things in a better light.*

❧ Kyle had told Chrystel that he was going to try and hook up with David, so he could get Derek off his mind. He knew that it was a bad idea, but he also knew that at one time things were good with them and maybe they could be again if he would let himself do it.

Kyle knew that David wanted him, and he had to admit that sex with David was always perfect. He also knew that it would be just physical sex and not making love like he had done with Derek, but it would help him ease the tension building inside of him … the ache he felt every time he thought of Derek. He had to do something to take that ache away, or he was going to go crazy. He picked up his phone and made the call.

David saw that it was Kyle on his caller ID, so he grabbed it right away. He wanted to ignore it and make him suffer for all the pain he had caused him, but he couldn't do it because he wanted him so much. "Hello, Kyle. To what do I owe the honor of this call?"

"I wondered if you would like to have dinner with me tonight after we got off work. I thought maybe we could talk and see if there was anything left of our relationship that we could salvage — that is, if you want to try again."

"You know I do, Kyle. I have *always* wanted that. Are you saying that you might want to be with me again like we were nine years ago?"

"I don't know if that is possible, but I do think we should see if there is anything left that we might build on, like I said."

"What about Derek?"

257

"He is no longer an issue. I will never be with him again. It is truly over, but I don't want to talk about him with you, now or ever. You have no part in that area of my life. Do you understand? If you can't leave it at that, then I don't think this will work."

"I am okay with that. What time and where do you want to meet?"

"I thought we could meet at Jean's B&B and eat there. Will that work for you?"

"Yeah. I will tell Galen not to expect me for dinner. We have been trying to eat together when we are able."

"Okay. I will meet you at 7:30 in the hotel lobby." Kyle was apprehensive about this and was already starting to second-guess it as he hung up the phone, but he was determined to try, like he told Chrystel. He had to do *something*.

✎ Kyle arrived at the hotel at 7:30. David was already there. He was so excited that he got there at 7:00. He jumped up to meet Kyle as soon as he saw him come through the door. He was extremely nervous about this dinner because he didn't want to do anything that might ruin it. This was what he had been waiting for: another chance with Kyle.

"You look really nice, Kyle."

"Thanks. So do you."

Both men had tried hard to look as good as they could for the other. Kyle hoped that this would work, so he could stop yearning for Derek. David was glad Kyle had said that he was truly through with Derek and wanted to try again with him.

"Let's go into the dining room and get something to eat and drink," Kyle suggested. "We can talk while we eat."

They were getting along fairly well, and it seemed promising that they could develop some sort of understanding. The dinner was good, and both had some wine. They mainly talked about the hospital and the cases in which they had been involved. It was like old friends talking instead of old lovers. This disappointed David, but he was willing to play it however Kyle wanted.

When they finished dinner, Kyle said that he had an early meeting and had to go home to prepare. David didn't want to push his luck, so he said okay. As they were leaving the hotel, Kyle surprised David by taking hold of his arm and leaning in to give him a short kiss goodbye. As their lips met, both felt a little twinge of wanting more, but they knew it was not what they should do at this time.

As Kyle moved toward his truck, he said, "Thanks for an enjoyable evening, David. We should do it again soon."

David agreed, and both went their separate ways.

Kyle sat in his truck for a while, pondering if this was something he would do again. It was not as hard as he thought it would be. He did have a genuinely nice evening with David, and that small kiss did stir something in him. *He is not Derek, but he might do. What a horrible thing to think about David! He does not deserve this. But it is true … he is not Derek! No one will ever take Derek's place. God, do you really know what you are doing here? You are an idiot.*

ᴈ The next day at the hospital, David came to Kyle's office to thank him for the great date the night before. He also wanted to get Kyle's help in convincing a mother of one of his patients that she should take her son off life support. She was not willing to let her loved one go, even though there was no brain activity on three separate tests.

Kyle agreed to go with David to see her. As they headed to the ICU, David noticed that Kyle was very friendly to him, and he really liked this change.

The family was holding vigil at the bedside of David's patient. He was 23 years old and had suffered massive head trauma in a motor vehicle accident a week earlier. David had operated on him to relieve the pressure on his brain, but he was not breathing on his own and had never gained consciousness from the time of the accident.

After testing the brain activity three times, David told the mother that her son was brain dead and that she should let him turn off the machines. Through her tears, the mother said that she couldn't do it and did not believe that her precious son was not going to recover. He was all she had. She had lost her husband a year ago to cancer, and this was her only child. Her sister was with her and hardly left the bedside to eat or sleep. Something had to be done, so David asked Kyle for help. Maybe he could get through to her.

As David and Kyle walked into the room, the mother grabbed David's arm and said that she saw her son move his hand. The sister stood behind her, looking at David and Kyle, and shook her head "no." David held the mother and assured her that she could not have seen his hand move. She was sobbing, and David just held her.

Kyle noticed how compassionate David was with her. He had to admit that, no matter what else David was, he was a competent doctor and always good with his patients. Watching David with her gave him a warm feeling. This reassured Kyle that maybe he and David could make a go of it again.

The mother's sister looked on with heartfelt sympathy for her sister but kept in the background as did Kyle. Kyle saw that David didn't need his help with her but just needed support for him to do what he knew was the right thing. After about an hour, David convinced the mother to turn off the machine and let her son rest in peace. It was always the hardest thing that he had to do in his career, but turning off the machine was the right thing. Kyle held her while David took care of it. It was very peaceful, and David's heart went out to her. The mother was now all alone except for her sister.

When they left the room, Kyle took David by the hand and told him what a great job he did and that he really didn't need him.

David told Kyle that he would always need him, but he knew what Kyle meant. "I just needed someone to help support me with her. I knew that it wasn't going to be easy, and I was right."

As they walked back to Kyle's office, David asked him if he would mind going out for a beer. He needed to shake off this doom and gloom, which had taken over since the young man's death.

"Sure, David. Let me finish up some paperwork, and then we will go. I will come by the OR and let you know when I am done."

"Great! That works for me. See you soon." David left with a spring in his step, which he had not had for a long time.

Kyle finished the paperwork and sat for a few minutes. He felt good about last night and today. *This has to work. Derek will always have a big piece of my heart, but I have to move forward and forget the past … forget about what was not meant for me to have.*

Old Loves

Chrystel came by the Walker farm to see how Derek was doing. She knew that things were still strained between him and Keith and thought that maybe he needed to talk. She also knew from Kyle that his date with David went well and that Derek was out of Kyle's life for sure. Kyle was trying to move on and was determined. She knew that he was stubborn enough to stick to this ridiculous plan with David, which she thought was a big mistake and that something bad was going to happen because of it. She could feel it in her bones. Call it women's intuition, but she believed it.

As Chrystel pulled up, Derek came out of the barn. "Chrystel, why are you here? Did Keith call you about one of the horses? There is nothing wrong as far as I know."

"No, Derek. I came to see how you were doing. I was hoping that we could talk."

"Sure. Come into the house. Keith is in town getting supplies."

"Good. I want to talk to you without interruptions. How are you doing, and how are you and Keith doing? Have you come any closer to getting over all the troubles that have separated you?"

"No, Chrystel … I am still not able to get back into Keith's bed, and it really hurts him. I see that, but I can't get Kyle off my mind."

"Well, dear, you had better start because he is dating David now, and they seem to be getting along much better. He says that he wants to give him another chance. You know that they were together for a long time, and it was good for most of that time until he caught him in bed with another man."

"How can Kyle forgive that? What am I *saying*? Keith is trying to get past me sleeping with Kyle, but it is not the same thing, I think."

"This whole thing is just too messed up. You love Kyle, and he loves you but can't be with you. Keith loves you, and you don't want him. David loves Kyle, and Kyle wants you. God, what a fucking *mess!*"

They both burst out laughing. It was funny in some sick way.

"Has Kyle been talking to you a lot? Is that how you know he is dating David again?" Thinking about Kyle being with David killed Derek. *Why won't Kyle believe that I love him and want to start a life with him? I've screwed up in the past, always thinking the worst of Kyle, but I don't feel that way now. Why can't Kyle see that?*

"Where did you hear about Kyle dating David?" Derek asked again. "Has he been talking to you?"

"Yes. He comes to me and talks about you. He told me that he was going to start dating David again. I told him that I thought it was a bad idea."

"What does he say about me? Is he no longer in love with me? I can't stand this, Chrystel! I love him so much, and I thought he loved me too. We were so happy, finally admitting how we felt about each other, and now we are so far apart."

"Derek, I know how much he loves you, but your hateful feelings, which always seem to surface when something doesn't go just right, have destroyed any chance you two may have had. Kyle says that it feels like a knife in his heart every time you turn on him. The last straw was when he made love to you and showed you how much he loved you, and then you turned on him and once again thought he was a horrible person. He is done, Derek, and I think you should try to except this and move on. Maybe with Keith — or not — but you need to move on."

"I don't know how I am going to do that, but …"

Keith walked into the kitchen, which stopped the conversation. "Hi, Chrystel. How are you? We should go out sometime soon and have dinner and catch up. What do you guys think?"

"Sounds like fun," Chrystel stated matter-of-factly. "Why don't we go tonight? I have no plans."

Keith and Derek answered at the same time. "Okay. Let's do it."

As Chrystel left, Derek thought that it might be good to get out and just have some fun for a change. He and Keith had been so strained, and this might be a good thing — especially after the news she just dropped on him. While they got ready, the phone rang. It was Jamie.

"Hello, Jamie," Keith said. "We are on our way to meet Chrystel at R&J Steakhouse for dinner to catch up. What's on your mind?"

"I was just calling to tell you guys that our plans have changed regarding coming to Berea. Little Mary has a thing at school that we don't want to miss, so we will have to make new arrangements to get the horses. We will call you back when you have time to talk."

✺ Kyle went by the OR and found David waiting in the doctor's lounge. "Are you ready to get that beer, David?"

"Sure. I was thinking of R&J Steakhouse. Is that okay with you?"

"Let's go. I like that place. Maybe we will grab one of their great hamburgers while we are at it."

"Sounds like a plan," David said as he started to grab Kyle's hand, but he stopped himself.

Kyle saw what David was about to do, and then turned around and took David's hand instead. Several people in the OR saw it and, of course, whispers started to flow.

✺ Kyle and David arrived at R&J Steakhouse and were seated right away. It was pleasant not having animosity between them, and they relaxed and enjoyed each other's company. They talked about what had happened earlier with the young man's death; later, they changed to lighter topics. They were laughing, and David reached for Kyle's hand on top of the table.

At that moment, Keith, Derek, and Chrystel walked in, and Keith was the first to spot them. "Well, well … it looks like Kyle and David are pretty cozy!"

Derek looked in the direction that Keith was looking and thought someone had punched him in the gut. He saw the man he loved holding hands with another man. He knew then that Kyle had really given up on him and that there was nothing he could do. He would show Kyle that he was over it too.

"Hey, guys. Let's go over and say hello to Kyle and David," Derek said as he started to move toward their table.

Neither Chrystel nor Keith had a chance to do anything but follow.

Derek had no idea what he planned to say but just wanted to make light conversation "Hi, guys! How are things at the hospital?" He didn't want Kyle to see how much it was killing him.

"Hi yourself, Derek!" David responded.

It was obvious that Kyle had lost his voice. Chrystel and Keith just stood behind Derek, not knowing what he was going to do next.

"Would you guys like to join us?" David said with a smile on his face. "We are having a beer." He knew that he had won. Kyle was going to be his. He could feel it.

"Sure! We would love to. *Wouldn't* we, guys?" Derek turned to look at Chrystel's and Keith's shocked faces.

"Don't you think that we should get a table of our own, Derek?" Keith asked as he grabbed Derek's arm. "We were going to eat, and it looks like we would be interrupting Kyle and David."

David kept it up. "No. You wouldn't be interrupting."

Kyle was dying a slow death. All he wanted was for Derek to get out of his line of vision, so his growing hard-on under the table would go away. Just looking at Derek made him feel things that he needed to put away for good.

Keith was extremely uncomfortable, but he also saw this situation as potentially positive. If Derek could sit and socialize with Kyle and David, it could finally mean good things for him and Derek.

"Okay," Keith said. "I guess we will join you for at least one beer."

Keith, Derek, and Chrystel pulled up chairs, and everyone ordered beers. Derek ended up sitting right next to Kyle, and Kyle would not look him in the eye. Derek felt heat and nervousness coming from Kyle. It really bothered Derek, and he wanted Kyle to feel like he was feeling when he saw Kyle and David holding hands.

Kyle squirmed in his seat, and their legs touched. Derek felt Kyle jump. Derek reached under the table and touched Kyle's thigh. Derek saw how much this affected him. Kyle was really fidgeting now.

David was busy talking to Chrystel and Keith and really hadn't noticed anything going on — or, if he did, he was pretending that he didn't. Derek moved his hand up Kyle's thigh toward his groin and loved the torture he was putting Kyle through.

Kyle reached under the table and grabbed Derek's hand, pushing it away before Derek moved farther up and felt his hard-on. Kyle knew that he was giving himself away. Derek could still move him like no other man ever had or ever could. *This has got to stop!* He downed his beer and turned his attention to David. "Are you about ready to go? We have some talking to do."

"Sure, Kyle. Whenever you are." David had no idea what he meant by "we have some talking to do," but maybe Kyle was going to tell him that he wanted to give him another chance and that he realized Derek was not for him after all.

"No, Kyle. Don't leave yet," Derek insisted. "We've only had one beer, and we have things to celebrate. It looks like you have found David again, and Keith and I are doing great."

Keith jumped up and grabbed Derek's arm. Enough was enough. "Come on, Derek. Let's get out of here." As he pulled Derek out of his seat, he asked, "Chrystel, are you coming?"

Chrystel was stunned. Keith didn't even look to see if Chrystel had followed or said goodbye to Kyle and David. He dragged Derek outside, and then grabbed both of his arms. "What was that little show for? David, Kyle, or me? I don't appreciate being made a fool of."

"I am not making a fool of you."

"We are far from 'doing fine' like you said. What were you doing back there?"

"Keith, I want us to get back to the way we were before all this mess. Please take me home and make love to me. I want us to be together, if that is still what you want."

"It is, Derek. You know that, but what were you doing in there?"

"I was just showing everyone involved that things are over with Kyle and we can live in the same town and act like adults when we run into each other."

Derek knew that he was lying through his teeth, but the hurt of seeing Kyle with David was so severe that he had to put up a front and try to give Keith another chance. Derek knew that they could not keep going on like they were. Keith had talked about leaving Kentucky and moving back to Cheyenne. It was also painfully clear that Kyle had meant what he said to Chrystel about moving forward with David, even though he knew that Kyle still responded to him.

"Okay. Maybe that did clear the air," Keith said. "Did you really mean that you want to come back to my bed? I would be the happiest man in the world if you did, but I want to make sure that I am not some rebound for you now that Kyle and David are together again."

"You are not a rebound. I do love you, Keith. I just need to remember what it was like to be *in* love with you. Seeing Kyle and David together made me realize that I want to forget what happened and move forward with you. I think that coming back to our bed will help get us back on track. I do want to be with you again. We were happy before both of us strayed, and I believe that, if we try, we can get back to being happy. I want that!"

᭧ "What was *that* all about?" Chrystel said to the table in general.

"I am totally baffled as you are, Chrystel," Kyle answered.

Meanwhile, David suspected what was wrong with Derek. He knew that Derek had seen Kyle holding hands with him and finally realized who won.

"I had better go too," Chrystel said as she got up to leave. "Have a nice dinner guys … see you soon."

"Wow, that was really weird in so many ways. Are you okay, Kyle?"

"Sure, David. Why would you think I wouldn't be? I told you that Derek was not an issue and that I would not discuss Derek with you now or ever. My relationship with him — or lack thereof — is not your business. Let's forget the whole episode, order some food, and pick up where we left off." Kyle reached across the table for David's hand and motioned for the waiter to come over and take their food order.

David and Kyle ate their hamburgers and had a pleasant conversation, totally enjoying the rest of the evening. When they got outside, David said that he hated for the nice time to end.

"Why does it have to end? Let's go to your place and have a few more drinks. What do you think?" Kyle asked as he put his arm around David's shoulder.

"Are you sure? I would love that! Galen might be there though."

"Oh, that's right. Well, come to my farm then." Kyle didn't want anything to stop what he had in mind after Derek's touch on his thigh got him so horny.

"Great!" David said. "I would like to spend more time with you."

"Okay. Let's go."

Kyle opened the door to his truck for David, and then walked around to the driver's side. As he got in, he leaned over and gave David a small peck on his lips. David was shocked but thrilled. He trailed after the lips that had just kissed him, but Kyle had already started the truck. When they got to the farm, Kyle got out and started around to where David sat, but David jumped out before he could get to the door. Kyle led the way to the house with David right on his heels.

"Come on in, David. You have not seen my house, have you? I would love to show you around."

"I have never been here. I'd love to see it." David was incredibly nervous that he would do or say something that would turn Kyle off. He was thrilled that he was even there. He had begun to think that it would never happen. As he walked into the giant living room, he stopped dead in his tracks and said, "Wow! What a nice place!"

The room was amazing. It was all done in huge, overstuffed leather furniture with a large table in front of the couch, which looked like a foot stool. In the center of the room was a big, colorful area rug that looked like it was made by Indians. The pictures on the walls were Western in nature, with cowboys on horses rounding up cattle and Indians. The room was so masculine. David loved the whole look.

Kyle was pleased at David's reaction, but little did David know that all of it was decorated for Derek. Kyle knew that Derek would love this room and the whole house. He secretly dreamed that someday he and Derek would live there.

Kyle had made up his mind that he would not show David his private den because, above the fireplace mantel, there was a large, framed picture of Derek, riding a magnificent golden palomino with a light tan mane. Derek's hair was close to the same color as the horse. The two — horse and rider — looked amazing together, like they were one. Jamie had sent this picture to Kyle, and he had it blown up to fit a 60 x 60-inch frame, which he had built and carved. Kyle knew that he should get rid of it but could not bring himself to do so. It was all he could have of Derek, and he would not spoil it by having David see it.

After he took David around the bottom level of the house, he offered him a beer.

David approached the door off the living room. "You didn't show me this room, Kyle."

"No one sees that room. It is my private den. It is where I work, and I don't take anyone in there," he lied. He didn't want to share that room with David. He knew the picture of Derek over the mantel would give away the fact that he was not over Derek.

"I understand," David said as he walked back to take the beer that Kyle offered him. "Do you want to sit and talk for a while?"

"How about bringing your beer and I will show you around upstairs?"

David got excited because he knew that Kyle's bedroom had to be up there since he did not see one downstairs. "Lead the way."

When they got upstairs, Kyle led David to a massive bedroom that was also decorated with a very masculine taste. David assumed that it had to be Kyle's bedroom. In the center of the room was a huge, four-poster king bed with large, heavy, burgundy-and-cream curtains behind the headboard.

"This room is great, Kyle. How do you bear to leave this house every day and come to work? If I had a place like this, I would hate to leave it …"

David didn't get another word out because Kyle moved toward him, took the beer out of his hand, placed it on the dresser, and took David in his arms. David groaned as Kyle rubbed his cock against his.

Kyle kissed David passionately and started to move his hands down David's chest to his belt buckle. Kyle slowly undid the buckle while kissing him hard, searching his open mouth with his tongue. David was on fire … he wanted this very much and was already hard and ready to blow. Kyle continued his downward pursuit by unbuttoning the top button of David's pants and slipping in his hand to feel his hard cock. David was having trouble breathing because he was so turned on.

Much later, after Kyle had taken David over and over in several positions, both were satisfied and proved to each other that, regardless of their problems, the sex between them was always good. It was just sex on Kyle's side because he was in love with another man. But, to David, it gave him hope that he was finally going to get Kyle back. They lay in each other's arms for a long time, deep in thought.

Because Kyle was so quiet, David asked, "Are you okay, Kyle?" He snuggled up closer.

"I am fine, David. I was just thinking that I should get you back to your place soon."

"Oh, no! Do we have to go so soon? I love being back in your arms."

"Yes. I have an early morning shift tomorrow at the hospital, and so do you. Don't you have a surgery scheduled for 6:30 a.m.?"

"Yes. I know you are right. This was just too good, and I am greedy."

"There will be more nights like this, I promise you." Kyle kissed David and told him to get up and get dressed, so he could take him home.

◂ᔆ Keith drove as fast as the law would allow in order to get Derek home and in his bed. He pulled up to the farmhouse, jumped out, and dragged Derek out of the truck and into the house.

"Wow, Keith! Can I get my footing?" Derek joked. "Are you a little bit anxious?"

Keith knew what Derek had said, but he also knew that he was reacting to seeing Kyle and David together. *I have got to do this. We can't go on like we have been.* "Sorry, Derek. I am a little anxious. I have wanted you back in my bed so much that I can't help rushing you upstairs." He took Derek by the hand and pulled him to their bedroom. As Keith closed the door behind them, he turned and asked Derek if he was sure that this was what he really wanted.

"Yes, Keith," Derek said as he moved in close and put his arms around Keith's neck.

Keith could not stop himself. He leaned in and claimed Derek's lips. As he kissed him, he started unbuttoning his shirt, taking it off his shoulders, and letting it drop to the floor. Derek let Keith undress him and went along with anything that Keith wanted to do, but his heart just wasn't into it. He kept having visions of Kyle making love to him. Keith could feel the difference too, but he wanted Derek so much that he ignored it.

Much later, they lay quietly side by side, neither one wanting to talk about how unsatisfied they were. Keith knew what was wrong, but he was convinced that things between them would get better. It was just going to take time. At least Derek seemed willing to try.

❧ The next day, Keith and Derek ate breakfast together, hugged, and then went about their chores, tending to the horses like nothing was amiss.

Last night was far from perfect, but I think we can get back to where we were, Keith thought as he exercised Shadow. *I will make him remember how much we loved each other. I have to. I can't lose him!*

Trying Hard

As the days passed, Keith and Derek got along better. Their lovemaking was still really off, but both men were determined to make it work. Neither wanted to walk away from the other, and they focused on the stables and running the ranch.

Mr. Hawthorn was pleased to see them working together again. He had reported to Jamie that things seemed to be better, and the stables were doing well. Jamie was happy to hear this but was still a little concerned because he knew how Derek felt about Kyle. Jamie decided that he would try to talk to Derek soon and find out how he was feeling.

Chrystel stopped by to check on the horses and to see how the guys were doing.

Derek saw her first. "Hi, Chrystel. How have you been? We haven't seen you since last week at the bar."

"I'm fine. More importantly, how are you and Keith? I have had you on my mind all week and hoped that you weren't doing anything stupid."

"What would *that* be? Keith wants us to get back to where we were, but it is not totally working yet. It is hard for me to sleep with him because I want to be in Kyle's bed, and Keith knows that. He is really a great man because he keeps trying, and I am also trying as best as I can."

"I just worry about you guys — all of you. That includes Kyle. He is my friend as you guys are, and I see that he is struggling too."

"Oh, *sure* he struggles," Derek said sarcastically.

"*Who* struggles?" Keith asked as he walked up to Chrystel and Derek.

"No one important," Derek said a little too abruptly.

Keith knew that it must be about Kyle, but he let it drop. He also knew that, if he commented any further, it would put up a wall between him and Derek, and he couldn't let that happen. Things were so much better. It just wasn't worth the risk.

Chrystel excused herself and went into the barn.

Keith walked up to Derek and pulled him into a hug. "Do you want to take a break and go to Cheyenne with me? I thought that we might get away for a few days and visit with Jamie and Marc."

"I would love that actually. When do you want to leave? I have been thinking about visiting them myself, and I miss my talks with Jamie as I am sure you do with Marc." He squeezed Keith and said, "Let's make the arrangements. I will talk to Mr. Hawthorn, and you call Jamie and Marc. Check and see if it is a good time to come."

Keith was encouraged to hear Derek say that he wanted to go away with him. *This could be just what we need — getting away from Berea and anything to do with reminders of Kyle.*

⤴ Derek went to the barn to see if Chrystel would keep an eye on the horses. "Chrystel, Keith and I are going away for a few days to visit with Jamie and Marc. Can you oversee things here with the horses? I will have Mr. Hawthorn take care of the fields."

Chrystel knew why Derek was going — to get far away from the chance of running into Kyle — and had a strained look on her face. "Sure. I will take care of things, but do you really think that you can run away from your problems?"

"Of course not, but Keith and I need some time away from here, and I always feel better after talking to Jamie. This might even help Keith and me get back to where we were before I was stupid enough to let myself fall in love with Kyle again. It was a mistake 20 years ago, and it still is. I need to get him out of my blood and my heart if Keith and I are ever going to make it."

Derek didn't realize that Keith had entered the barn and heard what he said. The hurt was devastating. He felt as if his heart were ripped out of his chest. He had a stupid notion that Derek had come to him again. But, after hearing those words, Keith realized that Derek was Kyle's no matter what he did.

Keith turned and walked out of the barn without either of them seeing him. *What should I do?* Keith thought. *Should I go with Derek to Cheyenne as if all was okay, and then tell him when we get there that I am not coming back to Berea with him? I need to let him go. He is in love with Kyle, and the love is deep. I can see that. Do I love him enough to give him up? Yes, I do. I will do anything to make him happy.* Keith was resolved to make these thoughts into a plan. He would stay in Cheyenne where he belonged and try to make a life with Jamie and Marc at the Three M Ranch. Hopefully, Marc would give him his old job as the groom for the horses. Keith would take a few extra clothes with him but not enough to raise any question with Derek. He would send for the rest of his things later. The plan was made.

֎ Jamie and Marc were thrilled to hear that Keith and Derek were coming to see them, and they prepared the guest room. Little Mary was glad to hear that she was going to see and play with her two favorite uncles and danced around the house with excitement. Karen tried her best to get Mary ready for bed, but there was no calming her.

"When are they coming, Daddy J?"

"Tomorrow, Mary. We promise that you will see them when you get home from school. Now go with Karen and get ready for bed. You have an exciting day tomorrow."

Mary gave Marc and Jamie a hug goodnight and went off with Karen.

"Since they are coming to Cheyenne, Marc, can we put off our trip to Berea to sell the one-year-olds they have there? I think it would be too hard to ship them. Maybe we can have one or both of them drive the horses to us at a later date. What do you think?"

"Sure. We can put it off for a few months. I'm sure the buyers will wait a little longer. Maybe in a month or two."

֎ Kyle's day started at 6 a.m. He had many pressing and important issues to take care of before the hospital woke up, with the first shift mostly coming in at 6:30 a.m. David knocked on the door.

"Come in!"

275

David came in, all smiles. Last night had been a dream come true, and he needed to see if Kyle was thinking like he was.

"Good morning, David," Kyle asked as he walked from behind the desk and took David into his arms for a big hug. "Aren't you supposed to be getting ready for surgery?"

David was thrilled by this greeting, and he knew that they were still on the same page. "Yes, I do, but they are prepping the patient, so I thought I would say good morning and thank you for a great night last night. I am a little sore," he joked as he rubbed his butt, but he loved every minute. Kyle had taken him to such great heights that he would do anything to feel that sensation again and again.

Kyle laughed a deep, guttural laugh that brought David's cock to immediate attention. "You are such a whore boy, David." He reached and grabbed David's erect penis. "I will take care of this later." He turned David around and pointed him to the door. "You need to get your mind off sex and go do your operations. I promise that there will be more punishment for that sweet ass of yours later."

David reluctantly did as he was told but left thinking that he would offer his ass to Kyle anywhere or any way he wanted him. Sex with Kyle was amazing, and he would make sure that he kept Kyle remembering how good they always were together.

Kyle went back to his duties as chief of staff but stopped periodically to relive the night before at R&J Steakhouse and afterwards at his house. *Why did Derek put me through that little display when he sat down with us at the table? There didn't seem to be any good reason except to slowly kill me by touching me and totally enjoying how much he knew it was affecting me. Diving deeply into David's ass really helped ease the pain. That is what I will keep doing to relieve the stress and sexual need. Fucking David was always good, and I will accept that this is how I will get over Derek.*

Kyle went to the doctors' lounge in the surgery suite to see if David was out of his first surgery. He had three scheduled that Kyle knew about, so he thought he might catch him between one and two. He needed a break from his desk for a while. He was in luck. David walked into the lounge, taking off his surgery cap and heading to the coffee pot.

"Wow, Kyle! What are you doing here? I just got out of my first surgery and was taking a coffee break while they turn over the room for the next one."

Kyle looked at David. He always looked good in scrubs, and he was instantly horny for him.

David could see the expression on his face. "What? What are you thinking?"

"I want to take you somewhere close and fuck you. Let's go into the linen closet. We can lock the door. I need to be inside you," Kyle said as he dragged David along with him.

David was no fool, and he was not going to let this opportunity slip away. "I am with you … let's go!"

They entered the linen closet and locked the door behind them. No one would come in there at this time of day. All the warming cabinets had been filled for the day's surgeries the first thing that morning, so there was no need to worry about getting found out. Kyle roughly threw David against the wall and started his descent to the drawstrings of David's scrub pants. They dropped to the floor, and so did his boxers. David's rock-hard cock pointed straight at Kyle's mouth. Kyle took him in one big movement, hitting the back of his throat, and sucked up and down for several strokes.

David moaned, "Kyle, I don't think I can last much longer!"

"Go for it … let me taste you, and then I am going to fuck you hard."

David came fast and furiously. Kyle never let any escape his mouth. He came off David's cock and turned him around to face the wall. "Spread your legs for me, David."

"Wait! We don't have any protection."

"Did you think I didn't come prepared? I have a condom and lube right here in the pocket of my lab coat."

"So you *did* come down here to fuck me!"

"Yes! Enough talk. Spread your legs for me." He prepped David for his entry and rolled on the condom. At first, he went slowly, entering David. Halfway in, he lost control and plunged deep and hard.

David moaned and squirmed against Kyle, and then begged to be taken faster and harder. As Kyle hit David's prostate, each stroke produced the moans that he knew David would give him. Kyle plunged in one last time and filled the condom as David sprayed the wall in front of him. As both came down from their orgasms, they stayed very still, with Kyle's balls deep inside David. Kyle slipped out slowly, took off the condom, and wrapped it in paper towels.

David pulled up his boxers and scrub pants as he turned to Kyle. "Wow! That … was … amazing … and … unexpected." David was still having trouble slowing down his breathing. "What brought *that* on?" He had just been plugged deep and hard, and he loved every minute of it. Kyle had never taken him that forcefully before. He thought that maybe he could get used to deep and hard all the time.

"I just needed you and couldn't get your sweet ass off my mind. I wasn't getting any work done, so I thought I would work out on you to relieve some of the tension. Any objections?"

"No. Hell, you can use me as your workout sessions anytime!"

"That is the plan, whore boy!" This was going to be his new name for David. He was a whore. He loved sex, and Kyle knew that he would do it with anyone who pushed up against his butt. He was under no illusions about that. He could never make a permanent life with David, but he certainly would not deny himself the sexy ass anytime he felt like it. He was just a juicy piece of ass for him these days.

"Thanks for the exercise, David. I feel better now. You had better check on your next surgery, and I have to get back to work." He threw David some paper towels to clean up his cum all over the wall and left the linen closet.

David knew that he should feel used, but he didn't care. He had Kyle back in his life. He would show him that, even though he did love sex, he would be faithful to him if it meant having him for good.

Kyle went back to his office and shut the door. He sat down behind the desk and thought about what he had just done and how he had treated David … like a piece of meat. *I know this is wrong, but I need a way to occupy my mind and body, so I can stop crying and hurting from the loss of Derek. I do regret pushing Derek away, but I had to do it for my own preservation. He would turn on me again … I just know it. I have done the right thing and will just satisfy myself with David.*

278

Heartbreaking Decision

Marc picked up Derek and Keith at the airport and drove them to the Three M Ranch. Keith thought of how good it was to be home. Derek was apprehensive about the whole trip because Keith was noticeably quiet and deep in thought on the airplane, and he wondered what Keith was thinking.

Jamie and Mary were waiting outside when they pulled up.

Mary jumped into Derek's arms as soon as he got out of the car. "I am so glad you came to see me, Uncle Derek!" Mary squealed with excitement.

"What about me, little one? Aren't you glad to see me too?" Keith smiled and held out his arms.

"Yes, Uncle Keith. I am so happy to see you too," she said as she attacked him next.

They all laughed at how excited she was. It had been a while since they both came for a visit.

"Let's all go inside and catch up while Betsy makes us something to eat," Jamie suggested as he wrapped his arms around both of them. "I am sure you guys are hungry since the airlines don't give out snacks anymore. It is great that you came for this visit. We have missed you."

Betsy made lunch, and they all gathered around the table.

"How are you two?" Marc asked. "Are you working through your problems?"

"We are doing much better, and we feel connected again. I believe that we can get back to where we were before I screwed up everything with Kyle."

"He wasn't the only one who messed up. I did too with Galen, but we are working on our problems and will work this out together." Keith lied about the last statement because he was secretly planning to leave Derek and stay with Marc and Jamie, if they let him.

"You guys get settled in and come down to the stables when you are ready," Jamie said. "Marc and I have some work to do. Take your time!" He winked at Derek before getting up from the table.

Keith and Derek took their suitcases upstairs to their bedroom. They unpacked in silence until Derek couldn't stand it anymore. "Keith, why are you being so quiet? You don't seem happy to be here."

"I am just tired, Derek. Nothing is wrong." He was lying but was not ready to tell Derek what he planned until he talked with Marc privately and found out if staying here was an option. Keith finished unpacking before Derek and told him that he was going down to the stables.

When Keith walked into the stables, Marc was saddling one of the horses for a workout and said, "Hi, Keith. It is really good to see you back here again. We have missed you guys. Is the farm doing okay? How is Shadow?"

"It is going very well, and Shadow is as great as ever. You know what a magnificent horse he is. Marc, I want to talk to you privately."

"Let's go riding. It sounds serious, and I could see when you two arrived that something was amiss. You are both talking like all is right with your world, but I can see on your face that it is not."

They saddled the other horse, and both mounted and walked their horses outside just as Derek and Jamie arrived at the stable door.

"What's up? Where are you two off to?" Jamie asked.

"We are going to go riding together like old times. You two don't mind, do you? It will give you and Derek a chance to get caught up with things at the farm," Marc said as he blew Jamie a kiss.

"You guys have fun. We will be here when you get back," Jamie said, smiling back at Marc as he watched them ride away. "Okay, Derek. Tell me what is *really* going on with you two. Are you working on your problems, or are you just going through the motions?"

"I don't know, Jamie. I hate where we are in this relationship, and I thought that I could do this, and I really wanted to make it work, but … I'm in love with Kyle and always will be. We both know that Keith deserves so much more."

"Yes, he does, Derek, but I want you to be happy. You will always be my first concern. You know that you are not being fair to Keith if you are just going through the motions. He is a good man. If you keep leading him on, then he will never have a chance to find someone who can love him like he should be loved."

"I know that Keith loves me, and we were incredibly happy at one time. Oh, god, why did I have to run into Kyle? Why was he put back in my life again? Why can't he trust me enough to give me the chance to show him that I want only him? I have messed up three lives so badly, and they will never be normal again." Derek hung his head and gave into the emotions that he had bottled up ever since Kyle turned his back on him and said that he was done.

Jamie let him cry until all the tears were gone. "We will keep talking this through until you know what you should do."

ے Marc and Keith rode a long while until they came upon a group of beautiful pines that surrounded a private area on the ranch. It was Keith's favorite riding destination when he wanted to be alone and think. They dismounted and let the horses graze while they sat down on a blanket that Marc had thrown onto the saddle as they left the barn.

"Okay, Keith. Let me hear what is on your mind and what is *really* going on with you and Derek. No matter what you two said, it was obvious to Jamie and me that things were not right with you guys."

"No. They are not right. I thought that getting away from Berea and Kyle Douglas was going to be the answer for us. But, as we were making plans to leave, I overheard Derek telling Chrystel that he needed to get Kyle out of his blood and heart in order to give us a chance. I knew then that he had not come back to me.

"Of course, if I were honest with you and myself, I already knew that he was just going through the motions. Our lovemaking is so forced now. I was just holding out hope that eventually he would fall back in love with me. I know he loves me, and that is why he is trying, but he is not *in* love with me, and there is a big difference. His heart belongs to Kyle and always will. He never truly got over him. I feel like I deserve better than someone just pretending. I want a chance to find someone who will love me the way he loves Kyle."

"Why is Derek not with Kyle then? If he loves him that much, then that is where he should be."

"Derek has hurt Kyle so much that Kyle can't bring himself to let Derek in again. I am sure it hurts Derek's heart as much as it does mine. Every time something goes wrong in the least little way, Derek always thinks the worst of Kyle. It is really sad. They both want each other, but it is just not working for them. Old hurts won't die a final death."

"So what are you going to do?"

"That is what I want to talk to you about, Marc. Will you and Jamie let me live here and give me my old job? I cannot go back to Berea with Derek."

"Have you told Derek what you are planning to do?"

"No, not yet. I had to first know if I could stay here. You haven't answered me. May I stay here?"

"Of course, if you are sure that is what you want to do. I will have to run it by Jamie because we are in this together, but I know that he won't have a problem with it."

Keith and Marc mounted up and headed back to the ranch. They arrived at about the same time that Jamie and Derek walked out of the barn.

"Did you guys have a nice ride?" Jamie asked as Marc dismounted and led the horses into the barn.

"Yes. It was nice to be back there with Keith," Marc answered.

Keith walked in front of Marc and tied up his mount. Derek followed him.

Marc pulled Jamie into a hug and whispered, "Keith wants to stay here, Jamie. Is that okay with you?"

"Sure. He can stay here. Let's talk about it privately."

⮜ Keith took off the saddle and brushed his horse. He turned to Derek and said, "We need to talk. Can you come up to the room for a few minutes?"

"Okay." Derek was very worried. He knew that something was not right with Keith since they arrived in Cheyenne. "What is wrong, Keith?"

"Let's go up to our room, so we can have some privacy."

"Oh! You can't even wait until tonight to make love to me, right?" Derek said a little too loudly, trying to be flirty, but nerves were governing his comment.

"No, Derek. We need to talk!" Keith walked out of the barn to the house, leaving Derek standing there and watching him walk away.

Derek followed Keith into the house and up to the guest room.

Keith closed the door behind them and sat down in a chair close to the bed. "Please sit down, Derek."

Derek sat on the edge of the bed, waiting for the worst. From Keith's body language, he could feel that it was not going to be good.

"Derek, I know that you love me but are not in love with me. I deserve more than you can give me." Derek started to protest, but Keith waved his hand to stop him. "Let me continue, Derek. I know that we have tried to get back what we had, but it is just not working. You are deeply in love with Kyle … always have been and always will be."

Derek started to protest again but Keith was not hearing anything from him. "I heard you tell Chrystel that you were in love with Kyle just before we came here, so I don't want to continue trying. I am not planning to go back to Berea with you when you leave. I have asked Marc if I can come here and get my job back. He said I could, so that is what I am going to do. I hope you will respect my decision and go back home without me. I will send for the rest of my things later." Keith waited until the shock on Derek's face changed. "Do you have anything to say?"

"I can't believe that you are done trying, even though it has only been a few weeks since we have been sleeping together again. I told you that I want to make this work and that I will never be with Kyle again. Why isn't that good enough for you?"

"Because, Derek, even though you say that you will never be with Kyle again, that is where you want to be. When we make love, I know you are trying to imagine that it is Kyle in bed with you instead of me. I deserve better than that. I want a man and partner who is all about loving me and only me. I can't help that Kyle does not want you anymore. But, at this

point, neither do I. I hope we can always remain friends, but we will never be lovers again. I am also hoping that you don't drag out this visit too long because it is awfully hard for me to be around you right now. Maybe with time it will be easier. Please tell everyone back in Berea that I have decided to stay here and that I will miss all of them. Tell Chrystel to keep in touch with me and let me know how things are going, but please …
I do not want to hear from you for a good long time." Keith left the room and slammed the door behind him.

Derek broke down on the bed and cried. *How could I have hurt Keith so much? What is wrong with me?*

Jamie heard the door slam and came up to see if Derek was okay. When he saw him crying, he took Derek in his arms and held him. "I assume that Keith told you his decision," he said gently. "I know that this is a shock to you right now, but it really shouldn't be. You had to know that you guys were going to have an extremely hard time recapturing what you had in the past. Cheating is never an easy thing to get over. What is the situation between you and Kyle now?"

"We are over. He has gone back to his boyfriend David whom he was with for a few years. David is back in the picture, even though Kyle said that he was done with him. He has been seeing David, and I am sure they are having sex again. There is no chance there. I guess I am doomed to live a life of loneliness and celibacy, which is what I deserve after what I have done to Keith and Kyle."

"Derek, you are just feeling sorry for yourself right now. You will get through this and someday look back on it and know that this was the right thing to do. Keith is right. He deserves to have someone who can love him like you love Kyle and like I love Marc. Go home and busy yourself with the horses. I will send a helper to work with you, and I will make sure that he is straight," he said jokingly.

They both laughed at that statement.

"I don't want any more drama with you and some guy I hire," Jamie added.

Derek smiled at his friend and hugged him. "I will go back home and let the Hawthorns and Chrystel know that Keith is not coming home."

ॐ They all had dinner together, and everyone was sad. Keith tried to make light conversation and, of course, Little Mary helped. She was sad that Uncle Derek was leaving so soon but was really happy that Uncle Keith was staying. Karen and Betsy were surprised by the news but kept it between them. Derek asked Karen if he could take Mary to bed. Mary was so happy that Uncle Derek was going to tuck her in and read her a story. They left and went up to her room.

"Are you going to be okay, Keith?" Jamie asked. "You are certainly welcome here with us. It will be like old times having you around. I am incredibly sad for you and Derek though. I love him like a brother and want him to be happy. Hell, I want you *both* to be happy. If it is not with each other, then you guys should find someone else."

"I will be fine, Jamie. I love Derek, but I don't want to be second best. He is so in love with Kyle, and he will never get over him. You know better than anyone that you only have a love like that once in a lifetime. I will find it someday. I thought I had it with Derek, but maybe someday I will say 'Derek who?' No … I am lying about that. Derek was my once-in-a-lifetime love."

"I know that, Keith. Life throws us curve balls sometimes, doesn't it?"

Derek left for Berea on the next plane, and Keith settled into his home.

Loneliness

Derek arrived in Berea after a long, hard flight. He had a lot of time to think about what to do next. He saw Mr. Hawthorn and went to the stables to check on the horses. It seemed so quiet with Keith gone. He decided to wait until morning to start packing Keith's stuff to send to him. He would also let Chrystel know tomorrow. Right now, he just wanted to unpack and go to bed. He was physically and mentally exhausted.

The next day, Derek called Chrystel to see if he could stop by and talk to her. He also went into the big house and let Mr. and Mrs. Hawthorn know what had changed. They were a little shocked but not as bad as he thought Chrystel was going to be.

Derek arrived at Chrystel's office. She was finishing her work and heading out to the farms she takes care of.

"Hi, Derek. Welcome home! I will be ready to talk in a few … get yourself a cup of coffee."

He got some coffee and thought about how he was going to tell her that Keith had left him.

"What's up?" Chrystel asked as she sat opposite Derek. "How were Cheyenne, Jamie, and Marc?"

Derek didn't answer at first. "Cheyenne was fine as was Jamie and Marc. Keith stayed there."

"Oh, so when is he coming home?"

"He *is* home. He left me."

"*What?* What do you mean? He would not have left you. He loves you!"

"Well, he knew that, no matter how hard we tried to get back what we had, it was not working. He knew that, even though I will always love him, I'm not *in* love with him. I'm in love with Kyle, and that is not going to change. Keith could not settle for that. He wants someone who will love

287

him and only him. He asked Marc and Jamie if he could have his job back, and they agreed. He wants me to send him the rest of his stuff."

Chrystel sat in silence and disbelief, and then she finally spoke. "So what now? Are you going to let Kyle know what is going on?"

"No. I see no reason to do that. He has made it clear that he will never take me back, and he is dating David. You know that I deserve all this. I was so mean and hateful to Kyle from the first day he came to Berea, and look how I hurt Keith, who is a great man and so in love with me."

"Did Keith tell you that he doesn't love you anymore?"

"No. He still loves me but doesn't want me. He doesn't want a man who is in love with someone else. He wants to be more than second best with his life partner, and that is what he should hold out for. I can't be that for him, and he had the courage to walk away."

Chrystel knelt in front of Derek and gave him a hug. She knew how much he was hurting. "Why don't we go out for dinner and drinks? I don't want you to go home to an empty house right now. We could eat and have a couple of beers and talk some more."

"Okay, but I thought you had to do your rounds at the farms."

"I can do them tomorrow before I open the office. Let's get out of here and go to R&J Steakhouse. You know how I love that place. We can order two big steaks and sit and talk."

"That really sounds good. I didn't want to be alone. You are my best friend, Chrystel. What would I do if I didn't have you to talk with? Let's take my truck."

⁓ They drove to R&J Steakhouse in silence. Derek was thinking about Kyle and, oddly enough, so was Chrystel. She was wondering what he would say when he found out that Derek was single again. She knew that he would stay away as long as Keith was here, but would he be able to stay away now that he was gone for good? She doubted it, no matter what he said.

When they arrived at R&J Steakhouse, Chrystel saw Kyle sitting at the bar by himself. The right thing to do would be to go up and say hello. Derek couldn't stop her when he saw where she was headed, and, in reality, he didn't want to. It was a chance to be close to him.

"Hi, Kyle!" Chrystel said as she tapped him on the shoulder.

Derek held back a little, his heart beating like crazy.

When Kyle turned around on his stool, he saw Derek and his heart stopped. He spoke to Chrystel but kept looking at Derek. "What are you two doing here? Where is Keith? Are you guys meeting here for dinner?" He was trying to be polite.

"We are having dinner, just Derek and me. Are you waiting for David?"

Derek remained quiet. His stomach turned just hearing David's name. "No. I'm here alone."

"Would you like to join us?" Chrystel asked as Derek poked her in the back.

Kyle looked at Derek as he answered, "Sure, if Derek doesn't mind."

"It's not a good time, Kyle. I hope you understand, but I really need to talk with Chrystel. It is not anything against you." With a pleading look on his face, he asked, "You know that, right?"

Kyle studied Derek's face and could see that he was sad. Kyle knew it must be something really big. "That is okay. I do understand. I won't bother you two."

"Sorry, Kyle. Maybe next time," Derek said. He did not want to let Kyle think bad thoughts about him. He was not rejecting him like before. Truth be told, he would have loved to spend time with Kyle, but he really needed to talk with Chrystel.

❧ Chrystel and Derek were shown to a table close to the bar — close enough that Kyle could possibly hear some of what they were saying. Derek picked the chair with his back to the bar. He did not want to see Kyle sitting so near. Chrystel took the chair opposite him where she could see Kyle. They ordered their steaks and beers and settled down to talk.

"Okay, Derek. Tell me the whole thing. You said that Keith left you because you were in love with Kyle, and that was not going to change."

"Yes. Just before we were leaving for Cheyenne, Keith heard me tell you in the barn that we had been trying to get back what we had but it just wasn't working for me. He heard that I would always be in love with

Kyle. So, when Keith and I were making our plans to go to Cheyenne, he planned to stay there. He deserves not to be second best to anyone. He told me that he loves me. But, like I told you, he wants to find a man who will love him and only him."

Kyle heard Derek say that Keith had left Derek and was staying in Cheyenne. *How do I feel about that? I need to find out what is going on.* He sat quietly at the bar, trying to hear more.

"So why don't you have a heart to heart with Kyle and let him know?"

"Because it would serve no purpose. You know he said that he was done with me. It hurts so much to be around him. I love him with all my heart, but I will have to live with the loss of him for the rest of my life. On the positive side, you know that there is nothing wrong with a gay man living alone and making a life. I can do this!"

"How are you going to run the stables without Keith's help?"

"Jamie is going to hire someone and send him here." Derek chuckled and said, "He's going to make sure that he's straight!"

Chrystel laughed. Kyle heard it and smiled to himself. Chrystel and Derek ate and had a couple of beers. Derek felt so much better after talking with his friend, and he was glad not to have gone home alone yet.

⤚ Kyle's thoughts were all over the place. He had heard all that Derek had said, and he was processing this new development. While deep in thought, he felt a tap on his shoulder. David had walked into R&J Steakhouse and saw Kyle at the bar.

"What are you doing here, David?"

"Hey, Kyle. I came looking for you. Why are you not glad to see me?"

Kyle was not glad because he thought that he would be able to have more time to listen to Derek. Derek saw a change in Chrystel's face and followed where she was looking. When Derek saw David, he knew then that he could not stay.

"Chrystel, let's get out of here."

When they paid the bill and got up to leave, David saw them for the first time. Chrystel said goodnight to both of them and asked David if

Galen was home. Derek said a polite goodbye and moved to the door. Kyle wanted to grab his arm but couldn't, so he returned the goodbye.

"Yes. He is home," David replied.

"Good," Chrystel added. "I need to talk to him for a few minutes. Well, see you both later." She met Derek at the door and left the restaurant.

"So that is why you didn't seem glad to see me!" David said, letting his jealousy and insecurity take over after seeing Derek.

"I'm glad to see you, David," Kyle lied. "I was just taken by surprise because you said that you had to brush up your skills for tomorrow's surgery."

"I did, but I needed a break and went by your house. I didn't see your car, so I thought you might be here."

"Well, sit and have a beer. I only have time for one more because I also have some reading to catch up on."

"So I saw that Chrystel and Derek were alone. Where was Keith?"

"I'm sure I don't know. I didn't ask. They only came over to me briefly, and then got a table. Drink up. I have to go unless you want to stay, but I can't."

David drank the remainder of his beer and got up to leave. "No. I will go out with you."

The two men walked out of R&J Steakhouse, and Kyle headed for his car.

"Aren't you even going to give me a kiss before you go?" David asked coyly.

Kyle walked over and gave him a quick kiss, and then walked to his car. "See you at the hospital in the morning, David," he said as he climbed in and drove away. As he was driving home, all he could think about was Derek. *God, what should I do? Should I try to talk to him and get more details, or should I leave this alone? Does this really change anything?* In the end, he decided to go home.

Derek drove Chrystel back to her place and thanked her again for the talk. He thought about Kyle on the drive home. It was good to see him, but seeing David just solidified the fact that it was over. Kyle was with David.

Awkward Moments

A month passed. Jamie had been interviewing almost constantly, trying to find someone to send to Berea. They were either green, didn't know anything about horses, or didn't want to move from Cheyenne. Derek told him that he was having trouble keeping up. Mr. Hawthorn was trying his best, but he was busy with the farming end of Walker's homestead. Jamie knew that he shouldn't ask Keith if he would consider going back until he and Marc could find someone, but he could also see how miserable Keith was here with them, so he decided to ask.

Jamie found Keith in the stables. "Keith, I have a big favor to ask. Would you consider going back to Berea to help Derek until I can find someone? I know it is a lot to ask, but he is really struggling with all the horses on his own. None of the people who answered my ad are working out."

Keith was shocked that Jamie was asking him to do this. It was true that he had been missing Derek more than anyone really knew, but he could not even consider it. "Are you sure that you can't find *one* cowboy who could help him? I don't think I could do it, and I'm sure Derek would never agree. He's probably already back with Kyle. I'm also sure that he wasted no time getting back in his bed," he said bitterly.

"You're wrong, Keith! He is *not* back with Kyle. As a matter of fact, the last time I talked to Derek, he had not even told Kyle that you two broke up. He asks about you every time we talk. He loves you Keith, and he misses you."

"I will have to think about it." Keith turned and went back to caring for the horse he was brushing down. *Can I really do this? I miss Derek so much, but I know that I made the right decision.* He also hated to let Jamie and Marc down. That night, he tossed and turned, dreaming about

293

making love to Derek. He woke up with a hard-on and was sweating. Finally, he got some decent sleep.

~ The next morning, Keith told Jamie that he would go back but only until they could find a replacement. He found himself getting excited to see Derek again, and he wanted to go right away. He asked Jamie to make the arrangements for the following day.

That night, Jamie called Derek to tell him that he was sending Keith back until he could find someone suitable.

"*What?* Is Keith okay with this arrangement?"

"Yes. He said he'd do it until I found someone. He is arriving tomorrow at 3:45 p.m. Delta #639. Will you pick him up?"

"Sure! I hope it will be okay. I'm a little worried as you can imagine. My thoughts are all over the place. I have missed Keith. It is so lonesome around the farm, but Chrystel has been a big help."

"Have you talked with Kyle since you have been back?"

"Yes, but only when I first came back. Chrystel and I ran into him at dinner, and we just spoke. That's all. Nothing since."

"Derek, I don't understand why you have not been in contact with Kyle. You should have at least tried. He needs to know your change in status. Maybe he would give it another try."

"No. I cannot go through the rejection again. Besides, I told you that he is back with David. They have been back together for a while, so I think it is probably serious. I have also been too busy around here to be bothered. I need this time to adjust to being alone."

"Okay. I will respect your decision, even though I think it is wrong. You belong with Kyle. I used to hate him for how he treated you so long ago, but now I know that he loves you, and I am convinced that David is just rebound stuff … nothing more."

~ Derek got off the phone with Jamie and tried to decide how he felt about this new development. *It will be so good to see Keith again! It has only been a month, but it feels like forever since I saw him that night in the bedroom at Marc and Jamie's ranch.* Derek had a fitful night while trying to get some sleep after Jamie's news.

The next morning, Derek got up and did the chores, fed the horses, and then went to the main house to tell Mr. Hawthorn that Keith was coming back for the time being until Jamie could find someone to work here.

"Are you sure it is just temporary, Derek?" Mrs. Hawthorn asked. She always thought that he and Keith were meant for each other and held out hope that they would work it out.

"Shush! That is none of your business, and you should not be asking such a question," Mr. Hawthorn scolded her.

"Don't you shush me! I will say what I please." She turned her back on her husband and continued. "I can't wait to see him! He has been missed around here."

"Derek, do you need me to do anything while you drive to Lexington to pick him up?" Mr. Hawthorn asked, trying to change the subject and shut up his wife.

"Yes. Let out the horses into the far field to graze later this afternoon. I am going to clean up the house a little and get the guest room ready for Keith before I get him."

⁓ Derek drove to Chrystel's veterinary office to let her know that Keith was coming back for a short time until Jamie could find someone.

"Wow! That is great news, Derek. Maybe you could work things out with him. How long do you think he will be here? I know you have been missing him."

"I will be glad to see him. I have missed him terribly, but this is just temporary. I know that he has made his decision, and he will stick to it."

"Well, anyway, I am glad that he will be back for a while. Do you think he would like to have something to eat at R&J Steakhouse when you get back from Lexington?"

"I don't know, but I will ask him and send you a text."

⌐§ Keith sat on the plane. He was excited to come back to Berea but apprehensive about seeing Derek again. There had been no communication between them since Derek left over a month ago. *I am going to have to handle this very professionally while I am around Derek in order to keep my sanity until I can get back to Cheyenne again.*

Derek was waiting for Keith outside of the baggage claim area. When Keith came out, his stomach turned over when he saw Derek inside the truck. *Okay. Get yourself together,* he thought.

When Derek saw Keith, he jumped out of the truck and walked around to help him with his suitcases. He wanted to hug him but was sure it would be a very wrong move at this time. "How are you doing, Keith? How is the ranch? Have you been getting any new horses since I left? How are Jamie and Marc?" He knew that he was running off at the mouth, but he couldn't help it. He was nervous and just kept talking. He finally realized that he hadn't even given Keith a chance to answer any of his questions.

Keith was also extremely nervous but tried to calm down enough to answer all of Derek's questions. "The ranch is great. We bought three new studs, and I think Jamie is going to send at least one here when he gets you some help. Jamie and Marc are perfect. They couldn't be happier." He laughed. "What are we doing, Derek? We are acting like two strangers. I will tell you that I have missed you."

Tears rolled down Derek's face. "Thank you for saying that. I have missed you terribly. I have thought about you every day since returning to Berea. I know this is only temporary, but I am so glad to have you back home."

When they got into the truck, Derek laid his hand on Keith's knee, causing Keith to jump at the unexpected intimacy.

"This is only temporary!" Keith emphasized.

Derek immediately took his hand off Keith and pulled away from the airport. Tension was high, and they drove in silence for the first half of the 50-minute drive from Lexington to the Walker farm.

Finally, Keith broke the silence. "How are things at the farm? How's sweet Mrs. Hawthorn? I think I have missed her the most besides Shadow — and, of course, you."

Derek was hurt that he was added as an afterthought, but he let it go. "The farm is okay, but it has been really hard by myself. Mr. Hawthorn has been taking care of the fields, and he lets out the horses to graze when I am away, but you know that the horses are a full-time job with breeding and everything else. Mrs. Hawthorn said how much she has missed you, so I think the feeling is mutual. Shadow is spectacular as usual."

"And you?"

"I am miserable. Thanks for asking!"

They both got quiet again until Derek broke the silence and asked Keith about going to dinner with Chrystel after he unpacked. Keith agreed, and Derek sent Chrystel a text message that they would meet her at R&J Steakhouse at 7 p.m. He thought it would be a good way to help everyone relax a little.

As they pulled into the farm, Mrs. Hawthorn heard the truck and came running out to greet Keith. He barely got out of the truck before she was on him. She gave him a big hug and told him that she was glad to see him back where he belonged. "You know you belong here, Keith, and we are going to do everything we can to keep you here this time." She hugged him again and went back into the house.

Mr. Hawthorn told him to ignore her. "She is an old, crazy woman," he said while laughing. "It is good to see you back here though."

"Thanks. It is good to see you guys too. I want to see Shadow before I unpack," Keith said as he walked toward the field where Mr. Hawthorn had put the horses. He had to admit that it felt like he was returning home. *Watch yourself, or you will be drawn back in, and you know what kind of hurt that would bring back to you. Keep your distance and just hope that Jamie gets someone to replace you sooner than later.*

⮬ Chrystel finished seeing her patients and got ready for dinner. She was anxious to see Keith again. Kyle pulled up to see if she could talk and catch up. He had been really busy at the hospital and had not seen much of her lately.

"I can't talk too long because I am meeting Keith and Derek at R&J Steakhouse at 7."

"What? Wait! Did you say *Keith* and Derek? I thought that Keith left Derek. I heard him tell you that about a month ago."

"You mean to tell me that you have known over a month that Keith left Derek, and you have not said one word to me or haven't tried to see Derek? What is *wrong* with you? How could you have stayed away knowing what you know? I thought you had no idea, so it would make sense that you would not have tried to see Derek, but you knew and still stayed away? Well, that says volumes, doesn't it? I guess you are back into David, like Derek said.

Chrystel was incredibly angry and continued. "I am extremely disappointed in you, Kyle. You have known all this time and thought that Derek was not worth trying to make it work. God, Kyle, you are so stupid for such a brilliant man! Derek loves you with everything in him, and you didn't even want to see if it could work now that Keith was out of the picture."

There was no doubt in Kyle's mind. "You know why I can't go there. But I guess it was short-lived since you just said that you were meeting both of them for dinner. It was obviously just a lover's quarrel, and now things are back to normal," he said bitterly.

"Oh, you stupid, stupid man! They are *not* back together. Not that you deserve to know this, but Jamie sent Keith back to help Derek temporarily with the horses until he could find someone who would work permanently. He was having trouble finding the suitable employee for the job, so Keith reluctantly agreed to come back just for now. He is not returning to Derek, as you so readily assumed. Now, if you don't mind, I am too angry to talk with you right now and don't want to say anything that I can't take back."

"Okay, okay! I am so sorry that I made you angry. I love you, Chrystel, so I will go. But you need to know that, even though my actions are what they are, I love Derek." He got into his car and drove away.

Chrystel calmed down after he left, and then felt bad for chewing him out like that. She always got so frustrated with him and Derek. They were throwing away their love, and she would give anything to have Derek's love.

᷍ Chrystel arrived at R&J Steakhouse first and expected to run into Kyle since she had told him 45 minutes earlier that she was meeting Derek and Keith there. She figured that his curiosity would get the better of him. But, when she arrived, Kyle wasn't there. She put in their name for a table and sat down at the bar. About that time, Keith and Derek came in, acting very apart and withdrawn. She hoped that would change, at least while they had to work together.

After they were seated, Chrystel told Keith how great it was that he was back, if only for a short while.

He said it did feel good to be back. "I have missed you, Chrystel. I hope you have been checking up on Derek in my absence."

"I have tried, but he has been very standoffish."

"Hey, you two … I'm right here. Don't talk about me like I am not in the room!"

They both laughed. They had not even realized that they were doing it.

They ordered their food and spent the whole meal without getting too personal about the situation between Keith and Derek. They relaxed and talked as friends. It turned out to be a very productive evening: The casual conversation lessoned the tension, and Keith and Derek were more like themselves.

Driving home, Keith told Derek that he enjoyed the evening and hoped they could keep on this same way. Derek agreed that it was good. When they got alone in the house, the tension returned because they both wanted to get close but knew it was not a good idea. They said goodnight and went into their separate rooms.

Second Chances

Neither Keith nor Derek slept well, tossing and turning and dreaming about the other. At sunrise, Derek was already up and out at the stables. He couldn't stay in bed. He wanted so much to go to Keith's room and lie next to him, but he knew that he would not be welcome anymore. He told himself that he just needed to keep busy.

Keith was awake also, thinking about how much he missed Derek and how much he wanted him in his bed. *I have got to stop this, or I will be right back where I was before: second choice. No! I want more. I have to keep telling myself that.* He got up and showered, and then went down to the stables. "Good morning, Derek. I see that you have already started to feed the horses. Can you tell me what you need me to do?"

"What? Since when do you not know what needs to be done around here?" Derek asked, sharply. He regretted his attitude immediately after the words came out.

"Derek, we need to find some common ground so we can work together. Don't you agree?"

"Yes. I'm sorry for the way I snapped. I'm just tired."

"So you didn't sleep well either?"

"No, damn it! All I could think about was you in the next room." Derek walked around to the next stall, just to be doing something. "I wanted to go to your bed and lie beside you, but I knew I couldn't. You would have thrown me out."

"You don't know that! I don't know that! But I hope that I would have been strong enough to toss you out."

Derek was lost in thought about what Keith had just said. All of a sudden, the horse in the stall kicked him, causing him to fall back into Keith. Keith grabbed him around the waist to keep him from falling, and tension, arousal, and wanting immediately came into play. Keith turned Derek around in his arms and kissed him with such passion that neither expected. Just as suddenly, Keith broke the kiss and pushed Derek back, almost making him fall again.

"Sorry," he said breathlessly. "I should not have done that. It was not fair to you or me. Just instinct, I guess!"

"You can't chalk it up to instinct. You still love me and want me. That kiss said it. I love you and want you as much as ever."

"You say that, but we both know that Kyle is who you really want to be with — not me! He will always be your first choice, and I can't accept being second. God, this was probably a big mistake. I knew better than to come, but I promised Jamie and I will see this through. Just know that I'm truly sorry for kissing you. Now tell me what you have or have not done, so we can get to work."

They worked hard all day, not saying too much. When the day was done, they went back to the house and found a big surprise. Mrs. Hawthorn had made a pot of stew for supper and left it with homemade bread.

"That was sweet of Mrs. Hawthorn to do that," Keith said.

"Yes. She has missed you. You know that she is hoping we will work this out and you will stay with me."

"Yes, I know, but I need to move on and find someone who will love me and only me. I know you love me, Derek, but you are not *in* love with me, and that is not enough."

They got plates and sat down to eat.

"Have you seen Kyle lately?" Keith asked. It was killing him to wonder about it. "Have you told him that you are free?"

"No. There is nothing there for me now. He has moved on."

"Why do you say that? I don't like it, but I know that he is in love with you and always will. You two have a love that will never go away, even if you are too stupid to work it out and give into it."

"Wow! We are talking like friends instead of ex-lovers," Derek commented.

"It would be nice if we could try and be some kind of friends while I am here working with you. I sure don't want to be enemies."

They came to an understanding after that talk. One week later, things were working out well on the farm. Keith and Derek were acting more like themselves. Mr. and Mrs. Hawthorn noticed. Of course, Mrs. Hawthorn was always holding out hope for more.

⮝ David had heard through the grapevine that Keith was back at the Walker farm and felt such joy. He assumed that he had come back to Derek, so he no longer had to worry about Derek going after Kyle. Nothing seemed to be happening between Derek and Kyle in Keith's absence, but David still worried because he knew that Kyle was not completely his. He went to Kyle's office to see if he had heard the news.

"Kyle, did you hear that Keith has come back to Berea and to Derek?"

"Yes, I know. Chrystel told me. Why is it any business of yours or mine? I'm thinking that it is a good thing. Maybe they are working out their problems."

"You're right," David said. "It's not our concern. Are we going out tonight, Kyle?"

"No. I have too much work. Maybe tomorrow night."

"Okay. See you in the morning."

Kyle had to be alone. He had been wondering what was happening at the Walker farm. He couldn't get Derek's words out of his mind. Even though he heard Derek say that he was in love with him and that Keith knew how he felt, were they getting close again? He knew that Keith loved Derek and being around the man you love would be hard to resist. That was the reason he kept his distance from Derek.

Kyle drove home, went into his private den, opened a beer, and went to the couch opposite the picture of Derek over the mantel. He sat quietly, looking at Derek and daydreaming about making love to him. He did not hear the sound of someone coming in.

David was worried about Kyle's nonreaction to the news. He felt that Kyle was hiding his true feelings, so he had followed him home. He got the shock of his life when he saw the picture of Derek and gasped.

Kyle came out of his daydream, turned around, and went wild. "What the fuck are you doing by coming into my home uninvited and invading my privacy?" He grabbed David by the neck and pushed him against the wall. He was so angry that the look in his eyes scared David. He looked like he could kill him. "Again, I'm asking you … why are you in my house uninvited?"

"I was worried about you and the news of Derek and Keith, so I followed you. You left the door open."

Kyle let him go and walked out of the den. David stared at the picture and knew that, no matter what Kyle did or said, he was not into him. Kyle was in love with Derek. David left the room and found Kyle standing in the living room, seething with anger.

David felt his own resentment and anger welling up. "So you were just playing me. You do not want to get back with me permanently! You are just using me because you can't have Derek."

Kyle once again turned on him with a venomous stare. "You are just a great piece of ass, David. I like pounding your ass because you are just a whore who would have sex with anyone who wanted to fuck you. Oh, don't get me wrong. I love diving deep in your ass, but that is all you are to me … exercise … a means for me to get off my sexual frustrations. You will never be any more than that to me. I do care for you because of our years together, but I'm not in love with you and never will be. Now, if you still want to be my boyfriend, knowing what you know now, then fine. We can continue as we have been. If not, then we are done."

"I will forget about all this," David said, "because I love you and will take you any way I can have you. I think you will someday let us be a permanent couple again, and I will always stay faithful to you. I will prove it. I know you loved me once until I messed up."

"Okay, whatever! Now get upstairs and do what you do best."

David and Kyle walked upstairs to the bedroom. Kyle fucked him even harder this time because he was angry with him and frustrated about thinking of Derek.

As David drove home, he was still upset about seeing the picture of Derek. *Oh, god! How I hate him!*

Reconnecting

Jamie called the farm to see how things were going and to tell Keith that he had no luck finding his replacement. "How is it going, Keith?"

"We are actually doing rather well. It has been great being back here. I have missed everyone."

"You are not mentioning Derek in particular. How is that going?"

"We have been getting along really well. We had a good talk, and it has been better ever since. The horses are great, so take as long as you need to find my replacement. I really don't mind hanging here."

"Okay. I'll let you know when I find someone. Give Derek a hug for me please."

Keith hung up and thought, *Can I honor Jamie's request and hug Derek?* He decided that he would.

Derek came into the house from the stables and said that he would start supper. Keith came up to him and took Derek in his arms.

"Whoa! What are you doing?"

"Jamie asked me to give you a hug from him, but this is really from me." Keith did not let Derek out of his embrace. He leaned back, still holding him, and looked into Derek's eyes. He knew then that he wanted him. Keith moved in closer and kissed Derek.

As their lips touched, all the feelings came rushing back. The old connection was still there.

Derek broke the kiss first. "What are we doing? Does the feeling I am getting from you mean what I hope it means?"

"Yes. I want you, Derek. Will you come upstairs with me?"

Derek grabbed Keith's hand and led him to the stairs. They went up to Derek's room and closed the door.

"Are you sure that this is what you want, Keith? I don't want to hurt you again."

Keith moved in close to Derek and grabbed his hand, placing it on his hard cock. "Does this answer your question?"

"Yes, it does."

Derek kissed Keith again and started to undress him. He couldn't believe that Keith wanted to make love to him again. They moved to the bed when both had their clothes off. Derek positioned himself under Keith as Keith took him completely. His mind was only on Derek as he pushed into him over and over. Derek took every stroke that Keith gave him with such wonder. He was getting him back. After they made love, both men were so happy to lie in each other's arms.

Keith spoke first. "Derek, I love you, and I do not regret this at all. I know that you don't love me in the same way, but I did feel that you were totally with me this time, unlike the past, so I'm willing to give us another chance if you want it too."

"Yes, Keith, I do. Please make love to me again and again."

They made love all night, and the next morning Derek could barely walk, let alone sit down. Keith laughed at him when he came down to breakfast.

"I think I'll stand and eat my eggs," Derek quipped.

"Oh, honey. Are you sure you don't want more of what you got all night? I could accommodate."

"You are very funny! We should call Jamie and tell him that he can stop looking, if you want to stay with me."

"Yes, yes, yes! I want to stay with you. Can we go back for round eight or nine? I've lost count."

"NO!"

Keith laughed and patted Derek on his very sore ass. "You are too cute, walking funny like that. It does my heart good to know that I caused it."

When they called Jamie later, he was so happy that his hug caused this great reconnection. He couldn't wait to tell Marc. Derek wasn't much good all day, so Keith took up the slack.

⌁ Chrystel came by to check on the horses and saw how funny Derek was walking. *Oh, my. I know there is only one thing that can cause that!* She smiled and asked, "How are you, Derek?"

"I'm fine, Chrystel. Why would you ask?"

"Oh, I don't know … just wondering." She went to the barn and found Keith brushing down Shadow. "How are things, Keith?"

"Couldn't be better, Chrystel."

"Yeah, I see that. Derek is walking funny, and you are smiling from ear to ear. I took that as a good sign."

"Yeah, we are going to try being a couple again."

"I am so happy for you both! We will have to go out and celebrate sometime soon. Maybe when Derek is back to normal," she said, chuckling.

"I may not let him get back to normal for quite a while," Keith said with another big smile.

Chrystel was happy for her friends. As she was leaving the farm, she yelled back at Derek, "Take care of yourself!"

Days and weeks went by with Keith and Derek working all day together and making love at night. They also told the Hawthorns that Keith was back for good, making Mrs. Hawthorn happy. She told her husband that she just knew it would happen.

"Yeah, yeah, woman!" He smiled as she walked into the house.

Life without Love

Kyle stopped by to see Chrystel and to check what was going on at the Walker farm. He had not seen Derek or Keith in town, and his curiosity was killing him. "Well, Chrystel, how are they doing?"

"Who?"

"Don't be cute. You know who. Are they back together again like I suspect they are?"

"Why don't you ask them?"

"Okay. So you just want to see me suffer! I thought we were friends."

"We are. To answer your questions, yes. They are working through their problems, but you and I both know that it is different from what you and Derek feel for each other. He loves you, Kyle, and always will. But since he can't have you, he will work on rekindling what he had with Keith. They were in love once. He loves Keith but, as he says, it's not the same as being *in* love with him. Keith is willing to settle for that because, in Keith's heart, Derek is the love of his life. He is happier with him than without him."

"Well, I guess I'm happy for them," Kyle said with a crack in his voice, walking toward the door.

Chrystel grabbed his arm. "I'm sorry, Kyle. I know that was not what you wanted to hear."

Kyle pulled away. "It is what I thought would happen," he said as he left. When he got to the car, he sat there for a long time.

Chrystel watched him from the window. Her heart was breaking.

⁓ The next day, Kyle was in his office and still not in the mood to do anything.

David walked in. "Are we still on for tonight? I'm really looking forward to it."

"Sure. I'll pick you up at 7:30. Now please go back to work. I have a lot of charts to catch up on, and I'm sure you have another surgery scheduled."

"Okay. See you tonight."

As the day went on, Kyle's mood deteriorated even more, and he decided that he could not face going out with David. He called him and begged off with a made-up excuse of not feeling well. David wasn't happy but said that maybe they'd get together the next day.

Kyle left work and sat once again in his car with no plan in mind. He wanted to be alone but also felt the need to be close to Derek. He drove to the Walker farm but parked way off the normal road that led into the farm, and he walked to Walker's Pond. The air was crisp, and the only light was from the full moon. He felt secure that no one would be out at the pond because of the crisp air and the time of night.

He sat on the ground and thought about how he had messed up his whole life from the first time he shunned Derek in high school until the time he sent him away from his barn so long ago. *Chrystel was right. I am such a fool. I pushed away the only man I will ever love and for what? MY PRIDE!* He sat quietly, watching the moon reflect on the pond. He agreed with Derek that this was the most beautiful place to be. He was deep in thought and didn't notice anyone approaching.

Derek's breath caught in his throat when he saw Kyle sitting in the moonlight. "Kyle?" He could barely get his name out.

Kyle was startled out of his thoughts, and he jumped up. He turned to face the object of his thoughts, red-faced and speechless.

"What are you doing here, Kyle?"

"I'm sorry to intrude, but I needed a place to be alone and I remembered the pond. I figured that you and Keith would not be here because of the cool, crisp air, so I took a chance." He wanted to say that it was close to Derek but held his tongue. As he started to walk away, he said, "So sorry. I'll leave!"

"Stop. Tell me what brought you here."

"You!" Kyle said louder than he intended. "I heard that you and Keith are back together, and I was reflecting about what a fool I have been. I have to go. Be happy, Derek." He walked as fast as he could to get away from Derek.

Derek just stood there stunned. *What was that? What did he mean? I can't go back there. Keith is my steadfast partner, and I should be with him. I can't hurt Keith again by rejecting him for Kyle. Just forget this encounter ever happened.*

Kyle was a mess while driving back home. *Why was I so stupid going there and opening myself up to this hurt?* Seeing Derek again opened all his wounds. He drove home and walked around the house like a lost soul. *Okay, Douglas. Get a grip on yourself. Derek is out of your life. Move on.* After a restless night, he decided that he would concentrate on his work at the hospital.

ᕗ The next day was really busy, and Kyle had not run into David all day, for which he was thankful. David wanted to check on Kyle to see if he was feeling better but had a busy surgery schedule, so it was not working out. He texted Kyle several times between cases but didn't receive any response.

Kyle was in meetings off and on for most of the day. He saw the text messages but didn't feel like talking. He left the hospital early while David was still in the OR to avoid seeing him. He had signed up for a medical conference in Lexington the next day, which was mentioned in one of his meetings. He just needed to get away.

Kyle went home to pack an overnight bag and get on the road before David was done at the hospital. He had no intention of telling David where he was. As he was driving to Lexington, he did a lot of thinking. He wanted to end it with David after last night at Walker's Pond. He couldn't keep it up even though he told David that, if he was still willing to be his exercise equipment, he would stay with him. *Maybe if I cut David loose, he could find someone. It's not fair to him or me. I can do without sex although I know David can't.*

311

Kyle checked into the hotel and went to the lounge for a sandwich and a beer. His phone was blowing up with text messages from David. He had finished his schedule and was trying to get Kyle to go out. Kyle ignored all of them. "Not tonight, David!"

The bartender looked up. "Sir, did you say something to me?"

"Sorry. I was just thinking out loud."

↬ David looked all over the hospital for Kyle. He finally went to Dr. Mitchell's office. "Dr. Mitchell, do you have any idea where Dr. Douglas went? I know that he is not in his office, and I have not seen him around the hospital. I asked several nurses and interns, but no one has seen him since earlier. He was sick yesterday, so I am worried. He is not responding to my texts."

Kyle had told Dr. Mitchell not to mention the conference to anyone and that he needed alone time and wanted to catch up at this conference without any diversions.

"I have no idea, Dr. Jenkins. I saw him in a meeting today, and he seemed to be fine. I'm sorry, but I really have to get to another meeting," he said as he left his office, ushering David out with him.

David was worried and confused. *I thought we were supposed to go out tonight. Where is he?*

David drove all around Berea, stopping at their favorite places. He also drove by Kyle's house, but his car was not there. Finally, he decided to go over to the Walker farm.

Derek answered the door and couldn't believe his eyes. *First Kyle was at the pond last night, and now David is at our front door today!* "What do you want, David?"

"Is Kyle here?"

Keith walked in the room at that moment and came to the door. "Why would you think that Kyle would be here?"

"Because I can't find him anywhere, and I have looked all over town. I thought he might show up here, but I guess that was stupid since he knows that you guys are back together."

"Yes. We are back together and out of both of your lives. When you do find him, tell him that Derek is mine!" Keith slammed the door in David's face.

"Was that necessary, Keith? Please don't ever speak for me again," Derek said as he walked to the kitchen.

"What is your problem, Derek? Please don't start this again. We are doing so well."

"I'm not starting anything, but I just don't see the necessity to be rude to him. He is not worth the effort. Just a simple 'no, he is not here' would have been enough."

"You're right."

⮜ David was elated to hear that Derek and Keith were back together, but he still wondered where Kyle was. He decided to go by Chrystel's place to see if she might know. When he got there, Chrystel was doing her rounds at a farm according to Galen, who was waiting for her.

"What have you been up to, David?" Galen asked. "We keep missing each other at the house."

"Just working and dating Kyle. With you working on computers at the hospital at night and me working in the day, we are like ships in the night!"

They both laughed.

"Do you want to get a drink, David? I'm not working tonight, so we can catch up."

"Sure, I would like that."

They went to a bar close to their house. "Have you found anyone since you have been here, Galen?'

"No. Just a couple of guys to have sex with but nothing serious. You said you were dating Kyle. He told me that you were a couple nine years ago but not now. Has that changed?"

"Well, sort of. We spend time together, but we're still not a couple."

They drank until late, both feeling the effects of too much to drink. Luckily, they could walk home from the bar. When they got there, they stumbled into the house.

"You want a nightcap, David? I have some really good scotch."

"Yeah, I do!"

They drank some more, and then finally decided to call it a night. Both went to their rooms. David got naked, which is the way he always slept. He needed some water, so he went back to the kitchen to get some. Galen heard him get up and worried, so he came out to see if he was okay. Galen saw David naked and couldn't help himself. He came up behind David and rubbed his cock against David's cute ass. David pushed back toward Galen out of instinct, inviting him.

"I want you, David. I'm so horny, and you walking out here naked, showing me your cute ass, made me hard."

David leaned back so Galen could kiss his neck and rub up against him again. David wanted it too. Galen bent him over the counter and wasted no time shoving his cock into him. With balls deep, he moaned and moved in and out.

David was lost in lust and wanted more. "Fuck me hard, Galen ... oh, that feels so good!"

Galen reached around to find David's hard cock and started pumping him as he pushed into him over and over. They both came almost together. Galen fell forward onto David's back and just lay there.

"You are a great piece of ass, David. I'm going to want you again soon." He pulled out and cleaned them both off. "Let's go to the bedroom and do this right."

David was lost in want and did not care that he was breaking his promise to Kyle. *Why shouldn't I enjoy this? Galen is really hot and horny and at least he wants me, not someone else.*

They went to Galen's bedroom and kept the lust going all night.

Kyle had fucked David over and over before, but this was addicting with Galen. David did not want to stop. *I will keep this my little secret and enjoy Galen any time I want. Kyle says I'm a whore, and he is right about one thing: I do like to be fucked. Who knew that I would have my own sex toy right here at home with Galen? I'll have to offer him my ass any time I feel in the mood. I am sure he will oblige.*

ᗖ David woke up in Galen's bed with a horrible hangover and the smell of sex all over him.

Galen stirred and reached for David. "Good morning! Are you okay, David?"

"Yes. We really hung one on, didn't we? My head sure feels it."

As he patted his ass, he asked, "What about here?"

"There too!" David said with a smile.

"Come on. Let's take a hot shower together." In the shower, Galen said, "You are really good, David. The best I have ever had. I loved being inside of you. Do you think you will want to do this again when we are sober?"

David moved against him. "We are sober now. What do you say we go another round?"

Galen couldn't believe his luck. "Oh, yeah. Let's go for it." He took David again while the hot water ran all over them. "Wow, we are good together!"

After the shower, David said, "Let's get dressed, Galen. I have to get to the hospital. I don't have any surgeries, but I have charts to catch up on for medical records."

"Okay. I will see you soon, I hope. I have to work tonight, but if you want me again, just come to me."

David dressed and headed to the hospital. He felt great after a coffee and a few aspirin. He had no guilt. He went to Kyle's office to see if he was in, but it was still empty.

ᗖ Kyle woke early, showered, shaved, and called room service. He felt much better and decided that, since he was here, he would attend the conference. At the end of the day, he called Dr. Mitchell to tell him that the conference was good and that he was staying another day. Dr. Mitchell told him that Dr. Jenkins came by the day before, but he had told David that he had no idea where to find him. Kyle thanked him and said that he would see him Monday morning.

Kyle stayed around the hotel, relaxing and trying to figure out what he should do next. He was deep in thought, mostly about Derek as usual. He was never far from his mind. *I wish I had never pushed Derek away when he came to me at the barn so long ago. Things would be different now. Why couldn't I let it go and accept him? He was giving me his heart, and I tossed it back in his face. Well, now he is back with Keith, and that is the end of it. I have really lost him forever. He will never leave Keith now. Knowing Derek the way I do, he would not hurt him again.*

I have to decide if I can stay in the same town and watch them in love and happy. Although I do want Derek to be happy, I just don't want to watch it. I think I need to look for another hospital far away from Berea, Kentucky. I will see what is out there for a chief of staff. Going away from here would also get me away from David too. That is something else I need to take care of. I really want him out of my life. I wish that he had not followed me here. I should never have picked up with him again. What a mess!

◈ Saturday morning, after Kyle came back from Lexington, he drove over to see Chrystel. He wanted to tell her that he had done a lot of soul searching and about what he had decided. "Hi, Chrystel. I want to talk to you. Do you have to do your rounds, or do you have time? May I take you to breakfast?"

"Sure, Kyle, I would love that! I have lots of time before I have to start my rounds." When she got in his truck, she noticed the overnight bag. "Where have you been?"

"I just drove back from Lexington. I was attending a conference and decided to stay an extra day to do some thinking."

"Let me guess … Derek!"

"Yes. I was trying to decide what to do about throwing Derek away and this whole mess with David. Chrystel, I really hate David. I have decided to make him go away and leave me alone. That is the easiest part of what I have to do. He is not worth much of my time. The hard part is figuring out how I am going to deal with Derek and Keith."

Kyle and Chrystel drove to her favorite breakfast place and ordered pancakes and coffee. Kyle was very quiet, and Chrystel decided to let him talk when he was ready. Their food arrived, and they ate in silence.

Chrystel was studying Kyle and wondering what he had on his mind. She could tell that it was quite serious. "Tell me what you are planning on doing. Whatever it is, I am sure that I'm not going to like it by the look on your face and your total demeanor."

Kyle took a sip of coffee and simply stated, "I'm going to hire a headhunter to find me another chief of staff position, far away from Berea and my heart."

Chrystel was speechless. Her mind was all over the place as she tried to process this information. It was certainly not what she expected to hear.

Betrayed Again

On Monday at the hospital, Kyle contacted the headhunter who got him the job in Berea. Kyle told him that he would like to go out west, maybe to San Jose, California, or somewhere else in that area. He really didn't care where. *I just want to be as far away as I can get from Berea and Derek,* he thought. His headhunter told him that, at this time, there was nothing, but he would keep looking.

⌁ Chrystel decided to go see Kyle at the hospital. She texted him: "Could I talk to you for a minute if I come to the hospital?"

"Sure. Come on," he texted back.

Chrystel drove to the hospital and knocked on Kyle's office door.

"Come in, Chrystel. What is so important that you came here?"

"You can't be serious about leaving."

"I have already hired a headhunter. I'm *very* serious! I can't stay here and watch Derek be with Keith again. I just can't."

"Where are you trying to go?"

"I'm going to try and go out west, far away from Berea."

"You know that it will kill Derek, even though he is with Keith. He loves you!"

"I don't know about that. He is always angry with me. Maybe it will be a good thing for him too. But, even if that were true, if they have a chance at making it work, then I have to go."

"You are my friend, Kyle, and I will miss you terribly."

"You can always come to visit. Besides, it's not going to be anytime soon. The headhunter said that there was nothing out there right now for a chief of staff job."

"Well, good. I don't want you to go."

After Chrystel left, Kyle decided that he needed to have a talk with David. *He is tied up in surgery, so I'll go by his house later tonight.* He was deep in thought when Dr. Mitchell knocked on his door. "Come in!"

"Hey, Dr. Douglas. I was wondering if you would be willing to do me a big favor."

"Sure, if I can."

"I need to travel to Africa for a three-month program with some professors from Berea College, and they need a doctor to come along. I would like you to run the hospital in my absence. I know that this is huge for you because you oversee all the staff and would have to do my administrative duties as well, but you are the only one who I feel can do it."

"Oh, I don't know. Like you said, that is a big undertaking. May I think about it? When do you leave?"

"In three weeks."

"Okay. I will give you my answer tomorrow."

"Thank you. I know that this is asking a lot, but it is very important work."

After Dr. Mitchell left, Kyle thought about it. If he ran the hospital for three months, he would have to put his plans to leave on hold. Dr. Mitchell was someone whom Kyle respected, and it would be a good thing if he helped him. *I will do this for Dr. Mitchell, but is it just an excuse to stay in Berea?*

When Kyle left the hospital, he headed to Chrystel's house. Just as he pulled up, he saw her on the porch, getting ready to leave. He got out of the truck and approached her.

"Hey, what are you doing here?" Chrystel asked. "Please tell me that you have changed your mind about leaving!"

"I did. Dr. Mitchell needs me to do his job at the hospital while he goes to Africa."

"*What?* Why is he going to Africa?"

"I don't know the particulars. I just know that he is going with some professors from the college for three months."

Chrystel grabbed him and gave him a big bear hug. "I'm so glad! You need to put that foolishness about leaving out of your head!"

Kyle laughed at her. "I'm so glad that you are my friend and want me around so much."

She hugged him again. "Always!"

"Well, I've got a million things to do, and you were headed somewhere when I pulled up, so I'll talk to you later." Kyle went back to his truck, and Chrystel went to hers.

"Later!"

Kyle called Dr. Mitchell to let him know that he would cover for him. He decided that there was no reason to make him wait until the next day for his answer. He headed home to shower and change before going to talk with David. He was really dreading this conversation.

꧁ Keith called Marc to check on the horses that they wanted to send to Kentucky for breeding.

"Hello!" Marc answered.

"Hi, Marc. I'm just checking about the horses you wanted Derek and me to take."

"How is that going, Keith? Are you guys still working on things between you?"

"Oh, yes. We are doing great. I'm glad that I decided to stay. I should have known that I would not be able to leave Derek."

"I'm so happy for you! By the way, I was thinking of having you drive the semi-truck with the horse trailer. I need you to bring the four horses that we are planning to sell here, and then have you pick up two horses for breeding and take them back with you. I'll let you know when we will be ready for you to come."

"I can do that. It will take me at least four to five days to drive from Berea to Cheyenne, and Derek will have to stay here and help Mr. Hawthorn. It will just be me coming."

Keith went to the stables to find Derek and let him know that he had the conversation with Marc regarding the horses. "They will call when they are ready for me to drive there."

"I guess I'll let you go without me, but only if you tell me that you plan to come back."

Keith laughed and gave Derek a big hug. "You are so silly. The horses can't drive the semi back themselves! Of course, I will be coming back."

◈ David was too busy to try and talk with Kyle at the hospital, so he went home to clean up and go find him. He was still upset that it had been days since he talked with him. He got home at 6 p.m. and found Galen, who had prepared dinner with wine and candles.

"What is all this, Galen?"

"I thought we would have a nice dinner together since we are hardly ever on the same schedule."

"I was going to clean up and try to find Kyle, but I guess we can eat first since you went to all this trouble." *How considerate of Galen*, he thought.

They ate and drank some wine.

Finally, Galen got up and pulled David into his arms. "I want you, David." He kissed him passionately.

David melted against him with no reservations, even though he was supposed to be faithful to Kyle.

◈ Kyle arrived at David's and knocked on the door. No one answered, so he knocked again … still no answer. He knew that David's car was there because he saw it when he pulled up, so he went over to the window to see if he could get his attention and open the door. When he looked inside, David and Galen were naked and going at it hot and heavy on the couch. Kyle became instantly sick to his stomach. He could not watch another moment. He went back to his car and drove off in a hurry. He didn't know where to go, so he just started driving. Suddenly, he looked up and saw that he was driving toward the Walker farm.

I can't go there, he thought. He pulled off the road and sat there, trying to wrap his head around what he just saw again. It was like reliving nine years ago. *Well, that finishes it once and for all. I will never be drawn in again. David made it so easy!*

Kyle put his head in his hands and leaned onto the steering wheel, lost in thought. All of a sudden, a knock on the window brought him back to the here and now. He had no idea how long he was there. He looked up and saw David standing outside the car. He opened the door, almost knocking David down.

"What are you doing on the side of the road, Kyle? I was coming to see you and saw your car," David said.

Kyle pulled back his fist and struck David right on the jaw, knocking him to the road.

David grabbed his jaw and looked up at Kyle. "What was *that* for?" He started to get up, and Kyle put his foot to David's chest, shoving him back down. "Kyle, what are you doing?"

"You are a disgusting human being, and I never want to sully my hands on you again." Kyle turned his back on David and started to walk away.

David jumped up and grabbed his arm to stop him. "What is wrong? I *love* you!"

"LOVE?" Kyle screamed. "You don't know what that is. Take your hands off me. You made me want to puke when I saw you with your legs in the air and Galen shoving his cock into you! It was shades of before, and we have nothing more to say. You are garbage and out of my personal life for sure, and I will get you out of my professional life ASAP. Don't *ever* come near me again!"

"Stop! You don't mean this, Kyle. Galen means *nothing* to me!"

Kyle looked at him and drove off, leaving David yelling after his car.

❧ Kyle drove home and went into his den. He sat on the couch for hours, staring at Derek's picture. *Derek, how could I have let you go? How am I going to live my life without you?* His phone kept going off … David was texting him. He even wrote that he was coming over.

Finally, Kyle texted back: "DON'T!"

Kyle called Dr. Mitchell and told him that he needed to take a couple of personal days. He wanted to close off the outside world and be alone. He texted Chrystel that he was going to stay home for a few days and just be alone. He said that he would contact her when he was ready to see anyone.

Chrystel got the text and was really worried. *What is going on? Something must have happened.* As she drove up to Galen's house, she saw David walking up to the door. "David, have you seen Kyle today?" As David turned to answer her, she saw his face. His jaw and eye were already turning blue. "What happened to *you?*"

"None of your damn business, and yes, I have seen Kyle." He turned and walked into the house.

Chrystel decided not to pursue it any farther. It was quite obvious that Kyle had hit him.

❧ The next day, Chrystel called Galen to see if he had any information about what happened to his roommate. Galen confirmed that Kyle had hit him because he saw him and David having sex.

"You what? You and *David*? When did that start?"

"We have been attracted to each other for a while and finally acted on it. It was just bad timing, but who cares? We are grown men who like sex."

Chrystel knew then why Kyle said that he was going to stay home alone for a few days. *Another big mess,* she thought. *Well, I'm glad he is through with David. I knew that was a mistake.* She couldn't wait to tell Derek the news, even though he was with Keith now. She knew that it would lessen the hurt in his heart knowing that Kyle was not with David and never would be again.

Chrystel went to see Derek right after she finished cleaning up after seeing her patients. When she arrived at the Walker farm, she found Derek in the stall with Shadow. "Hi, Derek. I have some news that I thought you would like to hear. Is Keith around?"

"No. He is riding today, getting four of the horses ready to take to Jamie and Marc. Why?"

"This is for your ears only. Kyle is done with David for good. He caught him having sex with my cousin Galen and totally ended it."

"Why should that matter to me at this point, Chrystel?"

"I know that you are with Keith now, but I thought this news would ease the hurt in your heart a little. Kyle has closed himself off from everyone. He said that he would let me know when he was ready to see people again. He told his boss at the hospital that he needed a few days for some alone time."

"Thanks for telling me, Chrystel. I'll have to process this to see how I feel."

When Chrystel left, Derek took Shadow for a ride to think. After a short while, he decided that he would go see Kyle, but not today. *I need to figure out what I will say to him.*

Trying to Be a Friend

The next day, Derek told Keith what Chrystel had told him and that he wanted to talk with Kyle.

"Sure, if you feel you must, Derek. I trust you because you said that you are with me for good. But may I ask why you feel the need to see him though?" Keith knew he shouldn't ask, but it was out before he thought about it.

"I know that he is probably hurting, and he is important to me, even though we are not together. Are you sure it is not a problem?"

"No, it's not. Go see him. I know you well enough to know that this will eat at you until you do." Keith hugged Derek, and the two men went out to do the chores.

∽ Derek drove to Kyle's farm after he and Keith finished their care of the horses. He got out of the truck and knocked on the door.

Kyle answered and was almost knocked off his feet when he saw who it was. Almost in a whisper because he hadn't gotten his senses back, he asked, "What are you doing here, Derek?"

"May I come in?"

Kyle stepped back to let Derek enter.

"I heard from Chrystel what happened to you with David, and I thought that maybe you could use a friend about now."

"We are not friends, Derek. I think you should go. I really don't want to talk about this — especially not with you!" Kyle knew that he said this a little harsher than he intended, but he was shaken by him coming here. He so wanted to beg Derek to stay, but he knew that it was long past them being anything to each other. "Please go, Derek. It is too hard for me to see you and be this close to you, knowing that you are committed to Keith. I just want to be left alone right now."

"Okay, Kyle. I don't want to add to your pain. I only wanted to try and show you that, even though we are not together, I don't want to see you hurt. I know that I have done enough of that toward you already."

"Please go!" Kyle pleaded, his heart broken. He opened the door for Derek to leave.

Derek felt incredibly sad for Kyle — and for them — because they couldn't even be in each other's lives as friends. He drove back to the Walker farm feeling defeated and heartbroken. When he got back, Keith wanted to know what had happened. Derek told him that Kyle did not want to talk or even have him there, so he did not try to stay. "I guess he will work through it without my help."

Keith hid his pleasure after hearing that Kyle didn't want him there, so he changed the subject. "Derek, what do you think about us going out to celebrate our getting back together? Maybe we could see if Chrystel wanted to go. We could go to that great place in Richmond where you can shoot pool or play darts and have a few beers."

"Yes, Keith. That sounds like fun. Let's call her. She usually likes to go there." Derek thought that it would help if they went out somewhere fun to take his mind off Kyle and how much it hurt him to see him in so much pain.

Keith called Chrystel and asked, "Do you want to celebrate with us tonight and go to that place in Richmond that you like? We want to play and just have fun."

"Sure. I would love to go! What time?"

"We will pick you up at 8."

⤚ Later that night, Keith and Derek picked up Chrystel and headed to Richmond.

"Wow! It looks a little crowded," Chrystel said as they pulled into the full parking lot.

"We will find a place when we get in there," Derek assured her.

As they walked in, Chrystel got whistles and cat calls from some of the men who were standing by the pool table. Chrystel ignored them as they walked up to the bar and ordered their beers. Keith found a table close to the bandstand, and they all sat down.

After a few beers, Keith asked if they wanted to shoot pool. Chrystel loved to play pool and agreed that it would be fun. The table was open, so the three of them got up to play cutthroat pool. Several of the men stood in the way of letting Chrystel pass. She continued to ignore their efforts to get her attention.

As the game progressed, the guys were starting to get a little more annoying, and Chrystel finally told them to back off. They left her alone for a few more shots. Keith won the game when he sank the last of his opponent's balls, and Derek came up and gave him a congratulatory hug.

The guys noticed the hug and immediately were all over Chrystel. Two of the five men grabbed her and pulled her against them. "What are you doing, hanging out with these two faggots? We will show you what *real* men can do for you," they said as they started to fondle her.

Keith and Derek approached them immediately, trying to get them off Chrystel. Keith was punched in the jaw, which caused him to fall on the floor. Two of the guys held Chrystel while the other three threw tables out of the way to go after Keith and Derek. Derek was still trying to get Chrystel away from the ones holding her when he was thrown over a table, sending bottles of beer flying. He landed on his back on the floor.

Before Derek could get up, one of the men started to stomp on him. He stomped and kicked Derek in the gut and side until he no longer fought back. All hell broke loose, with two of the men fighting Keith. Chrystel screamed for someone to help her friends. No one helped.

Keith threw punches at the other two men, but then one grabbed his left arm and pulled it back in an awkward position. Everyone heard a *snap*. Meanwhile, Chrystel was still screaming for help as she was being assaulted by the other two men, who were kissing her and pawing at her clothes.

Suddenly, everyone in the bar heard sirens, and the fight stopped immediately. The two men let Chrystel go and were trying to get out of the bar with the other three when they were stopped at the door by the police. The bartender had finally called the police when he saw what the men were doing to Chrystel. He didn't care that they were beating up the two gay guys, but he was not going to tolerate them raping a woman in his bar.

The police called an ambulance right away when they assessed the injuries. Derek was still unconscious on the floor, and Keith sat next to him, holding his arm. Chrystel was trying to get her clothes in order when one police officer came over.

"Miss, are you hurt?"

"No. Please take care of my friends."

The EMTs got there first and started taking care of Derek. The ambulance arrived right on the heels of the EMT truck and brought in a stretcher. The EMTs had already started an IV and put an oxygen mask on him, so all ambulance crew had to do was get him on the stretcher and transport and assess his vital signs.

One of the EMTs came over to assess Keith's condition and determined that he had a broken left arm and a broken nose. They checked his vitals, and all were good. They asked Keith if he wanted to ride in the ambulance with Derek, and he said yes. The ambulance left the bar and headed to the hospital in Richmond, which was just down the road. Once they got Derek stabilized, they transported him to Berea upon Keith's request. He told the EMTs that Derek's friend was chief of staff there, and he wanted him to take care of Derek.

In the meantime, the police questioned Chrystel about the incident along with the people in the bar. Chrystel told them that five guys started attacking her without any provocation, and her two friends came to her defense. The bartender told them the same story, so Chrystel was permitted to leave. The police had also talked with Keith before he left with Derek in the ambulance, and he told them their side of the story.

As Keith was getting in the ambulance, he told one of the guys who was sitting in the police van that they would be sorry they hurt his partner.

The guy yelled, "You and your faggot friend got what you deserve, and you will pay for getting us arrested."

The police arrested the five guys and took them to the county jail.

↜ Chrystel got into Keith's car and phoned Kyle.

Kyle answered after several rings. "Chrystel, what do you want? I told you that I wanted to be left alone."

"Kyle, shut up and listen to me." She was crying so hard that he could barely understand her. "Derek, Keith, and I went to a bar in Richmond tonight to have some fun, and we were attacked by five guys. We were minding our business when two of them grabbed me and started to fondle me. Derek and Keith came over to help, and a fight broke out. Derek is being rushed to the hospital in serious condition. They beat him badly. Keith is also hurt with a broken arm and nose. Other than that, he seems okay. I think they took them to Richmond Hospital."

"Where are you now? Are you okay?"

"Yes. Don't worry about me. You need to find out where Derek and Keith are and help Derek. He never regained consciousness. I don't know if he is even alive. Call me back and let me know where they took them."

Kyle immediately called Richmond Hospital and got the ER department. They told him that Keith and Derek were there and, after stabilizing the one patient, they were being taken to Berea Hospital. Kyle called Chrystel and told her to meet him there.

On the way to Berea, Derek's vital signs got worse, and the squad called ahead to the ER and reported the situation. His blood pressure was dropping dangerously low. The doctor on call told them to increase his IV fluids and the oxygen and that they would have doctors waiting for them. They were also told to get more vitals and reports as they were driving to Berea.

Kyle was walking in the ER just as the ambulance arrived. He ordered a CT scan STAT. He also called the OR to get a room ready for emergency surgery. He was dying inside, seeing Derek so pale and beaten, but he needed to be a doctor now. Derek's life could depend on it. He called David and told him to come to the hospital for an emergency laparotomy, even though he hated doing it. No matter how he felt about David as a person, he was an excellent surgeon and wanted the best for Derek.

The scan showed internal bleeding, which Kyle suspected all along, probably from a ruptured spleen. He noted extensive bruising when he looked at his abdomen as the squad brought him into the ER. Kyle ordered them to take Derek directly to the OR after doing the CT scan.

Chrystel arrived at the hospital and found Keith in an ER room. He told her that things were really bad with Derek. He had been in the ambulance when Derek's condition started getting worse.

"I have not seen Derek since we arrived, Chrystel. They took him into some other area. I got a glimpse of Kyle, but he was too busy barking orders to talk."

"I will find out what is going on, Keith, so don't worry. Just let them take care of you."

The doctor walked in to see Keith. "Hi. I am Dr. Scott, the ER doctor on staff. I have come to set your arm and your nose. The nurse will come in after to clean your face and dress any wounds you have."

Kyle walked into the room as Dr. Scott got ready to set Keith's arm. "Dr. Scott, these are friends of mine. Can you give us a minute? I want to let them know what is going on with Keith's partner."

Dr. Scott left the room to give them some privacy. Chrystel ran into Kyle's arms. He gave her a hug and told her to sit for a minute.

"Hello, Keith," Kyle said. "Are you injured any other place besides your nose and your arm hurting like a son of a bitch?"

"I'm okay, Kyle. Please tell me how Derek is."

"Derek has been taken to the OR for emergency surgery. He is bleeding internally, and I suspect it is from a ruptured spleen. I have called David to do the surgery."

"What? Are you crazy? Not him … he *hates* Derek! He will kill him!"

"Calm down, Keith. He may be a lot of things, but he is a doctor and a great surgeon. He would never break his oath, I assure you. If I thought otherwise, I would never have called him. You know how I feel about Derek. That is no secret. Now please excuse me. I have to get to the OR. I'm going to scrub in and observe." Kyle left the room and headed to surgery.

When he got there, David was coming out of the doctor's lounge where he had changed into scrubs. He asked him coldly, "So, Kyle, what is this emergency, and who is the patient?"

"The patient is Derek, and it's a ruptured spleen, I suspect. He is bleeding internally and is still unconscious."

David started scrubbing while Kyle checked the OR to see if everything was being set up. The anesthesiologist was taking care of Derek, and the scrub nurse and circulating nurse were getting everything ready.

The whole time David was scrubbing, he was thinking about doing this surgery. *It would be so easy to do something to Derek, and I would be rid of him forever.* His ethics as a doctor would stand in his way, and he knew that.

Kyle scrubbed in as well but was strictly there to observe and help if he were needed. He was sure that he would be useless because he was too upset to be much good. The surgery went longer than anticipated due to all the bleeding, so Kyle broke scrub to give Keith and Chrystel an update. He knew they would be worried.

"He will be in surgery a little longer," Kyle explained. "The internal bleeding has been hard to control, and we had to give him several units of blood. David is doing a really good job, so I have the utmost faith that Derek will be out of surgery soon. I will be back when I have more news."

"I called Jamie and Marc, and they are on their way," Keith told Kyle as he headed out the door.

Kyle turned back and said, "Good. He will need all his friends around him."

When Kyle got back to the OR, David was coming out and said, "Done! Derek is on his way to recovery."

"Thank you for operating on him, David. I know that it was hard for you, but you are the best surgeon I know, and I wanted the best for Derek."

"Does this mean that you will give me another chance?"

"No, never! You are a great surgeon but a horrible person. We are done!"

Kyle left David standing in the doctor's lounge and headed back to the ER to update Keith and Chrystel again. Dr. Scott had set Keith's arm and was putting on the cast when he got there.

"Derek is in recovery and will be there for at least an hour. He came through the surgery but is still unconscious. We will be watching him closely. I will come back and let you know when we get him in a room, and then you can see him. The surgery went well. Now we just have to wait and see." Kyle turned to Keith and asked, "Keith, are you *sure* you are okay? You really look pale."

Dr. Scott told Kyle that he was sure Keith was in a lot of pain from setting the fracture. "It was a hard one. I have ordered a shot for the pain. The nose was easy to put back."

Keith had been cleaned up by the nurse, and the bandage was across his nose. "I'm fine. I could use a cup of coffee though after this cast is done. Is anything open at this time of night in the hospital?"

"There is a snack bar where you can get hot coffee and something to eat, which you should do after getting that pain shot. I will find you guys when Derek is taken to his room in the ICU."

Kyle left them and went back to the recovery room to check on Derek. At this point, he was ready to collapse and give in to his feelings. He decided to go to his office. He shut the door and locked it, so he could be totally alone. He sat with his arms crossed on his desk and his head down and started to cry. He had been under enormous stress, seeing the man he loved in such bad shape and having to keep up the façade.

The staff finally moved Derek to the ICU and notified Kyle and David. He was still unconscious but stable.

Kyle went to the ER to notify Keith and Chrystel. "He is in ICU 104. They will let you see him after they get him settled. David will check in later."

Keith said, "Thanks for keeping us updated, Kyle. I know that this has been really hard on you too. I will always be grateful and glad that you were here for him." He shook Kyle's hand.

Chrystel gave Kyle a big hug. "Thank you from me too."

᪽ Kyle left the ER and stopped by the nurse's station before going home to tell them to call him with any changes. He needed to get out of the hospital and rest in his den where he could feel close to Derek. At home, exhaustion took over, and he dozed off while looking at the picture of Derek over his fireplace. When he awoke, it was still dark outside, so he decided to go back to the hospital. He wanted to see Derek and make sure that he was still doing okay.

When he got to the ICU, he checked with Derek's nurse to get a report on his condition. She said that he was holding his own but was still unconscious. Kyle went into Derek's room and sat on the side of his bed. He took Derek's hand and sat there for a long time, just looking at him.

"Derek, please don't leave me. I love you with all my heart … I never stopped. I could not go on if you were not here. I was so stupid when I pushed you away. Please come back to me." He lowered his head on Derek's hand and cried softly.

David came by to check on his patient and heard every word that Kyle said. *I hate Derek so much! I will never let Derek have Kyle. I should have gotten rid of him when I had the chance.* He turned around and left the unit.

Kyle was still in Derek's room when Keith came to the door. He stood there a moment and watched Kyle holding Derek's hand with his head resting on it, crying. Keith understood how Kyle felt. He had no more jealous feelings toward him because he helped keep his love alive. *How can I hate him now?*

❧ The next day, Jamie called Chrystel from the airport in Lexington to find out about Derek's condition.

"Hi, Jamie," Chrystel said. "He is still not awake, but Kyle assured us that it is not uncommon after such a loss of blood. They are giving him another unit this morning and think that this will be the last one. Hopefully, he will wake up soon."

"What? Are you telling me that Kyle was his doctor?"

"Yes, Jamie. Kyle took care of Derek from the time he left Richmond in the ambulance to his whole stay here in Berea Hospital. I thought Keith told you that when he called you guys last night. He also called David to do the surgery, and he assisted. They saved his life, Jamie."

"Okay! Well, you can tell me more about it later. I have rented a car, and I am headed there now. You know that Marc had to stay in Cheyenne because of problems on the ranch, so it is just me. I should be there in about 45 minutes."

◈ While Kyle was checking on Derek, he started to stir.

"Derek, come on! Open your eyes!"

"Keith? Keith?" Derek mumbled.

Kyle, hurt and dejected, turned and left the room and ran into Keith. "He is starting to wake up, and he is calling for you."

Keith saw the pain on Kyle's face. "Thanks again, Kyle, for all you have done."

Kyle just wanted to get away, so he nodded his head and left. When he got to his office, he sat for a minute and rehashed hearing Derek in his groggy state call out for Keith. He knew then that Derek wanted to be with Keith and not with him, so the only decision left was to walk away as soon as possible and leave Berea.

◈ Jamie arrived at the hospital and found Keith and Chrystel outside of Derek's room. He went in with Keith and stood at Derek's bedside. When Jamie saw that Derek's eyes were closed, he asked, "Keith, is he awake?"

"No, not really."

"Keith … is that you?" Derek asked with his eyes still closed.

"Yes, my love. I'm here with Jamie. Can you open your eyes?"

Derek opened his eyes slowly and looked at both of them with a puzzled look. He was confused and did not know for sure where he was or what was going on, but he thought he had heard Kyle tell him that he loved him and wanted him back. He must have been dreaming. *Kyle is not here. He would never come to see me.*

◈ While Jamie was visiting with Derek and Keith, Chrystel tried to find Kyle, and she found him in his office. He had not started rounds yet.

"Kyle, Derek is completely awake now and talking with Jamie and Keith. I wanted to check on you. How are you doing?"

"Not very well, Chrystel. I poured my heart out to Derek when he was unconscious, and the one name he said when he started to wake up was 'Keith.' It's clear to me that Keith is who he wants to be with, so I have to walk away and let them be happy."

"You can't go by that, Kyle. You don't know that he really heard you. As a doctor, you know we all think that the unconscious patient can hear what we say, but we don't know for sure."

"I believe in my heart that it's true, so as soon as my commitment to Dr. Mitchell is done, I am leaving Berea. I will find another job somewhere else. I'm not worried about that. I feel that it is just no use for me to keep hoping that I can be with Derek. He must never know that I was at his bedside other than as a doctor. Swear to me, Chrystel, that you will never tell him."

"I feel that he would want to know, Kyle. It's not fair to him."

"No, Chrystel. You can never tell him. Please!"

"You have my word — although I don't agree with you. It is your life and your decision." She left his office and went to say goodbye to Derek. She had to get back to her practice and take care of things before going out to the Walker farm.

Recovery and Judgment Time

Derek improved each day and was transferred from the ICU to a regular medical/surgical floor. When he moved out of the ICU, Jamie decided that he could go back to Cheyenne. He found out that he was needed at the ranch after his talk with Marc the previous night. Marc called every night for news of Derek and Keith. Jamie also told Marc what Chrystel had told him about the Richmond incident and about being in the hospital with Kyle.

Jamie visited Derek one last time, and then went to the farm to talk with Mr. Hawthorn. He agreed that he could handle most of the farm work and help Keith with the horses since his left arm was in a cast. Chrystel also told Jamie that she would help Keith with the horses. With all in agreement, Jamie went back to Wyoming on the next flight out of Lexington.

⤷ On the third day after being out of the ICU, Derek went back to his room after his physical therapy walk with the nurse and saw Chrystel waiting for him. "Hi, Chrystel. It is so good to see you!"

"I'm sorry that I wasn't here yesterday and earlier today, but I was at the farm, helping Keith and Mr. Hawthorn with the horses. Kyle has kept me updated about how you are doing though."

"How would he know? He has not been to see me at all. I have only seen resident doctors since I have been here. You know, he could have at least come in once, especially since we meant so much to each other."

Chrystel wanted to tell Derek how wrong he was, how much Kyle did for him, and the fact that Kyle was there every day when he was not awake, but she had to stay quiet.

"I have to get back to my office and clean up things there, but I will be back sometime tomorrow."

When Chrystel left Derek, she saw Kyle in the nurse's station, so she stopped to tell him what Derek said. "He doesn't realize that you are taking care of him. He said that all he has seen on morning rounds are residents. You need to see him and let him know that you are the doctor on record for his care. No excuses. It is the right and human thing to do." She turned before Kyle could respond and left the floor.

After she left, Kyle knew that Chrystel was right. He would go when he knew that Keith was there because it would be easier to act professionally. About two hours later, Keith arrived. The nurse called to let him know, just like Dr. Douglas had asked her to do.

Kyle walked in and saw Derek sitting in a chair with Keith by his side. "Hello, guys. I came in to give you the good news. I'm discharging you in the morning if you are okay tonight and if your vitals are good in the morning. You are doing very well, so I see no problem for tomorrow. The nurse will come after your morning medications, vitals, and breakfast to give you your instructions." Kyle was proud of himself for keeping his professionalism and acting as if Derek were any patient under his care.

Of course, Keith knew it was an act but went along with it.

"Wait!" Derek said. "Since when can you just walk in here like you are my doctor? I have not seen you this whole time!"

"Stop right there, Derek!" Keith shouted angrily. "You have no idea what you are talking about. Kyle saved your life. He has been taking care of you since we were brought in here over a week ago. He ordered all the tests and even called in the best surgeon in Berea. By the way, *David* did your emergency surgery! We could not have gotten through this without them."

"Please, Keith, it's okay," Kyle said. "Don't be angry. He didn't know."

"If that is so, then why haven't I seen you before now?"

"Well, in the beginning, you were unconscious. Then, when you did wake up, I didn't want to disturb your time with Jamie and Keith. I got all the news about how you were doing from my residents and your nurses. Plus, I checked your chart at all times. I didn't want my presence to cause any setback in your recovery. Believe me, I always knew what your status was. So, when you go home, you will not be doing any work on the farm. But, like I said, your nurse will go over the discharge instructions with you."

Derek didn't know what to say.

Keith got up to shake Kyle's hand. "Thank you again for all you did for us."

"You're welcome, Keith. Make sure that you aren't doing too much also with that arm. By the way, your black eyes are getting better!"

They both laughed.

"Yep!" Keith said.

"Bye, Derek. Take care of yourself when you go home and follow all the instructions. You had a serious surgery." He left the room and went back to the nurse's station to write his final orders for the day. Depending on the vitals in the morning, he told the nurse that he would write the discharge orders.

Kyle left the hospital and headed home. On the way, he called Chrystel and told her about his visit with Keith and Derek.

No more was said by Keith and Derek about Kyle's visit. They mainly discussed the horses and what needed to be done when they got home. Keith left close to the end of visiting hours.

After Keith left, Derek thought about the news that Kyle took care of him and, of all people, David. *So did I dream that Kyle was at my bedside, or was he really there?*

⁓ The district attorney called Keith at the farm and asked if he could come in the morning and talk with him and Derek about the fight.

Keith told the DA that Derek was still in the hospital but was supposed to come home the next day. "We can talk before he is discharged, if you can come to Berea Hospital."

They arranged to meet in Derek's room at 9 a.m.

Keith called Chrystel to tell her about the DA coming to meet them. He thought that she should be there, and she agreed.

The next morning, Derek was doing really well, so Kyle wrote the discharge instructions. The nurse brought his breakfast at 7 a.m. and told

Derek that she would be back a little later to give him his discharge papers and instructions.

"Is Dr. Douglas still on the floor?" Derek asked her.

"Yes, I believe he is. Do you want to see him?"

"Yes. Can you ask him to come in please?"

The nurse went out to the nurse's station and told Kyle that the patient wanted to see him.

Oh, no. What does he want? Kyle thought. He walked into Derek's room and asked, "You wanted to see me?"

"Yes. I wanted to apologize for how badly I treated you when you came into my room earlier and to thank you for taking care of me."

"No problem, Derek. I understand."

Derek watched Kyle carefully before he spoke again. "Kyle ... one question. Did you sit at my bedside and hold my hand when I was unconscious?"

I was afraid that this was why he wanted to see me. "Well, Derek, I had your hand in mine when I was checking your pulse, so yes, I guess you could say I held your hand."

"So that's all it was? Nothing else happened?"

"No. I was just checking your vitals. I'm really glad you that are doing so well now. That was a pretty serious fight you guys were in. Chrystel told me there were five guys against you and Keith."

"Yes. They started messing with Chrystel, so we had to protect her. It looked like they did that to get us to come forward. Keith thinks it was a hate crime against us being gay. The more I think about it and how it went down, he must be right."

"Well, I'm glad that you are both going to recover from this, and I hope they pay for what they did to you."

"I think they will. The DA from Richmond is coming here this morning to talk with us about it."

"Okay. I have to finish my rounds, so make sure you follow what I wrote when you get home. You should be able to get out of here before noon." Kyle left the room and was glad to be out of there. He was afraid that, if he stayed any longer, he would end up saying too much. *Wow!*

I dodged a bullet there. He cannot know that I did more than just hold his hand.

⁖ Keith and Chrystel arrived to meet with the DA. Derek had finished his breakfast and was already cleaned up with the help of the aide. His nurse had been in right after that to give him all of Kyle's discharge instructions, so he would be able to leave right after the meeting with the DA. Derek was sitting in a chair, waiting for all of them to come into his room. Keith and Chrystel came in first.

The DA came in right after and introduced himself. "Let's get right to it, if you don't mind. This should not take that long. I know that you are waiting to get out of here in a little while. The five guys who attacked the two of you were taken to jail in Richmond the night of the fight. They have been held without bail and arraigned on assault-and-battery charges, drunk and disorderly conduct, and damages to the bar. I have come here to get your side of the story and see if you want to file any additional charges against them."

Derek spoke up first. "Well, I don't want to have to go through lengthy court proceedings, so I would say no."

Keith agreed and asked, "So what does that mean for them moving forward?"

"Their court-appointed attorney wants a plea deal, if you both agree. They could face six months in jail if you are not in agreement. The plea deal that the attorney is proposing is for six months suspended with time served, community service by attending a program dealing with gay rights, plus a fine to repair the bar they damaged and all court costs. What are your thoughts on that?"

"That works for us," Keith and Derek said at the same time.

"Okay. I will take your statements regarding the incident and will go back to their attorney with your answer. I have papers for you to sign, agreeing to this plea deal, and they should be released shortly thereafter. This is very generous of you guys to do this. They should be grateful."

Keith spoke up. "We don't need gratitude. We just hope they learn something about us."

The DA shook their hands, said goodbye to Chrystel, and left.

"Okay, Derek. Let's get you out of here and home."

"I'm ready to get out of here and get on with our lives, Keith."

They drove home and got Derek settled in. Chrystel came along to make sure that he was okay before she went home. She was also glad that this whole ugly mess was over and Derek was on the road to recovery.

৶ The next day, the five men were brought in front of a judge to plead guilty and hear their sentences. The judge gave them six months with time served, community service attending a program regarding gay rights, a $1,000 fine to fix the bar they heavily damaged, and $500 in court costs. The judge told them that they were lucky that Keith and Derek did not press any additional charges because he wanted to send them to jail for the entire six months on a work gang.

When the five men left the courthouse, a guard heard them say, "WE DON'T NEED ANY CHARITY FROM SOME FAGGOTS! They will pay again."

৶ After four weeks, Derek and Keith had recovered nicely. Keith had just gotten off his cast and was anxious to get back to taking care of all the duties in the stables.

Derek was still a little weak and was not able to do any heavy lifting but was getting stronger each day. "Keith, let's take the rest of the day off and visit Chrystel. It has been a week, and I know she will be glad to see that your cast is off and your arm is good."

"We can do that, but first let me give you a proper hug with both arms," Keith said as he wrapped his arms around Derek and kissed him. "It's hard to believe that it has been six weeks since the bar fight, but it's totally over now and all behind us."

"Right. Let's go celebrate with Chrystel!"

Devastation and Loss

Jamie and Marc called Derek to find out how they were doing and if they were ready to drive the horses they had buyers for. It was scheduled a while back, but the bar fight happened and put the plan on the back burner.

"Hello, Derek. How are you feeling?" Jamie asked.

"I am doing much better. Still a little on the weak side but getting better each day. How are you and Marc?"

"All is well here. Keith got his cast off, right?"

"Yes. His arm is completely healed. He is actually in the stable with Shadow as we speak. He was so glad to get back to taking care of the horses. You know that Mr. Hawthorn does great work, but he would rather be in the fields on his tractor and not with the horses."

"Well, talk to Keith and see if we can get those horses here. Let us know."

"Okay. Will do."

Derek went to the stables and said, "Keith, I just got off the phone with Jamie, and he wants us to get the horses to Cheyenne soon. I think I should drive them there. Don't you?"

"No. You are not ready to make a trip like that. I'll go."

"We need to make plans soon because they need the horses, and they have already put the buyers off because of our injuries. That really put it on hold long enough. Don't you agree?"

"Okay. I'll call Jamie later and work out the details."

Later that evening, they made a dinner reservation with Chrystel for the following night.

∼ On Monday morning, David went to Kyle's office to see if they could talk.

"David, what do you want now?"

"I know we are done, but I was hoping that we could at least be friendly colleagues. We *do* have to work together."

"That is true until you or I leave here. I'm hoping that you find a job somewhere else, so we can end this personal and professional relationship."

"Well, that is another reason I came to see you. I want to go to a conference in Louisville for two weeks to learn about this new robotic surgery. It could help my resume and get me a great job somewhere else. I cannot work while at the conference due to the distance. I need you to sign off on it and get me coverage while I'm gone."

"When is the conference?"

"It starts next week for two weeks. I will leave here on Sunday."

"Go ahead and sign up for it. I'll clear your schedule."

David couldn't resist asking. "How is Derek, by the way?"

"I have no idea. I haven't seen him since his discharge a month ago."

"Well, that surprises me since he is the love of your life," David said bitterly.

"Please leave my office!"

David left but swore to himself that he was not done with Kyle yet.

~ Chrystel, Keith, and Derek arrived at R&J Steakhouse for dinner and were seated close to the bar. They ordered beers and steaks and talked about the horses that need to go to Cheyenne. Chrystel had gotten a call from Jamie, saying that he and Marc wanted her to go to the farm to make sure that the horses were in good health and ready to make the trip.

Keith said, "Chrystel, I am going to drive them to Cheyenne next week, and I would love it if you would come by the farm often to check on Derek and Mr. Hawthorn."

"Sure, I would be happy to! I have to come by before you leave and give them a good checkup, like Jamie asked me to do. How long are you going to be gone?"

346

"I will be gone at least two weeks. Pulling a trailer with four horses from here to Cheyenne is a slow process. It will take less time coming back but going there will be the longest."

While the waitress was getting each of them another beer, Chrystel looked toward the bar and saw Galen. Because of Derek and Keith, she decided to ignore him. She didn't want to bring up bad memories for both of them. Keith noticed Galen but didn't react either. They both hoped that Derek never saw him. They drank their beers, paid the bill, and left. Nothing was said regarding Galen.

Galen overheard the conversation about Keith going to Cheyenne. Later that night, when he and David were at their house, Galen made an offhanded remark about how Keith could leave Derek alone when, according to Chrystel, he was still pretty weak.

David thought about how he would love to see Derek gone. It still griped him that he had a chance to get rid of him during the surgery, but his oath stopped him. "Who cares?" He moved toward the bedroom. "I don't want to talk about Derek. Come here and do what you know I love."

Galen was eager to oblige.

The next day, David thought about how to get Derek completely out of Kyle's life. He came up with a tentative plan but would have to think it through. *Keith will be gone, leaving Derek alone on the farm and very vulnerable. I could set a fire in the barn while Derek was taking care of the horses. But how could I do this without anyone knowing that it was me? Oh, I know! I will be out of town at the medical conference in Louisville. That will be perfect! I was planning to go anyway. I will sneak back to town without anyone knowing that I'm not in Louisville, set the fire, and then return to the conference.*

᎗ Kyle had been too busy at the hospital with Dr. Mitchell gone to catch up with Chrystel and find out how Derek was doing since he was discharged from the hospital. It had been a month, and he really needed some news.

Chrystel was seeing her last patient when Kyle arrived at her clinic. She was really happy to see him. "Be right with you, Kyle. I'm almost done, and then we can talk."

Kyle waited in the reception area.

Chrystel came out and gave him a big hug. "How have you been, stranger?"

"I'm good … just have been really busy at the hospital. Dr. Mitchell is in Africa. How is Derek? I'm sure you have seen him."

"He is doing well —still a little weak but getting better each day. As much as I hate to say it, David did a really good job on Derek."

"Yeah, he is a lot of horrible things as a person, but you can't find a better surgeon. It's a shame that he can't be a good a person too."

"Yes, I agree, but I'm glad that you are finally done with him. You *are*, aren't you?"

"Yes. I told him that we are done. He knows there is no going back."

"Good! You want to get a beer or a glass of wine? I could use a drink right now."

"Me too. I had a rough day at the hospital. David came to my office to see if I had changed my mind and to get time off for a medical conference in Louisville the next two weeks. Thank God he will be away from the hospital, and I won't have to worry about running into him every day."

"Let's get out of here. We will talk more at R&J Steakhouse. I'll drive, Kyle. Leave your car here," she said as she locked up.

"Okay by me."

At R&J Steakhouse, they got a table way in the back, so they could talk without interruption. Chrystel ordered a glass of wine and Kyle ordered a beer. They caught up about how things were going at the Walker farm.

"Have you thought about going over there and checking on Derek yourself, Kyle?"

"Yes, of course. Many times. I have the urge to go over there, but I figured it would be best if I didn't."

"You are wrong, but I'm not going to push this anymore. You and Derek have decided how or where you are going from here, so I have to be okay with that."

◈ David left for the conference in Louisville and checked into his hotel for the two-week stint. He also checked into the conference itself, so his attendance would be documented. He spent the first week making his plans to sneak back to Berea without anyone knowing.

He bought gasoline in a small town outside of Louisville, away from Berea, so it could not be traced back to him. He knew that Derek and Keith fed the horses at night as they put them in their stalls. He planned to go back on the weekend between the two-week conference. He knew that Keith was leaving that week for Cheyenne, so now he just had to wait.

◈ Derek told Keith that he wanted to drive the horses, but Keith disagreed.

"Derek, I'm not sure that you are up for it."

"I need a change of scenery, Keith."

"Are you upset about what Chrystel said … about Kyle asking her about you and not coming to see you instead?"

"Yes. It bothers me a little because I thought that he would have come at least once, but it is what it is. I just need a change. Also, I don't think I'm strong enough to take care of the horses like you can, and we have leaned on Mr. Hawthorn enough."

"I understand. Let's call Jamie and Marc about this change. I'm going to suggest that we send two horses this time instead of all four, and then the other two in a month, if that is okay with the buyers."

Keith called Cheyenne. "Hi, Jamie. It's Keith. We have a proposition for you and Marc. Derek wants to make the drive instead of me. He feels that he could handle it better than doing all the work here. He also feels like he needs a change of scenery right now."

"Okay, Keith. What is your proposition?"

"Can we send two horses this time and bring the other two next month? We feel that it would be a lot for Derek to handle four horses."

"I don't know, Keith. I will have to check with the buyers. I do agree that, if Derek is driving them, he would have a harder time dealing with four horses. If the buyers say that they have waited long enough, we could ship the other two by train. I'll talk to Marc. He is out at the stables right now. I'll get back to you. Derek is planning to leave on Thursday, right?"

"Yes. That was the plan, so it is just two days away. Can you get back to me ASAP? We will need to switch trailers too."

"Sure. I will talk to Marc now, and then we will call the buyers. I'll call you later tonight."

"Great. I hope this works out because Derek has been through so much. I would like to give him this chance to get away for a couple of weeks."

After Keith hung up, he gave Derek a big hug and asked, "What would you like to do tonight?"

Derek flinched a little because he was still tender from the surgery.

"Oops! So sorry, Derek. I didn't mean to squeeze you so tightly."

They both laughed.

"It's okay ... I hurt more when I laugh."

Jamie called back to let them know the decision.

"Hi, Jamie. It's Keith. What did the buyers say?"

"Well, one buyer backed out altogether, so that leaves three horses," Jamie explained. "Do you think Derek can do that? The owner who is buying two of them needs them soon. The last horse can wait, if you think it would be too much for Derek."

"I would rather he only had to deal with two of them. I can bring the last one later."

"Okay, Keith. We will just have Derek bring two horses."

"Good enough. I'll tell him. He is taking a hot shower. He is a little sore tonight. I think he is trying to do too much around here."

"Let us know when he gets on the road."

"Will do. 'Night to both of you." Keith hung up the phone and went to their bedroom to wait until Derek finished his shower to let him know the decision.

⚘ The next day, Keith and Derek got ready for the trip to Cheyenne. On Thursday morning, Derek loaded the two horses with Keith's help. They hugged, and Derek assured Keith that he would be fine. He would keep him updated on how the trip was going.

"Okay. Please drive safely, Derek. I love you."

"I love you too, Keith," Derek said as he pulled out of the driveway and headed to Cheyenne.

The trip went well. It only took Derek three and a half days. Derek called Keith every night to let him know that he was okay and where he was. Derek arrived in Cheyenne on Sunday afternoon. Jamie, Marc, and Keith were glad that all was well.

⅋ On Sunday night, David drove back from Louisville, arriving close to the Walker farm. He parked down the road under some trees and walked with the gasoline cans in his gloved hands toward the back of the barn. He noticed that no one was around. Lights were on at the farmhouse and at the main house.

David quickly poured gasoline around the back and sides of the barn and threw a match on the ground. He quickly ran back to his car and watched for a minute to see the whole barn in flames. He drove away from the farm and back to Louisville, smiling all the way back. He was very proud of himself.

Keith was sitting at the kitchen table and saw the flames out the window. He heard the horses and ran out. Mr. Hawthorn saw it too and told his wife to call 911 and have them send a fire truck. They both ran into the barn to get the horses out of their stalls.

"Hurry! You work one side, and I'll work the other," Keith screamed to Mr. Hawthorn.

They frantically released the stall doors and shooed out the horses. The horses were running in all directions. Keith and Mr. Hawthorn ran out of the barn, thinking that all the horses were out, but Shadow had run back into the barn in a panic. Keith ran back in to get him. Mr. Hawthorn followed, yelling after him. Shadow ran back out but, in all the smoke, neither Keith nor Mr. Hawthorn saw him.

Mr. Hawthorn yelled at Keith that the roof was starting to collapse. He couldn't see him in all the smoke. The firemen and ambulances arrived, and some hooked up the water and some headed toward the barn entrance. Neither man came out. Mrs. Hawthorn told the firemen that her husband and Keith were still in there, so they ran in to look for them. They found Mr. Hawthorn first, but he was down. Another fireman looked for Keith and found him a second later, but a beam had fallen on him. The firemen worked frantically to get Keith out from under the beam and outside where they could work on him.

Mrs. Hawthorn ran to Mr. Hawthorn where the EMTs were doing CPR on him. He was not breathing. He had burns on his face and arms. They got him breathing again and transferred him to an ambulance with Mrs. Hawthorn by his side. She rode in the ambulance to the hospital.

Keith was put in the second ambulance. His breathing was labored, and he was unconscious. They put an oxygen mask on him and started an IV on the way to the hospital. The hospital was notified that they were bringing in two ambulances. Mr. Hawthorn coded again in the ambulance but did not recover. The ER doctors were updated regarding his status.

Kyle was still at the hospital doing some paperwork when he got the call from the head nurse of the ER that two patients were being brought in from the Walker farm where there was a barn fire. His heart sank with that news. Keith was rushed in, and Kyle and the ER doctors were waiting.

Oh, my god! I can't live without Derek, Kyle thought. *Please let him be okay.*

When Kyle looked at the patient on the gurney, he sighed with relief when he saw that it was Keith. The EMTs told Kyle that a beam fell on his chest in the fire. Kyle went into action, barking orders to the staff and getting Keith intubated and hooked to life support. The chest X-ray showed a crushed chest and collapsed lungs, so chest tubes were put in immediately. Keith was unresponsive and was in a coma. His vital signs were critical, and he suffered severe smoke inhalation. The EMT also told Kyle that the other patient, an elderly man, did not make it. Kyle asked if these two were the only ones at the Walker barn. They said yes, and the elderly man's wife was waiting in the emergency waiting area.

Kyle told the nurse to call Chrystel and have her go to the farm. The horses were probably scattered. Upon getting that call, Chrystel sprang into action. She raced to the farm, rounded up the horses, and put them in an outside corral.

Chrystel called the ER and told the head nurse that the horses were good, the firemen had put out the blaze, and they were still there because they were starting their investigation as to how the fire got started. She got into her car and headed to the hospital. When she arrived at the ER, she found Kyle. "What's going on here? How bad is Mr. Hawthorn and Derek? Please tell me that they are alive."

"It's not Derek. It's Keith. Mr. Hawthorn passed away in the ambulance. Keith has smoke inhalation, a crushed chest, and collapsed lungs. He is in a coma. Where is Derek? I have to admit that I was really scared when I got the call from the ambulance that the two coming in were from a fire at the Walker farm. I don't know what I would have done if it were Derek."

"He must be in Cheyenne. Keith was supposed to drive the horses this week to Cheyenne, but Derek must have gone instead. So what are you saying about Keith? Is he going to make it?"

"No. He is dying. We are trying our best, but he is hurt too badly. I need to call Derek and tell him that he should come back. We have Keith on life support, but he will not come off of that. I'm so sorry, Chrystel. I know he is a good friend of yours, and I grew to like him a lot after I got to know him while Derek was in the hospital. This is such a shame."

"Thank you, Kyle, for doing what you can for Keith. Derek is going to be devastated. Do you want me to make that call to Cheyenne?"

"No. I think it should be me," he said as he stepped outside of the ER to make the call.

Marc answered the phone.

"Hi, Marc. This is Kyle Douglas. Is Derek there?"

"Yes. You don't sound good. It must be serious. I'll get him."

"Hello, Kyle," Derek said. "You are the last person I expected to be on the phone."

"Derek, listen. There was a fire at your barn, and Keith is here in the hospital. You need to get on a plane as soon as you can. Keith is dying. I hate to tell you on the phone, but things are dire. I am so sorry, Derek."

Derek was crying so hard that he could barely speak. "Kyle, please tell me this isn't so! I'm begging you … save him! Please *save* him!"

"Derek, put Jamie on the phone please."

"Hi, Kyle. It's Jamie. What is going on?"

"Jamie, there was a barn fire on your farm. Mr. Hawthorn and Keith were getting the horses out. Mr. Hawthorn died on the way to the hospital with burns on his face and arms and smoke inhalation. He coded twice, and his heart just couldn't take it. Keith is alive but is dying. He has a crushed chest, collapsed lungs, and smoke inhalation. We have him on life support and is stable for now, but he is not going to make it. He is in a coma and unresponsive. I hope he can make it until Derek can get here. Mrs. Hawthorn is going to need you guys here too. Can you please all get on a plane and come? I'm sorry to be so short with my words, but I need to get back to Keith. We will talk more when you get here."

Kyle went back to the ER and had Keith moved to the ICU.

Chrystel came up to him outside of Keith's room and hugged him. "I know that you are doing your best for Keith."

"I can't save him, Chrystel. Derek begged me on the phone, but medicine can only do so much. The rest is for the man upstairs to decide."

"I know. This is the worst night I have ever lived through. Have we heard how the fire got started? My heart breaks for Mrs. Hawthorn. What will she do now?"

Kyle just shook his head.

Hope

C hrystel looked for Mrs. Hawthorn and found her in the emergency waiting area. She looked lost and was just staring into space, not focused on anything.

"Mrs. Hawthorn, it's Chrystel. I'm so sorry for your loss. We need to get out of here and get you somewhere, so you can rest. You can stay with me until you figure out your next move." She hugged her and again said how sorry she was.

"I need to stay here and take care of my husband. The doctor said that he would release him to whatever funeral home I want him to be at. They are making all the arrangements for the funeral director to come pick him up. I have to stay here."

"Okay. I'll stay with you until they come for him, and then we will head over there tomorrow and make the arrangements. You should not be alone tonight. Do you have any family that you want me to call?"

"No. We have no one. It's just the two of us. We have been together all of our adult lives."

The ER doctor had contacted the coroner's office regarding Mr. Hawthorn's death. Following their discussion, the coroner released the body and agreed with the ER physician that the death certificate should read "acute respiratory failure from smoke inhalation, cardiac arrest, and third-degree burns on face and arms."

The funeral director came in to get Mr. Hawthorn, and Mrs. Hawthorn stood up to meet him. They took Mr. Hawthorn in the hearse, and Chrystel took Mrs. Hawthorn home. She would not go with Chrystel to her home, so Chrystel told her that she would stay with her. She didn't want her to be at the Walker farm by herself.

"We will go the funeral home tomorrow whenever you are ready."

"Okay. I want to go to my bedroom now and be alone. I hope you understand."

"Of course!"

"A guest room is ready whenever you want to go to bed. It's upstairs to the right of the steps."

"Thanks. I'll be fine. I need to call Dr. Douglas to see how Keith is doing. You try and get some rest." Chrystel watched her walk upstairs to the Hawthorn's bedroom, and her heart was breaking. She sat down in the study and called Kyle. "Any change with Keith?"

"No. I just hope that we can keep him alive long enough for Derek, Jamie, and Marc to get here. It's going to be really rough on all three of them, especially Derek. I know how much he loves him."

The next day, the fire marshal came to the hospital to let Dr. Douglas know that the fire was started by arson and that Keith was the target. He said that the police had been notified, and the men who were responsible for the bar fight were picked up that morning. They were heard saying that they would not let some faggot give them a break and that he "will pay." They were questioned and the alibis were being checked. The fire marshal said that he would let them know what will happen to them. Kyle notified Chrystel about the results of their investigation.

⌇ Jamie, Marc, and Derek arrived at the hospital and were directed to the ICU. Kyle had been notified that they were coming and was waiting for them.

As Derek walked into the ICU, he asked, "How is Keith?"

"There is no other way to say this: He is dying."

Derek collapsed in a chair, and Jamie put his arm around him.

"Kyle, you promised me that you would save him! I want to see him."

"Okay. Do you want someone with you, or do you want to go in alone? Only two can be in the room at the same time."

"Jamie, will you go in with me?"

"Sure, Derek. Let's go." He held onto Derek as they entered the room.

"Oh, my god … look at him! He looks so bad." Derek swayed, almost passing out. "I can't *believe* this is happening! It should be me lying there instead of him. How did this happen? Please, Keith, open your eyes. I love you so much. Come back to me." He sat and held Keith's hand and cried.

Kyle watched Derek for a minute, and then left the area. He went to call Chrystel to let her know that they were all here and to see if she could come and be with Derek. Marc waited in the waiting area until Jamie came out, so he could go in to see Keith and try to comfort Derek.

"Chrystel, this is Kyle. Can you come to the ICU soon? Derek, Jamie, and Marc are here."

"I'm with Mrs. Hawthorn at the funeral home, arranging things for her husband. I can come when we are done and I have taken her back home. I think that Jamie should stop by later to help her. She is really hard to read. She has hardly spoken a word since her husband's death, but I feel that seeing Jamie will help her since she has worked for him a long time."

"Okay. I will pass that along. Come when you can."

Kyle went back to the ICU and checked on things there. Derek came out of the room and walked up to Kyle, who opened his arms. Derek went straight in Kyle's arms, and Kyle was shocked with this unexpected closeness.

"Please, Kyle. You promised me that you would save him," he said against Kyle's shoulder. "I begged you. Do something to bring him out of this!"

"I can't save him, Derek. He has a crushed chest, collapsed lungs, and smoke inhalation."

Derek beat Kyle's chest as hard as he could and screamed at him, jerking away at the same time. "You don't *want* to save him! You are a miserable excuse for a doctor. You promised. I *hate* you! You could save him, but you won't. I will *never* forgive you if you let him die!"

Jamie pulled Derek aside and said, "This is not Kyle's fault. He can't work miracles. You don't mean anything you are saying right now. Calm down, and don't say anything else that you will regret later."

Chrystel arrived at the ICU and caught the tail end of Derek's rampage. "Derek, listen to Jamie. This is not Kyle's fault. He has been by Keith's side ever since he was brought in. You don't mean anything you are saying."

"Yes, I do! If Keith dies, I will *never* forgive Kyle."

Chrystel looked at Kyle and saw the hurt in his eyes. This was too much for her to witness. It was all so heartbreaking.

Jamie went over to Kyle and grabbed his arm. "Can we talk somewhere?"

"Sure. Follow me to my office."

Jamie told Marc to stay with Derek and Chrystel while he talked to Kyle alone. When they got to Kyle's office, Jamie spoke first. "Please don't pay attention to what Derek is saying. He doesn't mean any of it. He loves you, Kyle, and always will. He loves Keith too but in a different way."

"I know that he is beside himself with worry and grief. I will do my best to deal with his anger again. By the way, Chrystel said that Mrs. Hawthorn really needs you too. She took her to the funeral home to arrange things for Mr. Hawthorn before she came here, so can you and Marc go see her? Chrystel will stay with Derek, and I will be in the background if he needs me. The nurses in the ICU will keep me informed as to what is going on with Keith."

"Sure, Kyle. We will go over to my house and see what she needs. Kyle, please know that Derek is in a bad place right now. Again, don't take anything he says to heart." Jamie gave Kyle a hug before he left to get Marc and go to the house.

ᦗ When Jamie and Marc got to the farm, they found Mrs. Hawthorn in the sitting room, looking at old photos of her and her husband. She looked up and saw Jamie. She ran into his arms and finally let out all her grief. Jamie held her and let her cry until she was composed again.

"The funeral is going to be on Friday, Jamie. I want to bury him in your family cemetery on the farm, if that's okay with you. We have always felt that this was home."

"Of course he can be here, and I want you to stay on in the house. This is your home."

"Oh, thank you! I wasn't sure what I was going to do. It's always been just Hiram and me. We have no family."

"You have us. We are your family, and I want you to stay here."

"How is Keith? I heard from Chrystel that it's not good. Poor Derek!"

"Keith is dying. Derek is not taking any of this well, which is understandable. I will make the arrangements to have Hiram buried on the property. Don't worry about it."

❧ Marc and Jamie put their luggage in the upstairs guest room and went back to the hospital to convince Derek to eat and rest. When they got back, nothing had changed. Derek was sitting at Keith's bedside, holding his hand. Chrystel was on the other side, just sitting quietly.

The next day, Kyle got a call from the fire marshal that the guys who threatened Keith were arrested formally and back in jail. Their alibis did not hold up. Kyle went to the ICU, looking for Jamie and Marc, and found them in the waiting area with Chrystel. Derek was still in Keith's room.

"Has Derek had any rest or eaten anything, Jamie?"

"No, Kyle. He has hardly moved from his bedside."

"If we don't get some food in him, we will have another patient on our hands. I heard from the fire marshal just now. The men who were in the bar fight with Keith and Derek have been arrested and charged with arson and the murder of Mr. Hawthorn."

"Good. I hope they get the maximum sentence," Marc said.

❧ David headed back to Berea. He decided to leave the conference in Louisville early because he couldn't stand not knowing what was happening. He was sure that he was going to hear the great news that he was finally rid of Derek. *I will have to comfort Kyle in the wake of Derek's death,* he thought gleefully.

❧ Alarms went off in Keith's room, and Kyle and the nurses ran to the bedside.

Derek was frantic. "Do something, Kyle! *Do* something!"

"He is actively dying, Derek. There is nothing I can do. We should let him go in peace and shut off the machines."

A distraught Derek grabbed his hand and screamed, "No! You can't do this!"

The nurse went out to ask Jamie, Marc, and Chrystel to help with Derek.

When Jamie entered the room, he grabbed Derek's arm. "Stop! Let Kyle and the nurses do their jobs."

At that moment, the cardiac monitor started to go off.

Kyle examined Keith and said, "I'm sorry, Derek. He is gone." He walked over and turned off the monitor and the ventilator. "Derek, you can sit with him as long as you want," he added as he left the room.

Jamie stayed with Derek.

Keith looked so peaceful, and Derek told himself that he was still here with him. "Keith, please … open your eyes. Please!"

"Derek, he is gone," Jamie said as he tried to get him to come out of the room and sit with Marc and Chrystel while the nurses prepared Keith.

"No. You go out," Derek said. "I'm staying here. I will *never* forgive Kyle for this."

Chrystel was standing with Kyle when they both heard that comment. Kyle recorded the time of death, turned away, and headed toward his office. Chrystel followed him. She knew that he needed her because she saw how hurt he was.

"Marc, why don't you go back to the farm and wait there for me?" Jamie asked. "I will stay with Derek until I can get him to leave."

"Okay. I'll stay with Mrs. Hawthorn," he said as he kissed Jamie and left.

Jamie decided to leave Derek alone with Keith for a while. He went to get a sandwich and coffee to bring back to Derek in the hopes that he would finally eat something.

While he was gone, David came into the hospital and looked for Kyle. He asked one of the staff if they had seen him. He was told that Kyle was in the ICU. David went there and couldn't believe his eyes.

David saw Derek at Keith's bedside and started to scream, "No, no! I *killed* you! You are supposed to be dead! What are you doing here? You were supposed to be in the stable. I found that out through Galen. Chrystel said that Keith went away on business."

Derek turned around to look at David. "I went instead. Are you saying that *you* started the fire?"

David lurched forward, pulled Derek out of the chair, and threw him to the ground. He put his hands around Derek's throat, trying to choke him. Derek couldn't fight back because of his weakened state.

The nurses heard the yelling and called security, paged Kyle to the ICU STAT, and the others ran into the room. One of the male nurses pulled David off Derek and threw him against the wall, restraining him. Kyle ran into Keith's room with Jamie right behind.

Derek yelled to them, "David killed Keith!"

Kyle and Jamie stood there, puzzled and in disbelief.

The male nurse, who was restraining David, said, "I heard Dr. Jenkins yelling, 'What are you doing here? I *killed* you!'"

Security arrived and took charge of David, and the police were called.

"Derek, are you okay?" Kyle frantically asked him. "Let me check you out to see for myself. I don't know what I would have done if anything happened to you." The words poured out without Kyle thinking what he was saying.

"Don't *touch* me! You are responsible for Keith and your lover David."

"Okay. I won't examine you since you can't stand the thought of me touching you. I'll have another doctor check you over." Kyle turned away with tears in his eyes and went into the waiting area just as the police arrived and handcuffed David. They told Kyle that they were taking him to jail.

"Kyle, I love you!" David screamed. "I did this for you. I thought it was Derek. I wanted him out of our lives!"

"You are scum! Please get him out of my sight and out of my hospital," Kyle told the officers.

David was taken to the police station, and the Richmond police were notified that they should release the five men they were holding for the fire because they had the responsible person in custody. Witnesses in the hospital had heard him admit to starting the fire. The five men were released immediately. David was arraigned on one count of arson and two counts of murder. The police notified Dr. Douglas of his arraignment and, as far as Kyle was concerned, he was done.

Chrystel came into Kyle's office a little later. "Wow, Kyle! I can't believe that David did this."

"I can't either. I never thought he was that sick of a person. You know that Derek will blame me for this too."

"Yeah, I know, but he is not in his rational mind right now. He is really hurting. Give him some time."

"I have done that over and over. I can't do it anymore. I know that Keith's death is one of the hardest things he will ever have to endure but …" Kyle stopped because he didn't want to say something he couldn't take back.

Chrystel gave him a big hug and went out.

Jamie finally got Derek to leave the ICU. "You need some rest and food. We have to arrange things for Keith. After you eat and rest, we will talk to the funeral director. We will have a funeral here for the people who want to say goodbye to him, and then we will take him home to Cheyenne where he wanted to be … in Mary's favorite spot."

"He would love to be there with Mary."

꙳ Jamie took Derek back to the farm. Derek didn't want to stay in the farmhouse, so he asked if he could stay with Jamie and Marc at the main house. Jamie took him there, and he fell asleep right away. Jamie told Marc and Mrs. Hawthorn of the development regarding David.

Later that evening, once the coroner had released Keith's body, he was moved to the same funeral home as Mr. Hawthorn. Jamie and Marc talked to Mrs. Hawthorn, and she agreed that they should have both funerals together on Friday. After, they would take Keith home to Cheyenne for burial.

Derek came downstairs to get something to eat. Jamie and Marc informed Derek of the funeral plans.

"Derek, I will let everyone who was close to Keith know about the plans," Jamie assured him. He then called Chrystel and Kyle to tell them what arrangements had been made and invited them to come. They both agreed to be there.

Kyle called Chrystel and asked if she would go with him on Friday. "I don't think I can go by myself."

"Sure, Kyle. We will go together."

ᐌ Friday came, and Kyle picked up Chrystel to go to the funeral home. When they arrived, Derek saw Kyle coming in and ran to stop him.

"No! No way do I want you here, Kyle. You let this happen, and you are not welcome here. I told you that I hate you, and you are the last person I want to be here."

Jamie tried to calm down Derek, but nothing would work. "Derek, I invited him," Jamie explained.

"I don't *want* him here. He is the reason we are here now."

"Okay, Derek," Kyle said. "I will leave. I'm sorry that you blame me, and someday maybe you will see that there was nothing I could have done to save Keith. Once again, you only see what you want about me. Be with Keith and know that I'm out of your life for good. You never have to see me again."

Chrystel followed Kyle out of the funeral home. "I am so sorry, Kyle."

"It is what it is. I understand a little. You stay here. If you need a ride home, call me. I will come and get you."

Kyle called Dr. Mitchell when he got in his truck, letting him know the circumstances and asking when he would be returning from Africa. "I am calling my headhunter to find another hospital far away from Berea. If he finds something, I will stay until you get back. Then I am gone."

"I will be home in two weeks," Dr. Mitchell responded. "Our work here is done, and we are just wrapping things up. If you get an offer before I get back, just put someone whom you feel can handle it in charge. I hate to see you leave us, but I totally understand your reason. I'm sorry things are so bad there. We need to replace Dr. Jenkins also. It is such a shock what he did. I still can't wrap my head around it."

"Thanks for understanding, Dr. Mitchell. I'll get things started on my end."

Kyle hung up the phone and called his headhunter, who said, "I'll get back to you on this. Do you have any idea where you want to go?"

"Anywhere far away from here. As I told you, I prefer to go out west. Hopefully someone there needs a chief of staff."

"I'll get right on it and let you know what I find."

❧ The funeral was short and incredibly sad. Jamie and Marc had asked the funeral director to make all the arrangements for shipping Keith's body to Cheyenne, so his body stayed behind as they took Mr. Hawthorn to the family cemetery on the Walker property. Burial went without any issues.

A forlorn Derek stood motionless. Jamie told him that it was time to take Mrs. Hawthorn and Chrystel home and, the next day, they would travel back to Cheyenne to finalize the plans for Keith. Chrystel embraced Derek and gave him a long, loving hug when they dropped her off. She knew the days ahead were going to be hard for him.

Once inside, Chrystel called Kyle to see how he was doing.

"I'm fine. I have finally resigned myself that there is nothing more for me here, so I called Dr. Mitchell and told him my plans. I called the headhunter to get that ball rolling too. I plan to leave Berea for good … no turning back. Hopefully it won't take long before he finds me something."

"Where are you trying to go? Do you really think that this is the right thing? You know that Derek will regret what he has done and said when he gets past his grief. I know that he really does love you."

"It doesn't matter, Chrystel. He will always go back to blaming me for all that goes wrong in his life. Frankly, I'm tired of taking his verbal abuse. I need to let him go in my heart. He is poison to me."

"You don't mean that either. You love him and always will. To totally walk away from him will be like cutting out your own heart. I don't believe you can do that."

"Maybe so, but I can't live in the same town, knowing that he hates me so much that he blocked me from coming to Mr. Hawthorn's and Keith's funeral today."

❧ Jamie, Marc, and Derek left the next day for Cheyenne, and Keith's body would arrive on Monday. They arranged things with the funeral director, who took care of Marc's family funerals, to take Keith's body directly to the burial site by Mary's memorial stone. They had a small memorial service for Keith there and, after the burial, Derek stayed with him for a while.

Derek prayed to Mary, saying, "Take good care of him, Mary." He sat and cried for a long time.

After a while, Jamie came to get him. Plans had to be made about the Walker farm. "Derek, I'm going to have Chrystel take the horses to another farm until we can get the stable rebuilt. Marc and I will hire two farm hands to help you. One will take over Mr. Hawthorn's duties, and the other will help you with the horses. I have already hired contractors to work on the stables when the fire marshal says they are done. David will be tried and sent to prison, so all will be done there. That part won't take long since he confessed."

"Good," Derek said very quietly. "I think I will move up to the big house with Mrs. Hawthorn, if that is okay with you. The farmhouse holds too many memories. The farm hands you hire can live there."

"That is actually a good idea. That house is too big for her to live in alone."

All the plans were told to Chrystel, and she agreed to put the horses on another farm. She took care of it the day that Derek was due back at the Walker farm. When he got there, he moved his stuff up to the main house. Mrs. Hawthorn was so glad that he was going to be with her. He packed up all of Keith's things and gave them to Goodwill. Then he cleaned the house to get it ready for the new hands that Jamie was going to hire. He found this extremely hard but necessary in order to start healing. This was going to be a new phase in his life.

"Kyle," Chrystel said, "Derek is back from Cheyenne. Do you want to call and talk with him to see how he is? I'm sure he is in a better place."

"There is no need. As a matter of fact, I heard from my headhunter, and he has already found me a job in San Jose, California. They got my resume and interviewed me on the phone and then with Skype. They were so impressed that they already offered me the job. I'm making plans to sell the farm and find a place to live there. With help from my contact person at the hospital, I should be able to find a place to live very soon. I feel like a big weight has been lifted from my shoulders. I even promoted one of the great surgeons we have at Berea Hospital to move into David's position as chief of surgery. Things are falling into place. Dr. Mitchell will be back in a couple of days, so I will move very soon."

"God, I hate to see you leave here! I feel like I'm losing my best friend."

"We will always be close, and you can visit me in sunny California any time or as often as you want."

A couple of weeks later, after Derek came back from Cheyenne, Kyle was packing, and he had hired a moving company. He had flown to San Jose to look at a place his contact person found for him, and he loved it. It was within walking distance to the hospital, which was ideal, so he took it. Dr. Mitchell returned from Africa, so all was good there. He only had to touch base with the real estate agent about his farm, and he would be ready to leave.

∽ The two men whom Jamie and Marc had hired arrived and were getting settled at the farmhouse.

When Derek drove into town, passing Kyle's place, he noticed a for-sale sign in front. *Is he leaving town? I have to know.* He wasn't sure why this bothered him. When Chrystel came by to give him information about the horses, he asked, "Is Kyle leaving Berea? I saw that his farm has a for-sale sign out front."

"Yes, Derek. He is moving. He got another job."

Derek didn't ask anymore, and Chrystel didn't volunteer anything else. She knew that Kyle wouldn't want her talking about his plans with Derek.

Kyle called Chrystel later that day and asked if she wanted to go to R&J Steakhouse for the last time before he left. She agreed. While they were eating, she asked Kyle if he had any bids on the farm yet.

"Yes. I have a solid bid, so I think it is safe for me to get the movers over and load up."

"Are you taking everything or leaving some things behind?"

"I'm taking it all. If I find after I get there that it doesn't fit, then I will sell it there."

"Do you think you will ever get past the hurt and find out that you and Derek are meant to be together?"

"I will always love Derek. He is the love of my life, and you know that kind of love never dies. But I can't say that he will ever get over Keith's death, and I may not ever get over the venom he has spewed at me. I think the worst was when he wouldn't let me pay my last respects to Keith and Mr. Hawthorn. That cut me to the core and broke my heart. I will take one thing with me to have something of my love to look back on in the years to come: his picture. I can't bear to part with that … ever."

Chrystel was glad to hear this because it gave her hope.

꿍 After one and a half years, Derek moved on while living in the big house with Mrs. Hawthorn. He was still running the farm with the workers whom Jamie and Marc sent. The stable was rebuilt, and the horses were back, including Shadow. Kyle was gone, David was in prison, and Derek had been thinking a lot about Kyle. He was wondering what he was doing or even where he was. Chrystel had never told him where he moved, and he had never asked.

One day, when Chrystel was checking on the horses, he decided to ask her about Kyle. "Hey, Chrystel. Can we talk?"

"Of course! What's on your mind?"

"I have been wondering why you haven't told me where Kyle is. Have you heard from him? I have had him on my mind lately."

"Well, I didn't think you would want to know or care where he is. I have been in constant contact with him ever since he left a year and a half ago. I miss him terribly and plan to visit him soon."

"Can you tell me where he is? I just want to know."

"He is in San Jose, California. He is chief of staff there. He is doing fine and loves where he is. He has made a good life for himself. Why don't you call him? After all, it has been well over a year since Keith died and Kyle left Berea. I'm sure he would love to hear how you are doing. I also know in my heart that you need him."

"I am not so sure that he will want to hear from me. You know how bad I was to him the last time I saw him, but I'll think about it."

"His number is the same, if you do decide."

Derek mulled it over for another week, and then finally called him. "Hello …" Silence for a second or two. "Hello, Kyle. It is me, Derek."

"I know. I have caller ID, and I never removed you from my phone. What do you want, Derek? I'm really surprised to hear from you. How are you?"

"I'm good. I wondered how you were. I have had you on my mind the last few months. I don't know if you will believe me after all I said the last time we spoke, but I just want you to know that I love you and miss you." Again, silence on the other end, so Derek continued. He had to say this now or lose his nerve. "I'm wondering if you would let me come to see you, so we could talk." He held his breath, waiting for Kyle's reply.

"I don't know, Derek. I'm not sure it's a good idea. I'm really in a good place now, and I don't want any more pain from you. We have both been through enough while trying to love each other."

"I know, Kyle, but please let me come. I love you, and I'm hoping you still love me … that I haven't killed that love."

"I do still love you, but it hurts too much. I don't know."

"Please … at least let me come and talk face to face."

"Okay, Derek. I will agree to see you, but I'm not promising anything. Like I said, I'm in a really good place. When will you come?"

"Tomorrow, if that is okay."

"Well, let me know when you get here." Kyle got off the phone and wondered if he made a mistake letting Derek come. He called Chrystel to tell her about the conversation.

"I knew that he was going to call you," Chrystel said. "He is really lost without you. Give him a chance and just listen."

"I will, and I will let you know how it goes. I'm really hesitant to let him back in my life. You know, sometimes love is not enough, and the wound is very deep."

⮥ The next day, Derek got on a flight to San Jose. During the flight, he reflected on all the hurt he had caused both of them. He also thought about the love they had for each other and believed they still had. *I hope that Kyle can forgive me and will give us another chance to make a lasting life together. We love each other, and that kind of love never dies!*

When Derek's plane landed, he turned on his phone and called Kyle.

Kyle called back and said, "Derek, I'm outside of baggage claim, so come out when you get your bag." Kyle was nervous about this meeting. When Derek walked out of the airport, Kyle took a deep breath and noticed how wonderful he looked. He got out of the car to help Derek with his bag. He wanted to take him in his arms but thought better of it. Instead, Kyle took his bag and asked him how he has been.

"I'm good, Kyle."

Both men were unsure of what to say, now that they were face to face. As they drove to Kyle's apartment, they talked about the weather and the farm but nothing important.

Derek wondered why they were unable to have an important conversation. "Kyle, do you think we can talk to each other for real — not like strangers?"

"We can talk when we get to my place." All kinds of feelings were going through Kyle's mind. He had to admit that it was great seeing Derek again. He had never been far from his thoughts.

When they arrived at Kyle's house, Derek said, "Wow, Kyle! Your place is really nice." He looked around and something caught his eye, stopping him dead in his tracks. It was the first time he had seen the big picture of him on a horse. "Kyle, what is *this*? How did you get it?"

"Jamie sent it to me a long time ago, and I had it blown up and framed."

Derek was stunned and encouraged that Kyle had the picture and *still* had it after all this time — even after the heartache that he had caused. Unable to figure out what he wanted to say, Derek asked Kyle where he got such a beautiful frame.

"I made it and carved it myself. That's what I was making when you came back from Cheyenne to see me."

"That was when you kicked me out?"

"Yes." Kyle poured them both a glass of wine from the kitchen, and then came back in and sat down. "Okay, Derek. Say what you need to say."

Derek was a little put off how abruptly Kyle spoke but decided that he would continue or lose his nerve. "Kyle, you have been on my mind so much this last year, and I wanted to come here and tell you how much I love you. I have had time to figure out how to let my anger go. I believe I have done that and felt the need to make things right with you. You have always been in my heart. I tried to get you out, even when I was with Keith. I loved him, but I was not *in* love with him. No one can replace you in my heart.

"I know that it is probably hard for you to believe that my anger toward you is gone, but it is. I want to spend the rest of my life proving it to you, if you can bring yourself to let me. I love you so much and am hoping that you will give us another chance to be together. When we finally made love, I told you that I felt as if were home, and I meant that. I need you, Kyle. Our kind of love never dies."

Kyle sat quietly without answering him.

Derek was getting nervous. *What is he thinking?* "Kyle, do you still love me?" He had to ask, even though Kyle said he did when they talked on the phone. The silence was killing him.

Kyle's thoughts were all over the place. *Should I believe him? Should I take him in my arms? Should I make love to him? Should I send him away? I want him. Can I give up my anger toward him?* Kyle got up and walked over to Derek, pulling him out of his chair and into his arms and holding him tightly. "Yes, Derek, I still love you. I thought that I could go on without you, and I have been in a good place here, but what has been missing was you."

"Please kiss me!" Derek whispered.

Kyle kissed him passionately. Then he broke the kiss and took Derek to his room. "I need to make love to you, Derek, and I will show you how much I need you too."

Much later, they lay together, talking about how stupid they had been, and Derek took full responsibility for that. They happily fell asleep in each other's arms.

◈ The next morning, Kyle told Derek that he had to go to the hospital and for him to make himself comfortable until he came back for dinner.

Derek was content to just stay and relax, now that he knew he had Kyle back for good. Kyle came home with a pasta dinner, which he ordered and picked up for the two of them.

He hugged and kissed Derek. "I am very happy, Derek. I am so glad that you took the chance and came here and that I listened, like Chrystel told me to do."

After dinner and another great lovemaking session, they called Chrystel to give her the good news. She was so excited. Then they started talking about all they needed to do. It wasn't going to be easy since they had lives in two different states, but they would do what it took to be together.

Derek left the next day for Berea. Kyle planned to visit when he got time off from the hospital. When Derek got to the farm, he called Jamie to let him and Marc know the turn of events. They were both happy for Derek.

"We have some news of our own!" Jamie said. "We are finally getting married and would love for you and Kyle to come."

Derek called Kyle and told him the happy news about Jamie and Marc.

"Great … let's go!" Kyle agreed. "Call them back and say that we will be there."

⚬ One month later, Jamie and Marc's wedding day arrived. Chrystel, Mrs. Hawthorn, and Derek flew in from Berea, and Kyle flew in from San Jose.

After the wedding at the Three M Ranch, Kyle pulled Derek outside under the moonlight. "I couldn't wait to get you alone." He hugged and kissed Derek tenderly, and then got down on one knee.

Derek was speechless.

"Will you marry me, Derek? I want you to be mine for the rest of our lives."

"Yes, yes! I will marry you, Kyle. See? I *knew* that our kind of love never dies!"

The End